Henry Hall Dixon

Scott and Sebright

Henry Hall Dixon

Scott and Sebright

ISBN/EAN: 9783337153175

Printed in Europe, USA, Canada, Australia, Japan

Cover: Foto ©Andreas Hilbeck / pixelio.de

More available books at **www.hansebooks.com**

TO

RICHARD AND EDMUND

TATTERSALL,

FROM THEIR FRIEND

THE AUTHOR.

PREFACE.

A THIRD work of the same class scarcely calls for a preface, except as pure matter of form. In writing it I have adhered strictly to my original plan of endeavouring to fill up from oral evidence, some blanks in the sporting history of the last seventy years; and where I have had the good fortune to meet with an especially well-known character, I have got him, Dick Christian fashion, to give the public the butt end of his mind in the first person. The three books must be taken as a whole, and hence any seeming omissions, or very slight notice of a celebrated man or horse in the present one, will generally be accounted for by reference to its predecessors. The difficulty of the task has been great, as no two men ever seemed to give precisely the same account of any thing, and on some points I have despaired of getting more than an approximation to the exact truth, amid so many conflicting statements. Poor Dick Christian's memory can aid me no more, and I can only again trust that in his present impoverished and bed-ridden state, his friends of other days may not wholly forget him.

The name of " Post and Paddock " could cause no mistake, but " Silk and Scarlet" deluded a few into the belief that it was a contribution to Church Polemics. When I had to think out a third title, I did hope that by adopting the names of two of their most accomplished practitioners, as the types of The Turf and The Chase, I ran no risk of being mis-understood ; but still I found one of my old Rugby school-fellows under the firm belief that by the heading " Sebright" I must be taken to contemplate a treatise on Bantams.

As regards the first three chapters, I have nothing to remark, except that I have handled the great win-ners as nearly as possible in chronological order, and separated man from horse, by a pony chapter, which, with about twenty pages more, has already appeared in print. " The Flag" part of the fourth chapter is a mere fragment, for the sake of illustrating the career of one of its most celebrated riders, when steeple-chasing really was a sport; and both "The Stag" and "The Drag" might have been worked out much more fully if there had been space at command.

I have, in fact, been able to make only a very sparing selection from the mass of sporting evidence which I collected in the course of three years. Still, "Field and Fold" is a very comprehensive title, and although I have now a new love, I dare say I shall not be found quite faithless to the old, in my proposed August and September rambles, and that I shall often turn aside from farming stock for the sake of a note on those two earlier subjects, which are connected in my mind with so many pleasant friendships.

10, *Kensington Square,*
　　June 10*th,* 1862.

ENGRAVINGS.

TABLE OF CONTENTS.

CHAPTER

CHAPTER IV.

CHAPTER V.

HORN AND HOUND.—Visit to Joe Hewitt —Service under Mr. Frank Fawkes—Joe's staghunting in Norfolk—Fox-hunting in Norfolk—A new light on foxhunting—Fox-hunting lecture—Fox-hunting 1790-1810— The late Earl of Darlington—Squire Draper—The Yorkshire Wolds—The Wold Hunts—The Sykes hounds—The Badsworth—Engagement of Wild Danby—Waifs and Strays for Holderness—Kennel building—Life in Holderness— Will Danby's sayings—Dreams of the chase—Holderness foxes—Mr. Hodgson's Scurry Stakes at Beverley—Practical jokes in Holderness—The biter bit—Captain Percy Williams—Mr. John Bower—Mr. Ralph Lambton—His habits of life—Mr. Lambton on the flags—His hound feeding—Mr. Williamson's mastership—The late Sir Harry Mainwaring —Tom Rance's history—The late Dick Gurney—Tom in Cheshire—Tom's table talk—Head, Maiden, and Markwell —Foxes and their troubles—Tom's disasters—The Cheshire green collars—Old Zach Goddard—The snooze in the Park—Celebrities at Bicester—Sir Thomas Mostyn and the B.D.C. — Stephen Goodall — Stephen in kennel — Tom Moody—Griff Lloyd—Griff Lloyd's power of bearing fatigue—Jem Hills—View from the kennel—The Heythrop covers — New kennels near Chipping Norton — Heythrop foxes—Making up forty brace—Jem and the badgers— Glories of Cribb, the terrier—Jem's early days—Special day for the Duke of Beaufort—Blooding future Masters of Hounds — Scent symptoms — The South Warwickshire's triumph—Dislike to water—Cricket reminiscences—Clarke's sanctum — The kennel beauties of Badminton — Recollections of Will Long—The dawn of Leicestershire— The Quorn country—Mr. Assheton Smith—Hunting field

SCOTT AND SEBRIGHT.

CHAPTER I.

TURF WORTHIES.

"Mr. Percival and Lord Sidmouth were Premiers, and that is all that is known of them; but if they had been great racing men, there would have been hundreds of enthusiasts who would treasure up the minute descriptions in which a Turf writer would have collected all the traditionary stream of knowledge bearing on their physical and mental gifts, on their successes and failures, the way they carried their heads, and the way they turned out their feet."

"I'LL *tell you what it is, my old* A word at starting. *friends,*" said a candidate, when he had been met at the station, and duly conducted to a dais at the end of his Committee Room; "*I'm not going to stand up here for a speech to-night, but I'll just come down and smoke a pipe with you.*" It was six to four on him at once, and the takers had the worst of it on the polling day. Such a homely solution of the starting difficulty might make the Jockey Club prick up its ears, and fill the author-world with the direst envy. It suits our own humour to a nicety. We want to settle down quickly into our stride, and tell from our note-book, as of yore, the post and paddock recollections of many an old English and Scottish worthy. Our appetite for moralizing is not sufficiently athletic to grapple with the morbid anatomy of The Turf, or to trace every dark episode in its annals. We simply feel proud, that an institution, so fraught with temptation, and exposed to the ken of so many millions of ignorant or crusty critics from within and from without, should

B

continue to furnish us with Premiers, and to show
such wonderful fibre and endurance under the
chronic onslaughts of that lop-sided morality, which
almost denies the existence of an honest owner,
trainer, or jockey.

Horse traditions. But second-hand homilies are not in
vogue, and nearly every tradition for
good or evil has been already moulded into shape.
We may have to take the Venerable Bede on trust,
when he tells us that in 631 the " English first began
to saddle horses;" but the same genius of stable
gossip which was at hand to note for posterity how
Lord Falkland's son bartered away his father's
library for a horse and a mare, has stayed the two
centuries well. A rich harvest of facts, down to
I'Anson's last Leger orders to Challoner, never to
raise his hands from Caller Ou's withers, has been
gathered in by its agency, but there is still much
work for the gleaner. And if our version of some
events differs in a measure from that which was
given of them at the time, it may be that we have
traced them more thoroughly to the fountain head,
when all motive on the part of the actors for gloss
or concealment had long passed away.

Old sporting writers. " 'Tis seventy years ago" is a phrase
of edge not to be matched now, and we
may well not care to go back further. We can still
reach by the light of living memory (the only book
we have cared much to consult), that great historic
age of "Genius Genuine," the Prince Regent, and
John Bull. Of thousands of good sportsmen, who
rode the hill towards Black Hambleton, on the
King's Plate day, to see the judges place 16 out of
31 for posterity behind the Belvoir "Bonny Black,"
or decide the delicate question between five Marys, we
must fain be content with the simple record that they
were born and died. No newspaper had then made
sporting its specialty, and the *Old Sporting Maga-*

zine only began in 1792 to " woo the votaries of Dian and the frequenters of Newmarket," with intelligence and " lyric compositions of the sylvan, rustic, and Anacreontic kind." The field of Turf literature had lain comparatively fallow, and when the writers did begin to work it again, they stuck too much to one kind of cropping. They were careless of the fame of great horses, or considered them to be sufficiently provided for in the *Racing Calendar*, which extended its earliest favours to Jamaica as well as Great Britain; and embalmed the Royal Rules of Cockfighting as solemnly as the pedigree of Coughing Peggy, or Skipjack from Old Mother Neesome. Men who had completed a zealous novitiate of folly or eccentricity, and risen to the dignity of a character ; the careless cassock, fonder of brewing an October posset than writing a fifteen-minutes sermon, and yet ready, like his ancestors, to melt his last tankard for Church and King; and the wealthy Corinthian who had run the gauntlet of the coffee-houses before he was three-and-twenty, were the subjects they delighted to honour.

The Prince Regent was their Mœcenas, *Eccentric turf* and Sir Harry Vane their Suwarrow of *characters.* the turf. Lord Barrymore, who was known as " Cripplegate," while another brother became " Newgate," and a third owned to a still warmer and more expressive title, was a most fruitful study with them. Inspired by the account of the countryman, who consumed a pound of salt, a cabbage, and a cabbage-net at a sitting, his Lordship *Lord Barrymore's* made a bet that he would produce a man *bets.* who was equal to eating a live cat ; and he won by a few yards at Brighton, when he challenged the Duke of York to try who could wade farthest into the sea. Well might his Boswell exclaim, on hearing of his early death, " Could the emotions of grief restore his vital heat, my lamentations should fatigue

Echo." Earl Orford's eccentricities, wrote another,
"are too firmly indented upon the tablet of the
memory, ever to be obliterated from the diversified
rays of retrospection," and then feeling refreshed by
this prelude, he proceeds, with his usual kindness,
to give them in detail.   Major Topham earned a
mention both for the drama's and Snowball's sake.
Sir John Lade (who " stood in" with " Leader, the
great coach builder of Liquor Pond Street,") was
a fund in himself for them, whether he was
driving his phaeton and four across the ice of the
Thames, or riding his mule for a thousand pound
match over the Ditch In ; and they loved to tell
how O'Kelly would fumble among a quire of bank-
notes just to set the caster, when he had got every
floating guinea in the bank.

Old Q.   Sonneteers and satirists all laid vio-
lent hands on Old Q, who still stuck to
his Piccadilly bow window, his green *vis à vis* with
black horses and long tails, his Richmond beauties, his
muff, and defied them. His body physician had only to
look in the *Morning Post* occasionally to be reminded
that he had strictly a life-interest in his patient, and
that his prescriptions of a warm milk bath scented
with almond powder, and a veal cutlet at 3 a.m.,
might as well have been posted at Charing Cross.

Colonel Thorn-   Colonel Thornton's thirst for notoriety
ton.   was also slaked to the full.   If he sat
down next to Oliver Goldsmith at the *Sçavoir Vivre*
Club, or jumped a five-foot-seven gate, or ran down
a hare on horseback, or coursed a bustard, or shot
a dotteril, or unhooded Sans Quartier amid the
elastic wold breezes round Falconer's Hall, the feat
never lacked a chronicler. His greyhound Major,
his beagle Merryman, and his terrier Pitch were all
accepted types of their order ; and Juno, whose fame
caused Lord Grantley to pay half-forfeit in a match
of thousands, was the queen of the twenty brace of

setters and thirty-five pointers, which composed his "partridge preparations."

Lord Orford's kennel was worsted by the Snowball blood over the Wharram *The Swaffham Club.* Wolds, but the plains of Swaffham had no mightier champion. It was at his bidding, that the club was limited to the number of letters in the alphabet, and each member selected a colour. If The Heath knew well the orange and black cap of the dashing match-maker Grosvenor, the green and white stripes of Foley and Fox, and the mazarine blue of Standish, coursing men watched with equal zest in Norfolk, whether brimstone, quaker, or pompadour would be the steward's cockade for the week.

While the turf and the leash thus held their alternate six months' sway, *Cricketing and Archery.* the Marchioness of Salisbury was tasting the delights of the chase and the quiver. A golden bugle-horn was sometimes the Hatfield prize, and it sounded the *reveillé* for many a county muster of the Woodmen of Arden, the Bowmen of Cheviot Chase, and the Hainault Foresters in their green and buff. While the Essex archers were keeping summer trysts at Fairlop Oak, the Men of Kent knew well how to handle the willow. Earls Winchilsea, Darnley, and two more dashing spirits thought nothing of pitting county elevens against each other at Lord's for a thousand guineas; and in 1792, fourteen matches were played for that sum, and six for half of it. The cricketing picture of the period is strange to look upon. The players are attired in round hats, knee-breeches, and pig-tails; the umpires are all frill, and two scorers sit contentedly with slates on a form.

Goodwood subsequently achieved renown, as the spot where Lillywhite *The dawn of Goodwood.* and James Broadbridge first took the hint for their round bowling from Lambert. In 1801 its racing was of a very lowly kind. One writer, in fact, seems to have carried away nothing more than an indefinite idea of " five or six roving tents, and plenty of ice and pickpockets." Ascot basked earlier in the smiles of royalty; its sports were regularly opened by beat of drum, and its cords bounded South by *E O* tables, some fifty strong, and North by four-in-hands. Never were the pigeons more heavily and more openly winged, and one *E Oite*, plaintively referring to his rich dividends of the previous year, seemed almost to consider that in a bad summer he was entitled to compensation from the Crown on its native heather, for " the poverty of one, the death of a second, and the compulsive abdication of a third."

The driving era. The new driving era was just beginning to dawn in '93, and the procession of a score of freshly-painted mail-coaches up St. James-street from the Bull and Mouth and The Swan with Two Necks, &c., after the birthday drawing-room, on June 4th, with their drivers and guards in new scarlets, and the horses in particoloured streamers, was becoming one of the most popular sights of the season. The Driving and the Whip Clubs were not then in being. The landlord of the Black Dog, at Bedfont had no visions for himself or his successors, of eleven teams of bays at his door, with Mr. Villebois, Mr. John Warde, and Sir Thomas Mostyn on the box. The Buxton bit, and the Hawke head territ still slumbered in the brains of their inventors, and the wildest dreams of the future "Baron Stultz,"—who gained Beau Brummell's love by putting a £100-note into each of his dress-coat pockets, and destroyed 'Schweizer's and Dawson's monopoly by the two hussar-jackets which he begged to make as a favour for " The Seventh," in Lord Anglesey's time,—did not as yet compass that double-breasted drab driving coat, with three tiers of pockets, and Spanish five-dollar pieces for buttons, in which Sir Godfrey Webster found no followers. Sir Henry Peyton had not brought four greys, or Squire Annesley four strawberry roans with "Harlequin" as off-leader into fashion; and a really crack team seldom showed at Ascot, except each horse was of a different colour.

Nothing pleased "Farmer George" so much as to find that there was a good entry for his four-mile Hunter Plate. His Majesty on his white horse, which did duty long before Hob was foaled, never missed the Windsor Forest Meet, on Holyrood Day (September 26th) : and until the melancholy twilight of his powers stole on, he cared quite as much to calculate how many of the horses were about to try for their ten qualification tickets, as to look at his hounds and men. Owners or grooms might ride them, but it was a *sine quâ non* that the Royal Huntsman should see them, both at the uncarting and the take of the deer. It made no matter how forward they might be during the run, if both those cardinal rules were not complied with. If three horses succeeded in winning their tickets at the end of a severe chase, it was thought to be a good day's work; but in an ordinary run, very few failed, and Mr. Davis has granted one, as an especial honour, to a lad on a pony. *Ascot qualification tickets.*

The early history of the Ascot of the North has been told so often, that there is no need for us to go back to the £5 5s., which was voted by its corporate body in 1681, for five years, to encourage the sport on their Town Moor. The return list began in 1728; and the meetings were held in July, and after shifting all over the summer months, they finally settled down into September, about 1750. Eight-and-twenty years after, the uncle of "Handsome Jack St. Leger" gave his name to the race, and so the ball has been kept rolling to *Doncaster Moor to wit.*

the present day. In 1794 the light skirmishes between the mayor and the gamblers began, but His Worship won, and like another Lord Elgin, at Pekin, burnt the E O tables in front of the Mansion House. Less martial mayors succeeded, and in 1825 another civic sally had to be made, or the very mace and meat-jack would have been in danger. The skulking which that defeat entailed upon the E Oites exasperated them to such an extent, that they joined forces with the thimble-riggers, and on Monday, September 14, 1829, was fought that sixteenth " decisive battle of the world," on Doncaster Moor, between the " Confederates," with legs of tables on the one side, and His Worship, with mounted constabulary, militia, yeomanry, volunteers, and a *posse comitatus* on the other, which eventuated in a series of exciting chases and prodigies of private valour, whose recital still furnishes many of the older inhabitants with an annually lengthening story over their wine and walnuts.

The Bibury Club was also in great force each June, with Lord Sackville, the Hon. George Germaine, Delmè Radcliffe, Ferdinando Bullock, and " Splitpost Douglas " (an undying name conferred on him by the Prince Regent himself) at the head of its silks. It was there, too, that John Scott, when quite a little Oxford lad, had his first glimpse of Sir Tatton in the saddle. The Prince Regent- seldom failed to show, and never passed the gate of Christ Church without calling upon his old tutor, Dr. Cyril Jackson. On one occasion he presented himself in his full Club uniform of green coat, buckskins, and top-boots. The Dean was as cordial as ever, but he felt, that in those cloistered precincts, discipline must be maintained even with The Heir Apparent. His stately hint at parting was on this wise:—" *Now re-*

member I'm always glad to see you, except when you're dressed for Bibury, and then I don't know that Your Royal Highness exists." Racing was a different matter, but the Dean did not in his heart object to hunting, and rather held the belief that a few fast men were not without their use to the hard readers in a large college, by giving them something to talk about. In fact, with rare and beautiful candour, he went so far as to say, to Lord Foley at the beginning of an October term; *" Well, you've come back amongst us, my Lord; I suppose you've brought your red rag with you."* Hence under his dynasty, and before the Duke of Bedford's political " crops" became legion, or the Duke of Rutland's raven wig was voted the best scratch in New Bond-street, those who wanted a gallop with Lord Sefton could do the thing correctly, and have their pigtails powdered for the field, after morning chapel, in peace.

Dean Milner, the President of Queen's, had also rather scandalized the Cambridge dons at this period, by the report that he had, on crossing over in the packet boat from Hull to Barton, been observed by curious eyes to make his way towards Mendoza, and enter, with his wonted energy, into a long conversation on box- Dean Milner's interview with Mendoza. ing with him. However, he would brook no admonition on the point, and curtly replied to his questionists: *" Ah! I knew he was at the head of his profession, and I wanted to get something out of him."* Mendoza's conqueror, Humphreys, had (as Tom Cribb did afterwards) retired into the coal line, near the Temple, and Mendoza after joining a party of " The Fancy" at the Lyceum, had accepted office as a sutler in the Notts Militia. The regiment was then (1798) encamped on Dorlington Heights, and " Jack Musters," who was considered, when blue coats and leathers came in, to divide with Brummell the honour of being the best dressed man on town, was helping, as ensign, to keep the coast from Bridlington to Spurn Point.

Sir Tatton Sykes and his sheep tastes.   When the Dean and the Professor held their discussion, Sir Tatton Sykes was a young banker in Hull, and employing his intervals of business between the camp and his Leicesters. Seven years before, Barton Ferry had been a memorable spot to him in connection with his first purchase of ewes. He had been smitten at twenty-one with a desire to have some pure Bakewells from the late Mr. Sanday's flock; and after selecting half-a-score at 20 gs. apiece, he met them afterwards at Lincoln, where they arrived from Holmpierrepont by wagon, and drove them home in person, a three days' journey, to Barton. He soon became a ram-letter, and last September was the fifty-eighth anniversary of his show; and until he was upwards of eighty, he never missed his annual June ride into the Midlands, to Burgess's, Buckley's, and Stone's. This love of Leicesters has always fought hard for supremacy with thoroughbreds at Sledmere. It peeped out in the naming of the bay colt, "Holmpierrepont," on which Sim Templeman in his seven-stone days was beaten in a canter, at York, by the dam of Charles XII.; and a somewhat expensive complication arose because of it at Cat-

A little difficulty with Mr. Baker of Elemore.   terick. Mr. Baker, of Elemore, in his chagrin at being defeated for a Hunters' Stake, construed Sir Tatton's gallant wave of his whip to the ladies on The Stand, into an expression of triumph over himself, and accordingly made matters so hot for him at Mr. Robert Collings's sheep sale, that he had to pay 156 gs. for the shearling Ajax.

His early days in London.   The forty miles behind his ewes from Lincoln was as nothing in Sir Tatton's eyes, as he had walked from London to Epsom and back to see Eager's Derby in '91, starting at four

on that June Thursday, and landing back at Lamb's
Conduit-street about eleven at night. Next year he
rode down to see Buckle win it on John Bull, and
he has never been at Epsom since. He had first
looked on London as a Westminster boy, with his brothers Mark and Christopher; and it was a cherished
recollection with the three, that after often lingering for that purpose at their tailor's, in Bolt-court,
they once caught a glimpse of Dr. Johnson, as he
handed a visitor to her carriage. In Sir Tatton's
case, a probation with Messrs. Farrar and Atkinson,
the solicitors of Lincoln's Inn Fields, followed
hard upon Westminster and Brasenose. Edwin as
Jemmy Jumps, Ranelagh, or the rope dancing at
Sadler's Wells, where a pint of punch, " and very
good punch too," was dispensed to every box visitor,
after the third act, might be the evening's amusement, but the young clerk had no easy time of it by
day. When he was not indirectly fostering his future
Holmpierrepont tastes among the sheep-skins in the
office, he was dutifully bearing the green bag after Mr.
Farrar to Westminster Hall, or to con- His probation in
sultations at chambers, in one of which Lincoln's Inn.
Erskine and the two Scotts were engaged. Hol-
royd was then great as a special pleader, Kenyon and
Buller were on the Bench, and Thurlow's tenure of
the Great Seal was rapidly waning to its close.

Hullock and Bayley were still hard working stuffs,
but Sir Tatton met them both in their ermine, when
it became his turn to put four bays into " the
Chameleon carriage," at York Assizes. That wonderful county conveyance was popularly supposed to
have heard some of " The Squire's" best hunting
stories, as he conveyed his learned charges and his
chaplain to and from the Castle, and to have been
the scene of that inward resolve to challenge Clinker
four miles over Leicestershire with Clasher, which
he reduced into his own queer manuscript before he

had been ten minutes in court. It is also in the
Humours of the Yorkshire shrievalties. recollection of some of its annual masters, how at the magistrates' dinner,
Baron Hullock invariably proved him-
self fonder of two bottles than one, and quizzed " my
Brother Bayley," whenever he lighted by mistake on
his special bottle of toast-and-water; and how strict
the latter was with Sir Tatton and every other High
Sheriff about conducting him home to his lodgings
after a late sitting, lest, as he was wont to phrase it,
" there should be an assassin behind the door."

While these stories were current of the Puisnes,
Lord Thurlow earned no mean fame in the eyes of
Sir Tatton and the Holderness men by his conduct
in the little affair of Spaxton Vicarage. The Chan-
A word with Lord Thurlow. cellor had sworn up to his usual mark,
when a young clergyman (Mr. Jaques)
encountered him on the sands at Scarborough, and
asked him, without the smallest introduction and with
a very slight preface, for the then vacant living.
" *But I won't go about my business*," rejoined the
intrepid divine, " *and what's more, it now becomes my duty, as a clergyman, to reprove you
for swearing.*" The man of the awful eyebrows was
fairly brought to his bearings, at last. " *Will you,
indeed?*" he began; but " *hang it, I see you're a
———— good fellow—you shall have it,*" was the rest
of the sentence, and the Chancellor shook hands over
it and kept his word.

Sir Tatton's race-riding. But we must glance off from these
woolsack recollections to the saddle, and
the " orange body, blue sleeves, and cap" of Sledmere,
in which the then Mr. Tatton Sykes won his maiden
race, on his brother's Sir Pertinax, at Beverley.
" Bob Lascelles," of Thirsk, was second, and Sir
Henry Boynton, Mr. Burton, and, " Hamlet Thomp-
son's" father were in the ruck. Sir Tatton had on
that occasion to ride 13st., but eleven was his regu-

lar racing weight, and he scaled ten-and-a-half over
Morpeth, at a pinch. No one ever loved a mount better, and he rode till he was above sixty for any one
who asked him, without a thought about fatigue or
distance. On one occasion, after riding 63 miles
from Sledmere that morning he was second to Mr.
Lindow (half-brother to Mr. Rawlinson, the owner
of Coronation), in the four-mile Macaroni Stakes,
at Pontefract, slept at Doncaster that night, and was
beaten in another four-mile heat race against " Splitpost Douglas," at Lincoln next day. Twice over he
journeyed from Sledmere to Aberdeen, with his
racing jacket under his waistcoat, and a clean shirt
and a razor in his pocket, for the sake of a mount
on the Marquis of Huntley's Kutusoff, and Sir
David Moncrieff's Harlequin, when the Welter Stakes
was the greatest race in Scotland; and without
stopping to dine went back to sleep at Breeching
that night, and reached Doncaster after a six days'
ride, just in time to see Blacklock beat for the St.
Leger. Kutusoff, whom he thought to be decidedly
the best he was ever on, did not win that bout, but
the victory in "the white and black cap" of Sir
David, in '22, squared up his Scottish luck. The
360 miles were done, principally in the forenoon, on
a little blood mare, and with the exception of a
slight stiffness she seemed no worse.

Caller Ou's St. Leger was the seventy- Visits to Doncas-
sixth Sir Tatton had seen, with only one   ter.
break, from illness, in Charles XIIth's and Euclid's
year; and he lodged for forty years with a cow-keeper
in Sheffield Lane, who offered him a bed by accident,
when he arrived late one night, and not another roost-
ing place was to be had in the town. Since Tom
Carter's death in 1854, he has ceased to ride to Doncaster; but when Tom was at his side, they used to
meet at Pocklington, and come through between
four and four, and sleep at Booth Ferry on the Cup

His rides to London. evening. The first of his rides to London was in 1805, when he sat for his portrait to Sir Thomas Lawrence in the scarlet coat, and black silk breeches, &c., which formed the evening costume of the Castle Howard Hunt. Sir Mark and Lady Sykes, who are also in the group, returned from the easel to the North with him. It was Christmas week, and his little blood mare required sharping twice a-day, but after spending two evenings with the carriage party at Eaton and Newark, her rider supped with them at York on the third. The ride three-and-forty years after, to Mr. Grant's studio was accomplished quite easily in June, partly on the black horse (by Colwick, from Lord Chesterfield's grey mare, Mad Moll), which with its rider numbered 108 years, when Sir Tatton was last on him at the cover side, and partly on the chesnut Revenge, by Recovery; and a peep at Buckley's and Burgess's beguiled the way.

Death and time combined had wrought a mighty change among the familiar faces of " Sportsman's Hall" between those two visits. Colonel Mellish, who commanded the Prince's crack " German troop," in The old race of the Tenth, and whom a few can still reTurfites. member raising his white hat ironically to his friends in the Grand Stand, as he sat behind his four browns, and saying, " *If Sancho's beat, I hope some of you will take me for a coachman,*" had died in his prime. Martin Hawke, of whom it was told that he always clove the air with his hand, whenever he saw a magpie, had failed to avert the omen. Within a year of each other, Sir Charles Turner, who swore by King Fergus, Sir Hedworth Williamson, who twice had good reason to bless his " saucy Arethusa" when the Derby was over, Mr. Wentworth, whose Chance found few save Haphazard to beat him, and Mr. Gascoigne, the great liegeman of the Delpini blood, had been laid under the turf of their hearts, and scarcely a jockey save Sammy King was living, who had begun the century at York or Epsom.

Up to that very visit the Jockey Club authorities had been faithful in practice, <sub/>The old Derby course.
as John Scott and nearly all the elder trainers and jockeys are in heart to the Old Derby Course, with its nice gentle rise of three-quarters of a'mile, which "nearly settled the thing before Tattenham Corner;" and it is somewhat remarkable that Sim Templeman should have won the last Derby and Oaks on Cossack and Miami over it, and opened the new era with another double benefit on Surplice and Cymba.

Betting had been as tardy in its growth as the American aloe, during <sub/>Early betting.
the first few years of this eventful interval. Owners were ready enough to put down money for a match, but did not care to speculate deeply about other people's horses. Much of that spirit still lingered which had made Lord Grosvenor offer to match any three out of his stable against the same number of the Duke of Bedford's for ten thousand; but till bookmaking gradually became a profession, getting the odds laid was always a matter of difficulty, and it was told as quite a marvellous thing, that Sir John Shelley should win nine thousand guineas on Phantom's Derby in 1811. Another kind of ring had risen so high in '17, when Molyneux was open to " fight any man born of woman bar Tom Cribb," that the first wits of the day flocked round Incledon at Tom's anniversary Tavern dinner near St. James's Square, to hear Edmund Kean return thanks for the drama and take a second in " *All's Well.*" It was in this year, that the two greatest certainties The certainties
in the North and South came to naught. of '17.
The first favourite Student was beaten to a standstill at Epsom by his own " valet" Azor, and, like

him, the mighty Blacklock was also snapped by the very last horse in the betting at Doncaster. Still, despite these turns for the fielders, the betting was at least forty per cent. below that of the two preceding seasons. Chester seems to have been the one bright exception. Such was the crush and excitement during the heats, that "two ladies fainted and two gentlemen betted over them, two course-clearers were knocked down, and nobody picked them up."

This difficulty about course-clearing effected an important alteration at Epsom. In the Prince Regent's day, it was the custom for the royal party to leave the Grand Stand, and lunch with Mr. Ladbroke the banker at Hedley, as soon as the Derby was over. The trainers and spectators whiled away this interval between two and four, by dining in the town or the tents; and hence the running for the plates was conducted, like those memorable evening sittings at the Old Bailey, in a very vinous mist. There was not much value received by the authorities after dinner from the Surrey labourers, who got eighteen-pence per diem to "make a waie for the horse-race;" and regard for human life called loudly for reform. The crowd broke in when Gustavus and Reginald "worked together from end to end in the Derby, as if it was run a match." Buckle's horse stared about him as Russborough did in a similar dilemma, and the old man's nerve rather went; while Sam Day, who kept close at his girths, thus graphically describes their journey from Tattenham Corner, "*We wound in and out, for all the world like a dog at a fair.*"

How they kept the course at Epsom.

If Sam's shabby little grey, which was purchased for a pony at Hampton Court, was not worthy of his steersman, Robinson proved to the world next day, that Augusta was one of the soundest and best mares that ever

The year of Gustavus and Augusta.

dared to make all her own running and win the Oaks. There was no little disappointment that autumn, when the terms of a match could not be arranged between her and Jack Spigot, on whom Bill Scott had just verified that favourite axiom, which came booming out to the end of his days, whenever turf-scale rogueries were mooted : " *Only give me a good horse, and quicksilver be hanged.*" If Augusta did not measure conclusions with the St. Leger winner, she defeated Emilius (of whom Robson, whose word was law, declared that there " had been no such horse since the days of John Bull") three years after, in nearly as heavy a match as that between " the hen-speckled Sultan" and Banker ; but neither she nor Jack were in the great A.F. race, that First October, for the Grand Duke Michael Cup. Its Royal donor stayed with the Duke of Rutland at the Palace during the races, and saw Sam Day win it for Lord Grosvenor on Michaelmas, with four others not beaten a length.

The afternoon parade on Easter Sun-day was looked forward to year after *The Warren Hill parade.* year at Newmarket, as the great Warren Hill prelude to the first Craven meeting of the morrow, and " half Cambridge came over." Trainers who never took kindly to the Robsonian system of having their horses out at four, morning and afternoon, for six months of the year, relaxed their code for that day ; and vied with each other in their new lad-liveries. The Jersey and Shelley lot of Tiny Edwards, than whom none knew better when to slip it into them, and when to let well alone, was distinguished as the " brown, and white metal buttons." The Duke of York's, under the command of Frank and Will Butler's father, formed " the drab division ;" blue with red waistcoats marked the approach of Lord Foley's ; drab with red and white stripes (borrowed from Tom Panton The Squire of New-

market, for whom **Jim Robinson's** father trained)
of the Brothers **Chifney**, with the **jaunty and wide-
awake Will** at their side; while the Heath in-
separables, **Lord Henry Fitzroy** and Robson, headed
the long **Indian** file of the Grafton grey-coats and
leather-breeches. As **time went on,** those two
clerically-dressed **figures were seen** no more, and
Bob Stephenson **was in command for the Duke as
well as** Lord Egremont. **Boyce was there on** behalf
of his good master from Belvoir, **John Howe** represented the **Sowerby interest, and** Cotton **that of
Lord Verulam ;** while **Cooper was** on duty for
" **Payne and Greville,"** and **sturdy** little Pettit **for
Mr. Stonehewer, whose love of** neatness extended to
having his **boot-soles** blacked. **Nearly all of that
trainer** band **have** passed away, and so has the King's
Chair Pond, with the odd practice **to which** it gave
rise, of taking the horses to the troughs to drink, and
giving them **a final canter "to warm** the water."

The Nomination
night at York. The same afternoon produced nearly
as great a **Yorkshire parade** at Hambleton ; but the **spirit of racing never** glowed
more brightly at " **Old Ebor,"** than on the evening
of each New **Year's Day. The** trainers held their
nomination dinner, over which John **Scott** for **many**
years presided, at Sylvester Reed's of the **Old Sand
Hill** Tavern ; **and all** that **varied turf** artillery **of**
talent **which had** been laid **up in** ordinary since
Richmond, was brought into action by night-fall **at
The Star in** Stonegate. Lord Kennedy, Mr. **Rhodes
Milnes,** Mr. **Milbanke, and** Sir William Maxwell could · have **hardly been** happy **away ; and
the Earl of Darlington** never failed **to** drop in and
do a smart stroke **of business on the St.** Leger.
When that great **problem of the** Northern year **was**
about **to be** solved, **the** scene was changed **to the**
The Leger eve at
the Salutation. front, **and the** long room of The **Salutation.** Those who were there to mark

the feverish anxiety of the crowd as the loyal phalanx
of "Croft's men" bore up for their stable against
the dashing assaults of Mr. Gully in his kerseymeres
and top-boots—with Crockford and his curious half-
grammar, the terrible Justice, and the reckless
Ridsdale, to aid him—could never forget it more.

Kirby was waiting for an innings, and, as often as
not, scoring badly when he got one; Tommy Swann
(who detested betting with a captain who had a
patch on his boot, as much as booking the odds on a
Sunday), and Michael Brunton were doing a safe little
game on the quiet, and Crutch Robinson would lean
against the outer wall or make his *Crutch Robin-*
way to the horse-block, and sit there *son's sayings*
full of his gammon, and yet watch- *and doings.*
ing the market with the eye of a glede hawk.
He made it his rule of life to "lay agin the
Manchester pick." It might be that it was his
peculiar mode of upholding the rival dignity of Staley
Bridge, but he never swerved from it. To hot
favourites he had a deathless dislike, and as he
maintained that it was the specialty of the Manchester mind not only to back them, but to run
after them, when they came on to the course, he
found himself perpetually ministering to its enthusiasm, by laying the odds. " *I may just as weel have
thee five pun as anybody else,*" was the phrase in which
he graciously signified his intentions of operating.

If any one said that a horse was dead amiss, or fit to
run for a man's life, he never believed it; and he was
equally sceptical about their doing such great things
in private. " *Nar, nar! thou knawest a great deal
aboot it, I dar say,*" was his stereotyped reply, when
he heard of those marvellous trials, which are so rife
before the Derby; and then came his inevitable
proposal, " *I'll bet thee five pun; I may as
weel have my expenses, &c.*" This antipathy to
favourites was so rooted, that if anything was backed

against the field for a large stake, he would invariably stand the latter for five hundred. He seldom drank anything himself, but when he was fairly ensconced of an evening in the Black Bear at Newmarket, he was far from happy, if Joe Rogers, who was always staunch to his friends and Spaniel, Sam Darling, and a few more of them, did not look in to "pull up the score." His jockeys were not much troubled with orders from him beyond, "*Ride as thoo likest, only mind and win.*" Of all his racehorses he loved best to discourse of Stockport, and he ought to have known his form to an ounce, as he never wearied of trying him on Delamere Forest. His Liverpool was also a favoured theme, but when he boasted about selling him for seventeen hundred, he always wound up the recital with some dark grievance of "*thirteen pun for the toys.*"

Michael Brunton. Any one who conversed with Michael Brunton about horses, was sure to hear of Atalanta. "*Bless you,*" he was wont to say, when they pressed him with modern cracks, "*Old Atalanta would have snuffed them up her nose.*" Physician was always his delight, more especially for his delicate step, which "wouldn't crush an egg." His betting creed was concise, and based mainly on the principle, that "none are so good to bet with as trainers; if there are twenty of them in a race they've all got a good horse." He never took less than 3 to 1, or laid more than 5 to 2, and if he lost, he watched night and day for his man till he paid him. No one lost with better grace, and "*Bubbled again!*" was his only ebullition.

The old school of Yorkshire trainers—Thuytes. The trainers in drab-breeches and gaiters of the period were strictly in keeping with these old-fashioned odd-dealers. Thuytes of Middleham was quite a character among them, and hailed for a time from Tupgill. It was there that he first enunciated to a friend his great theory of Perpetual Motion. "By the Godlins, I can find out how to save a horse's legs, and mak him run for ever :— tak a feed of corn off a day." He was one of the first Northern trainers who adopted long tails, and he did it on the ground that "horses came into the world with them, and didn't want besom stumps." He thought His views on tails and training. a good deal on this subject, and highly approved of the old horse-dealer, who, to all seeming, seldom cared to do more than pass his hand down to the dock. If it was a strong one, he took the backbone for granted, "only a continuation of it,— Maister."

Mark Plews was a mixture of a blacksmith and a farmer, and if there was a Mark Plews. Richmond horse in the St. Leger, he invariably stood it. When Vingt'-un from Belle Isle was all the rage, Mark and his wife got on without telling each other, one to win £25 for himself, and the other £4 in partnership with Mrs. Pierse. These daring ventures got bruited about, and hence when the town express, which was managed on state occasions by sending horses on to Ferrybridge the day before, arrived at midnight, with the news of the defeat, one of the large party which sat up for it, could think of no other consolation than hoaxing "Old Mark." The window was not far from the ground, and the delegate was enabled to report, word for word, the matrimonial colloquy, which followed the shout of "*Vingt'-un's won.*" Mark was furious when the truth came out in the morning, and threatened in vain to walk all over Yorkshire, if he could only discover the owner of the voice.

He always delivered his mind about man or horse, without fear or favour ; and was looked upon by some as no His interview with the Marquis of Queensberry. mean authority. When the Marquis of Queensberry, whose waist was quite as capacious as his own, requested him to come and give him his confidential opinion of Caledonian's chance for the Leger, he mounted his spectacles and took a protracted survey. His rainbow neck he dismissed in silence, and then he broke out with, " *He wants what you and me has gitten, my Lord—hinder ribs, hinder ribs;*" and in went his spectacles to their case once more.

John Smith.　　The Marquis had John Smith for his trainer both in Scotland and at Middleham, and then he went to the Duke of Cleveland at Raby. In all these wanderings, his heart still turned to the Streatlam of his younger days (where he first wooed and won his Peggy, who was housekeeper at the Castle), and the lot he trained for Lord Strathmore. If a friend came to see him, as soon as "only some thin ribs of mutton and a *craw* pie," which is, being interpreted, a most excellent dinner, was over, his first toast was to that master's memory. "*He was the best master,*" he used to say, "*that I ever served; he made me a Tory.*" Still his loyalty to his dead Lord was quite equalled by that which one of his own Middleham stable lads showed towards himself. As he was setting out with his horses for Lancaster, he suddenly recollected that he had left his hair-brush, and sent Jem Alderson *alias* " Botty"* (who was under-valet at the time to Cartwright, *alias* " Harrogate,") in immediate search of it. " Botty" began doing up his mare, and for a time quite forgot his commission; and then snatching the brush out of the dressing-case rushed wildly after the lot on the road to Kettlewell, which was the first stage. The horses were nearly done up for the night, when one of the lads ran to tell his master that they had caught a

---

* In the Yorkshire dialect " above himself."

glimpse of "Botty," running in his shirt-sleeves, and without his cap, and brought him out of the inn with a rush, under the firm impression that some disaster had happened at home. "*Please, sir, I've brought you your hair-brush,*" said the gasping lad; but "*Get into the stable, and don't let any one see that I've such a fool about me,*" was his only welcome. However, Smith gave him the fullest credit in his heart, and had him conveyed the eighteen miles back in a miller's wagon, which happened to be passing. Such perseverance was certain to succeed, and when "Botty" became too heavy and had saved a good deal of money from presents, he became groom to Mr. Christy the great hat-maker, was eventually placed in one of his farms, and is there, we believe to this day.

Smith was severe with his lads, but he always hedged by saying during the ash-plant process, "*Thou'lt come to me in ten years' time, and thank me on thy knees for saving thee from the gallows.*" "Only cruel to be kind" had never a finer exemplification. His "poor Peggy" was a rare helpmate, but she still sighed for Middleham (where their charity and kindness will long be remembered), during her Raby sojourn. "Anything that comes from Middleham must be fed at all ends," was her spouse's invariable remark, when he found her giving an apple out of the window to Maria, the dam of Euclid and Theon, or any of her especials, which would regularly stop to claim it on their way from exercise; and he lived under a moral conviction, that "poor Peggy and Maria betwixt them will break all the glass about the place." The wish of the former to return to Middleham was fulfilled, and she and her John died at their house directly opposite "Croft's old stables," from whence the four first horses for the St. Leger, and three of them

Mrs. Smith's love for Middleham.

Comuses, set out for Doncaster in Theodore's year, and had their deeds recorded on their trainer's marble.

Tommy Sykes was a great advocate for long

Old Sykes and his card inspection.

steady work on Langton Wold, and he could have stayed any distance over cards. He was of grim aspect, and most rigidly orthodox in his silence during the game, except when he felt it salutary to say to his partner, " *Thoo maks a very poor tew of it.*" A Malton landlady, who knew his *forte*, implored him to counsel and shield her husband, when he had got up a little card party on the sly. " *Do go up, Mr. Sykes,*" she said, " *and see after my poor Jacky; I fear he'se only got among a baddish lot.*" A very few minutes satisfied Tommy how matters stood, and he was shortly enabled to descend with a clear conscience, and beg the anxious wife " *not to trouble yourself, for Jacky's the biggest rogue amongst them.*"

Billy Pierse had a wife who looked

Billy Pierse.

still more wisely after his interests, and made the most admirable Clary wine. It was, in fact, quite a moot point with him, whether he did not prefer it to that pipe of port, which Sir William Gerard sent him when he won the Oaks on his Oriana, and which, with another from the same hand, lasted him his life. His belief that " If I ever saved a shilling, my wife saved sixpence," was fully verified after his death, as his son Tom succeeded to a stable full of horses, with six hundred bushels in the corn chamber, and no debts. For three years he had no luck at Belle Isle, and was about to migrate to Hambleton, when his wife entreated him to stay "just one year more," and then came their harvest home. Mr. Kay, the banker, who used occasionally to invest a fiver on his advice, admired his character so much, that he was always believed to be the invisible friend, who presented him with the place. Billy was never known to quarrel with any one in Richmond, and he was so popular with the little freehold owners round there, that by way of homage they used to lead manure on to his land, and top-dress it without leave.

Mrs. Pierse took a large share in the management of the stable, and her husband always said that she had the quickest eye of the two for finding out if a horse was lame. She was, in short, the exact counterpart in the North, of Grandmother Day, with her walking-stick and black crunch bonnet, in the South. Morning after morning, Mrs. Pierse's she would stand at the door, with her training tact. hands behind her, marking each horse as it left the yard; and if there came " *I say, turn him back, mun, that horse is leame, I see,*" in the broad dialect of Yorkshire, there could be no mistake about it. In domestic matters, Billy never interfered, except, firstly by enforcing a goose every Sunday during the season (which he never thoroughly believed in, " except my wife roasts it"), and secondly by always buying and spreading out triumphantly on the dresser, when it arrived, just twice as much meat as was wanted whenever, purse in hand, he had chosen to sally forth to market. On this one point he was so proof to the last against all experience, that the poor people who shared the overplus began to think that his good soul of a wife secretly backed him in the habit. She was always her own almoner, and her plain useful education and sound sense made them quite a pattern couple.

The excessive shortness of his legs rather spoilt her Billy's seat on horseback, and he could not always use them to advantage when he was wasting. Jacques and Ben Smith walked with him once from Lancaster to Ashton Hall, on the morning of the races, but they were obliged to leave him behind at last on the road side, and he returned rather crest-fallen in a cart. Riding and training had taught him the great general rule, which he scarcely ever found to fail him—" If a two-year-old wins by half-a-neck, or even a length, with difficulty, depend upon it the whole squad's bad." As a powerful finisher and judge of pace, especially when he was on Haphazard, he stood in the first rank, and although he was such a one to dodge the lads, and knee their elders, when he had a chance, he was looked up to as quite a Lyndhurst in the profession. Mr. Tomline, the judge at Richmond, used often to tell how deftly he stopped a quarrel between Field and Mangles, who had ridden a very punishing finish, and got to high words about the issue. Trotting back past the chair to weigh in, he called out, " *How far did I win, Mr. Tomline?*" " *You, Mr. Pierse? why you were beaten three lengths,*" was the response; and even the belligerents could not help laughing when they saw Billy's polite bow, and heard his dry rejoinder, " *Thank you, sir; that alters the case materially.*"

His *test of two-year-old form.* appears as a marginal note beside the first lines.

Tact in stopping a quarrel. appears as a marginal note.

His whole book reading was confined to the Bible and Smith's Wealth of Nations. It was calculated that he had gone through each of them about thirty times, and they were his joy and solace to the last. With his arms folded on the table he would study Political Economy sternly for hours together. Although he gained largely by always paying ready money, he did not scruple, as we have seen in meat matters, to openly violate all the most cherished doctrines of supply and demand; but, armed with arguments at every point, he would occasionally open his mind to Sir Tatton, even when they were both dressed to ride, on the influx of bullion and the medium of exchange, subjects which threatened at times quite to weigh him down. Why John Day should be the only " Honest" man in the world also

His studies in Political Economy. appears as a marginal note.

puzzled him as sorely, as he did his own friends with the question, whether, in a commercial point of view, " the French will ever get us on to all-fours;" and he carried out his principle of selling in the dearest and buying in the cheapest market, by giving a few of the cordmen in Manchester an occasional stable tip, and carrying back as many yards of corduroy as breeched his stable lads for the year.

Mr. Joliff was the repository of one of his most cherished secrets. Billy The Borodino tip in the bed-room. went over to dine and sleep at his house, and after a very pleasant evening was ended, his host heard unmistakeable signals of distress in one of the guest-chambers. On entering, he found a little bare-headed figure, in a long night-dress, which turned out to be Billy, pacing about the room, quite on the fret, because " my wife has forgotten to put up my nightcap, Mr. Joliff, and I can't sleep without one." He was soon fitted with a substitute, and his peace of mind was restored. " *These are very high beds of yours, Mr. Joliff,*" he observed, " *I can't get in, do give me a leg up.*" This was also done with as much solemnity as if the St. Leger bell was ringing. Billy was tucked in, and felt at once warm and grateful. " *Mr. Joliff,*" said he, " *You've been very kind and neighbourly to me to-day, Mr. Joliff—I wish to make some return—it goes no farther—Borodino's a race-horse—Good night, Sir !*"

He never betted, and hated to hear of either trainers or jockeys doing much that way ; and his last mount was on Sir Walter, at Richmond, in 1819, for Col. Cradock, who thought very highly of him, and in later years always had him as his carriage companion to Doncaster and back. One of the most striking pictures of him is that in which he and Tom are looking at the Shuttle mare, with Simon at her foot. She was originally given to Billy by Sir William Gerard, after she broke her fetlock, and she nearly equalled the fame of Pratt of Askrigg's Squirt mare, (twelve of whose seventeen foals turned out well,) by throwing nineteen, with Swiss amongst them. Simon proved himself in a rough gallop, as a yearling, to be nearly as good as the three-year-old Canteen, from the Greystone In; but he died very soon afterwards from rupture of the heart.

Old Forth. Old Forth was another of those trainer-jockeys, of which Yorkshire has been pretty prolific, but he became so naturalized at Mitchell Grove, that the Southrons seemed to claim him. To the last he kept his "Frederick weight," and rode in trials with the same fine patience and tact. He loved to come through with the old one, and considered that " two year olds would do much greater things with each other than threes." Frederick, Little Wonder, and Merry Monarch were all trained by him, and through them he framed the rule, that " if you try a two-year-old a reeker for a quarter-of-a-mile at even weights with a Derby winner, and the young'un cannot win, depend upon it he's not worth backing for Epsom." The Goodwood Cup was the race he loved best, and he was sure, that " if a horse wins that really well trained, it is all up with him for the Leger." Even for it or anything else, he would never try more than a mile and a quarter, and if they could get that distance well, he was " quite ready to take the rest on credit." Buckle and Jim Robinson were his jockey idols, and he used to say that he would gladly have given £500 a-year to have the first call of " Old Frank." He delighted to dwell on those finishes in which Buckle brought his horse with such energy on the post, " that the very plates flew into the air."

Buckle, Robinson, & Chifney. John Day's decided opinion about " Old Frank" was, that if you threw him up in the air in any part of the country, he

would be certain to fall on a horse at the post, all
ready to begin. His courage was quite on a par
with the bull-dog's, which never left his heels; and
when a man nearly twice his weight annoyed
him at The Star, it took five or six to choke
him off again. His weakest point was his judgment in a trial and on horses generally; and it
was calculated that he must have lost hundreds of
pounds by bad hack bargains alone. Still, take *him*
for all in all, Jim Robinson, with his short heads on
the post, and Sam Chifney with his mighty rushes,
we cannot wonder that the old school of Turfites
dwell very fondly on the past, and declare that it
was " quite worth all the meeting's expenses to see
those three ride." As for Sam, they said that it
was equal to a tenner, just to watch him canter an
awkward horse. " *Of Newmarket*" may well be the
solitary and stately comment on his headstone at
Hove; but still our senior jockeys generally acknow-
ledge, and none more cordially than John and
Alfred Day, that Jim was " the schoolmaster" from
whom they formed their style.

Old Chifney rode so long that he
hardly seemed to rise in his saddle, and
his son as well as Tom Goodisson carried the practice to an extreme. Tom suffered from
it two or three times on the Heath, and more especially when Grandfather Day, who was two-and-
twenty stone, and always the boy for a lark, caught
him upon the road after Exeter races, and gammoned
him to put on his cap and jacket, fasten his hack to
the gigshafts, and ride it as leader for him into De-
vonport. The crowd, which rolled up like a snowball
to see the great sight, frightened the hack by their
cheers, and bolting into a shop window, it landed
Tom headforemost among a pile of shawls. He
rode no more leaders to the day of his death,
and never at any period of his life did he look like

a jockey, although he was a very good and fortunate one. There was no absence of mind in the saddle; but if he asked a friend to dine, it was just as likely as not that he would take up a little thumb-piece, walk round the table chewing it in silence, and depart to a glass and a pipe elsewhere, for the remainder of the evening. Owing to his height, Wheatley had much difficulty in wasting, and although he won the Derby on Prince Leopold and Spaniel, and was entrusted with Velocipede for the St. Leger, the impression left on posterity was, that he had great splay feet, and would always stick them out. Copperbottom was the first horse that Clift looked after, when he went into the Marquis of Rockingham's stables, under Kit Skaife, and the name well foreshadowed the future riding and walking powers of the lad. He was forty-four when he received the Fitzwilliam green jacket, and he held it till he could ride no more, and Harry Edwards succeeded him. Once only did he win the St. Leger, and then it was snatched not out of the fire, but the ditch, into which he and Paulina were driven. The lodge on the North side of Wentworth Park still retains his name, and if no jockey can say *ditto* to his winning the Derby in a trot, they are equally unable to boast that they ever judged at Ashdown.

Wheatley & Clift.

Bill Arnull infinitely preferred cock-fighting to coursing, and saving money to both. His friends used to tell him that he would go without victuals for a month, if he saw his way to a sovereign. This feeling grew upon him after he lost an action at Cambridge, and for years, as he reflected on those painful costs and damages, he would remark " I've never swallowed that four hundred yet." To realize when you can was his prevailing idea, and " I'd put my horse in Button Park," was the mode in which he conveyed it. Robinson could always outride him; but he had a

Bill Arnull on money matters.

high saddle repute, and quite a mania for winning both in public and private. Hence he would stop the pace so cleverly on the trial horse, that he could invariably win on him, and then blame the lads for not getting theirs out. The thing happened so often, that the Exeter stable at last put some one else up to come right away. He was very gouty, and a wretched walker in consequence, and it was curious to see him get off " his great grey like a giraffe," and helped with a straight leg on to the horse he had to steer.

William Edwards (who won his maiden race over Newmarket, in 1800), is the Southern Nestor among jockeys; and he and Sir Tatton had all the wins to themselves on the last day of Doncaster, four years later, one with Gratitude and Lady Brough, and the other with his brother's Sir Pertinax. What Will most grudged losing was the Doncaster Cup, which was then nearly a four-mile race on Lord Fitzwilliam's Orville. He was a mere feather at the time, and he begged hard for a curb-bridle; but the trainer knew his colt to be such a slug, that he only said " *the farther he runs away the more he'll beat them.*" Jackson on Alonzo and Shepherd on Sir Solomon thought very differently, and decided, in a hasty council of war, that it was their bounden duty to make the Leger winner run away. Accordingly they got the lad between them, and one, by sly taps of the whip, and the other by sundry toe administrations, waked up his colt most effectually for him. It was in vain for him to shout when he saw *their* game, " *I'll tell the Jockey Club of you;*" and Jackson finished up the matter, by kneeing him on to the rails. Three hundred guineas was Mr. Watt's present to George Edwards for winning the One Thousand on Cara, and that daring horseman well deserved such a sweetener. His brother Harry had still more power, and fairly

William Edwards.

Plot to make Orville run away.

drove his horse before him, sitting back in his set-to
like Robinson, and spurring in front of the girths.
No man got himself up better, and when he and Sam
Darling were side by side, the one might be seen
turning up his cuffs for the fray, and the other pulling down his ruffles.

John Jackson.   Although Jackson was only one Leger
short of Bill Scott, and had for many
years the finest practice in the North, he just lacked
Bill's dash, and with a first-class rider he would get
into difficulties at the finish.   John Shepherd was a
splendid judge of pace, and very fond, as a young
man, of coming to meetings in a chaise and pair,
when others were glad to hack it.   Some of his
finest races were won on Sir Solomon, whose power of
making his own play in a four-mile race was as remarkable as his rider's seat.   Shepherd held himself so
bolt upright, that there was quite a hollow in the
middle of his back, and he kept his foot straight out
before him, to the point of the horse's shoulder.

Ben Smith.   Ben Smith's patience and loyalty were
nobly conspicuous, when he refused to
dismount from the Duke of Hamilton's Ironsides,
after a horse had broken his leg with a kick, and he
won the race as he deserved.   It was a deed worthy
of the good, simple-hearted creature, and the connection with the stable was only ended by the Duke's
death.   Two St. Legers fell to their lot in the course
of it, and it is remarkable that the two he won for
Mr. Gascoigne, resulted from the only mounts that
gentleman ever gave him.

Malaprop sayings   His Malapropisms formed a fund of
of Ben.   amusement to the county, and were duly
repeated as " Ben's last."   When, however, it transpired that he had gone forth to commune with Nature at Studley, and had spoken on his return to
Middleham, of " fine ravenues and turpentine
walks," Yorkshire shook her head, and wouldn't

have it. There was plenty of the genuine article without drawing on fancy. An affidavit could have been sworn, if necessary, that on more than one occasion he had observed to an owner, " *I should say, Sir, that horse of yours is fifteen four or five.*" " *If you'll only buy that horse, Sir,*" he remarked to another, " *I'll warrant he'll win all the Maiden Plates in Scotland.*" His only comment on three Sir Peters, which Mr. Baillie of Mellerstein showed him, was to the effect : " *I'll lay, Sir, thou maans them to be in the rear ;*" and he used his favourite adjuration, " *By the Lord Harry, that's a fine colt,*" to such an extent, when Mr. Henry Peirse of Bedale invited him to a similar inspection, that his host might well ask rather tartly after his departure, " What on earth did the fellow mean '*Harrying*' me every minute?" With all his quiet ways, he did a little of the kneeing business occasionally ; but when he began it with Jackson, there came the fierce North Riding challenge ; " *By the Heart, my lad, thoo'se trying it on. I'll gie it thee,*" and at it they both went, and after fairly cutting each other's jackets off their backs, returned to scale in peace.

Bob Johnson was an equally good-hearted fellow, though much rougher in his speech, full of activity and a quick starter, but in far too great a hurry to get home. He was born at Sunderland, and was apprenticed to a quack doctor. This gentleman also did a little in smuggled spirits, and often sent Bob out to his customers, with two tin cases full of gin on his shoulders. On one of his journeys, he met the Lambton hounds, and his pony becoming excited by the cry, and the flapping of the empty cases, carried him with a tremendous cannon against Sir Hedworth Williamson, who was at first disposed to be very angry. However, the lad's enthusiasm under difficulties disarmed the

Early humours of Bob Johnson.

D

baronet, and he often told the story when Bob had become famous. The budding apothecary soon deserted the herb and spirit business, and after a probation at Ellerker's of Hart's, he became a light-weight at Croft's. Ottrington, who, as he elegantly remarked, "had tired like muck," in all his other races, was the first St. Leger winner he rode. His orders were to watch Manuella, and when he found his horse living on, and the Oaks mare sinking, he irreverently exclaimed as he swept past the old Richmond jock; " *Hoo do ye like me, Mr. Pierse?*" Well might Billy say afterwards, in his anguish, that " for cheek that Bob Johnson beats them all."

First mount on General Chassé. His first connection with General Chassé was brought about rather oddly. Sir James Boswell came to see his string, which were at Ashgill for a short time, and consulted with Fobert, as to whom he should get to ride the chesnut, in his maiden race at Liverpool. " *Yonder's Robert Johnson breaking sticks, Sir James; he'se nearly as good as any of them,*" said Fobert, pointing in the direction of Tupgill, where the ever-busy Robert then resided; " *he'se just the man for him.*" " *In course I can ride him,*" said Bob, when he had been waved up ; " *we've nought in, have we, Mr. Fobert?*" This question was absolutely necessary, as he left everything to his brother-in-law Watson Lonsdale, and Robert Hill his head lad.

Even if any one asked him about a pedigree (which they took care to do pretty often), he gave his invariable answer " *In course thou knaws, he'se by t'aud horse, out of t'aud meer.*" However, if he forgot their pedigrees, or rather never learnt them, he gave a pretty vivid sketch of their capabilities when he had scaled in. He had not ridden Chassé in his trial, and did not therefore expect to find him such a lurcher, and Sir James was equally unprepared for his definition of the chesnut, as " *a nice donkey of a divil—donkey I tell ther."* Still, owners felt great confidence in him, and if Bill Scott carried off four St. Legers in succession, Bob, Mangles, and Ben Smith were the only jockeys who could boast of having won it three years out of four. Relying on this prestige, his friends were wont to consult him at Doncaster as to his chance; but they never got much more out of him than *"In course, thoo may back me to be third—likely enough t'aud place—I never get for-* His perpetual thirds for the St. Leger. *warder."* That was true enough after St. Patrick's year. When the Barefoot St. Leger was run twice over, he held that place each time on Comte d'Artois; and Emancipation, La Fille Mal Gardée, Bedlamite, General Chassé, and Beeswing only rivetted the spell. Bedlamite suffered severely from that terrible shower which almost washed away horse and man during the first parade that was ever made for the great race, and Bob, who was always up early, and away towards the distance to "try his stirrups," resolutely refused to accept the umbrella and great coats which were pressed upon him, and ended, as in General Chassé's case, with making his run too soon.

He got an ugly fall over Doncaster on the Nutwith day. Trainers were His fall at Doncaster. then allowed to ride on the course when the horses were running, and Tom Dawson, in galloping up from the distance to encourage the sulky Aristides, ran against him on his pony, and left him lying on his face with the force of the concussion. He picked himself up just in time to hear that Job had beaten the Malton crack, and subsequently informed Tom Dawson of his accident, which, he stuck to it, had been caused by " a great divil with a red coat on a grey meer," and quite fought out the point with Tom, when he explained and apologized.

Colloquies and correspondence with Mr. Ord.

A perfect Ordiana might be made up of the scenes between him and the lord of Beeswing. They duly decided, after accepting sixpence for the purpose from a facetious friend at Ascot, to " let t'aud meer win first, and get shaved afterwards." Again they were heard to take counsel together about the state of Mr. Ord's betting book. " *I've taken fifteen sovereigns to two, Robert, about the mare,*" said that gentleman, most meekly. " *Shall I hedge?*" " *In course, nowt of the sort,*" was the prompt answer, " *Stan it out ; be a man or a mouse.*" Once when this comical pair were separated, Bob suddenly felt constrained by a sense of duty to communicate stable intelligence ; and Will Beresford, who used to tell the story in his best style, was requested to act as his secretary. " *Sir, the meer's weel, I'm weel, we're all weel,*" was the result of Bob's dictation, and he declined to furnish any other address than " Ord, Esq., Northumberland." It must, however, be explained that the original draft was much more voluminous, and that Bob had thus remonstrated when it was read over to him : " In course, thou knows, Mr. Beresford, I din'nt tell thee to put in ' *In course*' all that number of times. Now, I'll gie it ye plain." After this, he felt it more politic to commit his own feelings to paper, and having left Tupgill with a cause of anxiety upon him, he announced his return to convalescence at Liverpool, in these spousal words : " *Peg, all's well ; Robert Johnson.*"

The Pilgrim's Rest, at Gosforth.

In his wasting days Bob was an eminent member of that School of Industry, which met during the Newcastle race-mornings in the Servants' Hall at Gosforth. Mr. Brandling liked the custom kept up, and often a muffled troop of Sim, Jacques, Scott, Harry Edwards, Holmes, Garbutt, Cartwright, Lye, Oates, Gray, &c., would be found there about ten o'clock, sipping the warm ale

which the butler always had in readiness for them
after their three miles' walk from the Grand Stand,
and listening, if Bill Scott was not just i' the vein,
to Bob Johnson's comments on nags and men. One
morning Bob did not get on with his ale, and Mr.
Brandling asked him if there was anything else he
would like better. "*I don't knaw, Sir,*" he said,
"*but I should like a bottle of your champeagne.*" It
was accordingly brought, and Bob considered that
he put his host up to such a good thing for the day
while they were drinking it, that he wound up with
"*Weel, I think I should like another away with me,
Mr. Brandling, to drink your health when I've won.*"
His companion protested in vain, but Mr. Brandling
was intensely amused, and sided so energetically with
Bob, that another was fetched, and duly stuffed into
his pocket, and away he went rejoicing, and verified
his Gosforth tip by beating Sim cleverly. Jacques
turned that Pilgrim's Rest to high account once, as
he was in it three times in four-and-twenty hours,
and in spite of the butler's request to consider his
health, took off about 17lbs. in the time, rather than
lose his mount. Two ounces of Epsom salts, a little
tea with gin in it, to make him break out freely, a
dry biscuit, and a poached egg with vinegar, were all
that passed his lips. He excelled as much in wasting,
as he did in corner-cutting, and if fifteen or sixteen
started on a Doncaster morning to Rossington Bridge
and back, he and Sim and Jack Holmes would invariably be seen leading up the old elm-avenue at
the finish.

Sam Darling, who has ceased to ride *Sam Darling's*
since 1844, was another of the hard *wastes.*
wasters, and seemed to view it merely in the light
of a constitutional. His walks in the sweaters alone,
for fully twenty-five years, averaged some five hundred miles, as he often went, whether he had weight
to get off or not. To the last he could manage

eight two with hard pinching on a 4lb. saddle, to which he was peculiarly partial. He quite knocked up John Day junior, who was always a bit of a piper, in a strong twelve mile walk from Newmarket to the Swan at Bottisham and back. John's sweaters got slack, and he was so completely beat that he gave in near the toll-bar. Coach-riding was Sam's aversion, as travelling in that style, especially by night, has an immense tendency to put on weight, although it "comes off like butter." He perhaps never galloped from Manchester to York in an afternoon, as Sim, Gray, and Garbutt once did; but in 1832, one of the best seasons he ever had, he rode in 174 races, and won seventy-three, many of them heats, in all parts of the country. One year after riding in the St. Leger, he borrowed a clever hack from a brother-jockey, and catching the coach at Sheffield, won twice at Shrewsbury the next day, and had time to waste as well. His delight was to get a great raking horse to make play with, and in the science of going in front to stop or force a pace, there was no more able practitioner.

Mr. Horsley's story of Sam. The habit of rather closing one eye gave him a very knowing look, and his friend Horsley used to have a joke against him on this head. He had backed a horse with some stranger on the course for two sovereigns, and was asked for the money next day. "*Dash me,*" said Sam, opening both his eyes as if he was quite astonished at the request, "*I bet you two sovereigns!*" "*Oh! I beg your pardon, Sir,*" said the man, quite submissively, "*The gentleman I bet it with had only one eye—I've made some mistake,*" and he was moving off to renew the search when Sam called him back and paid. Such was poor Horsley's version of the story, but Sam always said that he made it. Isaac is the horse with which his name is linked, but Major Ormsby Gore's Hesperus, which he also trained, was the luckiest for him. The Gloucestershire Stakes, one of the earliest and most important handicaps, made part and parcel of this horse's thirty-four victories in his hands, and he was beaten in the only race in which Sam did not ride him. Four times over was Sam cheered as the winner of the Chester Cup, and perhaps no one ever rode so many different animals, all by the same horse, as he did when Lord Exeter and Mr. Houldsworth were making such a run upon Sultan.

Only one of the three great races, to wit, the St. Leger with Rockingham, fell to his lot, and he never took a mount *Winning the St. Leger on Rockingham.* with less heart. He was engaged, as he considered, by Mr. Watt to ride Belshazzar, and was about to dress for him, when Dick Shepherd called him aside, and said, "*I want thee; thee must ride in the white cap to-day; thee'd win.*" Sam's countenance fell, as he had just put a pony on Belshazzar, but there was no remedy. "*Thee'd win, I tell thee,*" resumed the relentless Dick in a louder key; "*coom and have a glass of sherry for luck, and doan't look so sulky.*" Under these grim blandishments, he very reluctantly gave up the harlequin cap to Nicholson, and saddled the big pheasant-looking son of Humphrey Clinker, whose temper seemed none of the sweetest. The joints of the narrow-looking Belshazzar fairly "snocked" as he walked, and Tommy with his "spurs down-hill" as usual, made all the running with him; but long before they reached the Red House, Sam found out that it was the white cap's day, and got two hundred from Mr. Watt for wearing it.

There were only a few years between John and Sam Day, and clever as the *John and Sam Day's first pony race.* brothers were, they got regularly picked up in the morning of life, when they went off together to the diversions at Lyndhurst. John had a

wonderful little brown pony, with which he expected
to clear out the whole lot of Hampshire yokels, and
he was so haunted with the fear of her being " got
at," that he persuaded Sam, nothing loath for a game
of that sort, to get into a crate in the stable, and
watch her all the forenoon.   Sam's position was one
of undoubted peril.   He was a tight fit

Sam in the crate.

to begin with, and the truss of hay,
which the cautious John had piled over him, gradually became so diminished, that at last he was
within an ace of having the pitch-fork in his spine.
Those who have known him, whether on Mendicant
at the Oaks post (where his mare was nearly kicked
out of time) or in later years as banker at the Danebury Stewards' Stand, will feel assured that he bore
up under the dispensation; but when he did rejoin
the outer world, it was only to face worse things.
The brothers proceeded to the course, but it got
buzzed about who they were, and how high they
had tried their pony, and no one cared to be beaten.
However, a country lad suddenly came forward in an
apron and high-lows, and very humbly trusted that
John would not take it amiss if " I run my old pony
out of a cart there against you."   " *Who are you,
Sir, may I ask?*" said John drawing himself up with
native dignity ; " *put down your ten pounds, and then
I'll see about it.*"   The money came out so promptly,
that John rather began to smell a rat, but there was
no retreating.   John mounted, and the young man
mounted with his butcher's apron twisted round his
arm, and when the Danebury pony had been beaten
some twenty yards, John learnt that he had been
matching her against Gulliver, whose fame was in
all the West Countrie.

    Sam had quite his share of winnings in the pony
way, but he had the ill-luck to meet Macdonald on
Mat o' the Mint at Sherborne, and to find that
Mat's sister was pounds below his form.   He also

John Day (1836), p. 41.

rode at Barnet for the Duke of St. Albans, and then he had six years with Cooper, who trained for the Duke of York at Newmarket, while "Our Jim" was riding exercise at Robson's. His brother John learnt his rudiments from his father, " an out and out fellow," as Hampshire says to this Grandfather day. Sitting in his low-crowned hat Day. and brown leggings, on his pony Black Jack, and with Lord Palmerston at his side, watching Hougomont at work on Houghton Downs, he was as completely the model of the old John Bull trainer, as his son Sam was of the elegant muscular jockey, when Lord Rivers placed his statuette by the side of Tom Cribb's in his collection of man-models. John was first apprenticed at Newmarket with Smallman, who then trained the Prince Regent's horses. His salary was only ten guineas a-year, and two suits of livery; but he steadily rose the ranks, and when he did get into riding practice, his hack's shoes had scarcely time to cool. With a saddle round his waist, and huge saddle-bags flapping at his side, he might be seen year after year on circuit, and two summers in succession, with Tom Dilly to cheer the way, he rode through the night from Exeter to Southampton, so as to catch a mount at both the meetings.

Perhaps he was greatest as a jockey John Day as a in his earlier days, when he had not so jockey. much training and betting on his mind. Latterly he presumed very much on his own training, and liked to "feel my own condition under me." He was all activity, and very fond of a rush, and no one could handle a hard-pulling or bad-mouthed horse more ably. Touchstone, for instance, he held as if he was in a vice, and unlike Sam Chifney, who abhorred them, he gloried in curb-bridles. Still there was a lack of ease and style about his seat, as well as his son Sam's, whose patience and hands

were undeniable. Strange to say, old John never
won a Derby, though he made up for it by five Oaks.
Some of his pleasantest jockey recollections were his
beating Priam and Conolly on Lord Berners's Chap-
man, and the recital of how he made play, and then
stopped his horse for a few strides, and let the crack
reach his girths, was given with a solemnity and em-
phasis befitting a passage out of the Old Fathers.
Defeating Buckle for the Riddlesworth was another
sunny memory, and so was The Column, which he
His race on Am-
phitrite. snatched out of the fire on the Duke of
Portland's Amphitrite. "*His Grace*,"
he would say, "*gave me his own orders; 'John, you
make play behind !' and I did. Jim Robinson went
on Mixbury; and then he suffered; and I came
thirty yards from the post, and I got first run, and
he never quite reached me—that was a great victory
for me.*" Coldrenick was a rare miler, but he did
not deceive him at last, and there was nothing for it
but to "bear up for him," and try and save some of
the Derby money. John's severe system of training
hardly suited a horse of that stamp, as he worked
him instead of stopping him, and made matters
rather worse than better. Still he wrought wonders
in his time, and it would have made half-a-dozen
trainers' reputations to have brought Crucifix with
such a faulty sinew to the Oaks post, or get Grey
Momus through The Port on such doubtful fore-legs.
His waste walk, Never did any one lead a harder life
in and out of the saddle. He went to
bed quite early, and was never asleep after four in summer, or letting any one else sleep. He took nearly
an hour to dress, always tying his white cravat
with the most scrupulous care. The horses were
all done up again by eight, and then after a slender
breakfast of tea and bread and butter, he went
wasting for a couple of hours. The wind might be
high, and the rain might pelt, but in that path of

duty he defied the elements. A mile walk, which Alfred Day still uses, was cut out for him round Sadler's Plantation, and when the March winds whistled keenly round young John's home at Longstock, he too deserted his daily trudge to Tidcomb Bridge or "the Lily Roarer" (*Anglicè* White Lion) at Wherwell, and piped away towards the afternoon in the same sheltered grove. The umbrella, which never left Old John's grasp except for a whip, was not forgotten in his waste walk; and he held it aloft on a wet morning, and swung his arms by turn. He generally began at nine stone ten, but it came off very freely, and at his latest effort in '45 he rode 8st. 1lb. on Wilderness for the Ham Stakes *and Danebury discipline.* in a 3lb. saddle. His stable lads were kept in the highest state of discipline, and after the two Sunday services, he never failed to assemble them in the dinner-room, and read one of Blair's Discourses. His whip hung up behind him, and with a rush as electric as that on Amphitrite, he had it down from its peg, and across the back of any of the unlucky sleepers.

With his round hat, scarlet coat, and massive silver-handled whip (which John Day rigidly preserves as his staff of office) he made up admirably as a clerk of the course at the Stockbridge Meeting. When he had resigned that office and the stables to his son, he never missed coming over to the meetings to shake his old friends by the hand, and we remember how in 1854, he solemnly indorsed John's demand that "my boy William,"—who whipped in for the Four-Year-Old Trienial on the peacocky Pharos, which he had just purchased for twenty-seven guineas at Tattersall's—should pass the post and "not disgrace the family by being distanced." Those were times when Sir John Mills with his four bays and the red-cuff postilions, *Sir John Mills at Stockbridge races.* was seen driving up to Danebury for lunch before the races began, and then leading the way to the Stand. But the cavalcade did not go straight back to Mottisfont from the Stand, when Aitchbone and Alfred in the " all blue" had won the Champagne Stakes. The postilions nearly pulled down one of the Danebury gate-posts in their zeal to come in at a trot. The old baronet had another cigar, and some more champagne, and gave the gout notice to look out for itself; every bit of blue ribbon that the ladies or the lasses could rifle off cap, bonnet, or watch-case, was pressed into the service for streamers and rosettes; and the church bells rung many a merry peal, as they did in after years for Giantess and the Warwickshire Handicap, when Mottisfont heard the news. Old John was in the thick of it, as delighted as any of them, at the success of the lord of the soil, but the meeting of '59 was the last both for him and Isaac Day.

Isaac Day. "No relation, but the best of friends," was always full of his kidding, and actively proposing during that visit to ride his black cob against a man on foot for a hundred yards. Good cobs were a great point with him, but he was happiest when he had a screw to doctor, and his very highest ambition was to be talked about. "The Vicar" had a remarkable time of it with his patron, before whom he used to stand most reverentially, hat in hand, as if he had been the Archbishop of Northleach. Still he could not make out what game Isaac would be up to next with him, when he once darkly observed on the authority of a late Duke of Grafton, that " no jockey was a jockey unless he could cross country," and that as he (The Vicar) was no longer a young man, it was high time that it should be seen by the world how he could perform in that line. The apparition of all John Osborne's lads, determined to eat out their entrance shilling, was not one whit less startling to the office-bearers at a recent Middleham

tea-fight, than the next announcement that Sparta
was in training for the Liverpool, and that he was
to ride her. However, to Aintree the trio went, and
Isaac had the laugh he yearned for, when he learnt
from Tom Oliver, through the medium of an image
of which Swift and Addison in their best form
never dreamed, that the face of "The Vicar" in the
scramble at Becher's Brook reminded him of a man,
"who had swallowed a wagon-load of monkeys."

Like his friend Isaac, the celebrated
"Uncle Sam" has always been a "light
'arted 'oss," and we may say, quite the

Uncle Sam in the Epsom paddock.

Sam Weller of the Turf. We hardly ever saw that
great steersman of Gustavus, Priam, Pyrrhus, and
Mendicant look perfectly grave, except when he was
lately leaning on his staff under the hawthorn canopy
in the Epsom Paddock, drawing shrewd mental paral-
lels between the past and the present, as twice the
eighteen walked round him, and finally delivering
judgment that one "was made at a pottery," and
another "at six." No man has had such a string of
accidents, and plucked up under them so wonderfully. He broke nearly every limb he had but the
right arm, "skull and jaw included," riding for Dick
Goodison, and then one leg was broken twice, once
by jumping out of a carriage into a rut at Goodwood, when an omnibus backed into it, and again by
slipping up in the Hall at Mr. Ben Way's. His spirits,
however, knew no decay; and music soothed his
soul. He would have hold of a tin-
pipe, when he was on his back after the

Uncle Sam on the pipe.

first accident for nearly nine months, and played a
variety of pastoral and martial airs with a taste and
brilliancy which astonished the Singleton farmers.
They never just knew where they had him on that pipe.
At times, he would blow a hurricane, or go as low as a
Southern Hound. "He could," as he was wont to
observe, "kill a town wasting, and when he was in

his golden prime, which, barring his leg, never seems to leave him, he was not far wrong. For instance, when he was at supper at Robson's, a letter came from Lord Henry Fitzroy, that the Duke of Grafton's mare Loo was to run next day in an A. F. race, and that the money was on. Sam finished his helping, and then mounted the weighing-machine, which made him 8st. 4lbs. without his coat, but he went at it like a Briton, and, with physic and a fourteen-mile walk, got off the 12lbs., and won.

His lecture on waste. The announcement of a lecture by him to the young jockeys and society in general on "My Wasting Days," would fill Covent Garden thrice over. First he would treat of liquors on this wise: " *Drink inflates you just like a balloon; champagne and light wines are all rubbish; they only blow a fellow's roof off.*" He would then tackle the eating part of the business in very different terms: " *No man can work if he can't eat; you can't get light without eating; have a good mutton-chop, that's my style; it gives a tone to the stomach.*" We might then have a pleasing digression to the days when he was an eleven-six farmer near Reading, and took to the racing-saddle once more, accompanied by a variety of Robson anecdotes; but most assuredly the curtain would fall to this great moral tag, " *Depend upon it a man does'nt enjoy the comforts of life unless he knows the wasting part of the business.*"

His London practice. The history of his residence in London when he was at that business for the second time, would be one of his finest " bits." He wanted to draw 8st. 7lbs., and he was two months doing it. Sometimes he showed his ruddy, streaming face among the quiet dwellers at Wimbledon, and departed like a flash, before they could make out his mission, leaving the very wildest surmises in his track. Again, he would be found walking in his

woollen attire on Greenwich Hill during Easter, and
not only getting scratched himself, but investing a
penny on the spot, running after a large field of girls
(who called him "The Mysterious Stranger,") and
doing immense execution with his scratcher in return.   At all events it was fine fun, and he was
not only "*fit to fight a wind-mill after it,*" but to
win the Derby and the Oaks as well.

John and Bill Scott began well by Early tuition of
John and Bill
Scott.
being born at Chippenham, near New-
market, but they were not in the same
stable, from the time they left their father, who became the landlord of The Ship at Oxford, till they
met in 1814 at Crofts of Middleham.   Mr. Scott,
sen., who had ridden for Sir Sitwell Sitwell when
he had Clinker and Gooseander (the dam of Sailor
and Shoveller) in his stable, destined them both for
the saddle, and placed John at Bourton under
Stevens, and Will at Sadler's of Allsworth.   Boyce
and Tiny Edwards gave them respectively "a Newmarket polish," and John had three-quarters of a
year with Franks at Middleham, before he joined
Croft, and looked after Sir William Maxwell's grey
cup horse, Viscount. Starting for himself he had a few
months at Hambleton, where he trained No Go, and
when the great match was made between Filho da
Puta and Sir Joshua, he was requested Filho da Puta's
match.
by Croft, whose health was very delicate,
to undertake the responsible charge of the crack of
the North on his Newmarket journey.   The training of this fine-tempered, leggy, and near-sighted
colt was a very anxious task, and John had not
much credit out of it after all.   True to the great
code of his life, he wanted to run him rather above
himself; but when Croft came, he thought he had
not done work enough.   The Brothers Chifney, who
had backed him, and were made Friends in Council,
sided with the elder, so he was sent along again, and as

John says with a sigh to this day, "*That cooked him.*"
Looking over the John's eye for condition is of a very
Squeers' lot. universal kind, and no one made a more
accurate calculation of the time it would require to
them "fit," when the supposed "young Wackford
Squeers" and a batch of pupils, rode down with him
on the coach from London to Yorkshire.

The fame of the match brought shoals of visitors
to Filho da Puta's stable, and one of them walked in
and made himself so much at home, that the young
trainer was quite taken aback, and supposed that he
must be a friend of the Maxwell family. However,
when the horse was sheeted up again, it struck him
The sporting that he had been a little too good-na-
bagman. tured, and he ventured to ask the stranger if he would favour him with his name. "*My
name,*" he said, "*with all pleasure—Mr. Hogg from
town,—in the silk way,*" and with a most magnificent
bow and strut he departed. The horse lost some
lengths at starting by nearly going on to his head,
and Goodisson drove him after that ; but the match
was the making of John Scott, and it ended in Mr.
Houldsworth's buying Filho for 3,000 guineas, and
taking the young trainer with him to Mansfield. It
is worthy of note that on the great match afternoon,
Sam Darling, who wore the Houldsworth colours so
long and well in Beresford's day, made his Heath
début on one of Mr. West's horses.

Performances of Bill Scott won the Doncaster and
Filho. the Richmond Cups on Filho, after
running clean out of the course in the latter race. As
a sire Filho paid well for a time, and Sherwood, the
second for the St. Leger, and Miller of Mansfield,
were his principal legacies to the green and gold.
His St. Leger was a very remarkable one, from the
fact that at the close of the betting, the four first
horses were exactly placed. The weight of money
which Filho and Dinmont carried was enormous, as

Croft had never been more confident, and hence Sir William Maxwell might well thrust his stick for a safety-valve to his feelings, at night, through all the pier-glasses at the Rein Deer, and long in his rapture for more. The name of his horse was rather a puzzler to the hardware youths, Dispute about his name. who had a vague notion that it was Fill the Pewter, and it led to a little difficulty between two of them, who had seen the race from a carriage-wheel. "*Noo Jack, what wil't have for a croon?*" said one; and "*Hang it man, I'll have Filler,*" was the reply. "*Will'er?*" said his mate. "*Dang it, then, I'll have Pewter;*" and anon when the winner's name was shouted, there came such an angry skirmish of "*I'se won; Filler's won; Dang it thoo'se a le'er; Pewter's won, &c.,*" succeeded by a battle royal, that the police had to interfere and explain.

John had quite given up the saddle John's riding. before he settled at Mansfield, and as he jocularly says, "Bill turned me out of training." His first win was the Freemen's Plate, four mile heats, at 4st. 4lbs. over the Oxford Port Meadows. Wasting never suited him, and after getting from ten stone to 7st. 7lbs. in a very short time, to ride for a Seventy Pound Plate at Lancaster, which he lost by a neck, and half killing himself by the effort, he was glad to let it alone. His last appearance was in a private trial of eleven cocktails at Malton, in which he rode Rufus, but his Brother Bill and Sim ran him out at the last turn, and "ruined my prospects entirely."

With the exception of a few of Pratt's Life on Sherwood Forest. leather-platers, not a horse had as yet been trained on Sherwood Forest, when John went into residence there, and began operations with a stable at the top of the Windmill Hill. The gallops were laid out on the Forest land, and extended nearly up to Sherwood Hall, and Filho and the

E

young stock stood at Farnsfield. Although Cata-
line and Magistrate by Camillus, a perfect beauty of
a horse and bought for £500 from Major Bower of
Welham, were the only other good things through his
hands, John had a pleasant enough time of it. Mr.
Houldsworth scarcely knew his horses by sight,
and to the end of his life, if he took a nomination,
he invariably said, "*I don't know what I have for it;
put down my name; and I'll write to my man.*" The
Rufford Hunt in "Black Jack's" day had few more
constant attendants than John in his drab-breeches
and cherry-coloured tops; and Bill, who was then
first jockey to Mr. Powlett, and also rode for
Mr. Houldsworth, was nearly as well known with
them during the season, as he was in after-years with
Sir Tatton's. John Jones (and latterly Sharpe) was
huntsman, and Jem Davis (father to the present Jack)
and "Johnny Walker of Wynnstay," whipped in to
him. It was a merry sort of life " under the green
wood tree" for the young trainer, as the master and
the Duke of Portland gave him full liberty of the
Forest. Railways were then undreamt of in those
sylvan solitudes, and no telegraph-posts in black,
white, and green array near Wellow Wood suggested names for foxhounds. He could

Forest privileges.

have coursed for twenty miles, and he
killed some ninety-three hares in one season, a feat
which pleased him nearly as much as beating thirty
dogs in a Scurry Stakes, with his Glaucus, after he
had been busy among the scuts all day.

If he had just missed one St. Leger

Birth of Matilda.

for Mr. Houldsworth with Sherwood, he
found "the missing link" to victory during the short
time which he spent at Mansfield, between leaving
that gentleman's service and entering on Mr. Petre's.
At his advice, old Juliana had come to Magistrate,
and was standing at the stable of a lawyer near the
Swan Inn. About four o'clock on May morning, a

lad came running to his lodgings with the news that
she had foaled, and that they thought it was a colt.
John thought so too, at first, from its excessive
activity, although in size it looked "like a buck
rabbit, with a black list stripe down its back." Its
arrival created a very great sensation even at that
early hour, and Mrs. Stirrup, the landlady of The
Swan, and own sister to the celebrated George Clark
of Barnby Moor, ran out to see it, in her shift. In
spite of his disappointment, John's gallantry did
not wax cold, when he found that she had come to
do honour to one of her own sex, and his offer to
"*stand you a new quarter piece, Mam, if this
Comus filly wins the Leger*," was quickly made and
accepted. The word was lightly spoken, but the
little bay, which was soon skipping everywhere about
the box, ripened into "Matilda,"—the first of Mr.
Petre's memorable St. Leger trio, and the first of
the Whitewall fifteen—and the silk was not forgotten.

She was in fact the load-star of John's fortunes, and
refusing a very tempting offer from Sir Thomas
Mostyn to go to Holywell, he cast in his lot with
Mr. Petre at Whitewall (whose twenty- Mr. Petre's
four stalls are now trebled), with Veluti, career.
Ivanhoff, and a few more cast-offs, in the Martinmas
of '24. A hundred sovereign match over the St.
Leger course that year with Tramper, was the first
Scott victory of "the pink and black," and it only
missed a 450 Sovereign Stake with Saladin, a half-
brother to Matilda, by half-a-head. It was somewhat remarkable that in this race John should beat
his old master, and that Mr. Petre should be worsted
by a mare of Mr. Lambton's, whose parties, equi-
pages, and racing stud had stirred up his keenest
emulation. His Whitewall career was as short as it
was merry. He was at the same time master of the
Badsworth, with Jack Richards from Sir Bellingham
Graham as his huntsman, and there "was a sound of

revelry by night" as well as day, at Stapleton Park.
Still, when all had crumbled in his hand, he had at
least something to boast of.   He had led back a
St. Leger winner to scale, who started at 200 to 1;
he had scored three St. Leger victories in succession,
and in this respect has never known his marrow,
save in Lord Archibald Hamilton.   His horses had
beaten Voltaire, Sir Hercules, Velocipede, Zinganee,
Lottery, and Laurel; and he had sold a six-year-old,
good enough even in his decline to give 17lbs. for
his two years, and collar the great Camarine for the
Ascot Cup.   Well may John Scott have a tender
recollection of his first Whitewall master, and say
in our hearing to one who had so often shared his
triumphs, " *If we were among them, Sim, with another
Mr. Petre, we should not take a deal of harm.*"

Bill Scott's jockey-   To write of Bill Scott is to master the
ship.   inner history of four Derbies, nine St.
Legers, and as many Champagne Stakes, three Oaks,
and a succession of the best stakes of the North and
South for thirty years, until we recall him wending his
way back to scale in his yellow and blue cap for the
last time, on Snowball, at York.   Still there is something in Tommy Nicholson's facetious boast that he
(Tommy) was best man over Doncaster; as in Jack
Spigot's year, he had a mount in fourteen out of the
twenty-one races, and only lost once.   Two years
before that, Bill's and Tommy's claim to have ridden
the St. Leger winner was in abeyance for sixteen
days, and then the Jockey Club decided that the
first start was valid, and that Tommy's Antonio win
must stand.   If Bill lost the St. Leger on Sherwood, it gave him an opinion of Barefoot which he
turned to good account, when that Tramp chesnut
ran for the Oatlands and carried seven hundred of
his money.   He often declared, " *It was the first good
money I ever won.   I knew from the Leger what a
game beggar he was.*"   Bill perhaps a little over-did

it in that race by making such a strong pace with
Sherwood, but his Doncaster recipe to the last was
to make severe running to the top of the hill. "*If
you can't get a pull and go on again,*" he was wont
to say, "*you'll never win; what's the use of condition
if you don't use it?*" No one ever knew him lose a
race if he once had the best of it, and if thirty were
in it, he could tell with one of his Parthian glances,
exactly what every one of them was   His riding of
doing. His brother always considers   Attila.
that his riding of Satirist in the St. Leger, and of
Mundig in the Derby were the finest specimens of
his style, which as far as daring and decision went, has
perhaps never been matched. He was out of humour
with Col. Anson for starting Attila, with 9lbs. extra,
and the St. Leger in view, and hence he cut the colt up
sadly in the Drawing Room Stakes, when Robinson
on Envoy had him as dead as a stone. In the St.
Leger again he went off with him at score, and enabled Heseltine on Eboracum before they got to the
Red House triumphantly to carry out his threat,—
"*I'll run at Bill Scott as long as my horse can wag
a leg.*" Strange as it may seem, ten out of the
seventeen jockeys who rode that day are dead, and
Sam Rogers is the only one left in *Ruff*.

    Bill was wonderfully fond of chaffing   His amusements.
Nat, and dropped it into him rather
heavily one day at "the Squire's;" but still his
pleasantry was very neat, when he chose. "*Well,
my Lord,*" was his salute to Lord Maidstone, when the
(1) was entered against the "gorge de pigeon" jacket,
in Mr. Clark's book, after the Molecomb, and his
lordship met him coming back to scale on The Caster,
who had run half way up the hill, "*We've set the
caster the first time.*" In his hunters he was very
choice, and the likeness between him and Ben Morgan, on horseback, has always been so striking, that
the East Riding men often say, that they seem to

have him still amongst them, at Firby Wood side. For one grey horse, Ainderby, he was bid 450 gs., and he rode the hollow-backed Heslington, of Northumberland Plate fame, with Sir Tatton's, for two or three seasons after he had steeple-chased him, but he never made much out.

In other respects he was not a keen sportsman. He liked to have his greyhound, Major, at his heels, but did not care to run him much. Sometimes he fished in the Ouse, and if the fish did not rise properly, away would go rod and creel into the water; and when, after frightening a few rooks, he eventually knocked himself down with his gun, he gave it away to Isaac Blades. He was always in high Visit to Harro- spirits when he got to Harrogate, and in gate. his latest visit, the Tewit waters seemed quite to set him up. Markwell was with him as *aide-de-camp*, and one day, at Bill's suggestion, the pair went to Brimham Rocks, not only in a donkey carriage, but in real state, with two more donkey boys as outriders.

Training of his William Oates and his father looked colt Sir Tatton after his colt Sir Tatton Sykes for him, Sykes. but he was very seldom " up" himself during his preparation. The colt took plenty of work, and Driffield had the schooling of him over a mile-and-a-half round Wise's Farm. They had only one spin together on Langton Wold, when his pupil gave him four stone easily. Old George Oates rode the young one in the trial, and despite his recollections of Lottery, he declared that he had never been on anything like him, and that he never half got him out. Still he was far riper for the St. Leger than he was on the Derby day; and William Oates was so anxious, that he went to the course all dressed to ride him, in case his owner, who had wasted very severely, should feel unfit at the last moment. How such a sluggish horse got through his task was a

wonder to every one ; as half-way up the distance
Bill fairly dropped forward on to his neck, from
exhaustion, and could'nt drive him at all.

Many a rich story has fallen from the *The Whitewall*
lips of " The Wizard" in that little snug- *snuggery.*
gery on the left, when he goes back to the good old
days, and dashes off in one pregnant sentence, the
form of each stable favourite, till we can almost see
Bill, and Frank, and Nat in the saddle once more,
and silently filing before us. What merry, and yet
what anxious groups have mustered there, round the
trio of spirit decanters, with their varied pace and
colour emblems of horse and game cock—white pile
and grey, dun and chesnut, brown-red and bay !
Colonel Anson knew that council chamber well, and
it was there that many a crafty Derby attack was
planned ; and " all white," " red and blue," or " all
black" was selected to silence the " Kentish fire," or
turn the Danebury flank. Sim, Jack Holmes, and
Nelson would all be on duty; and if it was a great trial,
Bill would start from his house at York after
nightfall, to put the double on the touts, who stood,
with a perseverance hardly natural to man, watching his every movement, about Epsom-tide. No one
wished for the dawn, when he had come with an
ever-fresh stock of anecdotes and ethics, enough to
set up half-a-dozen wits in trade.

As the light flashes back on the walls, *Pictures of the*
we read, from Herring's hand, the silent *cracks.*
canvas record of those days. Hornsea of the wall
eye, Don John, and Industry take up the Bretby
tale ; Mundig, the first " member for Streatlam"
is there to catch the eye and jog the memory of many
a speaker, and so is Cotherstone whose merits, to the
Colonel's utter astonishment, were enforced in Bill's
most emphatic speech, when the party had come
back from Langton Wold on that morning which
sealed Gaper's doom. There, too, among the family

pictures of the little girl in the red cloak on the spotted donkey, are the late General Norcliffe, the owner of the Wold, and Sir Tatton and his trusty henchman, Tom Carter, as they appeared when the scarlets were hung on the nail, and the cubs at play, with no Proctor or Cruiser to rally them. Harry Hall and Ferneley also bear their part among the "Cracks of the Turf." Holmes pulling Maroon double for the St. Leger, is the first painting on the left; and if poor Jack ever mourned over his riding orders of that day, within earshot of Sim, he was pretty sure to be reminded that his resolution had not always been so rigid, and that neither his memory nor all the shouting at his girths could prevail upon him, at Richmond, to pull Delphine to one side, and let Sim win the stable money on Matilda. Touchstone has his *In Memoriam* in the Doncaster Cup, in which Hornsea separated him and his old foe General Chassé once more. Attila, Canezou, " a good mare, but not a smasher," Fazzoletto, little Daniel, The West, and Songstress tell the story of their years: and there, too, in a pleasant tree and water group, are Frailty of Filho's blood, the dam of Cyprian, and Mrs. Bang-up, with Morgan Rattler by Velocipede at her foot.

The Whitewall dining-room. The elegant little Matilda, defying the rush of Sam and the mighty stride of Mameluke, has her place in the dining-room, with Charles and Euclid fighting out their dead-heat. Velocipede holds the post of honour over the sideboard, flanked by Cotherstone and Princess, the son and daughter of the great Ascot Cup rivals, and under their shadow, among Durham, Pontefract, and Malton Cups, the steel-armed shank bones of Tramp know no rest from man, when a round or silver-edge of beef is between them. The Petre chesnut days live again in Rowton and The Colonel; and Cyprian, of the vicious eye and ear, bears testimony to that punishing finish, in which she taught the Houldsworth stable that it was not their destiny to win the Oaks. Frank and John himself are on guard over the fireplace, and there, too, is the Roland which carried the flying huntress, who introduced the first three-pommel saddle into Leicestershire, and made Captain White's sing out as she topped her first fence, "*Look to yourself Heycock, or you'll be cut down by a woman!*"

What a multifarious miscellany of men have sat at that bountiful board!— The guests at Whitewall. peers, baronets, barons, and Queen's counsel learned in the law; foreigners, who have reverently journeyed to it and Sir Tatton's, within a week of landing, as if to a shrine; squires, farmers, jockeys, trainers, and authors,

"Pricking a Cockney ear,"

and jealously treasuring up each waif and stray for the time, when all Yorkshire is in its delicious September simmer, and the talk in every harvest field, and at every ram-letting, is of what John Scott will run for the Leger, and when he intends to try. Baron Alderson only wrote half Baron Alderson's visit. his recollections of his visit. He might have told how he questioned Frank, on the whole art of riding; how he wondered not so much at the condition of the horses, as where the supply of boys came from, and the solution of the difficulty; how he noted down, at Jim Perren's dictation, some of their most remarkable titles, "Spider," "Cudjoe," "Frog," "Weasel," "Squeaky," &c., and how, when the contents of Jacob's cock-bag were duly unfolded, nothing but the sternest Whitewall headshake checked Frank's itching fingers from having a regular carpet set-to.

And so we draw near Cyprian's barn, Old Cyprian. and turn aside to see that ancient bag

of bones, with nigh eight-and-twenty summers on
her head, and enough malice to make a short run,
and a finish of every visitor in turn. Her death-
warrant had been duly signed; and when John Scott
next took his way to visit Isaac Walker and "the
infants" at Streatlam Castle, the barn knew her no
more; but a couple of thousand guinea and three
five-hundred guinea foals, with Meteora to head them,
are placed to her credit, with Weatherby. Then
passing by I'Anson's paddock, where Queen Mary
and her daughter Blink Bonny raise their white faces
at our approach, we are through the wicket gate on
to the Wolds.

Scene on Lang-   Every one seems out that morning.
ton Wolds.   Cyprian's old friend Johnny Gray, who
could ride six stone seven when he was fifty, is there at
seventy-odd, and blazing away upon Willie Wright.
John Scott spies him forthwith, and does'nt forget to
tell of Bill's frisk at Knutsford races, when he slept in
the same room with Johnny and Ben Smith. Little
Baker with the big straw hat, "the tall man from
Newcastle," and eight or ten others, are on duty
along the outposts, gathering "such information as
no other gentleman possibly can have," from
their tan gallop survey. Balnamoon is there, and they
little think, as a despised brown ball of a filly bounds
along by herself, that she is duly fated to lower the
pride of the great Kettledrum. Cape Flyaway, as true
a tryer as Dilkoosh or Backbiter, leads Sweetsauce,
who, in his white quarter piece, and with Jack Charlton up, comes striding along as if the Goodwood
Cup field were at his heels once more. The next
are a lot of Barbatuses, and the Miss Whip colt
fresh from a Knavesmire Stakes victory at York;
and The Wizard, with Bob Cliffe still true to
him, in sunshine or in shade, comes up, nearly
pulling double over his schoolmaster, the ever bold
Benbow.

Then the green furze at the distance The schoolmaster at home on Langton Wold. is suddenly alive with sterns, and the word is passed :—"*There are Morgan and the hounds*" coming over the Wold from Birdsall. Ben draws them up on a little knoll, and John Scott gets out of his phaeton, to give them greeting, and beckons Jim Perren to bring up the horses, and "let them walk near us in a ring." *The Malton Messenger*, big with prophecy, and on his white steed of fate, keeps, like ourselves, to the scarlets, while Jack Charlton with his grey's rein on his arm, and Ashmall on I'Anson's rare eleven-season hunter, Kettle, half-sister to Fisherman, join the morning consultation. "*Don't take off too much at once, Jim, from The Drone.*" "*Now you may go home with Sweetsauce, you've done enough for this morning ;*" "*Walk Long-range, and bring him steadily along a mile ; mind keep your hands down, Ginger !*" *Jack, just get up again, and lead him !*" float to us occasionally, as John, with his adjutant scans each of the troop.

Now, the council is over, and he turns once more to the hounds. He has, of course, his old Arrival of "Ben" and the hounds. fling at Ben, for assuring him that his country was "like the Grampians, and even The West could'nt live with them." Then Bill is in his mind once more, and he tells us of the run from Millington Wood, when "he rode a Whalebone horse, and I was only nine stone." Gameboy and Warlock lie blinking lazily, and half-dreaming, it may be, of the greatest day of the next season, from Garrowby to Warter; or of the still more memorable Christmas Eve of '61, over three rivers and nineteen parishes. There, too, are Dexter and Dimity, of the Grove Duster sort, " and John Scott's commentaries. not a bad sort either," as John Scott observes. Again, he picks out Woodman, "one of the Proctor sort in the picture for a thousand ;" and "*hang it, he's a slasher*" is his terse commentary, as

Rochester, with his stern up, walks proudly past him. Now Perren has a word, and asks about a Grove Rector, in a spirit of anxious inquiry, which makes his captain predict that "Jim will be a great kennel huntsman yet." Then the scarlets and the "spotted darlings" are lost among the distant furzes, and once more the Whitewall thirty-nine, with Benbow still in command, file homeward through the Rifleman Dell, and the morning's work is over.

Pavis & Conolly. Robson delighted to see jockeys do their travelling on horseback, and he was once known to say to a very eminent one, " *Now, I saw you come in a chaise; you don't ride for me all this week.*" Conolly and Pavis were great epicures in this way, and liked to go about with their gigs and servants. On one occasion they passed Darling and Chapple riding into Abingdon, with their saddle-bags at their sides and their light saddles round their waists. When they again met on their arrival at The Lamb, Pavis told them that they were " *a disgrace to go about with their pots,*" but quiet Jemmy only clapped his hand on his saddle-bags, and retorted, " *I'll lay there's been more in these pots than there ever will be in all your fine gigs.*" Sam got his best rise out of Pavis, at Wells, whither the natty one had gone down for Mazeppa in *Isaac Day's descent with Little Boy Blue.* the Mendip Stakes. At the eleventh hour, Isaac Day determined to start Little Boy Blue, and brought Sam to ride him. Pavis had been elected king of the revels at the inn, and was bouncing most valiantly of what he was going to do next day, when the fatal forms of Sam and Isaac loomed in the door-way. Little Arthur nearly dropped under the table at the sight, and years after Isaac would go solemnly through the scene, with increasing humour at each performance.

Jemmy Chapple. Chapple's great country successes were with Spectre, and his forte was waiting

with a quiet horse, and taking a beautiful measure.
Somehow or other, the country knew his value better
than they did at head-quarters, and this he felt so
keenly, that it somewhat hardened and crisped his
manner. They were ready enough to offer him engagements after he won the Cesarewitch and Cambridgeshire, and it was no very cynical asperity in
him to decline them.

It was Nat's misfortune to have out-
lived his fame, and the baseless object- $\qquad$ A word on Nat.
ions which were taken to his mode of riding
Toxophilite (who was "never half a good horse"),
for the Derby, made it the fashion to call him
"old Nat," and to say that he was nervous. For
our own part, we believe that the public (who
had always praised his riding most extravagantly
up to that point) merely followed suit, and that
his brother-jockeys are right in saying that he
was as good as ever to the last. At no period of his
career had he been quite a first-class man; but still
a most efficient rider, a respectful servant, and as
honest as the day. He had been creeping well up
for four or five seasons; but the death of Pavis in
1839, at a time when he could ride 6st. 10lbs.
cleverly, and there were no "Tinies" or "Bantams,"
gave him an opening which he knew well how to use.
He was the first Newmarket jockey that ever regularly got a footing at the Northern meetings; and
Garbutt, whose practice had all but departed from
him, did not much like this innovation. On one
occasion, Jem made the running very good in a race
at Newton, and turning round in his rough way, he
contemptuously bellowed out to him as they returned to scale, "*There, Mr. Newmarket, what do
you think of that to a pace?*"

Weight always favoured him, as he was barely
11lbs. heavier at fifty than he was at twenty-nine.
His great knack was his quickness at a T.Y.C. post;

and, although he just kept within the line and avoided being fined, he often put the starter's temper sadly to the test by his determination if possible to anticipate the " *Go along.*" We should call him rather a good jockey by profession, than a great horseman by intuition. He seldom did anything brilliant, but his good head and fine patience served him, and he rarely made a mistake as regards measure in the last few strides. A tremendous finish, when a horse had to be ridden home from below the distance, was not his *forte;* and it put him all abroad if he had to make running. His thighs were so short that he had'nt sufficient purchase from the knee to use a sluggish horse, and if he had a free goer he was a little apt to overdo it. In his *annus mirabilis* 1848, he scored 104 victories; but it was generally believed that he made most in Orlando's year, and entered about £5,000 to the credit side of his riding book in fees and presents alone. His illness was very painful and wearing. As the spring came on, he seemed to recover a little, and got out, we believe, a few times, in a carriage; but when he went up to London to have the best advice during the July meeting, he learnt that there was no hope for him, and quietly returned to Newmarket to die. Strange to say, it was one of his last requests that he should not be buried in the cemetery at the entrance of the Heath.

Job Marson.   He was not very sociable in his temper, or popular with his brother-jockeys, and between him and poor Job Marson there was always a sort of secret feud, and nothing delighted the latter so much as to beat him in a finish. Job was best on a very free goer, as he could hold anything, and preferred it to having to ride them all the way. There was less of the Chifney style about him than Frank, as he was never fond of lying too much away, and then trusting so implicitly to the creeping business, which once put Frank quite wrong on Nunnykirk at York. According to his own notions, the A.F. match on Colleen Bawn when he beat Frank on Leopard in the Newmarket Craven of 1847, and his Humdrum victory over the same jockey and Wolfdog for the Queen's Plate the same spring, after a most terrific finish from the Plantation, were about the best things Job ever did ; and the men were worthy of each other. His anxiety to pull off a great race for Mr. Bouverie and his uncle, after their Derby disappointment, rather upset his nerve in the Chester Cup, and he always believed that he had won his race with War Eagle at the Castle Pole, and that if he had waited longer under that crushing weight, he might have landed their money.

It was somewhat singular that both Job and Frank should have been each specially known during their last season, in connection with the horse they loved best of all. Job made his last great finish for the Doncaster Cup on Fandango, and Frank's sun set gloriously in "The West." The first connection of the latter couple was rather an odd one. Frank had been on him at Whitewall, but never expected that he was coming for the Criterion. His astonishment was unbounded when he first learnt the news from John Scott's lips at the Newmarket Station. "*What!*" said he, "*you don't mean to say you've brought the big bay horse with you; we've tried a rare good 'un, and I've backed him for a devil of a lot of money!*" "I'm very sorry for it," replied John, "but we've had Sim and Jack up, and we like him, and Mr. Bowes has backed him for the Derby,—the money's all on —and you've to stand the odds to fifty." There was no help for it, and so Frank went and told his brother that Rogers would have to take the Sittingbourne mount. He strictly obeyed his orders to

Frank Butler's surprise with The West.

" ride him tenderly up the hill, for fear he flounders in the dirt," but the horse could not move in it, and Speed the Plough dropped on to him at the finish.

Colloquy with Isaac Walker on the Moors. Frank's opinion of " the big bay horse" underwent a great change after the Glasgow Stakes, and he thought all the winter of what he and "my hack" were to do. He had liked what he had seen of the colt in the previous summer, though he never expected him to be got fit that year. In the August of Daniel's year, when he was riding back with Isaac Walker from the Hunderthwaite Moors to Streatlam, he thus broke out, "Isaac, I've been thinking how wonderful it would be if we should win the Derby next year for Mr. Bowes. I've got a rough customer for them ; I've won with a little one this year, and I should'nt be surprised if I pull through with a big 'un next." He came down to Durham for the grouse-shooting both years, but there was a great change in him in '53. No day was too long for him in Daniel's year, but the next August he could not follow his game. He wanted constant flask refreshers, and he was glad to sit down on the heather with the daily paper, and talk about what they had been doing at Egham. His fund of anecdote and chaff, which he delivered in a thick, husky voice, and with a visage as grave as a mustard-pot, seemed to have failed him, and there was no "Fine Old English Gentleman," or " Return of the Admiral" at night. Isaac still sadly remembers how they visited Tom Flint at Raby, and how out of that party of six he alone remains.

The Old Victory Jacket. Frank never exactly alluded to his growing weakness ; but it was in these pleasant summer days, that he promised Isaac to give him his Bowes jacket, whenever he died. " *All the boys,*" as he used to say when he spoke of the bequest, " *when they don't go for the stuff, they put on the flash jacket, but I always put on the old Victory.*" Next

month when he came out of the weighing-house
after the St. Leger, and gravely asked Isaac if he
had ridden him quite to orders, he slapped his hand
on his jacket breast, and repeated the promise:
"*You'll never breed another West*," he added, "*I
never knew what he was, I only touched him with the
spur once in the Derby, and I was glad to get him
stopped.*" It was to Hobby Horse that he could positively give 6st. in a rough gallop, and strangely
enough, it was on that wretch that Frank weighed
in for the last time on the Houghton Saturday of '53.
Sore as the trial was, he kept at 8st. 7lbs. till this
last afternoon, and won two matches, the second of
them on Ariosto against his old opponent Nat.

Acrobat had been his Derby delight Last days of Frank.
ever since he got off him after the
Doncaster Two-Year-Old Stakes, with a prophecy in
his mouth, and Dervish was his abhorrence; but he
never saw them put together with Boiardo, at three
Two years old. He was at the Ditch Stables on the
Thousand Day, just about a stone over weight,
and led Sim on Boiardo their canter; and he took
his saddle down to Goodwood that July in the
hope of meeting The West once more, and getting
upon him at exercise. His first master, Colonel
Anson, lingered before going out to India just to
see The West win at Doncaster, and he had arranged
to meet John Scott when it was over, near the
Rubbing House, that they might say good-by. Both
had, however, a melancholy consciousness that they
should never see each other again, and when John
did not trust himself to come, the other knew "the
reason why," and with the kindest of farewell letters
they parted. Jockey and master died almost together, the one in his tent at Poonah, on Ellington's
Derby day; and when we pass by that low St. Mar-
garet's church wall, and glance over the "P. C.
1842" stone of little Conolly, and the grave of

F

cheery Will Beresford beside him, towards the rail-
ings in the Nunnery corner, we may well think of
the glorious time of Whitewall, and Frank in the
" all white," and trust that, like his old master, he
sleeps well.

Mr. Theobald, of   Mr. Theobald, of Stockwell, was one
    Stockwell.   of the most remarkable of the Southern
patriarchs.   The manor house still defies change,
and his valued factotum John Lowry lives hard-by,
in the public line, cherishing both on his walls and
in his heart every fresh triumph of the Pocahontas
blood; but an Angel Town of brick and mortar is
built upon the site of the paddocks where she was
wont to roam, with seventy or eighty brood mares
in the season.   The old gentleman swore by
Whalebone, Whisker, and Orville; and Camel of the
Whalebone and Selim blood, whom he bought from
Lord Egremont, held the undisturbed premiership
    Camel.   of his stud. This horse was as good as
    an £800 annuity for some seasons after
Touchstone had brought him out, and Caravan,
Wapiti, and Callisto carried on the game.   When the
Americans arrived and bid Mr. Theobald 5,000 gs.,
he "gave a verdict without turning round in the
box."   In fact, he did not even allow Lowry time
to strip the brown, before he refused the offer.
The horse was then rising seventeen, and he lived
for six seasons more.   Nothing delighted the old
man more than to stroll into the paddock, with
General Wemyss and Bransby Cooper, to visit my
" bit of Whalebone," and his fairy genius the white
Mr. Bransby   rabbit.   Mr. Cooper used invariably to
Cooper's opin- visit Stockwell on a Sunday, and Camel
ion of him.   was always stripped as a relish before
dinner. The great surgeon always maintained that he
never looked over a more powerful piece of anatomy.
His gaskins were enormous, and his leverage and
mettle so great, that when Lowry lunged him, he could

leap mid air almost to the last, to the full extent of a caveçon-rein. Mr. Theobald used to tell how Banter came there from Moor Park in the shape of a low lengthy mare of fifteen-two, but she was on a visit to Peter Lely when her first fruits appeared in the frail-looking foal Touchstone.

Camel, Smolensko, and the little Other sires at Stockwell. thirteen-hand racing pony Mat-o'-the-Mint were buried in that paddock along with Laurel, Cydnus, Norfolk Phenomenon, and the rest, but there were no tablets. " That would have touched the old gentleman up," and there was not even a tree to mark them. He had another bit of Whalebone in the grey Exquisite, the second to Frederick in the Derby, and the subject of Old Forth's bet about placing two ; but he served only a few hack mares, and that was also the line, though in a more eminent degree, of the short, thick-set Caccia Piatti by Whisker. Cydnus, who beat Serab, was a chesnut by Quiz, and good for long distances in his day, and for half-breds in his decline ; and even old Flibberti-gibbet, a blind chesnut by Comus from a Selim mare, was added to his collection from Jemmy Messer's of Welwyn. Tarrare by Catton was a great strapping sire for job horses, after his mud tour with Tommy Nicholson at Doncaster ; but "the coarse and larky coach-horse " Laurel, who had under the same guidance avenged himself on both Matilda and Mameluke, and put Longwaist, Medora, Purity, and Mulatto to shame in the greatest of his eight cup victories, never made or had much chance of making himself a name at Stockwell, or any where else. The big, leggy Muley Moloch found a quiet refuge here, when he was compelled to abdicate in favour of Lanercost at Walm Gate Bar Without, and held it till the old gentleman died. Rockingham, Calmuck, Belgrade, and The Baron were also in residence ; Sorella was rather a favourite purchase ; and

Pocahontas came in the course of a city transaction from Mr. Greatrex.

His love of being in the fashion. Mr. Theobald's highest ambition was to have the best of everything, cost what it might. Mat-o'-the-Mint was the result of this feeling, and so was a dun trotting mare. He also owned Rochester, who did the five miles on the Bourne Bridge Road in 15 minutes 38 seconds, against the Squire's hunting-looking Rattler; and Macdonald never handled anything much better than his Rockingham, who, with his shaggy mane and low-set tail, reminded bystanders more of a lion than a horse. In short, the Squire of Stockwell carried out the fashion of the day in everything, and pushed it to the very extreme. Cost what it might, he would be in the front. Sometimes his harness was smothered in brass, and then plated would come up once more, and he had the best of that. All his bacon was cured on the premises, and he defied Yorkshire or Cumberland to beat it. He brewed ale, which he was ready to match for a hundred a-side against the Sledmere or Trinity College audit; and yet amid all this rivalry with the great, "he ne'er forgot the small," and kept four or five cows specially for the poor's milk.

His dress & dogs. At one time he dressed like the Prince Regent, and he finally subsided into buckskins, brown-tops, blue-coat, with gilt-buttons, buff-waistcoat, white handkerchief, and a broad-brimmed hat. His weight was about twenty stone. He breakfasted regularly at half-past ten in his little parlour, whose walls James Ward, R.A., and Herring had covered with their racers and trotters. The blood-hound lay blinking on the rug, and quietly waiting for his share of the plate with those mysterious eleven slices of thick bread and butter, which the housekeeper placed each morning at her master's side. Before starting for town, the old man made

it a rule of life to walk to the wicket-gate where
five cats and as many more dogs were duly in
waiting, but they learnt to know by the church
bells that they had to look out for Sunday's
breakfast elsewhere. A yellow "pill-box" always
took him to his place of business in Skinner-
street, and a roan, brown, or chesnut, *Trap horses.*
each of them worth about 200 guineas
at the very least, was between the shafts. The pace
was always first-class, and his man returned for him
in the afternoon with a fresh horse. After dinner,
if he was alone, John Lowry appeared, and read
The Advertiser, beginning, of course, with the racing and "Vates." On Saturday night *Trips to Doncas-*
his master would sometimes produce *ter and New-*
a roll of bank-notes, and be off betimes *market.*
in the yellow chariot, with John on the box, to Newmarket for the week. Such was his love of pace,
that he would not condescend to divide the Doncaster journey into three days, as others did, but he
dozed all the way and slept at the Bull at Witham
Common the first night, and arrived on the second
at his lodgings near the Betting Rooms, which he
shared with his friends Tattersall and Peter Cloves.
He was hearty and bulky, and had the keenest enjoyment of a race to the last, and it was not any
disease of old age, but a mere casual ailment which
laid him, at 85, low in Kensal Green, nearly three
years before Stockwell secured him his A 1 register
among breeders.

For three years before his death, Mr. *The late Mr.*
Richard or rather "Dick" Tattersall, *Tattersall.*
never mounted the rostrum, and even then his
memory had begun slightly to fail, and his son never
left his side. It was only on this point that he showed
signs of decay, as his general health continued good,
and he died very suddenly (1858), at Dover, in his
seventy-fourth year, merely from exhaustion brought

on by the heat; and was buried on the Goodwood Cup day. He was a man who from his simple
honesty and unusually straightforward, decisive manner it was impossible to misunderstand, and it has
been well said of him, that "the best men liked him
best." To rogues and dodgers he was a perfect
terror, as he spoke his mind to every one, peer or
groom alike, whom he did'nt consider to be going
straight, and always conveyed his sentiments in
pretty unmistakable terms. If the servant or any
other agent of the owner bid when the sale was " without reserve," he has been known to send the whole
stud away, after the first horse, declaring in tones
like the view holloa of " *The* Squire," " piercing
the heavens, Boys," that he " *would tell a lie for no
man alive.*"

To professional betting he had a most inveterate
dislike, and beyond perhaps taking the odds to a
fiver for the Derby or St. Leger, often only on the
morning of the race, and very seldom winning,
except in Phosphorus' year, (when he
Dislike to betting. took 100 to 1, out of respect to Lord
Berners,) he hardly risked a crown. In fact, when
young men wrote up to him about becoming members
of the Rooms, he as often as not wrote a line in reply
to say that betting was certain to ruin them, and
they had, therefore, far better keep their two
guineas in their pockets. His feelings, both on
this and many other points, kept very large sums
out of his ledger; but it was the confidence of the
public, not money, that he cared for. Still The
Rooms were an institution which hardly admitted of
being conducted in any other than a pure matter-of-
fact way; and as inconvenience arose out of his scru-
ples, he felt it best to hand over the management of
them entirely to a committee. His opinion, like
Bill Scott's, was made up by his first glance at a man
or horse, and his laconic analysis of a lot, which

seldom failed to put his audience in a roar, and the way in which he dropped on to any dodging bidders, or pert would-be questionists, were always grand in the extreme.

His father, Mr. Edmund Tattersall, His entry on the died suddenly from brain fever, and he business. thus assumed the sole command at The Corner, when he was only twenty-five. For some years he did all the business himself, and was then joined by his brother Edmund, and under their joint auspices, and that of his son and nephew, the present partners, the firm has well held its own. A stag-hound difference between " Dick " and Colonel Maberley led to the establishment of the Baker-street Bazaar, but as Horace Walpole said of a certain Court beauty, the old spot " required a vast of ruining."

His grandfather " Old Tat," who first established the concern, died some seventy years ago, and was buried near Highflyer Hall. That The yard at Tat- " family horse" was not foaled, and Bay tersall's. Malton had just made the pace strong enough in a four-mile race over York to burst a blood vessel in King Herod's head, when the 99 years lease of the place was first signed with Lord Grosvenor. Old Tat showed his loyalty by surmounting the pump cupola with a bust of the Prince Regent, modelled when he was only seventeen. It was lost during the repairs, and missing for several years, after being searched for high and low, and was then found by the merest chance among some waste stones in a builder's yard and duly replaced. When the lease was signed, in 1766, " The Five Fields" stood on the site of Belgrave Square, and cows and footpads shared them. There was in fact nothing but fields, where partridges still dared to "jug," as late as 1812, between Hyde Park Corner and Chelsea, and back fare had to be paid to the ancient jarveys if they took a fare

off the stones up to the present Prince's Gate. Mr.
Richard Tattersall's house was for many years the
London head-quarters of the Jockey Club, who had a
regular cook and coffee-room; and all the Newmarket business was transacted at the office of the late
Mr. Weatherby, who was in practice there as a soli-
citor.

Mr. Tattersall's
connection with
the Prince. Mr. Tattersall's father and the Prince
Regent had been partners in the *Morn-
ing Post*, and cast in £5,000 damages
for " a delicate Court disclosure." Although the
paper passed into other hands, the royal connection with the son remained firm, and only
once was there an interruption of good feeling on
George Guelph's part, and then only for a few hours.

Difficulties with
H.R.H. about a
challenge. Count Münster was the Hanoverian
Ambassador to the Court of St.
James, and shared with His Majesty the
guardianship of a certain reigning Duke. The
latter felt himself aggrieved at some money matters,
and his equerry requested Mr. Tattersall to convey a letter to the Count. Not suspecting anything, he took Wimbledon in his afternoon's ride,
and as the Count was not at home, he gave the letter
to the valet. His astonishment and indignation were
most unmeasured, when *The Times* of the next day
announced that a challenge had been sent to the
Count, and that Mr. Tattersall had been the bearer
of it. It was, of course, construed by the King
into an insult to himself, as co-guardian; but an
explanation soon set matters right between them,
and it transpired that, if the letter had not met
with such convoy, it would have been left by an
attorney's clerk.

His Majesty's care
for old chums. When George Guelph became King,
he honourably paid off every outstand-
ing liability, and sending for Mr. Tattersall, he said to
him, " You've known all the men I've known in my

youth; when any of them ever get into difficulties, send me word." And so he did most faithfully, and a royal cheque for all amounts from £100 to £500 would arrive, whenever the out-of-elbows office was given.

Mr. Tattersall's lameness began when he was quite a boy, and was always at- Mr. Tattersall as
a hunting man. tributed to the groom's habit of giving him a leg up very roughly on to his pony. He had been limping for some months before his family took much notice of it, and even Dr. Hunter pledged his word that the bone was not out of the socket. Time said differently, but not until all cure was hopeless. Still this sad misfortune did not dwell on his mind or stand in the way of his hunting, a sport which he loved far beyond racing; and after Lord Derby's grandfather gave up the Surrey staghounds, and Mr. Maberley tired, he managed them for three or four seasons.

He was one of the most regular staggers when his Lordship lived at The Oaks. Jonathan Griffin, on his grey, came out in state, with his whips and prickers on their 200-guinea horses, and Lord Fitzwilliam, Sir Hedworth Williamson, the Hon. Fitzroy Stanhope, the Hon. George and John Coventry, Lord Leaconfield and his brother General Wyndham, and the Hon. Berkeley Craven were seldom missing from among the scarlets, when Smitham Bottom was the meet. Mr. Tattersall was also a constant frequenter of the cover-side; and in order to meet Earl Fitzwilliam's, he would sometimes have three hacks posted for him, and starting as soon as his Monday's sale labours were over, ride all the way to Stamford where he arrived in the dead of night. In consequence of his infirmity, he liked to have the horse on his arms, and hence any one who had a very hard-puller or rusher, at about five-and-thirty pounds, knew pretty generally where there was a customer for it. He had no purchase with one knee, and simply rode by balance, steadying himself at a leap by a handle at the back of his saddle. If he could succeed in having three or four falls in a day, he was all the better pleased with himself; and said that he never had a good run without them. He quite enjoyed hearing those who did not know him, exclaim as he limped across the field after his horse,—"*Poor fellow! look how he's hurt himself.*"

Understanding with highwaymen. The days when the white horse of a leading road practitioner was styled "Auld Robin Gray" were not over, when he took his lonely night rides into the Midlands: but the highwaymen all knew him, and he rode unscathed among masks and pistols. The pikeman near Grantham once said to him, when he was on his way to meet "The Duke's," "*Don't go on, sir; I've had several through to-night, and they've all been robbed.*" "*Never mind, my man,*" said the little hero, "*no one ever stops me,*" and on he went. Two miles further, and a masked horseman was at his side, and they rode silently for some two hundred yards together. At last there came the husky voice of the night, "*I think your name's Tattersall.*" "*Tattersall!—of course it is,*" was the reply, "*Richard Tattersall all the world over.*" This was quite enough, and with the courteous rejoinder, " "*Ah, I thought so; I beg your pardon, sir,*" and a mutual " good night," they parted.

Sir Clement Dormer in difficulties. He was seldom heard to tell this story without dwelling in contrast upon the woes of Sir Clement Dormer, who was Master of the Ceremonies at St. James's. Sir Clement was fond of riding up to London on a very large horse, and talked on horse matters to every one he saw. Coming out of Beaconsfield one day he overtook another horseman, "*Going to town, sir?*" he began; "*Yes, Sir Clement, I am,*" was the reply; "*What! you know me, then? we'll ride together.*"

And on they went. "*That's a very nice horse you're on,*" said Sir Clement; "*Yes he is,*" said the man, "*Would you like to see him go?*" They were under Bulstrode Park wall at the time, and the man trotted away to a turn of the road, where he could see half-a-mile before him. The coast was clear both ways, and when Sir Clement arrived full of admiration, his new friend promptly put a pistol to his head. There was nothing for it but to produce his purse, and receive the sorry consolation in exchange, "*Now, Sir Clement, do let me advise you to give up that bad habit of talking to every one about their horse.*"

Mr. Tattersall bore a charmed pocket in town, and once when it was picked of a handkerchief, remorse seized the appropriator, when he was proceeding to pick out the name, and it was "returned with compliments—taken quite by mistake." One cracksman was, however, much less scrupulous, as he broke into the office and took £500. Suspicion rather His stories of fell upon the too celebrated "Slender Slender Billy. Billy," who was then a great man with the Corinthians, and had cocks, badgers, rats, bears, and terriers, ready to go into action at any moment. His crib in the Willow Walk, Tothill Fields, was a perfect conjurors' bottle in this respect, and if there was likely to be " a call of the house," on any very important occasion, he could knock up a bull-ring as well. The Bow Street runners were all terrified at him, and haunted with a legend, that when their august body had once girded up their loins for a descent upon him, Billy had vindicated the majesty of the spot in his peculiar way, by unloosing the bears. They knew him ostensibly as a knacker, but it was whispered that he " was wanted" for a little affair about the communion plate at St. Paul's. A still heavier suspicion hung over him, and " *Oh! master, to think that I should go* Boiling the Ex- *and boil an exciseman!*" was his invari- ciseman.

able mode of parrying the question which was so often propounded to him on that head. He seemed to look upon any allusion to it as rather a delicate compliment than otherwise, and there was an impression on the mind of the executive, that the unhappy gauger, who could never be traced beyond, had visited Billy's premises once too often, and had been popped bodily into the flesh copper.

Billy's warning voice;

Under all these rumours, Billy preserved a pleasing and courteous exterior, and in such perilous times it was prudent for virtue and respectability to stand in with him, just so far as to have his good word if they were robbed. One evening, a leading man was sitting down to dinner, when the presence of "The slender one" in the servants' hall was announced. "*Do ask Billy what he wants with me at this time of night,*" was the testy message; but Billy refused to unbosom by proxy. There was nothing for it, and as it was not safe to alienate Billy's affections by neglect, the parties met at once, and conversed on this wise: "*Well, Billy, what's up now?*" "*You've lost one of your fat pigs, master.*" "*Yes, I have, Billy, and I'll make the fellows pay for it pretty sharply.*" "*Now, look here, master, I'll just tell you what it is; if you go on as you're doing, kicking up such a confounded row,* YOU'LL LOSE THE OTHER." "*Well, Billy, it's a bad job; but, perhaps, I'll take your advice, and say no more about it.*" And so Billy departed, and the bereft one became bacon in peace.

and his execution.

Billy came to grief and the gallows at last, under the operation of the Forgery Act. It was proved that he could neither read nor write, but that mattered very little. When Bow Street, stimulated to unusual energy by the taunts of its superior, dropped upon him, he had the flash-notes in his hand, and not only thrust them into the fire, but held them there.

Having only his "left duke" at liberty, he could not defend his hearth position long enough, and sufficient fragments were rescued to give the assayer his cue. Mr. Tattersall visited him in the condemned cell, and urged him to confess his associates, and for a few minutes he sat on his box, with his heavily chained hands to his face, apparently absorbed in thought. Then he broke out: "*No, master, they'll never say that Slender Billy split on his pals; if every hair in my head was alive, and had to be hung separate, I would'nt.*" And die he did, walking second in the procession of nine on to the Newgate Scaffold, and some would have it that Dan Dawson, who wore the fatal nightcap on Cambridge jail next spring, when he had cost the Jockey Club £1,500 to prosecute him, had stood near St. Sepulchre's church that very morning, and marked that "Billy was game."

Parson Harvey was wont to hang about the office at Tattersall's on sale days, in his dirty white cravat and suit of rusty black. Mr. Tattersall would never let them wake him if he snored in his chair, with the butt end of a pound of mutton chops sticking out of his pocket. "*Let him sleep, poor fellow! it's a sweeter place than the garret in Pimlico.*" His only connection with the church latterly consisted in almost daily visits to Westminster Abbey, to hear the anthem, and he rode his stallions there by turn. To avoid ostler's fees, they were left at a farrier's while he lingered about the nave, and one new shoe was put on at a time, that he might have a pretext for the convenience as often as possible. Mr. Tattersall had always some fresh story about him, and if there was an odd anecdote about man or horse, the master of "The Corner" generally gave it first.

He delighted to tell of the great racing man, Mr. Vernon, who had been quite a Waterton in his wanderings, and rode a horse, which he had painted like a leopard, on his return. Long sermons were not to his mind. Hence he presented his parish church with a hollow sounding board, craftily connected by a secret string to his pew, and when on the first Sunday the sermon had reached a certain length, and showed no symptoms of ending, he dropped it like an extinguisher on to the preacher. Poachers and steel traps were alike his horror; and as his notices, spring guns, and steel traps gradually became stale, he wrote up in three-inch letters: "*Every one found trespassing on these grounds shall be spifflicated,*" and the menace of such unknown torture was effectual at last.

Coaching, dogs, and fists. Driving the Peterbro' coach was great fancy of Mr. Tattersall's, and he was quite as *au fait* at road language as John Warde, who invariably worked the Hungerford coach up, on his non-hunting days. Still he always confessed himself to be quite in shadow, when he told how the master of the Craven had admonished a " box seat," who wore immensely high collars, in language more graphic than polite, of the ultimate injury he might inflict on his health. Dogs he was exceedingly fond of, and the best one he ever had, wandered into his yard by accident. The groom misunderstood the extent of his orders to " give the poor wretch something to eat," and kept it for two months. There was then nothing for it but to be put through the mill, and by way of trying high enough, it was tumbled bodily into a tub with two badgers. A tremendous scuffle of five minutes was followed by an ominous lull; but the dog had won the day most decisively, and nothing would face it for 100 guineas a-side. Once it was challenged by its old owner in Piccadilly, but as it would let no one but Mr. Tattersall touch it, the offers to "*take him, if you can,*"—was a perfectly safe one.

It never left its adopted master's side in his walks, and waited for him outside the theatres. *Theatre rows.* It was well that it did not penetrate further, or it would have taken a most dangerous part in some of the light skirmishes, which came off there almost nightly. There were no police to keep disorderlies in check, and numerous "little difficulties" were arranged by fists in the lobby. Mr. Tattersall, who was immensely powerful, and had enjoyed many a private glove bout with Jackson in the old betting rooms, was not unfrequently engaged, and the box-keeper would seize up a bench, and run to him, in order that by seating himself, and daring his man to sit opposite him, and fight it out, he might never be at a discount. Sir Tatton promptly offered to act for him when the foe, who had been very offensive, seemed far above his weight, in the Doncaster theatre, but his blood was up, and he would'nt hear of it.

The great John Warde was one of Mr. Tattersall's most intimate friends, and *The late John Warde.* Monday after Monday his portly form would be seen at dinner there, facing Col. Dan Mackinnon. The room was in keeping with the company. Highflyer and "old Tat" looked down on them from its walls, and so did Warrior, Tandem, and Mambrino, and "Dick" himself on the bay Bonaparte, with his little white terrier at his side, going as if the dickens kicked them, across Surrey. This Monday feast commenced before his father died, and the old man, who said that hunting talk was hardly in his line, gave up his room for the day, and "left the boys to themselves." At these times the Doncaster Cup, of the two horse-handles, won by Crookshanks in 1781, always held the punch. The pipe of port, which the host and his brother Edmund laid down annually between them from Harmer's, had also a heavy tax laid on it, as each man had to drink John Warde and the Noble Science, in a silver fox-head, which held nearly a pint, and admitted of no heel taps. None stood the process better than "glorious John" himself, and he would rise from the table as steady as a rock, and never leave till he had gone up to the drawing-room, in the short hours, to bid Mrs. Tattersall good-by.

Mr. Tattersall's Derby dinner. The Derby dinner, which was held late in the week before Epsom, would have seemed as nothing without him to represent fox-hunting, and true as the dial to the sun, he would, a few minutes before six, issue from his yellow chariot, in his silver knee and shoe buckles. His servants wore that same style of low-crowned hat, which the Blue Ruin and Betsy picture has immortalized, and their brown coats were edged with silver braid. A large cold game pie held its pride of place at the feast, and the host especially plumed himself on the Rhenish hock, which his foreign friends sent him. The venison was from Goodwood, where he was often a guest during the races, and the present Duke and Lord Stradbroke were at his last festival. With his brother, and latterly his son Richard, to face him, no host held his party together better, or told such old-fashioned stories from behind his stiff white choker, and it was only when his memory began to fail him, and his jokes would not come out quite so crisp and neat as of yore, that he reluctantly gave it up.

The first guests. Death has been busy with host and guests since John Warde's place knew him no more, and the Hon. Fitzroy Stanhope is the sole survivor of "the old lot." Kit Wilson, the Father of the Turf, Jack Musters, and the florid Duke of Holstein,—who bought the Duke of York's mares,

and loved a field-day among the badgers in the Five
Fields Pit,—all dined there once, and adjourned to
a ball at Carlton House in the evening. There,
too, came Ormsby Gore, the master of Hesperus,
"Plenipo Batson" from Gogmagog, and Captain
Meynell, who won the Derby Club Cup for his host,
with a cocktail, when they were confederates in '16.
Val Kingston, a wine merchant, who had a share of
his Ruby and Ratcatcher, never failed to show; nor
did the hapless Berkeley Craven, whose Oaks book
would have brought back more than the amount for
which his Derby one beat him. Bedfordshire sent
her best Nimrod, Sam Ongley, to face John Warde,
and those who had

> " Seen him at the time,
> When Melon glittered in his prime;
> And one by one the scattered train
> Came up to question or explain,"—

dare not dispute the title. The stately Charles
Young, with his fine baritone voice, was another,
and the evening never passed without a call on
him for "The Old English Gentleman." Years
after he was gone, two rival authors quarrelled
about this song, and Mr. Fitzroy Stanhope knocked
them both out of the betting, by stating that he
had heard his friend Charles sing it almost before
they were born.

Young was a beautiful foil for his *Humours of Chas. Mathews, sen.*
vivacious friend Charles Mathews, who
always had a bet on the Derby, and was never more
"At Home" than at his friend Tat's house. He
would mimic his selling manner to the life, and
his " *Take Care!*" was absolutely tremendous.
Another of his annual encores was in the story of
the foreigner, who went to purchase blood-stock
at Newmarket, and utterly confounded the trainer
by asking " *What* years he has?" If he was in

G

his best form, he would go behind the curtain, and come out quite a different man, just as
when he dined with a rich pawnbroker, and slipping out of the room unobserved, appeared in
the shop below, and pawned him his own knives
Drawing the and forks. In the Derby Lottery of
Derby Lottery. the evening, he was, of course, Mr.
Tattersall's deputy. The stakes were two sovereigns
each, and of the eighteen or twenty subscribers one
always took the field. The lots were placed in a
claret-cup, and drawn after dinner, and those who
did not like their horse's chance, or wanted to hedge,
had it put up for sale. Mathews knew his Calendar and Corner quotations right well, and could di-
late to any extent on the merits of a favourite, which
he sometimes sold as high as £20. " Some say
Glaucus, some Forester, and others Whale, but I
say that Astra—*can* win the Derby," was one of his
neatest hits in 1833.

Frightening the He nearly frightened a post-boy out
Chesterford post of his wits, when he accompanied Mr.
boy. Tattersall and his son Richard to Newmarket. They had dined at Chesterford (whose old
waiter never wore a hat except when he came to London to receive his half-yearly dividends), and had got
about a mile on the road, when Mathews put his
head out of the window, and imitated the cry of a
child which had been run over. The post-boy pulled
up with a jerk, but being very short and hump-backed,
he was unable to get off, and had to run along the
pole, and so to earth by the splinter-bar. Once
there, he groped about hopelessly in the dark, for
the sufferer, till Mr. Tattersall ordered him to
ascend once more. Beyond Bourne Bridge, the
screams were again heard, and descending still
more swiftly, he was not content this time with
crawling under the carriage to make sure that he
had not committed infanticide, but drew the neigh-

bouring hedges blank as well. Again the same agonizing scream startled the night; but the little man could bear it no longer, and going at his horses, hand and heel, he raced them past Six-mile Bottom, roaring that he would stop for no one, and that there was "something evil in the chaise."

As a breeder of blood stock, Mr. Tat- Mr. Tattersall as a breeder of blood stock. tersall was not particularly successful. He always sold when he could, and his foreign customers cleared him out so often, that his brood mares and yearlings were but little tested. It seemed his duty to keep the thing going, and as he quaintly told a committee of the House of Commons, with a low bow, he "did not wish to see an end of horse racing and your humble servant." He bought The Colonel out of pure loyalty at the Hampton Court sale, because he did not consider that France ought to have him so cheap; but neither he nor Glaucus, nor Ratcatcher (a very great favourite) did much for him. Charles XII., Sir Hercules, and Harkaway were also hired by him to stand at Dawley or Willesden, and the chesnut was the last horse of renown that he sold at Doncaster. The "race Sunday" there never quite looked itself, unless Mr. Tattersall appeared in his wonted seat of honour at old St. George's, making the responses in a deep, sonorous voice, along with the Marquis of Westminster (who seldom quitted the borough all September), from the front row of the Corporation pew. Scarcely an alderman or common councillor was absent from the rear of the mace that day; and never did men look so important as they marched down Baxter Gate in procession.

His collection of horse portraits, Mr. Tattersall's scrap book. which is far the largest in England, was Mr. Tattersall's great delight, and each member of that congress of cracks, lies like a veiled prophet under silver paper, with its performances written out by the collector himself, in small round-hand. Lord Lonsdale's collection merged in it, and it goes back to Sedbury, 1734, who was " for justness of shape the most beautiful." Stubbs begins in 1768, with Mambrino, of the lofty style, and the forefather of some of the best American trotters. Firetail's head is a remarkable specimen; and in Jupiter we have the softer line of Gilpin, about 1790, and again in Sir Peter Teazle. According to the picture of Orville and Selim, they must have been giraffes of a trifle under nineteen hands, and their painter need hardly have made such a point of drinking " The Arts," as the last toast wherever he dined. Highflyer's 113 winners stand, in rows of nine, opposite him, and close by the original deed of conveyance which Lord Bolingbroke, literally sealed with his thumb. The new era of steel engraving seems to dawn with Ben Marshall, and Haphazard. Quiz (1808) is remarkable for its curious Newmarket back ground, in which the Duke's Stand, a heavy-sterned jockey, a soldier, and a man with a wooden leg, have not been forgotten; and Rubens, after Barenger, and supposed to be in training, is as fat as a Dutch vrow.

James Ward, R.A. The late Mr. James Ward, R.A., is well represented in that strange turf missal. He was related by marriage to Morland, and took to the same line of art, with such success as to become quite the first animal painter of the early part of the century. " He showed," as an eminent critic writes us, " wonderful facility in the management of white animals, particularly bulls; and painted the skins of his horses most delightfully, and his Earl Powis's Arabian and portrait of a Hunter, exhibited in the Royal Academy about 1818, are marvellous both in colour and execution. Unfortunately he did not let well alone, but began to study Rubens; and in all his after-backgrounds there were the heavy blues and purples so conspicuous in that great master's works, but which were quite out of place in the portrait of a horse or other animal. Instead of continuing his beautiful skins, he now sought to give more texture, and consequently exchanged the satin for the door-mat. He was, it has been considered, a good anatomist; but now he made a bad use of his knowledge, for some of his horses looked as if they were skinned. Arabians and thorough-breds show this to a great extent, but never as drawn by him. This he called "giving character;" but he forgot that, by adopting crooked lines where they should be straight, in many instances he introduced that which gave the appearance of disease—*i. e.*, curbs, thorough-pins, spavins, splints, and ringbones. He also introduced so many lines and veins into his horses' heads, and more particularly into the eyes and nostrils, that, instead of producing the effect he intended to express, they quite looked as if they were laughing. His "Doctor Syntax" has some strange drawing in the under-lip, and also in the hind-legs: but his "Phantom" is better."

Mr. Ferneley's father was a wheel- Mr. Ferneley. wright at Thrussington (where the future painter was born on the 18th of May, 1782), and obliged him to follow that trade until he was twenty-one. He had, however, chosen his own line long before that; and every leisure moment was spent in preparing his colours and canvas, and copying pictures lent him by a gentleman in the neighbourhood. His father soon found that it was no use contesting the point, and, accordingly, sent him, in 1803, to study under Ben Marshall, the great horse-painter of that day. After a year's tuition from his brilliant but lazy tutor, he started to seek his fortune in Ireland. In 1806 he turned up at Quorn, about the time when Mr. Assheton Smith bought the hounds;

and achieved, as it were, his Leicestershire diploma, by painting some hunting pictures for " *Le grand Chasseur*," beginning with little Will Burton and Manager. The next three years were spent between England and Ireland. He then retraced his steps to Thrussington, and was married ; and 1814 found him regularly settled at Melton Mowbray, where he painted two generations of Leicestershire hard riders and stable beauties, and received a very extensive patronage from other hunts. His works since that date amount to some hundreds, several of them of a very large size. Among the earliest of them was " Mr. Assheton Smith and his Hounds," for the Earl of Plymouth. He seldom recurred to this picture without telling how one day, when he strolled out as a lad to the meet, the Leicestershire hunting-field first became cognizant of Mr. Smith's existence by seeing a young man (of whom nothing more was then known, except that he was a guest at Belvoir) put his chesnut, Jack-a-Lantern, eight or nine times at a flight of rails, before he could get him over.

Principal pictures. The late Marquis of Westminster, Mr. Foljambe, Mr. Russell, of Brancepeth Castle; the Earl of Kintore, Mr. Ralph Lambton, and Sir Bellingham Graham were also among his large hunting-picture patrons; and the latter selected as his subject " The Meet at Kirby Gate." One also adorned the lobby of the late Master of the Hurworth; and Mr. Crawfurd, of Langton Hall, has a large " Scurry" from his hand, with portraits of Sir Harry Goodricke, Mr. Osbaldeston, and Sir Francis Holyoake. The study for these three was a very favourite one, and hung in his studio, like a sacred relic of the good old times, as long as the little, enfeebled form of the hoary devotee to art could bend over the easel. There, too, was another and a smaller " Scurry" of modern scarlets, which Earl

Wilton won in a raffle; a half-finished picture of Sir
Harry Goodricke, with Mumford and his whips,
Will Derry and Beers at the Whaw-Hoop; and a
sort of caricature of hard riding, in which Sir Francis Holyoake, on his white-legged chesnut Brilliant,
is trying to catch the fox, and within an ace of
succeeding. "Silver Firs" was also a well-known
shooting-picture of his, and the Duke of Rutland had
many hunters from his hand. Miss Burdett Coutts
honoured him, as well, with an order for an eques-
trian portrait of her late father; and his last professional journey was undertaken in company with his
daughter, to paint some hunters for Lord Middleton,
in Yorkshire. Racehorses were less in his line; but
a commission from Lord Jersey included Filagree and
Cobweb, with their foals; and Velocipede, and The
Cur (for Mr. Craufurd) are among his Turf memorials.

He was a man of unwearied industry   His habits.
and perseverance; and, although he
had been a great invalid for the last two years, he
never gave up his habit of early rising till a very
short time before his death. However sleepless and
painful the night might have been, it seemed a relief
to him to be back, with the morning light, in his
studio. Every June found him up in London for
his annual visit to the exhibitions; and, if we remember rightly, his last sketching expedition was into
the Vale of Belvoir; and he showed us the stable-
interiors he had gathered in that quarter with particular delight, from some connexion they had with
the hunting days of Mr. Musters. Amongst his
latest works were two very large ones of " The Horse
Fair" and The " Cattle Market," containing portraits
of celebrated horses and horse-characters in the neighbourhood. The chase was, after all, his great *forte*.
He loved it best; and hence he painted it best; and
his pictures were real bits of Cream Gorse memory.

In his plain groups of horses there was more mannerism, and his outline and shadows were often rather too hard; but although he lacked any very remarkable finish, there were the higher qualities of feeling and breadth about everything he handled. Beyond what they were doing at Belvoir, the hunting of the present had but little interest for him. He sighed for the old régime when "George the Fourth was king," and when Moore, Maxse, and Maher were names of Melton renown.

" Him go vip, vip, vip! Vot he know about horses ?"
said a jealous old artist, when Herring, the well-known coachman of the London and York Highflyer, had thrown aside the reins in Jack Spigot's year, and fairly cast in his lot with the mahl-stick. We thought of the saying, as, under the guidance of "Sailor Jack," another of the North Road men who had followed Mr. Herring's fortunes, and now looks after his Arabs, we bowled over the three miles from Tonbridge to Meopham Park. Even in the tender sunshine of a May morning, the hop-fields with their countless wigwams of poles wore a very dreary air, and made us long for the autumn, when their rich green clusters will once more claim to be Barley Brides. The carriage-drive shaded by oaks with large fantastic arms, which would have made Parson Gilpin of the New Forest gaze for a moment and then rush for relief to his pencil, is kept in faultless "Quicksilver mail order," as a memento of the old whip days.

Visit to Mr Herring at Meopham.

Scarcely a wheel has touched it since Charles Herring was borne over it, six years since, to his grave, and it is really sacred to his memory. And well it may be, as a better son or a more skilful lover of art for his years never passed to his rest.

White and red rosebuds just bursting into bloom, clustered round the verandah, and from it the

Mr. J. F. Herring, p. 89.

outline of the pleasant woods of Penshurst, which

> " Heard the sound of Sydney's song,
> Perchance of Surrey's reed,"

was just visible in the drowsy distance. Partridges
were feeding on the lawn, and scarcely caring
to rise on the wing, or run behind the purple beech
at your approach ; and the deep coo of the wood-
pigeons as they perched on the Scotch and silver
firs, which towered above the thickly interlaced
grove of holly and laburnum, so vocal with its song
of spring, was all in harmony with a painter's
home.

Jack, the thirty-seven inch pony, is *Horse & donkey
models.* nearly as free to range, and he mounted
the steps of the front-door and walked gravely into
the room, in search of his ginger-bread, or to enquire
if he was wanted for the basket that day. Favourite
as he is, we did not meet with him on canvas, and
in this respect he differs widely from the white Arab
Imaum, of which the story goes that he has not
been seen to lie down for at least eight years. He
sleeps leaning against his stall, and like the oldest
Alderney, and the donkey which runs unicorn in the
bush-harrow and roller team, and wins half the saddles in the neighbourhood when so disposed, he is
on canvas all the world over, in nearly a hundred
positions. Sometimes an Ironside stables him in a
cathedral nave, or he waits for some boisterous
cavalier, hard by an ale-house bench.

He was one of the four first horses *The Arab Imaum.*
that was ever sent over by the Imaum
of Muscat to Her Majesty; and was made a present to the Clerk of the Royal Stable, who sold him
at Tattersall's. When it became necessary to have
a model for the dead horses, which Mr. Herring was
to have introduced into the Battle of Waterloo at the
Gallery of Illustrations he sent for Pedro, a black man

from Batty's Circus, and had him taught to lie down. With a few lessons he became so complete a trick horse, that Pedro declared he wanted nothing but youth to beat the Bedas, and the other time-honoured pets of the horse ballet, quite out of the field. He looks peaky and worn now, and his tricks have rather departed from him; but in his prime, Mr. Herring was followed by a gentleman into a yard in Picca-dilly, and had 200 guineas bid for him there and then. In spite of the prejudice against Arabs, he was wonderfully stout, and when his master drove him from Camberwell to Stevenage and back, about 75 miles in one day, to paint The Switcher and other "Steeple-Chase Cracks" for Lord Strathmore, he was fresher than the English black, who was in the phaeton with him, and who had never shirked his work by comparison before. Her Majesty hearing of Mr. Herring's severe asthma, which has for some time past quite disabled him from leaving home, sent down three of her horses for him to paint. They included Korseed (a white Arab), Bagdad, a black charger of the late Prince Albert's, and Said, the Arab on which Mr. Meyer has instructed the royal children. The latter is among the Osborne collection, with a back-ground of white sand and Arab tents, in the composition of which, his friend Mr. D. Roberts, R.A., gave Mr. Herring the advan-tage of all his Eastern lore. .

The painting-room almost adjoins the stable, but it has been but little used since his son's death. A model of a coach in a case rests upon some packing-boxes, and the original sketch for the picture which he took of the beautiful Attila, just before he went abroad, is the only tenant of the easel; but the sketch, like that fatal journey, was never com-pleted.

Mr. Herring himself is about sixty-seven, or just the mean in age between his old friends John and

Mr. Herring's first efforts. William Scott. Doncaster and its Town Moor associations naturally whetted his zeal for the brush, long before he took to it as a profession, and many a little horse or mail-coach sketch by him crept on to the tavern walls, and the signs. His earliest anatomy study was the fractured leg of Spartan, one of whose small bones near the pastern was completely pulverized by his break down; and Smolensko and Comus were the racers on which his " prentice han" was tried.

A gigantic " Horse Fair" adorns the lobby, which is, as Mr. Herring's pictures so invariably are, " all daylight." The mail is again in requisition, following in the wake of a gig, whose horse trots right out of the picture, and whose driver casts a glance at the troops of nags and stallions, which are dispersing to their stalls when business is over. All kinds have mustered there, and the supply of ginger-nuts and ginger in the raw has been of course unlimited. Then we get among the Eight Day-Waggons and a pair of the blue jacket and white hat line, stopping for refreshment at one of the old road-side inns near the orthodox trough and tree. Wood-piling and hop-picking are not forgotten. It seems that there is a family in the neighbourhood, who especially pride themselves on the accomplishment; and accordingly, at half-past six, one summer morning, Mr. Herring sallied out, and caught them by appointment, just at the most picturesque crisis, when the timber is slung aloft, and the truck is being backed under it. In the other, the artist in a straw-hat, with a black ribbon and mahogany tops, plays " Farmer Oldfield," and does not look, as he gazes complacently at the fast-filling bins, as if the iron of Gladstone was piercing his soul so acutely. The jaunty ribbons and tunics of the hop-pickers blend very prettily with the green avenues which they are so ruthlessly rifling, and the farmer's daughter with her bonnet carelessly tossed back is taking the tally as the widow brings up her bin to be measured.

Interior of his studio. Mr. Herring now paints in his dining-room, which is hung all round with prints from his works, of which " Distinguished Members of the Temperance Society" is the premier. It is there that he loves to grapple with the Giant Foreshortening, who has given the cross-buttock to so many, and flings him in picture after picture. Leading lines have always been his great guide for perspective, and he invariably works from left to right. His great racing pictures have generally been got by the aid of a sketch-book, with ideal horses and jockeys, which a few strokes from life at the post converted into portraits. Of Vision he had no sight at all, but sketched her, years after her death, merely from the description of Will Beresford, who pronounced the likeness perfect. All the elder heroes caught our eye, as we turned from a gigantic* Dutchman galloping, and scanned the oil treasures of his portfolio. Sultan was there, with his beautiful Arab head and dish nose, not more beautiful,

Recollections of his " Book of Beauty." but more masculine in its expression than Attila's. Langar's was another of the glorious heads, and so was Dr. Syntax's, Mameluke's, Partisan's, and Venison's, with his deep jowl and tapering nose. Mr. Herring considers that the coarsest thorough-bred horse he ever painted was Ardrossan, the sire of Jack Spigot (the first of his St. Leger winning series), as his neck was really heavier than even Stubbs's sketch of the Godolphin Arabian ; and Welbeck the sire of the

---

* *Apropos* of this picture, Mr. Herring told a landlord of an inn, the sign of which was a half moon, that if he would get his licence altered to The Flying Dutchman, he would make him a present of a new sign, which Boniface considering too good for a sign, never hung outside, and refused a very long sum for, although painted on the Half Moon wood.

neat little Bedlamite ranks nearly as high in his list of the Ugly Club. Mr. Lambton's Don Juan by Orville, who wrought wonders among the Cleveland mares, was quite one of his delights, and so were Magistrate, and Filho da Puta ; while The Duchess (who always ran in high company) was his prima donna among the small, and Crucifix and Queen of Trumps among the larger-sized mares.

We traced in a pictured line the *Painting Bay Middleton.* Cotherstone pedigree on both sides, till the Whalebone and Whisker strains united ; and in essaying The Dutchman's, we came across the original sketch of Bay Middleton, just as it was left about a quarter of a century ago. It occupied only 1 hour 10 min., but it looks like the work of a day. No horse impressed Mr. Herring more firmly than this son of Sultan with the belief that he had the heart and the muscular energy to do what he liked with his fields. " George Villiers" too stood by the easel, watching every stroke as it was dashed in; and never had painter a higher stimulus to bring all his manhood to his hand.

If we want to sketch an enthusiast *Baron Petroffski.* among Continental sportsmen, we need only turn for a space to the Romanoff dominions and its Baron Ippolyte Petroffski. The Baron, who is better known in the thirty-six-letter alphabet of his country as " Ummoiuml Nemjsobevez," resides at Petroffski Park, a short distance out of Moscow. The house is a two-storied one, built in the oriental style, among beautiful gardens, and with a large set of stables attached. These are, after all, merely his head-quarters during the season of ice and snow, and hardly furnish any index to the magnitude of his possessions, which consist of three large estates in the interior. On each of them he keeps nearly a thousand serfs; but his sway is not of a very iron kind, and those who are not engaged in agriculture are all brought up to some trade. Everything necessary for himself and this huge family is produced on his own estates, from sheep-skins down to his renowned kish-le-shee, a species of mead of an aromatic rose flavour, and compounded from apple juice, honey, and flour and water.

His love of sport. Sixty-five summers have done very little towards blanching his hair or dimming his sharp hazel eyes, and he still carries his light wiry frame erect, as beseems a captain of the Imperial Guard. No one who has visited him can forget that quiet, courteous bearing, or the delight with which he speaks of everything English. Sir Joseph Hawley and John Scott are breathing types to his imagination of everything 'cute in connection with horse management; and if a Witch of Endor gave him his choice as to what spirit among the departed thoroughbreds he should recall from the Happy Pastures to his delighted gaze for a season, he would decide for old Waxy or Orville. His fowls, sheep, pigs, and dogs (not forgetting the favourite black terrier which has been painted in one of his pictures), are all English; but we are not so sure as to the nativity of his fighting geese. They are stouter than the common geese, and on shorter legs, and are put down just like game cocks on to the green sod for the fray, which they solemnly conduct by seizing each other by the beak, and striking furiously with the butts of their wings. Such is his passion for the sport, that for one of the most warlike he paid no less than 500 silver roubles.

His race-horse breeding. The Baron breeds his horses at one of his estates, and trains at another, where his string do their work in the winter, without shoes, on frozen snow regularly harrowed for the purpose. The ground is, however, mostly flat, without any extent or variety of gallops. His breeding farm is bordered by a noble river of great width, and in summer, when the flies teaze the young foals to distraction, they dash in and swim, while their dams watch them placidly from the bank, and occasionally join in the sport. If a ten-stone by five-feet-eight figure is seen standing by, in a blue tunic, and trowsers tucked inside his boots, it is even betting that it is the Baron himself, meditating on Moscow or Crenavoy Meetings to come. Many of them have excellent hind-leg action, and their owner invariably attributes it to their early swimming habits. The brood mares alone number about 160, some of which are still unbroken, and most of them never trained. The blood is, strictly speaking, a cross between the Russian and Arab mares, and the horses imported by Government—Memnon, General Chassé, Van Tromp, Andover, &c.; and the stock are generally browns, of great length and on short legs, having all the Arab deficiency of shoulder, but catching the Eastern character in their fine eye and small nostrils, and bearing the Sir Hercules crest at the root of their tails. In 1859 his racing stud consisted of seventeen horses in training, fifty brood mares, twenty-five two-year-olds, nearly as many yearlings and foals respectively, while Signal, Granite, and Bombardier were the principal sires, and the Signals his best racing stock.

The spring opens for training in April, Racing in Russia. and early in June the racing season begins at Moscow, where the Baron gives 500 silver roubles in prizes. The Moscow Meeting then lasts for a month; they race for three days out of the seven, and run off four or five races per day. The Jockey Club, of which Baron Petroffski is an active member, have a stand of their own, and the horses are entered the night before at their rooms. There is very little betting, and that has been principally introduced by the English jockeys, who are, alas! too true to their old Tattersall's instincts. The Toola meeting is on July 8th, and on August 18th the one at Tsarskey Sela begins. Lebedan, on September 12th,

is the fourth, and last meeting; and here, in 1859,
the Petroffski "boy in yellow" literally carried off
every prize.

Training troubles. Of his training troubles, however, the
Baron shall speak for himself: "You
like the horses of old stock," he says, in writing to
a friend, "and old form, just the same, which I prefer to the new-fashioned, who win great prizes on a
short distance. Such a horse is the same as the
card at the play of bank, only by accident ready at
time. I would like very much to try the best
English race-horse with my poor fellows. I call my
horses poor fellows. We have only two months to
prepare them for the races, that is May and June.
The horses are led 500 versts, with all the road in-
conveniences. They change water and food, and
suffer much before they come to the racing place.
All that is not easy to support for a racing horse.
Our prizes are not worth carrying food and water,
and the horse itself in equipage. It would be sup-
portable yet to run once, having passed 500 versts,
but they go again 200 versts and run, and then
again 500 versts, and yet 200 versts and run again."

The English Stud Book is his Koran, and in his
library may also be found every Racing Calendar and
Sporting Magazine that has ever seen the light.
He is himself an author, and has been at the pains
of publishing, in the Russian language, a most complete synopsis of the celebrated stallions in England
from 1811. It enters with the greatest accuracy
into the number of years they were at the stud, the
price at which they covered, and the dams of their
most celebrated winners. Upwards of 135 paintings
or engravings of racers and sporting subjects adorn
his rooms; and if there was an alarm of fire, we are
afraid that his valuable gallery of old Dutch and
Italian masters would be left to take their chance,
till those dearly-loved forms of Derby and St. Leger
renown were safe out of harm's way.

CHAPTER II.

EXMOOR TO WIT.

> " I ride as good a galloway,
>   As any man in town ;
> He'll trot you sixteen miles an hour,
>   I'll bet you half-a-crown ;
> He's such a one to bend the knee,
>   And tuck his haunches in ;
> And to throw the dirt into your face,
>   He never deems a sin."

DEVONSHIRE had done its best to naturalize us. Its clotted cream had appealed to our feelings through the tart and the teacup ; and its junket had whispered " Stay !" We had borne our part in its pleasant pastorals among the deep shady lanes and orchard clusters of Barton. We had viewed that grave Wittenagemote of the red-line elders of the West, which met under old Frank Quartly's picture in the black wainscoted parlour at Champson, and arose from their rump cuts and their cider, to " try a fall" for the Flowers and the Pictures of that grand old stock. Still the gipsy element of our nature was strong upon us, and we longed to wander afield. It may be that our labours had been too much in one groove. After four long days among the cattle, we might well wish for a change, and even consider that Locke of Lynemouth, who roasted an Exmoor pony for his friends after one of the Simon's Bath sales, judiciously sympathized with Tartar

The road to Exmoor.

H

tastes. Both sheep and ponies acted as a magnet in our case. We bade good-by to our kind host and his chesnut hack, without one ounce of saddle ache, as a forget-me-not at parting; and Flitton Oak, that far-famed tryst of the Poltimore hounds, was soon upon our lee. The time of nuts was not yet come, and it was rather exasperating to see them brush the gig with their clusters, as we toiled up the rutty lanes. Mist was fast closing over the land of the Devons when we reached North Molton Ridge, and then the long, dark line of forest wall bade us welcome to Somerset, and the pony glories of its Exmoor hills.

Emmett's Grange. The lights in Emmett's Grange, about a mile to the right, acted as a still more cheery beacon, and the white gates, dotted here and there, as guardians to the richly irrigated tracts, of which Philip Pusey so loved to talk, told too surely that the glorious days of hound and horse, when "Fred Knight" led the field over Exmoor, will ere long live only in hearth-side story, or the songs of the Somerset dames. The Red men of North America have already succumbed before the dread fire-water, and the red deer are equally certain in their turn to bow their antlered heads before Mr. Robert Smith and his water-sluices.

Mr. Robt. Smith's cob breeding. Ponies and mountain sheep were his first Exmoor aim, but as cultivation grew apace, and irrigation laid its green velvet hand on the meadows, where the rushy swamp and the snipe had flourished amicably since the days of William Rufus, the former gave way in the natural order of things to galloways. The necessity of sticking to mountain produce ceased, when only 250 acres out of the 700 were left unenclosed; and hence the only ponies on the Emmett's Grange holding consist of some twenty-five short-legged brood mares of about thirteen-two. Three parts of the

year these mares live on the mountain land, while
the farm is making beef and mutton below, and sup-
porting the Taunton sale lot of that autumn to
boot. Their foals are carefully wintered in paddocks
with the yearlings, and if the weather is very severe,
the two-year-olds have hay as well. The paddocks
are principally four acres in extent; little open
sheds, neatly thatched, nestle in cunning nooks, to
shelter the young stock, and when its whole array
is marshalled on to the lowlands, the stud is about
120 strong. At first Mr. Smith used neighbouring
sires, among whom Old Port, the first-born of Sir
Hercules and Beeswing, had the lead, and at length
started on his own account with "Exmoor." His
dam was one of the seven mares, with hunting
blemishes, which migrated to Emmett's Grange from
Burley; but they were all sold off with the exception of a Red Gauntlet, after adding some high-
priced entries to the ledger.

The renowned fourteen-hand Bobby
then came from Dr. Beevor, for two sea-   Bobby.
sons, and won the Champion prize, and a two-guinea
bonus at "The Bath and West of England," at Barnstaple. He looked more than his height, and the
officials measured him three times before the fourteen-
hand claim was allowed. The greybeards of Devon
were, one and all, amazed at his remarkable likeness
to the renowned Katerfelto of their youth. Both of
them had the same Eastern blood in their escutch-
eons. Bobby could trace his descent through two
degrees on his dam's side to Borax, who beat all the
best horses, under high weights, at Madras; and
Katerfelto's dam, after being stolen by some gypsies,
was recovered in foal with him to an Arab. Independently of his fine stock, which is still referred to in
nearly every pedigree, Katerfelto was a mighty hunter,
and earned deathless glory, both for himself and
his owner, a lusty farmer, by taking the bit between

his teeth on the Barkham Hills, and carrying him bodily over a twenty-foot gap in an old Roman iron mine. Bobby's stock so far have almost invariably fallen bays, and nearly all of them have a star. Twenty-five foals, with their chubby chieftain "Master Bobby," from a black mare were running with their dams, so that *The Life's* query, "*Where are the Bobbies?*" receives a highly practical answer from Somersetshire. They are so thick that the clerical visitor, who broke out into an exclamation, "*I can only describe them as bantam cocks!*" did not draw his description bow at a venture. An Arab has succeeded Bobby, and if he only proves a second Katerfelto, the day may come when the poet, who summed up mere human felicity under six heads, and placed "the gentle wife" behind "the haunch of good buck" and "the glass of Madeira old," may feel that the "Exmoor" has as good a right as the "Norfolk" cob, in the fifth

The Inn at Simon's Bath. The mist was thick upon Long Halcombe, and the rain was rattling down on to the devoted "Bobbies" as we took our first glance at Exmoor by broad daylight, and it seemed like an act of sheer self-immolation to wander forth on the hills that day. However, it cleared up towards ten o'clock, and we were soon on our road toward Simon's Bath Lodge. The most inveterate stickler for blood would have been satisfied with his mounts, as "Sambo," a grandson of old Beeswing, was allotted us for the first day, this being "positively his last appearance" before his departure for Cornwall; and as if to aid our Newcastle Cup recollections, we found ourselves next day on "The Comet," a grandson of Lanercost's,—who was also fourteen-two, and from an Exmoor pony dam. The original colour of the Exmoor seems to have been a buffy bay, with a mealy nose, and it is supposed to have preserved its characteristics ever since the Phœnicians

brought it over, when they visited the shores of
Cornwall, to trade in tin and metals. The climate
was propitious; and thus the private sale at the
Simon's Bath Inn gradually became a sort of rustic
fête. The aspirants to the Cann and Polkinghorne
line of business met there, and showed rude feats
of wrestling, not only with each other, but at the
expence of the ponies, which they seized and dragged
out of the fold, with all a giant's thew. "*Seventy
years ago, sir,*" said a bailiff to us, "*there were only
five men and a woman and a little girl on Exmoor,
and my mother was that little girl. She drew beer at
the Simon's Bath public-house;—they were a rough
lot of customers there, I promise you.*" And no
doubt they were. The Doons, who had retired to
Badgery, and carried out their Commonwealth
yearnings, by becoming the Moss-troopers of the
West, had taken their last leap from the cart, one
after another, at Taunton Assizes, or "saved their
lives by dying in jail." After them, the illicit love
of mutton extended to spirits. Smugglers slung
their kegs across their "Scrambling Jacks" at night,
and, if they did not care to hide their treasure in
the rocks, or leave it at a certain gate, till the next
mystic hand in that living chain should give it his
allotted lift on its road towards Exeter, there were
always friendly cellars under the ale-house at Simon's
Bath. The ale was decent, and the landlady was
judiciously deaf, and hence its old ingle, where the
date 1654 still lingers on a beam, shorn or built into
half its length, heard many a roystering tale of
prime brandy and extra-parochial enormities, bad
enough to make a beadle blush and an exciseman
groan.

The time of pony memory for all prac- Origin of the Ex-
tical purposes goes back to the present   moor Ponies.
Sir Thomas Acland, who rented a great part of Exmoor from the Crown. When it was disforested in

1818, the father of the present Mr. Frederick Knight, M.P., bought the 10,000-acre Crown allotment, and by the subsequent purchase of 6,000 more, became the owner of at least four-fifths. The ponies had for some years past only fetched from £4 to £6, and in spite of "the anchor brand," and the death code, the Exmoor shepherds took very liberal tithe of them, as well as the sheep, and passed them at night-fall over the hills to their crafty Wiltshire customers. Sir Thomas carried away his original uncrossed stock to the Winsford Hills, and only about a dozen mare ponies were left to preserve the line. Luckily, an after-dinner conversation led Mr. Knight, senior, to consider the great pony question in all its bearings. The party met at Sir Joseph Banks's, the eminent naturalist, in the days when Soho Square was equivalent to Belgravia in fashionable ears, and Bruce's Abyssinian stories were all the rage. Passing from live beef-steaks, they discussed the merits of the Dongala horse, which "the travelling giant" had described as an Arab of sixteen hands, and peculiar to the regions round Nubia.

The Dongalas.   Sir Joseph proposed to the party to get them some of the breed, and accordingly Lords Headley, Morton, and Dundas, and Mr. Knight then and there gave him a joint-£1,000-cheque as a deposit for the expences. The English Consul in Egypt was applied to in due course, and the horses and mares which he sent over bore out Bruce's description to the letter. It was said that they were got through the agency of a High Priest, who "had his price;" and after trying unsuccessfully for two years, dissembled most artfully at the end. The Moorish Princes felt that they had been duped, and a century of bullocks were offered in vain as the ransom. In addition to their fine height, they were rather Roman-nosed, with a very fine texture of skin, well-chiselled under the jowl, and as clear-winded as all their race. Their action was quite of the "knee-in-the-curb-chain-" school; and they had short thick backs, and great hind-quarters. Still, there were three or four points against these "gaudy blacks," in the shape of flattish ribs, drooping croups, and rather long white legs.

As *manége* horses they were perfect; and the dusky Nubian, who brought them over, delighted to gallop them at a wall in the riding-school, and make them stop dead when they reached it. About ten or twelve arrived, and Mr. Knight was so pleased with them, that, acting on the advice of the late Marquis of Anglesey, who considered that they "would improve any breed alive," he bought Lord Headley's share. Lord Dundas bred a good many from his lot in Scotland, and one especially nice white one sprang from the stock. Mr. Knight's two sires and three mares were brought to Simon's Bath at once, where he had established a stud of seven or eight thorough-bred mares, and thirty half-breds of the coaching Cleveland sort. A dozen twelve-hand pony mares were also put to one of the Dongalas, and the produce generally came fourteen-two, and very seldom black. The first cross knocked out the mealy nose, as completely as the Leicester destroys the Exmoor horn; but the buffy stood true to its colour, and thus the type was never quite lost. The half-Dongalas did wonderfully well with the West Somerset, which often came to Exmoor to draw for a fox, and they managed to get down the difficult hills so well, and crossed the brooks so close up with the hounds, that the vocation of the white-clad guides on chase days gradually fell into disuse. One of the Dongalas was never put to the stud, and preceded the Quicksilver colts in Mr. Frederick Knight's hunting stable. This cross-out was only intended for size, and not for character, as no sire of half

Dongala blood was used, and the mares which did not retain as much as possible of the Exmoor type were drafted forthwith.

Thorough-bred crosses.   Pandarus, a whole-coloured fifteen-hand son of Whalebone, was the first important successor of the Dongala; but though he confirmed the original bay, he reduced the standard to thirteen hands or thirteen and a-half. The fine breeding as well as the "Pandarus bay" were kept up by Canopus, a grandson of Velocipede, and while the experiment was in progress, the colts were better wintered on limed land, which enabled them to bear up pretty well against the climate. When, however, the farms were let by the present Mr. Knight, they had to go back *en masse* to the naked moor, and then it was found that even if the mares with the first cross could put up with the fare and climate, they grew far too thin to give any milk, while those which were of the old stock stood it well with their foals. Hence, about eighteen years ago, the whole pony stud was remodelled, the lighter mares were drafted, and Mr. Knight determined to stick henceforth to his own ponies, with the buffy bay sire. So strict has been this rule, that for many years, with the exception of the chesnut Hero, whose massive form and Pandarus dam preserved him from "Schedule G," and the grey Lillias, whose original Acland blood knows but little alloy, no other colour has been used.

The first pony sales.   They were disposed of by private contract until 1850, when the public sales were established. At the first, the whole of the hunting stock were sold along with some forty ponies. Sir Thomas Sebright gave £16 for a pony which had rather a large-sized cross in him, and Mr. Pole Carey, M.P., £41 for three, which were an exact bay unicorn match, with the exception of one slight star. The hunters had long been under the charge of

Robert Milton, Lord Portsmouth's present training groom, who got old Tory and the other steeple-chase denizens of the eight-stall stable, so well up to their "flag line" form, and they fetched good prices, along with the colts, which were principally of the Dongala and Quicksilver blood. The stock of ponies was sold up so close, that no more were brought out for sale until the autumn of 1853, when Stony Plot, the knoll with its belt of quartz boulders, on which the picturesque new parish church stands, had a hammer auditory of two hundred. The average was an improvement over that of other years; but the plan of selling in the heart of the wilds was far too primitive, and in the following autumn the venue was changed to Bampton fair, fourteen miles nearer the rail. Then they were broken and brought as far as Reading, with Kettledrum and Dundee, "names worth all the money" (as the auctioneer observed) among them; and in future the foals are to be weaned in October, and fed more highly, instead of running with their dams all winter. Philip Richards has very little trouble with them. When he once gets near enough to scratch their tails, he soon makes a rural Rarey of himself, and contrives to be on their backs, the very first day.

The present pony stock consists of _Mr. Knight's pony stock._ about 400, of which nearly a fourth are brood mares, of all ages from one to thirteen. The mares are put to the horses at three, and up to that age they share the 800 heather acres of Badgery, with the red deer and the blackcock, protected on all sides by high stone walls, which even Lillias, the gay Lothario of the moor, cannot jump in his moonlit rambles. The average height is 12½ hands, but the smaller mares are being gradually drafted. In order to keep up the size, one hundred and thirty acres of the pasture land and water meadows round Simon's Bath have been taken in hand, to winter the

foals and weakly yearlings. The foals came in for the
first time in '59, and the effect upon the two-year-olds
and yearlings has already been most encourag-
Their mode of
life. ing. This wintering begins after the
marking in November, and the meadows
are shut up for hay again on the 1st of May. The
older ponies live on the hills all winter, and seek the
most sheltered spots during the continuance of the
wind and wet, which are much more the features of
the climate, than extreme cold. These favourite
nooks are well-known to the herdsmen, who build
up stacks of hay, straw, and rushes, and dole forth
their out-door relief over the rails, without any regard to the Union dietary scale. Still, like honest,
hard-working labourers, the ponies never assemble
at the wicket, till they have exhausted every means
of self-support, by scratching with their fore-feet in
the snow, for the last remnants of the summer tufts;
and drag wearily behind them an ever-lengthening
chain of snow-balls.

Habits and bat-
tles of the sires. The bays and the buffy bays (a description of yellow), both with mealy
noses, are in a majority of at least three to one, but
there are several browns and greys, half-a-dozen
blacks, and a few chesnuts, which have strained back
to their great grandsire Velocipede. They are
grouped about on certain hills, and "The Sparkham
pony" (a son of the beautiful mare Bay Lillias), soon
earned his name from such constancy. He won the
head prize at Barnstaple in '59, with Cheriton
second, and a Pandarus pony third, and the instant
the three shook off civilization and its halters on
their return, they galloped off several miles, as
straight as a minié ball, to their respective hills.
The ten sires are all wintered together in an allotment, until the 1st May, apart from the mares; but
Lillias, who has more of the old pony blood in him
than any of them, twice scrambled over at least a

score of six-feet walls, and away to his loved North
Forest.

It is a very beautiful sight to see them
jealously beating the bounds, when they are once
more in their own domains; and they would, if they
wore shoes, break every bone in a usurper's skin.
The challenge to a battle royal is given with a snort,
and then they commence by rearing up against each
other's necks, so as to get the finest leverage for a
worry. When they are weary of that, they turn
tail to tail, and commence a series of heavy ex-
changes, till the least exhausted pony of the two
watches his opportunity, and whisking round, gives
his antagonist a broadside in the ribs, which fairly
echoes down the glen. In the closing scene, they
face each other once more, and begin like bull-dogs
to manœuvre for their favourite bite on the arm.
The first which is caught off his guard, goes down
like a shot, and then scurries off, with the victor in
hot pursuit, savagely "weaving," while his head
nearly touches the ground, and his "flag" waves
triumphantly in the air. With the exception of
Lillias, the ten are generally pretty content, each with
their one thousand acres of territory, and like Sayers
and Heenan they are ultimately "reconciled,"—in
November.

Stock is taken of the whole in the *Annual mark-
second* week of this month, when the *ing of the hoofs.*
hills are swept by the three "hard-riding Dicks,"
for a couple of days, and the four hundred are
brought into a paddock at Simon's Bath in lots.
The first process is the separation of them into
ages, and placing them in distinct paddocks for
marking. The foals are then branded on the saddle
place, with "the forest mark," which has been
changed from the Acland anchor, to the spur, which
forms part of the crest of the Knight family. It is
burnt in with a hot iron, just sufficiently to scar the

roots of the hair, and no age eradicates it.   If a pony
wanders away, and there is any dispute, the hair
is clipped off to make the identity more perfect, and
on one occasion a white sire was discovered by the
head herdsman's brother, after he had been lost for
three seasons.   The spur has only one heel, and as
the brand can be made with the rowel pointing in
four directions (beginning towards the neck), on
each side of the pony, it coincides with an eight year
cycle, and serves as a guide, in case the foot-marks
are prematurely worn out.   The foal is of course
not marked on the foot, but an exact record is taken
of his dam and all his marks, by the land-steward,
who stands book in hand under all weathers, for
at least a week, to act as the Weatherby of the
hills.

The mares then come under review, and if any are
absent, the stud-book tells its infallible tale.   A
mare and two yearlings were missing one November,
and the herdsmen set forth on their search so completely primed with these stud-book data, that the
two were very shortly discovered.   The register
hoof-marks are then renewed on the mares, &c.,
and the Dominical letter of their year of entry
is placed upon the yearlings.   The marks are two-
fold, to wit, that of the year, which began with
B in 1848, on the off hoof, and the register
figure of the dam from the stud-book, on the near.
They are marked as close to the coronet as possible, as it is found that in all the ages, the hoof has
the faculty of reproducing itself in twelve months.
In the older ones it grows more rapidly, and not
unfrequently the spur-mark has to be referred to as
a guide.   The letters A and I have proved exces-
sively troublesome, as the one broke away towards
the end of the year in the shape of a triangular
fissure ; while the other merged into a species of
sand-crack.

Average of casualties. Under the old system, when the mares and their foals were never separated, it was not unusual to see one of the matrons with two or three of her progeny trotting after her, and trying to get a stray suck; but since the foals were weaned, and drafted into their Simon's Bath quarters, the family tie is quite broken, and the new winter associations foreshadow the hill groupings of the summer. The percentage of deaths is comparatively small, and during the winter of '59, when many of the old ponies fairly gave in on the neighbouring hills, Mr. Knight's mares fought through it, but five or six of them died from exhaustion at foaling, or slipped foals at ten months. Their greatest peril is when they are tempted into the bogs about that period, by the green bait of the early aquatic grasses, and flounder about under weakness and heavy pressure, till they die. The stud-book contains some very curious records. *" Died of old age in the snow,"* forms quite a pathetic St. Bernard sort of entry. *" Found dead in a bog"* has less poetry about it. *" Iron grey, found dead with a broken leg, at the foot of a hill,"* is rather an odd mortality comment on such a chamois-footed race; while *" Grey mare C 22, and grey yearling missing; both found, mare with foal at her foot,"* gives us rather a more cheery glimpse of forest history.

Will Court, the head herdsman, and his two aide-de-camps, Bill Shapland The herdsmen. and Will Scott, form the staff of the pony department: and the latter has been gazetted from the Scotch hills, *vice* Jack Huxtable, promoted to be ground-keeper on Larkborough and Badgery. Will Court has been bred up among " our ponies" from a boy, and treats " the droop-rumped mongrels" on the adjacent hills with the most magnificent disdain. He is a perfect Follett in his advocacy of " the old sort" on the review-day, and unwavering in his

fealty to Lillias as a lineal descendant of the anchor
brand. The trio have two ponies a-piece, besides
occasional young ones in breaking; and Will's boast
about Exmoor endurance receives strong con-
firmation from the fact, that his men, who, like himself, are no feather weights, can ride a pony incessantly
through a ten-hour herding-day.

A ride by the Barle.   If we had prefaced all this pony lore
in the true G. P. James fashion, by
saying that it was morning, &c., and that two men
on horseback were seen in conversation, as they wound
their way, &c., we should be pretty nearly describing
ourselves on Sambo, and our informant on the stag-
loving Rattler, as we rode towards Simon's Bath
Lodge, with a very promising sky overhead. There
had been nothing but a common-place succession of
pasture and moorlands, varied with " Bobby foals"
and iron-ore piles (which a private railway is destined to carry Wales-ward to the Bristol Channel);
but a turn in the road brought us on to a sort of
plateau, and revealed the heather and gorse-clad
rocks of Cornham Brake, with the Barle rippling
quietly along its valley, to join the Exe, near Dul-
verton.

A herd of nearly three dozen Devons were marching in slow, Indian file along the opposite bank, and
foxhunters tell that nearly half as many cubs were
" at home" in the Brake, when the North Devon
drew it three seasons ago. Milton, by Old Port,
whom Mr. Knight has used for a good brown cross,
was grazing at the water's edge, with a pony mare of
Burley and Dongala blood. The patriarchs Hero
and Nelson, the son of the Forest *prima donna*
Nelly, then told by their joint pasture presence, on
the opposite side, of the proximity of the Simon's
Bath stables. The renowned Pocket Hercules of
Exmoor lifted his white Velocipede forehead, and
shook his shaggy chesnut forelock more assiduously

than ever into his eyes, as he gave back an answering cheer to our Sambo; while the massive Nelson (whose sire pined himself to death to escape the indignity of the breaking bit) ate calmly on, as befitted the deposed head of the buffy bays, or perchance reserved his greeting for one of his great namesake's lieutenants, who had long since risen to admiral's estate, and had just arrived, "as green as grass," for a cruise among the hills, in his poncha.

The day had quite broken long before noon, and hence there was nothing for *On Exmoor.* it but to mount a military cloak, which the rain of the tropics could hardly soak, and with a second companion cased in oilskin, and on a bit of Dongala blood at our side, and Will Court making strong running on his pet sister to the Sparkham pony, we were soon pointing across the deer park for the South Forest. Hundreds of red and fallow deer used to consider this as their sanctuary, but they have been shot or hunted down, or have fallen back for a last stand amongst the old haunts of the Doons of Badgery. The moor was like a sponge; but the clay pan which holds up the peaty surface is doomed to be broken by Fowler's subsoil plough, and a topdressing of railway-brought lime will complete this great measure of Reform.

A perfect parliament of sale ponies, sixty strong, was met at the corner of the South Forest, after the most active whip on the part of Scott and Shapland, who kept them steadily in position till we got up. Some of the draft brood mares had foals at their sides, and all the horse ponies dated from the May or June of '56. Buffy Bay was quite in the ascendant, and five or six Lillias greys formed that Stumps element which has hitherto given such pleasant character to the thorough-bred Sledmere park troop. Some dark browns added life to the whole, and one of them, with a piece of bracken hanging carelessly

in his mane tresses, would remind us of Herring's
fine study of Mulcy Moloch, and Rebecca.   A solitary Devon kept running among them, vainly claim-
ing kindred; but their sympathies had evidently
been too much for a brown in his strangles troubles,
as they had licked his ears till they were raw, and
the festering blast had converted him into a croppy.
Bringing up the ponies.   Our military-capped leader then gave
the word for the North Forest; and in
a few minutes the whole troop were dispersed into
little friendly knots once more, while Will and Bill
scoured wildly away, with their whips aloft, and
driving their brothers to Lillias and Tipton Slasher
with as much energy as if they were racing for life
or a bride.   The office was, to *gather the Sparkham
and Pinford ponies*; and, heedless of the Exmoor
cavaliers, who dashed carelessly down something very
little short of a precipice, we accomplished a more
cautious, but successful descent in the neighbourhood of an iron mine, whose water-wheel was lazily
resting till the railway era sets in.   Once across the
brook, in which our cloak, which already weighed
some fourteen pounds, went in gallantly for
another, there were no obstacles on the Honeymead
and Warren farms.   The latter is said to have sheltered a banished lord, who beguiled his unwilling
martyrdom by breeding and eating rabbits.

Not a trace of his furry fancy crossed our path; and
in fact, throughout our entire stay, we saw neither red deer nor "heather poult."   A leash
of wild ducks certainly sailed far above us, into
the Buscombe mist; while three other flying black
specks were seen against the outline of the horizon, in
the shape of the two Wills and Bill.   In utter despair
at their not bringing up the Sparkham pony—
the Barnstaple pet of his heart— Will Court had gone
off, with an expressive grunt and a Chifney rush on
" my Polly," into space, across bogs and heather,

to do the deed, or die ; and we watched _{The Sparkham}
him as he made a series of masterly ^{Pony.}
casts on the Sparkham hill, with his two whips waiting handy to turn them to him. It seemed likely
to be a twenty-minutes' job, at least ; but as we
quietly rested in our saddle—on a knoll near the
rushy Pinford bottom, where Mr. Knight saw his
first fox found—(a small clump of rushes is often a
sure Exmoor draw), a trampling behind us told that
Will's grand *coup* was achieved. Up came the
Sparkham pony, as if he had dropped from the
clouds, with his crest erect and his mane flying, in
the van, and, drawing himself proudly into attitude
for a moment, snorted his defiance, and paced on to
his companions. The second prizeman, Cheriton,
was not far behind ; and the Pandarus pony
promptly ran alongside of him, as if to move for a
fresh trial on the points which so puzzled the bench
at Barnstaple.

The bones of a pony, which the foxes _{The Doons of}
and the ravens had pecked bare between ^{Badgery.}
them, lay bleaching across our path, as we turned
for the Lillias hill. Badgery had been our original
point ; and as the sun shone out for a brief quarter of
an hour, and just lit up the yellow surface of the
dying brackens, and tipped the grey boulders in their
rich green setting, we felt inclined to make a pil-
grimage to its forty fillies, its desolate huts, and the
spot where the late Lord Alford got into a bog, and
named a pet Pytchley horse in its honour. However, the thin indigo haze on the Culbourne hills
behind soon died away ; rain followed hard on the
train of the rainbow, which spanned the Doons' valley ; and Lillias was still unseen. A little chesnut
colt, " as thick as a bear," raised countless surmises
as to whether he was one of the race of " Heroes ;"
while Will and his men, with a most energetic
volunteer on a chesnut to aid them, routed up the

I

crafty white from his lair, and drove him past at a smart trot.

After this specimen of Will's "old sort," which has no particular style about him, and looks, as they all do, much larger on the heather than off it, we beguiled the road home by seeing the little twelve-hand Brother to Tipton Slasher crawl up a six-feet wall like a cat, after Bill Shapland, and trot away, seemingly "as fresh as a kitten," after his eight hours' enjoyment of something beyond a thirteen-stone hamper. The Hero was waiting at the door of Simon's Bath Lodge, to give its young heir his third taste of saddle-life, as we passed it; and, leaving that last note to memory, we shook up "The Comet" into a smart canter, and chased the groom and our carpet-bag, over hill and heather, to "the boat" at Lynemouth.

CHAPTER III.

TURF CRACKS.

"If our author had lived in the days of the Emperor who made his horse a consul, he would undoubtedly have been the first to propose a vote of confidence in the Government."

IT is to the rivalry of the county fami- County rivalry in lies in the three great Ridings of Arabs. Yorkshire, even in the days when they were up to their very cruppers in politics, that we may be said to owe the foundation of our finest English blood. The cockfighter, who lies full length on the floor to judge of his champions' action ; the naturalist who nearly hatched a fowl's egg in his arm-pit; the gardener "who sat up all night with a sick cactus," and the lunatic lady who, for six long years addressed the editor of a stern Radical newspaper weekly, as "My dearest Alphonzo," had not one whit more enthusiasm than these jealous vendees of Turks, Barbs, and Arabians. "To winde their horn, to carry their hawke fair," and to see Matchem Timms riding the pick of their stables for the Gold Cup over Hambleton or Rawcliffe Ings, made up no mean portion of their ancestral pride. Timms went to glory on his own hook with Bald Peg at Hambleton, but his finest victories were on the Earl of Carlisle's Buckhunter, by the Bald Galloway. Not the oldest man who used to totter to Castle Howard, year after year, in the beginning of the century, to see the annual Buck's Head run for by Levy Eckersley and other crack foot-racers of Yorkshire, could remember that renowned chesnut, whose half-sister Roxana was the first consort of the Godolphin Arabian. This foreign blood still flourished long after 1770, and even Eclipse's 25-guinea Epsom advertisement, and that of "Mask* sire of Eclipse—witness my hand, B. Smith," are almost overshadowed in the *Racing Calendar* by a cloud of Arabs. One of them won the Arabian Plate at Newmarket, and another had been presented by the Emperor of Morocco, " on a particular occasion to Thomas Adams, merchant of Rotherhithe, whose groom could be enquired for at the Europa Inn."

Indian blood sire contract. Such were the flea-bitten and "bloody-shouldered" treasures which the East sent us, and it was not until last year, in compliance with Lord Canning's request that the Indian Council would export some young blood sires between fifteen-two and three, instead of such half-bred, actionless coachers, that we began systematically to pay back our heavy horse debt to the East. Sir John Lawrence, Sir Erskine Perry, and Sir Frederick Currie, three of the most " stable minds" of the Indian Council, undertook, with Mr. Jex, V. S., of the First Life Guards, the preliminary inspection of the twenty-two which had been sifted by Mr. Phillips, during six months, from upwards of 200. On the day after the private inspection, in which two only were put back, the rest of the Council arrived at Willesden, headed by the President Sir Charles Wood, a right good man with the Badsworth, and as fond as every other tyke of the side of the horse ring. The Council did not attend in the capacity of a Court of Error, but they freely endorsed the choice which had been made.

Willesden Pad-docks. Willesden Paddocks are very beautifully adapted for such an inspection. The place is so daintily kept, and the green ivy-clustered boxes are so nicely interspersed among the

* Another reading of " Marske."

foliage and the paddocks, where a choice Southdown
or a Leicester disputes the supremacy of the herbage
with a blood mare, that on a sunny day it reminds
us of one of Madame Vestris's drop scenes. We
had no need to dwell on the memories of Harkaway, Charles XII., or Ratcatcher. Vandermulin
and Ellington were there in the flesh under the same
roof where Pyrrhus the First dwelt; and a little
farther on, the tortoise-shell cat, with the leather-
collar round her neck, was snoozing on the yellow
sheet, which covered the haunches of Voltigeur.

When his friend is in the rack, the Voltigeur and Sir
horse will lift his head affectionately, and Edwin Landseer.
she will crawl along his nose and neck to the
old spot; and Sir Edwin was so delighted with
the partnership, when Lord and Lady Zetland
introduced him, that it furnished an idea at once
for his canvas. The groom, however, put in a
special demurrer, and convinced him, by removing
the sheet and placing the cat on the bare back, that
she was far too particular to rest on that natural
couch, and that therefore painting her there was dead
against nature. Fifteen times did Voltigeur wend his
way to St. John's Wood, and his canvas *carte de
visite*, which is to adorn the great staircase at Aske,
represents him as large as life, with his head
down, whispering soft things to his furry friend.
Martha Lynn, along with Hersey and Birthday (dam
of Lupellus) had departed after their visit to Ellington, and therefore we had not the pleasure of com-
paring sire and dam together; but The Lion Ram-
pant, the whilom champion of the carriage world,
passed the door just as we emerged (pulling at
his new mahogany-coloured water-cart with a
vigour worthy of the days when the most
languid of the park strollers would run to the
rails to have a look at "Batthyany's turn out,")
and we got up a pleasant contrast between

the two browns, so pre-eminent in their peculiar spheres.

The Willesden staff. About five-and-twenty men are employed about the spot, under Mr. Charles Phillips, who acts as his cousin's secretary. Independently of Mr. Phillips's own mares and foals, the stalls and paddocks are seldom less than half-full. Sometimes a troop of blacks are there, waiting to be passed for the Life Guards. Then there are chargers, hunters, or brood mares, for the King of Italy, or some other of the European potentates, resting a space before they are shipped; and Asia also takes her turn, as the Egyptian cavalry contract brought up four hundred. Newmarket, too, claims its place in the arrangements, and we found some yearlings preparing for Mr. Saville's trainer, and about, we trust, to follow in the footsteps of Parmesan, who drew breath here. The little fellow excited Mr. Phillips's attention so much by his action in the paddock, that he pressed Mr. Saville to overlook his lack of size, and buy him for 60 guineas, and a contingency of half his first five races, which made 250 more.

The selected sires. Besides Voltigeur, there were eight-and-twenty sires in residence that day, and the great majority of the Indian ones were on ship parade. They had been duly physicked, and cooled down with bran-mashes, and now they stood side by side in blinkers, fastened with white pillar reins, in order to drill them for the long voyage. Seventeen of them "all in a row" in one stable, and champing at their bits, was a sight worth remembering; but alas! *Field Marshal The Duke of Duty*, a chesnut with a very beautiful forehand, by Pyrrhus the First, was sadly belying Mr. Hutchinson's nomenclature, and misconducting himself far worse than any of them. Young Pyrrhus and Apollo were also there, to keep up the Gully chesnut line; and the rare-jumper Eremite bore solitary witness for his Hermit. Touchstone had only one son Jasper amongst them; but in direct succession came Garibaldi and Volcano by Orlando, Heart's Delight by Pontifex, and the mouldy-looking Sermon by Surplice, the most beautiful of the lot and the most uncertain in his temper. Mr. Rarey had been with him; and his remembrance of the system was still so keen, that he would go down the moment his foot was taken up. Brown Holland, with his dark glossy coat, was quite The Dutchman's son, and there too was the sturdy little, white-maned Lord Nelson, who would puzzle all the physiologists to discover where his dashing mile talent could have come from, unless they knew of his Collingwood and Velocipede descent.

Bumble Bee was a good-looking relic of the glorious days of Curraghmore, and beside him stood Young St. Francis, with many traces of the old horse, who learnt the language of the bit from Sam Chifney's hand. Æthiopian was one dark-brown level, from his ears to his croup, as many of the Robert de Gorhams are wont to be. Near him was Ryedale, long, low, and untried, and dubious as to his paternity between Vatican and John O'Gaunt. The Alderman by Knight of Avenel was so neat, that Tom Dawson could hardly bear to let him go; and Professor Dick and Young Marcian (h.b.) were of the hunting field order; Belgium had furnished Namur by Corban, with only three summers on his head, and Ackworth, half-brother to Mincepie, and the best of the score, carried the fortunes of Simoom.

Four grooms, two of them appointed by the company (for Mr. Phillips's responsibility ceased the moment the horses were on ship board), and two of Mr. Green's men, went to attend on them during their voyage. The stalls were built in two lines between decks, with a gang-

On shipboard.

way separating them, to admit of exercise in fine weather, and were five feet wide, well-padded and laid down with mats. The allowance for the ninety-five days was 10lbs. of compressed hay, 8lbs. of oats, and 1½ bushels of bran for each horse per diem. Twelve loads of hay was the general supply, with 33 quarters of bran, and 60 quarters of oats, the latter pure Riga, and not Scotch "potato." The great London job-masters have long held by the Riga, and old Bob Newman used to say that his greys could face Barnet Hill, and go the eleven mile stage in ten minutes' less time, when they were not stuffed up with that "thick-skinned potato stuff." There was also a medicine chest, with a good stock of directions, and as the horses were not allowed to lie down, stays were provided, and adjusted so as to prevent the pressure, which slings too often produce on the intestines. They hang loosely when things are going right ; and in case of a horse losing his sea legs by a sudden heave, or becoming unduly weary, he learns to drop and lie upon them. The embarkation was managed nicely enough ; as they started from Willesden Paddocks soon after daylight, with their twenty aid-de-camps and a blacksmith. Their shoes were then taken off, and after a little remonstrance on the part of Sermon and Namur, they were all in position between decks by eight o'clock.

The President of the Council, the examiners, and others of the Board, looked in upon them once more, and in ninety days their leagues along the watery way were over, and the Pilgrim Fathers set foot on Eastern ground, without one death in the lot.*

* "In Bengal there are two Government stud establishments—one called "The North-west Stud," and the other "The Central Stud." The former consists of two depôts, viz., at Hauppu and Scharunpore, with a breeding district ; and the latter of four depôts, viz., Ghazeepoor, Bunar, Kurruntadhee, and Poosah, also with a breeding district. The North-west breeding district is conducted on what is called the Zemindaree system. The mares belong to the farmers, but

Young St. Francis, however, broke from his picket one night on the way to his station, and dashed out his brains against a wall.

The prejudice against Arabs was not lessened by the strange mixed lot which were brought home after the Crimean war. About that time, if you saw a crowd in the city, and a turban elevated above it, you might be sure that it was some unhappy native on an Arab, as damp as if it had been dragged through a river. Those who have passed their lives in India wonder why the Arab sires never will take in England; and others wonder, in reply, why the "nabobs" who come over do not give them the chance themselves, by buying a

Arabs in England.

before being covered they are duly registered, and the man is bound to bring the produce to the Deputy Superintendent when he goes on his yearly tour of inspection. If the foal is approved of, and the price agreed to, the foal is purchased, and goes into the Government depôt at once. If the foal is not approved of, it becomes the property of the farmer. Formerly, when entire horses were ridden in the ranks (what a mistake that was, by the way, and what thousands of pounds have been lost by it, through not being able to make use of mares!), colts only were purchased, fillies always belonging to the farmers; now, however, fillies are also purchased, if they appear likely to make troopers.

In the Central Stud the system is different altogether. There the mares belong to Government, and they are given out to the farmers at four years old, under the following conditions: The farmer signs a bond that he will keep the mare in good condition—that she shall want for nothing—that he will bring her and her foal for inspection, when called on, &c.; and he has also to give a security. When the mare comes in season she is covered by a Government stallion, the farmer merely paying a groom's fee of two rupees, equivalent to four shillings—as I dare say you know. Both in the North-west and Central Studs the mares are classed to the stallions thought most fitted for them, by the Deputy Superintendents in their yearly tours of inspection. In the Central Stud the mares are inspected in the districts once a month by the district officers, when their condition and everything connected with them is noted down in a book kept for the purpose. Three times in the year the Deputy Superintendent purchases the young stock that are over seven months old. The prices vary from £7 to £13, being never under the former or above the latter sum, and the following is the system:

It is considered that, as both the mare and stallion belong to Go-

few thorough-bred brood mares, and boldly leading the way. Precepts fall dead from the lips of men who have plenty of time and money, and yet dare not back their opinions by stud practice, or claim the 32lb. allowance in the Goodwood Cup, or the 28lbs. in the Royal Ascot Stand Plate.

Mr. Wilson and Omer Pacha. To judge from Mr. Wilson and his late fifteen-hand bay charge, Omer Pacha, at Althorpe, the habits of some of these Arabs are remarkable. This horse was ridden ninety miles in one day without drawing rein, by Omer Pacha's messenger, with the news of the Russian repulse, from Silistria to Varna; and although *he* was none the worse, the unhappy rider

---

vernment, and she was classed to that particular horse by a Government servant, if the farmer has invariably done justice to the mare and foal, it is not his fault if the latter prove worthless, and consequently it is a standing rule that if a man's mare and foal have always been mustered good, he gets the highest price—£13 for the latter, whatever it may be like. If, however, the farmer has at any time neglected the mare in any way, he at once forfeits this privilege. You may probably think these prices low; but when I tell you that if a man sells a foal for 130 rupees (£13), he can, without loss, keep the mare for three years, even if she does not have another foal—in other words, that £13 will keep the mare for four years—you will, I think, consider the remuneration sufficient. When these foals are purchased, the colts go to the Bunar and Kurruntadhee depôts, from whence they are at three years old transferred to Ghazeepoor, where they remain till they go into the service at four years old. The fillies all go to Poosah (there are generally upwards of 1,500 there), and remain there till they are four years old, when the best go into the districts as brood mares, the second-best go into the Light Cavalry regiments and batteries, and the others are sold in the Calcutta and other markets, where they realize fair prices. The stallions are stationed in the districts, and each has about thirty mares allotted to him. The situation of the stable of course depends on the number of mares in the vicinity. At some stands there are six stallions, at others only one.

Those horses that are now coming out will be kept in the depôts until they are in good condition, when they will be sent into the districts; but if, when the hot weather comes on, any of them show signs of feeling the heat, they will be at once brought to the depôt again. From the 15th June till the 15th October all covering is stopped, and the horses come into the depôt.—*Sporting Magazine.*

died. Mr. Wilson does not wonder at that, as he
believes that "nothing short of a cast-iron man
could sit on him for six hours." He certainly speaks
from a pretty vast experience, as he rode him out every
morning on his rounds. Their matutinal progress
was not unfrequently marked by a succession of pirou-
ettes. Owing to his peculiar military training, he
has acquired a habit of always keeping a leg in reserve. If he is cantering, it is with only three legs,
and he is trotting with the other; and then he will
suddenly reverse matters. Again, seized by a sudden fit of martial enthusiasm, he will gallop across
the paddock at thirty miles an hour, then stop dead,
and wheel round on one leg for a pivot. He was
given by Omer Pacha to Sir Richard Airey, and was
bought by the late Lord Spencer for 200 guineas,
quite weak and almost hairless from the effects of
the voyage. When his present Lordship gave up
his stud, he was given to his agent Mr. Beaseley,
who has since let him to Mr. Smith, to follow up
the Katerfelto cross at Exmoor.

Mr. Elliot, late of the Bombay Presi- Mr. Elliot on Arab
dency, in an article in the *India Sport-* champions.
ing Review (1852), gives it as his deliberate opinion,
that up to that point the silver grey Barefoot* was
of the purest Arabian blood he had met with.
To The Child of the Islands he assigns the palm of
racing superiority at 9st. 7lb. and under; and

* The following is the description given by Major Gwatkin of
Barefoot in 1828: Barefoot is of the Nedgdee caste, eight years old,
stands 14 hands 2 inches; is a silvery grey, with a dark skin; blood
head, full eye, large thropple, light neck; the shoulders are flat, with
the muscular lines very distinct; withers well raised; a good arm;
legs flat, and the sinews large and well detached from the bone;
pasterns of a moderate length. His back and loins are particularly
beautiful, and convey the idea of great strength. His quarters are
finely turned and very muscular. His temper is exceedingly good.
When led out to start, he appears to great advantage, full of fire, yet
very temperate; and when at work no horse could evince more vigour
and determined courage.

selects Elepoo, whose race with the Cape horse Sir
Benjamin, was described in these terms—which,
if they had been embodied in a telegram, would
have sorely puzzled Lord John and the Foreign
Office,—"*Asia gave Africa a stone and a beating,*" as the Champion of the Heavy Weights.
Taking, however, purity of breed and goodness combined, there has, perhaps, been nothing to beat
Barefoot, who was imported in 1820, and after running at Bombay, and Baroda, passed over into
the hands of Major Gwatkin, and distinguished himself at Meerut and Cawnpore. He was only fourteen hands two inches, and of the Nedgdee caste,
and his owner at one time intended to have sent
him to the stud in England, but Mr. Weatherby did
not think he would take, and dissuaded him
from it.*

Landing of Arabs   Bagdad is the great emporium at
at Bombay.   which the Arabs are collected for India,
and shipped thence to Bombay in droves of forty to
seventy, where the great dealers from Calcutta and
Madras await them. They begin to arrive about
October 1st, and never cease till the middle of March.
Formerly they used to come as threes and fours, but
of late years the system has been changed. The
buyers like them with more age on them, and they
require at least a year's seasoning before they can be
got into racing condition. From 6,000 to 9,000 are
landed at the Apollo pier annually, the majority of
them grey sires, which become quite white at eight.
The prices range generally from £45 to £60, but no
good charger for a 12st. man can be got under £100
to £150, while a racer will fetch his £150 to £250.
The landing is a very picturesque sight, as the
native dealers in long yellow robes and turbans
struggle with their charges on the landing boards,
and hand them over to little African boys, who flock

* Mr. Elliott ranks Ruby next to Barefoot.

down to the pier, and ride them to the different stables with nothing but a halter.

Many of them have never seen a carriage in their lives before, and there is not unfrequently some terrible devilry among them in consequence. They rush from one side of the street to another, till they are one mass of foam, and occasionally dash head-long through the Bazaar, and perhaps kill a child. The voyage varies from thirty to seventy days, and reduces some of them to mere grey ghosts. Very few mares come, and those are generally barren. Their food on board consists of barley and dates, and what with this, day after day, following on their bad pasture, they get sadly heated, and their legs fill. Barbadoes aloes, and a little soap and ginger, is prin-cipally given them on landing, and it not unfre-quently removes a plate of pebbles, which they have brought inside them, as a most appropriate memento from Stony Arabia. Their food is changed to gram, which is a species of pulse, and very much resembles dry peas. It is so apt to ferment in the stomach, that it is not possible to give them very much of it, and it is usually mixed with English oats, which are very much better than the oats of the country.

Madras used to be the Newmarket of India, and its success from 1826-38 may Racing in India. be fairly attributed to the energetic system of the late and "lanky Will Hall," who was then training for General Showers. Till 1838 no Arab had ever run two miles under 3 minutes 54 seconds; but at Madras in the January of 1838, it was first done in 3 minutes 51 seconds, with 7st. 12lb., by the bay four-year-old Samnite.* The courses are measured to a yard, about 12 inches from the inside, in order to make the time test as perfect as possible. Racing at Madras is in a great measure a dead letter now, and the Company have rather set their faces against

* It has been done three times since, in 3 min. 48 secs.

the sport everywhere, on account of the great amount of gambling which went on. Calcutta and Barrack-pore were the worst in this respect, and the system of lotteries (which is somewhat elaborate and rather different to ours), had grown to such a height, that at times a lac of rupees (£10,000) would be depending on the issue of one race. There are still 100 courses in India, the principal of which are Bombay, Poonah, Mysore, Baroda, Guzerat, Calcutta, and Cawnpore. General McDowell had seldom less than fifty Arabs in training; Colonel Macleane had also a large string, and the late Sir Walter Gilbert's was very renowned at Cawnpore. In Calcutta they begin to race at seven in the morning, but have to wait till nine, some times, on account of the fogs; while at Madras and Bombay they begin at three or four in the after-noon.

The "Bombay ducks" consider their racing season to extend through January, February, and part of March. Heats have been abolished; from four to six races are run off in an afternoon, and seldom more than eight or nine start in each. The Maiden Plate at Bombay, for horses imported the previous year, generally ensures a capital start, and as there are sometimes seventy subscribers, it has been known to reach £1,200. The course on which it is run is circular, about a mile and a-half round, and very flat and hard, as in portions of it there are not more than eight or nine inches of soil above the rock. Arabs and Mahrattas and Parsees all look after the racers in the stables, and lead them at exercise for about three-quarters of an hour before they gallop. The native jockeys (which have been of late years nearly superseded by English ones), are principally Mah-rattas, and ride to the course on their hacks in true English style; and as a general thing, they do not extend their circuits out of their own presi-dency.

Arabs are invariably quick beginners, Breeds and pecu-
as most horses with hocks well under liarities of Arabs.
them are, and it is generally a case of trying to cut
down each other from the very post. In point of
speed they are not remarkable; but their *forte* is to
keep up to the very "top of their foot" for two miles.
Their legs are very good naturally, and none the
worse for being calf-kneed; but the fetlocks often
become ossified with hard work on hard ground.
Some of them will run three seasons in this state,
and the excessive stiffness only seems to tell against
them, by their getting off from the post rather
slower. As hacks they are inferior, and often
stumble most dreadfully. One of their greatest
peculiarities is, that owing to their compact form,
their over-stepping sometimes goes to the extent of
fourteen inches, whereas the English horse seldom
does more than just clear his fore-foot print. The
Arab dealers lay great stress on this talent, as indi-
cative of the highest racing capacity. With respect
to carrying weight, the real test is whether the
shoulder is well laid, and the girth deep. Hog
hunting is quite in their way, and if their master is a
cool hand (which they very soon find out), they are
not long in learning how to turn with the boar, and
receive his charge with the most unflinching courage.
The most approved colours are bays and light greys,
and in the case of the latter, it is easy to tell from
an examination of the subtle red and black shades
under the skin, whether they will be silver grey or
flea-bitten; and the tendency to the latter coat de-
velopes itself very distinctly at four years old. If the
Arabs have a golden chesnut, they love the accom-
paniment of a blaze, and four white stockings.

The two principal tribes are the Aneza, in the
centre of Arabia, and the Nedgdee, so called after the
capital of Stony Arabia. Several of a distinct tribe
are bred at Bagdad; but although they are very

handsome and showy, they are hardly so pure in
blood, and seldom stay a distance so well. The
Aneza horses have very great endurance, and during
the last twenty years they have gradually got ahead
of the Nedgdee, which scarcely ever exceeds fourteen-
two, while the Aneza is seldom less than that, and
occasionally reaches fifteen. Both are fine in their
tempers, though, perhaps, the Nedgdee has the pull
in this respect. The Anezas are mostly bays and
chesnuts, whereas the most famous Nedgdee tribe of
Saglowdie is almost invariably grey. As regards the
heads of these desert rivals, that of the Aneza horse
is the least pure of the two, and there is, perhaps,
a cross of the Turcoman (native dealers say the
English) horse in it, which makes the head larger
and more Roman-nosed, though the eye is equally
good.

In this point, the Nedgdee is remarkably beautiful, and retains the small head, fine eye, neat
ears, and clean jowl of his patrician race; and as a
general rule, these two tribes are not crossed with
each other. One of the leading marks
of the pure Nedgdee, is the line at the
root of the ear, arising from the practice of sewing
the ears together when they are young. As this point
is always looked for by purchasers, the dealers take
care not to disappoint them, and a hot skewer makes
a very fair fac-simile of it. In the Aneza, a white
mark above the near hock, caused by the chain
attached to the fore-leg, which prevents them from
straying in the desert, has been almost made a *sine
quá non*, since Major Seaton first noticed it;
but the " Fort Adjutant's mark" gradually came
up in horses of apparently such coarse caste,
that forgery and friction had no doubt been at
work.

Tricks of native dealers.

Horizon, the first of the Eclipses,
came out in 1774, and Competitor,

The early English cracks.

the last of them, died towards the close of 1816.
Neither the late Mr. Kirby, nor any other of the
Turf patriarchs we have talked with, can remember
seeing the mighty chesnut, and we have therefore no
fresh traditions, wherewith to rush into that profitless
controversy, which rages at intervals over his
bones. Good old Sylvester Reed is also gone;
but many a little hint of his, on man and horse,
is scattered through these pages. Of Champion,
he was wont to say, that he showed remarkable
breeding, and had no coarseness about him, except
his lop-ears. Hambletonian although " more of a harness horse," was another of his boyish Hambletonian.
darlings. This horse was not thought
much of as a yearling, when he was in the paddocks at Shipton, with Beningbrough, and his mares
were his best runners. In his seventeen starts he
was never beaten but once, and then he jumped the
cords; but his sister Gipsy gained a most unhappy
notoriety, by throwing George Herring (who won
nineteen races in succession) three times at Hull,
in 1796, and killing him at last on the spot. She
was sold as a maiden to Russia, and there have
been no races at Hull since.

Mr. Reed's invariable story of Crowcatcher, whom
John Smith insisted on so naming, when John Smith at
he had seen him deftly behead a wool Streatlam.
stealer *in ipso facto*, led us insensibly on to the Streatlam stud. It is quite the oldest in the North, and
well has it held its ground. John Smith entered
the tenth Lord Strathmore's service in 1795, and
was with him till 1808. Before this, his lordship
had quite a small stud at Esher, near Kingston, and
Pipator, one of Lord Clermont's breeding, and
Queen Mab, the nursing mother of the stud, both
came from there. Queen Mab was by " I see Queen Mab
Eclipse, from a Tartar mare, and has been with
the youngest of the ten chesnuts, five you."

K

colts, and five fillies, with Jupiter and Mercury among them, which her dam threw to Eclipse in 1772-85. Some would have it that she was foaled when the Tartar mare was thirty-six; but Isaac Walker, after making himself, as in duty bound, a perfect Strype on the subject, cannot find that she was more than twenty-seven.

She was trained at Epsom and Newmarket, but, like one of Captain Meynell's (who had four years of it on the Warren Hill) she never started. Lord Strathmore gave £296 for her, and she was sent, in 1795, to Tattersall's; but as 180 gs. was the highest offer, she did not change hands, and commenced a three hundred mile walk, to Gibside. As regards her looks, Isaac has all the facts and figures of the thing, down to " white nearly up to hock on near hind leg, and a few white hairs close to hoof on near forefoot, &c. ;" but it is enough for us to know that she was a thick and lengthy fourteen-three chesnut, with white mane and tail, and wide drooping ears. Her Remembrancer by Pipator won the St. Leger in Ben Smith's hands, and Cassio by Sir Peter, who was born when she was a desperate sufferer from a gathered udder, ran second to Fyldener, and performed most brilliantly the following year. It was, however, through Remembrance by Sir Solomon, and Oblivion by Jerry, that her blood descends in female tail to Forget-me-Not, the dam of Daniel O'Rourke.

The three other " blue ribbons" of Streatlam, only inherit a strong collateral dash of her blood through her dark chesnut nephew Hermes by Mercury, from a Woodpecker dam. He went blind from inflammation, at Winchester races, and Lord Strathmore rode him hack, and drove him in his curricle. John Smith was wont to say, that he never rode a faster trotter, and bade the farmers be of good courage, and not

The Queen Mab family at Streatlam.

mind a fifteen-shilling fee. Hermes died at Gibside in 1814, but not before he had united the Eclipse and Highflyer strains in his Gibside Fairy, from Vicissitude by Pipator. From the cross of this bloody-looking brown and Whisker, came Emma, the dam of Mundig, Cotherstone, and the grandam of West Australian, and as Isaac triumphantly observes, *"there we have it."* Vicissitude was foaled at the paddocks, and was forfeited with her dam to his Lordship, because her owner left her till the expenses of the keep were far beyond her seeming value. She was the granddaughter of Pyrrha, the produce of those two Northumberland flyers of Mr. Fenwick's, of whom a highly equitable poet observes, in allusion to there not being the weight of a stable-key between them :

> " Matchem he was the best of all
> But Duchess the flower of Bywell Hall."

In 1808, John Smith went to the Marquis of Queensberry, as stud-groom, *Streatlam trainers.* in Scotland, and from thence with his lordship's horses to Middleham. Dunn succeeded him as trainer at Streatlam, and then Charles Marson, who trained for his lordship till he died, and afterwards entered the Marquis of Exeter's service, taking with him a 2,000-guinea colt, by Ardrossan from Vicissitude. After him there was no more training at Streatlam, and a riband of rather greener turf in the park still faintly marks the course, over which he worked the Remembrancer stock, with Lord Foley and Sir John Shelley to look on during the grouse season.

Independent of all this Turf heraldry, *Isaac Walker at home.* the spot is as beautiful a one as you may find in the county of Durham. A large herd of Argyles formed a red, black, and cream array, as they gathered beef in the park, where the Pipators and Remembrancers got rid of it.   A herd of fallow deer, which had months before

> Hung their old heads on the pale,

were sauntering past the boxes of the fated Night-watch and the bay filly Culotte de Peau, a name just fresh from Paris, and over the meaning and pronunciation of which we found Isaac fiercely struggling for the mastery, in the recesses of his saddle-room. Among the inner and outer treasures of that cupboard are Obadiah the Quaker musing on the future ; and the Doncaster return sheet of The West's year in full. There, too, are the gilt plates of that hero, while one of a larger size represents Mundig. Isaac himself went as a stripling to Mr. George Lane Fox's, of Bramham, and first visited Newmarket, in charge of Macduff, when he beat the Duke of York's Moses, the Derby winner of '22. After a few years there with Bloss, he joined Perren, of Settrington, and putting into Hambleton, in stress of weather, with Euphrosyne, Macduff, New Baith, and Sir Tatton's Negotiator, he first saw his future ally John Scott. It was a rare harbour of refuge for Yorkshire trainers in hard weather ; and there, too, among others, came Dicky Shepherd, with Muta and Manuella, and Bobby Pettit, with Sir R. K. Dick's Ajax and Euphrates.

After this little interlude, near " the white mare of Whissencliffe," Isaac lived three years as padgroom

Isaac's interviews with Will Goodall. to Mr. Bowes, at Cambridge ; and when that gentleman sat for South Durham, in the first Reform Parliament, he still held his post. He met Will Goodall, who was there on duty for Mr. Drake, and " on the other side of the question," night after night, under the St. Stephen's horse shed ; and when their minds, like the Laird of Cockpen's, were not " ta'en up wi' affairs of the State," during a great division night, they exchanged many a reflection on horse and hound.

Isaac's father gave up his place soon after; but he lived to see his son hold it in his room for exactly a third of a century.

The earliest stud recollection of the latter was seeing his father help to drag out Hermes from his box, to be buried under the hawthorn, close by the precipice of the Lune bank, to the side of which he had galloped even in his blind days, and stopped short like a *manége* horse. A few nettles close by bloom over Pipator and Queen Mab; and the paddocks in which their progeny roamed, still flourish, guarded by those thick holly hedges which the stable lads planted, and John Smith watered with such care. The stones for their high walls came from the old buildings, and Frank never failed to tell Isaac that he knew he " shut up his yearlings for another twelve months, if they were not big enough, and only brought them up honest if they were." The West's paddock is generally reserved for the crack of the year, but Welcome and Ratomski were its doubtful denizens of 'Sixty.

Among the mares, which were a little further on, The Flapper looked like a lengthy, lame poster, and Mowerina, an own sister to Cother-stone, with her chubby-headed old Orange Girl at her side, was quite light enough below the knee. Still there can be no doubt, if you look at her, whence The West catches his beau-tiful head and shoulders, and Isaac observes to us as he tenderly passes his hand under her jowl, that " she has no chance of roaring when the machi-nery is so clean." The year that she went to Bay Middleton she was his only thoroughbred mare, and she lost her colt foal, owing to the man in charge turning idle and riding her for fifteen or sixteen miles. Forget-me-Not was there, with the first and last foal by The West they ever had at these paddocks; and when Isaac is called on for the other curiosities of his Streatlam experience; he will tell you that Balderdale and Lunedale have been the only roarers on the place, that in Cotherstone's year all seven mares produced colts, that he never had twins except the brothers to Klarikoff, and that Gibside Fairy carried Emma for a twelvemonth and a day.

The Yorkshire Greys. Phenomenon had the honour of making roaring as fashionable in the North, as the stock of Cervantes made two-year-old-running. Delpini filled it with rather leggy greys, most of which could go four miles. He was the sire of Mr. Garforth's Vesta, who, with her dam, Faith, and her half-sister Marcia, formed the most beautiful trio of greys that ever adorned a stud, Mr. Pierse's not excepted. There were three Delpini greys amongst the eight St. Leger starters in Beningbrough's year; and his grey Symmetry soon afterwards proved his claim to be the sweetest-looking colt that ever won that race. Delpini himself was very closely allied to the Arab in his look, light-bodied, and with a prominent eye and head, which told of desert descent; and even when he was wasted almost to a skeleton, he miraculously retained his beauty. During his last three years, he never shed his coat, and became like the woolly child of caravan lore. The fact was so well known in Yorkshire, that when an old gentleman with very long white hair sat on the Grand Jury for the first time at York, and went up to the foreman to pay his footings, there was heard this pretty audible aside from one of them, "Here comes the Delpini *colt*."

Turf doings at Sledmere. Golumpus was the first sire Sir Tatton ever used, when he began to keep a few mares at Westow, and Sledmere, by Delpini from a Gabriel mare, who went to Sir Bellingham Graham for 800 gs., was the first good sale he made. Half of this horse belonged to Sir Mark, who had four or five brood mares at Sledmere, in 1804, and among them the sisters Miss Teazle Hornpipe and Miss Hornpipe Teazle, by Sir Peter from a Trumpator mare. Both of them were sent to Sancho, and they returned in foal with Prime Minister and President. The former beat Tramp, after a most desperate finish in the Four-year-old Subscription at York, and the latter was a little brown horse, which passed into Sir Tatton's hands, and was given by him to an earth-stopper. To the donor he proved rich treasure-trove, as he soon ranked next to Screveton in the North Riding's eyes, and nearly all the young things were fathered on the pair. The Sledmere horses were then trained at Marramat, by George Searle, and while Mr. Bethell, of Rise (who was confederate with Mr. Pratt) confined his racing nomenclature to Green-gage and other fruits, Sir Mark bethought himself of the Knights-of-the-Round-Table, and went in for Sir Sacripant, Sir Bertram, Sir Marinel, and the like.

Sam Chifney, who had attracted his notice at York, was engaged as jockey at £100 a-year, but his dawdling ways were against him, and he was spoken of, in the Sledmere stable, as "the long, thin, lazy lad." As he lived at Newmarket, a hack had to be sent over frequently by appointment to meet the coach at Malton, and as often as not, it returned without him. When Woldsman was to be tried for his Shuttlecock match, over Knavesmire, Sam kept Sir Mark and his brother waiting three or four hours, and then arrived a stone over weight, from a venison feast.

After his discharge on the trial morning, Garbutt, who was, like Snarry, a lad with Searle, rode occasionally for the stable; but Jackson got the best

mounts, and never showed finer horsemanship
than when he met Petronius with Theresa, at
York.

Sir Mark gave 500 guineas for Camil-
Camillus & Stumps lus by Hambletonian from Faith, and
kept him for eight or nine seasons, till he died. He
was barely fifteen-one, and full of Arab quality, and
his portrait, with the old coachman at his head,
forms one of the *Penates* at Sledmere. One of
his fillies was the dam of Negotiator by Prime
Minister, a strong, useful horse, but rather a rambling goer, and sold to Lord Kennedy for 700 gs.,
at three. Stumps by Whalebone was the first sire
Sir Tatton ever bought, and he combined his
favourite fifteen-two standard, with rather light
bone, and an aptitude for heats, in which he had
beaten Goshawk. He had Delpini's style of head,
and it was from his light fore-legs, and his stumped-
up way of going on them, that he acquired his
name.

Two hundred guineas was his Doncaster price, and
he was finally given away after five seasons to a
Death of Stumps. tenant in Holderness. His end was a
sad one, as he broke away from his
leader, who was in his cups, and caught a fatal inflammation from wandering up and down a field in
a rainy night, with his sheets dragging at his
heels.

But Snarry in his snow-white jacket
An afternoon with Sir Tat- must step forward now, ashen plant in
ton & Snarry. hand, like the Chorus in the play, and
tell his experience of Sledmere past and present.
The inspiriting presence of Dick Stockdale, more
deep than ever in the Maroon faith since he became
his own, was not wanting that day. Both openly
and by implication he set forth his praises. We heard
of high stepping bays by him, which had worked
their way into the Royal Mews, and again that

A QUIET DAY AT SLEDMERE, 1863.

(FROM A PHOTOGRAPH, THE SOLE PROPERTY OF THE AUTHOR, TAKEN BY S. HOGGARD, AND REGISTERED ACCORDING TO THE ACT.)

mysterious story of a presumptuous rival, who only
lived to break two men, and well nigh caused another
to hang himself. And so, passing for the present,
over Daniel the delight of Snarry's
heart, Colsterdale with whom he has
never held more than an armed truce, and
Fandango towards whom he has always
preserved a highly dignified neutrality, we commenced our journey with The Dialls field. It was
high-tide with The Lawyer that summer and
Snarry's *Manchester Examiner* was perpetually
bringing good tidings. As luck would have it, his
dam stood foremost among the eleven mares; and
our interpreter spake on this wise,

*Diplomatic rela-
tion of Snarry
and the Sled-
mere sires.*

The Diall's field.

"That's Lawyer's dam; she's by
Hampton, dam by Cervantes, great grandam by
Smasher. Lawyer 'd have been a lost horse if he'd
not been sold at York; he's just got hold of four
Queen's Plates in four days. They rode her at
Birdsall when the hounds went there, hunter and
hack occasionally. That's a half-brother to him by
Caster, that chesnut Sir Tatton's on now; Mr.
Sykes has another of them in London. The old
brown horse, he was shot last week, not very safe at
last, he'd carried Sir Tatton sixteen years. I thought
I was right on that point, however; I don't think
he ever had a name. Hampton?—yes, we must go
back a bit; he'd be by Sultan out of Sister to
Moses; we had him first in '38; his mares are going
off now; Lord Westminster had him; gave 600 gs.
for him at the Hampton sale; he was a chesnut;
he got us short-legged, strong chesnut mares; Sir
Tatton gave three hundred for him; he was a slow
beast, did us a deal of good for all that. Cervantes!
you want to know about him? he was a compact-
looking horse; not so very big; they were pretty
fair stayers. That's a Fernhill mare, we had him a
season. That's sister to Odd Trick by Sleight, she's

got the best foal here, *that's by Daniel.* That's
Thornhill's dam; hers'll be by Colsterdale; like
him too; second best foal, but a long way behind.
We've thirty or forty Colsterdales. That's Greyling's dam there, and sister to Jack Frost, both by
Sleight. They've each got one, so has the Jereed
mare. That's a Knight of the Whistle; she's one
of the best bred ones in England, I'll be bound for
it; her foal's by Daniel, and a very good one it is.
We had a good way on to a hundred foals, five
double ones, seven or eight mares slipped, and some
not put to. That mare's by Hampton, dam by
Young Phantom out of sister to Barefoot, she's the
prettiest mare we have.

Swale's Wold. "This is Swale's Wold, that will be an
ash belt, oaks don't manage much of a
tap-root in these parts. We've four Fernhill mares
here; that's one of them, the chesnut; let me see,
she's by Pyrrhus from Odd Trick's dam; a Daniel
foal too, such a thick one. Pyrrhus was only here
one season, and left us large chesnut mares. That's
a Burgundy: we'll not say much about her looks,
rare bred 'un for all that, out of a Muley Moloch
mare, the foal's a Colsterdale; got his hind-legs to
a shaving. Do you mean that white-faced one
on the heap? Algebra, best of Mathematician's
get. Poor Mr. Drinkald, he *would* send him; she's
got a chesnut filly by Daniel, bloody-looking—the
white-faced one, I mean. They're ten foals here, all
of them fillies. That's a Caster mare, Colsterdale
again, and very like him. We had Caster seven or
eight seasons, I think you'd put thirty to him one
season, Sir Tatton; aye! it would be fully that; he
was a thick, short horse, got us little stumpy mares,
we've very few of them. That mare's off sister to
Spotted Boy's dam;— * * * Yes, it's a good
cow, I question whether we've a better about the
place.

" They call this The Cottage Pasture. The Cottage Pasture. There are the mares among those white thorns in the slack : sister to Sauter le Coup, she's a beautiful mare by Sleight of Hand out of Black Tommy's dam; we bred him, he was second for the Derby. That Orlando-looking colt's out of her own sister, and her first foal; you needn't ask it's if a Daniel, when we see the legs and limbs. Yon brown mare, she's by Sleight out of Darling; a grand mare; we've best mares of any body's, I don't care where they are, we can challenge any stud in England with our Sleight of Hand mares; bring what they like, we'll meet them. That's a Stumps mare, as like the family as aught we have; he had sweet legs and hind-quarters, his fore ones wern't much to crack of; she's got a grey, short-looking Daniel; it may make something yet; from grey mares Daniel gets as many grey as anything; we've put her to Fandango,—he's rather starved Daniel; that Stumps mare Wicket we had, she scratched her hip with a nail in the railway-box, and died of lock-jaw. This will be as good as ever she was. That's a Pyrrhus mare, dam by Sleight of Hand, she's sister to Baronet. Colsterdale, he got them half chesnuts the first go off; after that more bay ones.

" We're coming into Cherry Wood Cherry Wood End. End; there are five mares, all of them with fillies; three whites among them. That's Panmure's dam by Stumps; we had Stumps six or seven years; he'd be fifteen-two, Sir Tatton, and not very good measure either ; we've a granddaughter of Wicket, she's had nothing that's come to hand yet; Monge's dam by Bay Middleton, she's another of the whites; and that mare by Sleight of Hand dam by Cervantes, grandam by Young Phantom, we call her blue grey. That great, stout-bodied mare, she's sister to Grey Tommy by Sleight of Hand; Mr. Drinkald bought five or six that turn. The brown

mare next her (the Colsterdale's a twin), she's by
Sleight of Hand, dam by Comus, grandam by Golumpus. We've most stout mares by Sleight, he got
us nice bays and browns; St. Giles is from them.
Sleight of Hand, he was as narrow as a rail across
the hips; he hit with the Hamptons, they're low
and wide, with wonderful fore-legs, and the Comus
mares. Mr. Scott said he was good, but a bit delicate—bloody head and neck. Sir Tatton and Mr.
Osborne were a long time over the bargain, it went
on nearly all the Doncaster week—325 guineas at
last; he was a cheap horse to us. We had two
Comus mares last year, one's put down and one's
dead; he got foals, did the old horse when he was
twenty-eight; he got us chesnuts with white legs;
he had no white himself; Sir Tatton hired him for
six seasons. Grey Momus, he was the pick of the
basket, he was from a Cervantes mare. Many
Comus mares are grey, they get it from Camillus,—
he got them grey; Cervantes's and Young Phantom's, they come bays. Young Phantom never got
us a chesnut; he was half Bill Scott's; lame at three
years old, though; he got his foot into a rabbit
hole; Comus never had a spavinned one, and only
one ring-bone that I know of.

The Craggs Flat. "You'll know Craggs Flat again, we
put the cracks here; all colts looking
like yearlings, and all chesnuts but one; five Colsterdales and two Daniels. They're very forward
pastures; there are two black lambs to make stockings of. That chesnut mare's by Sleight out of
sister to Hamptonia; she only lived to have a colt
and a filly; that's the filly. The pretty dark chesnut
by itself, that's Thornhill's dam; that's the first
Colsterdale foal we had; there's Naughty Boy's dam
close by her; that's a rare thick chesnut Colsterdale
she's got with her, it's a horse now; Amati's
dam never made a mistake; Mr. Cookson came

here and found the name on a fiddle, that's why
we called him that. We must get it correct
anyhow; only four of them have ever had a bridle
on. Gorse Hill, Amati, Elcho, Bogle Hill—
Marquis of Bowmont they called him when he
won—all winners; bred nothing but what's won,—
what's been tried however. The chesnut's by
Sleight of Hand out of Darling; she has a chesnut; to'ther's a bay Colsterdale foal, and like him
too; that Darling blood's as good as anything
we have. Little Hampton was from the old mare.
That's a Pyrrhus mare, none of them's run but
Bayonet; I doubt he's not so good as he ought to
be; they keep matching of him; I don't know what
they're doing with him; they don't measure him
well, I think. Yes! he gave 22lbs., Sir Tatton.

"There are lots of mushrooms in this
Castle field; we get the best view of ^{The Castle Field.}
Sledmere from it; that's Marramat among the firs
and ashes over there. Sir Christopher planted the
woods; there's a good gallop two miles round among
those woods at Marramat; Sam Chifney's ridden in
it many a time. George Serle had the farm, and
trained Sir Mark's horses; I was there as a lad,
fifty years ago; aye! it will be fully that; then Sir
Mark's horses went to Joe Ackroyd's, where Mr.
Scott lives now; then on to Perren's at Settrington.
Tibthorpe Wold Farm lies over there; a good bit of
Boddle was a rabbit warren; those red roofs there,
that's it; then we get round—Marramat—Mow-
thorpe—Kirby and the rest of them. The separate
trees look like a wood. We're forgetting these
mares; there are five Sleights amongst them; have
you got that one down? I suppose you'll be bringing out something in the *Silk and Scarlet* style; one
of them's by Sleight out of Wicket, white mare you
were talking of; next her, let me see, she'll be by
Sleight of Hand, dam by Stumps, grandam by Oiseau.

The white-legged bay walking off ; that's Wynnstay's
dam, with a foal just the make of Colsterdale. Mr.
Sykes rode the little chesnut mare with the harriers; that's her Daniel foal, that thick 'un. Daniel's
fillies have a deal more grey at the root of their
tails than the colts; there are a deal of grey hairs
from Daniel; that's the Irishman; the tails always
witness of Daniel,—they used to be called the Matchem arms.   That big foal in the middle, he's brother to—Highflyer, and not fly so very fast either.
We only once brought up twins, they were a couple
of Riflemen.

The King's Field.
"There are only two Pyrrhuses in this
King's Field, and a sister to Wollaton;
the skewballed one's out of sister to Baronet; I
didn't know what was coming; so Sir Tatton says;
Well! there was a great white patch on the side,—
as like a calf as aught.   That other Pyrrhus, Sir
Tatton thinks her about his best.   Now, there is a
good halter full, Mr. Stockdale ! We had seven or
eight Pyrrhuses, Sir Tatton's never sold but two,
and those to the King of Italy; Mr. Phillips
came, and Count Cigar or Cigala, I think they call
him—well, it's some name like that.

Across the road
and into the
Park.
"We must cross the Driffield Road,
and through the wood ; that will bring
us into the Park.   This reservoir it's
about thirty yards across. We've only fifty-five
mares here. How many have we got? I never counted
them,—better than a hundred; Sir Tatton gave the
word, and we left off early in May; several good
mares have never been touched with nothing, four,
five, six, not one in this Park too young; we've that
Lanercost mare, dam of Monsieur Dobler, she's all
we've got or ever had of that sort.   That's by Caster,
she goes into a Muscat Arab, bought at Hampton
Court.   The great grandam of that mare, it's supposed to be by Grey Orvile from a pony that was

at Waterloo, Sir Tatton will tell you all about it;
Grey Orvile, he'd got a skip with a coach-horse
some way. There are nineteen on the other side of
Marramat; we've seen about fifty. There are eight we
haven't seen, other side of Colly Wood. There's one
Womersley here, sister to Gaspard, neither covered
or nothing else; most of them are Daniels, when
we get at them below. That's a Russian; this is
an Andover out of a Caster mare; it's a bit damaged
in the eye; the other's a Cossack out of sister to
Grey Tommy; three white legs, she's sister to
Baronet; there's sister to Juggler; that's a Young
Barefoot. This is either a Colonel mare or a Langar
dam; they're four-year-olds, I must look at my
book: *Woo! my lass! No.* 57, *what marks?* " *A*
star, a spot on the nose, far hind-leg white nearly up
to hock;" that will be Colonel. We've seven or
eight Andovers, they suit Daniel's, they're on a
longer leg.

"I don't see any Recovery mares; Sir Tatton sent
six to him: King of Hearts's dam is from one. We
had Sir Joseph here; he looked the yearlings over,
and King of Hearts was the only one he had out
the second time. He didn't buy him for all that; and
he just beat his Duke Rollo. It would be at Northampton, Sir Tatton. That's a Defence mare: we've
only one Andover and Pyrrhus; they both go back
to Lord Fitzwilliam's Amadis blood, Mr. Kirby
hired him; he came once a week to the kennels at
Eddlethorpe; he got the best hunters Lord Fitzwilliam ever had. He was got by Quicksilver, the
same horse as Cervantes. There's Gaspard's dam,
and the chesnut, she's by Sleight of Hand out
of Ragged Petticoat by Comus. That brown's
been ridden in the harrier stables a bit of one
season.

That black 'un's a Fernhill; I don't fancy the sort
much,—game horse too for all that. Most of them

down here are Daniels; that want's to be out of
sight, Poverty's been there since it came from Heslington Wold.   That Andover out of Caster mare
want's to be shown; she thinks herself better than
common. *Don't be so proud, Miss!* That Daniel's
out of a Lanercost mare; she's very like him. That
one never had a tail to speak of, and never will have.
That's by Fugleman; next her's an Andover, let
me see my book, a twin; yes! she will be, Sir Tatton, out of sister to Billy go Rarely.   That was one
of Lord Waterford's names; he put him in his drag,
and drove Mr. Legard down to Epsom first time he'd
been in harness.   That mare's the best of Daniel's;
the thin end of them we picked out to go to York,
the thick's not covered yet.

A little arithmetic. "We're through them at last; they're
middle-sized these Daniel mares; they're
not big, still they're wide mares.   How many have
we?   I don't know rightly, Sir Tatton; there are
twenty-five two-year-olds at the kennels; eleven
threes we picked out to keep, they're at Heslington
Carr; eleven three-year-old colts down in Holderness on the Marshes; the fours and fives are about
home : I can't just tell about the yearling
fillies; I've not cast them up lately; there'll be
thirty-two or thirty-three of one kind or another,
fifteen on farmers' seeds, eighteen left at home; I
don't know without looking at my book where they
are.   This is the tally-board, I've just done chalking
up all the filly foals with their marks.   I'll copy
them out some evening into the book; there we fix
them; there'll be twenty-five this year, one of them's
dead.   We'll begin swinging them at the stack, when
we've done with York, to teach them to lead; we do
two or three stack-fulls a day, eight a-piece about
two hours at a time, that's quite long enough.   We've
been a good deal bothered with these worms—they're
five or six inches long—but I think we've matched

'em; we give them a gill of cold drawn linseed oil, and an ounce of spirits of turpentine; it brings them away in scuttles full; they've forks at both ends, and they fairly eat through the bowels.

"Sir Tatton's had these laurels by the road-side cut down lately. Daniel gets *The sire paddocks.* plenty of swing here; he goes once round the paddock, whoever's here; now he does that nicely; Sir Tatton still says, I hang to him a bit; look at those legs moving, just like a fiddle for all the world; Derby course, indeed! he could have run to Derby that day, if Frank had asked him. He mastered them a bit latterly at Mr. Scott's; aye! it's a good colour; dark chesnut's as pretty as aught when it's blooming. Now, you Colsterdale men! he's up in that corner among the peacocks; he's as proud as any of them in his way; he needn't be; it's a very silky skin, but he's no credit to himself, he tears at himself; his thighs are straight enough, they'll just suit the Daniel crook; Sir Tatton looked at Loup-garou, and five or six more before he bought him. Take care of him; keep a look out or he'll begin his dot-and-go-one, and wheedle up to you. He's all wire; he was a great jumper with hounds in his pauper days, so they tell me; well, he's had a rare chance now. *Be off with you! None of your tricks!* We'll shut him up with his gay company. That will be the bell, Sir Tatton."

From Sledmere to Ashton Hall is a *Old times at Ashton Hall.* long leap, but we must make it for chronology's sake. It lies about three miles from Lancaster, and in the Duke of Hamilton's zenith, no paddocks were a surer find for a St. Leger winner. They are like a fortified town with walls seven feet high, which, with a belt of planting, form a good bulwark against the breezes of the Irish Ocean. Underley was twenty-five miles away, and Muley had not then made for it a name. The

L

Duke was very often at the Hall, and he had a jovial custom that the sailors, when they came in from abroad, and passed on their route from Glaston Dock to Lancaster, should make it their half-way house, and pledge Old England in a horn of ale. The Duke's and their Polls' healths were not forgotten, and if his Grace was about, they would huzza, till for peace and quietness he was compelled to show himself and bow. His own dress was quite of the good old fashion, and he was not above grey breeches and drab gaiters, with a double-breaster of blue and yellow stripes, and a large drab coat.

His horses were his great delight at home, but he cared very little for seeing them run, and had the results across the hills by express. When "The best of all good company." he did get as far as York, he stayed with Archbishop Harcourt at Bishopthorpe, and they would watch the running together from a stile It was said that they gradually shifted their ground nearly half-a-mile in six or seven years, and finally finished opposite the Gravel Road. Eyes as keen had been content to look on at the running from Middlethorpe Corner, and it was there that Mr. Bethell's Ruler broke his fetlock-joint in '82, and the three young Sykes's, then boys with a tutor at Bishopthorpe, were the first to get up to him.

Lancashire turf rivals. The era of 1808-10 was a merry one at Ashton Hall. The York Herald was *The Life* of that day, and "Nap's" battles were keenly looked for and talked over by the lads, amid the intervals of cricket, nine pins, and nurr and spell. Of all such games, his Grace was a great patron, and he engaged Mendoza, whose "limbs like an ox" were the astonishment of that little community, to come down and instruct his sons. Theakstone trained for him, and Charles Marson, who looked after Petronius and Ashton in turn, rode his light weights. There had been some little dispute between his Grace and Lord Strathmore, as to which should have the black jacket, which, by the bye, had no gold braid till Mr. Bowes came of age. The former gave way, and adopted a blue belt, and went to Lancaster to see Marson winning the first race in it on Ploughboy, and getting carried shoulder high into the stand. Preston was then quite the county race course, and His Grace made it a point of honour to go there, and pit his steeds specially against Lord Derby, Sir Thomas Stanley, and Mr. Clifton.

Sir Peter had long been the Touch- St. Leger sons of stone of Knowsley and Mr. Clifton Sir Peter. owned the first St. Leger winner Fyldener, and the Duke of Hamilton the last in that extraordinary triple succession of luck (1806-8), which has never before or since fallen to the lot of one sire. Petronius went to 100 to 3 at starting, as a report got wind that he had flung his lad behind the Rockingham, and lunched up to his knees in clover. Ashton was tried to be as good as him at 7lbs. that autumn, and hence the stable considered that they had four horses good enough to win the St. Leger, and pretty well proved it by running first and second. Ashton was quite a hunter-looking horse, with very hairy legs, which "took a life-time to dry," and none of the elegance of his reputed sire Walnut. The latter never ran, as he broke his shoulder, which united with a curious knot at the point, and brought about a complete wasting of the fore-leg and foot.

Sultan's head, Memnon's Doncaster The Waxy blood. coat, Oiseau's ability to "give his year away and win the St. Leger," and Whisker's quarters seem still to haunt the old school of sportsmen The Duke of Grafton was won't to say, "Let us find the horse, and then we'll talk about the jockey," and Penelope and Waxy furnished him with a worthy pair in Whisker and Whalebone. Short legs, high-bred nostrils, and very prominent eyes were the principal trade marks of the Waxy stock, and the mottled brown Whalebone was the smallest amongst them.

The standard could never make him more than fifteen and half an inch, and as he did not seem likely to become fashionable, he was sold at seven Whalebone at for 510 guineas. His old Petworth Petworth. groom Dayman enthusiastically says of him, "He was the lowest, and longest, and most double-jointed horse, with the best legs—eight and half below the knee—and worst feet I ever saw in my life." The latter were contracted and high on the heel, and became so Chinese boot-like and full of fever at last that he never moved out of his box.

The Earl of Egremont tried to train him after he bought him with Octavius at Mr. Ladbroke's sale, but he never ran, and his principal occupation in training was to rear and knock his hoofs together like a pair of castanettes, a freak which once cost him three tumbles in a day. His hunters were good and mostly bays and browns, and Myrrha and Sir Hercules were the last of his racing line. He was ten years at Petworth, but he did not seem to have created much private veneration. No enthusiasts helped to rob him of his tail, and the kennel copper and the knacker claimed every hair.

The Petworth Octavius had quite his share of the stud. mares, of which his Lordship had at least thirty at Upwaltham, and his son Little John from Greyskin got several hunters, which were often sluggish, and went blind. Among the thirty, only a tithe of which in one very slippery spring produced foals, were Wasp the dam of Chateau Margaux; and the Canopus mare, which twice over hit to Whalebone, with that natty little pair of Derby winners, Lapdog and Spaniel.. Wanderer by Gohanna was another great Petworth character, and grandsire on the dam's side to Sir Hercules. He was quite a slug when he was put in training, but all alive after his sweats, and so restless as a sire that he would fight a stick, or toss a stone or straws, about all day, and vary matters by kicking all night.

Blacklock's dam, the chesnut Rosalind by Coriander, was originally one of *Blacklock's youth.* the Wiganthorpe stud in Atalanta and Faith's day. Mr. Garforth also bred his sire Whitelock "a naggish horse with a big, coarse head and plumb fore-legs." He became the property of Sir Mark Sykes, who named him from the lock in his tail, and sold him to Mr. Sylvester Reed for three hundred. Mr. Reed had the offer of Blacklock as a foal for fifty, but he neither liked his fore-legs nor the remembrance of his dam, when he saw her crawling past his window to Mr. Moss's, through the streets of York, after she had been purchased for £3. Aristotle's fore-legs were not more "plumb" than Blacklock's, and hence Tom Dawson begged Mr. Meiklam, who was very loath to risk it, not to part with him as a yearling. Blacklock's most desperate *Racing finish of* race was four miles over York with Ma- *Blacklock.* gistrate, whom he barely defeated by a head. The severity of it finished them both; Magistrate never ran again, and after his defeat the next day by St. Helena, who had been pulled up in the first race, a mile from home, Blacklock was saddled no more.

He used to lead the unhappy Duchess such dances that Tom Peirse exclaimed in his anguish, when he saw the great half-moon head and seven-leagued stride at work, "*Father's going to kill the mare by following that half-thick.*" John Smith was of the same opinion, and thought that "if Eclipse himself came again he couldn't beat him;" and Tommy Sykes was so confident before the St. Leger, that he would

give Jackson no orders, but "*Rid him as thou likes,
lig thee hands down and let him stride away, and distance them.*"

Sire and sons of Tramp. Jemmy Rooke had Joe and Dick
Andrews on Wychwood Forest, when he
was sold up, and it was quite a novelty to see the
latter eat hay with his giraffe-like neck, from the
top of his rack. In ugliness of ears and head altogether, he was almost unsurpassable, and so light in
the body that he required next to no training.
Tramp was narrow like all his tribe, when a yearling, but he gradually became one of the grandest
boned horses in England, and Herring's likeness of
him at the Tickhill Castle Paddocks makes him well
worthy to be the sire of Lottery from Mandane.

Lottery. This horse's finest race was for that Doncaster Cup, whose wanderings and uses
by land and river were so varied and remarkable.
He made his own running all the way, and just beat
Longwaist by half a neck, and scattered his field
nearly half a mile. Sam Day still says that it "was
like going after a steam-engine," and that he "suffered to keep near him at all." He always went
like a machine, and the trainers declared that they
"could hear him a mile off." Sam was not on
Longwaist, when that horse had such a great finish
with Fleur de Lis, who nearly fell on his head, and
left Sam, as he pathetically says, "hanging by the
spurs." Lottery was a curious horse to meet, as he
Peculiar action of Lottery and Tomboy. threw his off fore-leg quite out. Still
he was not so eccentric as Tomboy, who
threw both legs clean round, and had
all his action so completely from behind, that Johnny
Gray said of him when he rode him at Durham, "*he
couldn't get on to his legs, without first sitting down
on his tail.*"

The last of Lottery. Lottery was an unsatisfactory, erratic
genius all his days. He was tried to

run away from Barefoot in private, but he would hardly make an effort in the St. Leger, and Mr. Watt did not care to run him after the false start. In his last race, he whipped in sixth to Fleur de Lis at Doncaster, and the first of his get, Chorister from the dam of Crowcatcher, won the St. Leger. Finally, he became a Government sire at the *Bois de Boulogne*, with Cadland and Physician, and the fame of the three quite spoilt the sport of Palmer at Viroflay, who had made £2,000 in three years, or sufficient to stock a farm in Poland, by fees from the Parisians. They came over by cartloads every Sunday to see Rainbow and the Viroflay mares, and clubbed from five to twenty francs, to have the door opened.

Catton by Golumpus was stout and The Catton tribe. useful, and with unsurpassable legs. Old Tom Taylor (or "Catton Tom" as he was then called), looked after him when he was with Sammy King, who had always the credit of being rather tender with his horses. Mulatto was more blood-like than the majority of the Cattons ; Royal Oak, the sire of Slane, ran first as Mr. Catton; and the game Ossian had to live the greater part of his time "on the muzzle." Slane had a sad aptitude for getting roarers, and there were no less than ten or eleven by him in one year. Like The Princess, who very much resembled Altisidora in her chief points, their specialty was to be game and slow.

Reveller was a thick-necked, fine goer, with square hips and short ribs, and ran with his head low. The defeat of Underhand and Beeswing at Newcastle, or Isaac at Warwick, never struck the beholders with such a chill, as did that of Dr. Syntax Dr. Syntax and Reveller. at Preston. It was there that the little brown won his Maiden Plate, and for seven years in succession carried off the Old Gold Cup. So sure did the Guild make of his winning the eighth, that

they had prepared gilt shoes, and marshalled the pro-
gramme of a procession in his honour. The race
was worthy of the anticipations it raised, as Reveller
and Jack Spigot came for it, but Dr. Syntax divided
them at the finish. If spurred or whipped, " Doctor"
would invariably swerve, and Bob Johnson and
Bill Scott, (who rode him in a few of his first races,)
would never venture to do more than talk to him,
and hiss at him in an extremity.

Death of Dr. Syntax. The old horse passed into William
Edwards's hands, with a promise to Mr.
Riddell, that he would never give him away. He became so paralyzed that a party of Newmarket jockeys
and trainers were invited to see him shot, and buried
in the paddocks behind The Palace. They gave
three times three over his grave, and then toasted

Ralph. his memory. Ralph, from a sister to
Altisidora, was one of the very few
chesnuts he ever got. He had the same prominent
eye, and such a velvetty skin that critics were
wont to say of him that he had no hair except on
his mane and tail. A very fine cross was lost by
his death, which was occasioned by his being poisoned
before the Ascot Cup. He won, but pulled up in a
desperate state of gasping, and the perspiration and
distension of the nostrils never seemed to leave
him.

Scottish cracks. Scottish racing was in its best form
when Mr. Sharpe became secretary, in
1827, to the Caledonian Hunt. He has stood to it,
and seen old friends drop off, year after year, till
very few of those who sat round the ordinary at
Edinburgh in 1828, and first drank his official health,
are left to greet him in his October tryst. Leda by
Filho da Puta, and purchased from Mr. Houldsworth commenced matters for him by winning two
races at that meeting, but although his own luck
with the white body and blue sleeves has been but

scant, he has held what proved trumps, either as dams or runners for others. From Leda he bred Martha Lynn, the dam of Voltigeur; he gave away Old Bessy, the dam of Myrrha, and grandam of Wild Dayrell; he sold Butterfly to William Oates, as a foal; he did not stand to the steeple chaser, Mauchline, and lastly he did not bid quite enough for Isaac. His brother, General Sharpe, Sir A. Ramsay, Sir David Moncrieff, and Sir William Maxwell were all thoroughly staunch, and so was Sir John Heron Maxwell, whose ancient brown cob was nearly as well known as himself.

The two Maxwells were exceedingly alike, and when Charles Lord Queensberry joined them, at the side of the cords, the three in their cool calico waistcoats made up, as the agriculturists have it, "a very thick and level pen." Sir William trained at Bogside, with Richard Greathead, and had Monreith, brother to Filho, while Springkell and Fair Helen flourished under "Old Nelson" and his lad "Finkle," in Sir John's own park. *Sir John Maxwell & "Old Nelson."* There was a good deal of quiet humour about Sir John, and on one occasion when "Old Nelson" rather demurred to his recommendation about taking Springkell back to his stable by the least crowded way, after winning the Cup, he stopped any further bounce by solemnly pulling off his hat in the streets of Carlisle, and saying, with a most courteous bow, "*I beg your pardon, Mr. Nelson, for presuming to give you a little advice about my own horse.*"

His Fair Helen was a red grey, with a most peculiarly arched neck and weaselly body, and the potions, which were administered to her during the season, no doubt affected her foals. Springkell was a round, useful, thick-necked hunter; but good as the two were, their names are quite wiped out of the studbook. Perlet, by Peter Lely, was one of the first ever trained in the Holme at Hoddom Castle, and he bettered the instruction at Dumfries : but it was when the neat little Canteen came from Brecongill to meet Springkell, for the Carlisle Cup, that Dumfriesshire made its great exodus Southwards.

Canteen & Springkell at Carlisle.

Even old Mr. Bird, the Hoddom butler, was persuaded on to horseback, for the first time in his life, and rode the twenty miles, with the tails of his dresscoat pinned in front of him. The course was too deep to suit Canteen, and hence the Cup returned in the Springkell carriage, and Mr. Bird retired into the fastnesses of his Border Tower, leaving his bark in the saddle, and his crowns in the hands of others. However, Mr. Kirby had a still more bitter recollection of Canteen, as he laid 1,000 to 5 against Jerry and him coupled, as first and second for the St. Leger.

Difficulties of the Hoddom Castle butler.

Matilda was sadly fidgetty, and in and out in her running, after the St. Leger. When she was taken up as a yearling late in September, she was only fourteen-one-and-a-half, but still she was half-an-inch bigger than The Colonel. Perhaps a handsomer little mare and big horse than she and Mameluke never met in a race. Eventually Mr. Petre gave her to the Duke of Cleveland, and she bred Henriade, Alzira, and Foxberry, and some other fair things.

Matilda.

Rowton had his beauty as a heritage from Oiseau and Camillus, and John Scott thus sums up the delight of his heart, as " long and low, not fifteen at the Leger, calf-kneed, straight hocks, no girth, and a regular tickler." He was rather light-fleshed, and not one to come every day. His dam Katharina was bred precisely like Augusta, by Woful from a Rubens mare, and he was bought at her foot, from Mr. Allen, after dinner. The bargain

Purchase of Rowton.

was a regular Dutch auction. During dinner, Mr. Allen was deaf to anything less than five hundred; but after the first bottle, he was down at four. With the second bottle, the colt stood at three; but John Scott had his guard up, and no business was done, so Mr. Allen offered to drive him home, and they shook hands for two hundred at parting. Never but once that his friends can remember, did John Scott miss anything peculiar when he looked over a horse, but it never struck him that Rowton had no warts on the inside of his legs, and his brother won a sovereign from him on the point. In his slow paces, he was not remarkable, and he lurched like a fox with his head down. To all appearance, his St. Leger finish with Voltaire was quite as *His race for the St. Leger.* desperate as Mundig's Derby one; but Bill Scott always said that he won quite easily. He certainly allowed to his friends that he " got the fog down his throat;" but his private report to his brother was, that he left off riding at the distance, after forcing the pace from the hill, and could not get his chesnut to begin again.

Like the sisters to Touchstone and Lanercost Moss Rose, sister to Velocipede, was a *Velocipede on the Turf.* very faint reflection of him, and not fond of more than half-a-mile. Her brother was bought for £120 from Mr. Moss, after Mr. Houldsworth had said that he would not give sixpence for such a slight-legged one. His mettle under leg difficulties elicited this eulogy from Bill Scott, " that if his legs had been cut off he'd have fought on his stumps;" and the way in which, four-year-old cripple as he was, he cut down Bessy Bedlam over the T.Y.C., at York, was his highest triumph of speed. His first great race was won at York August, during a meeting, in which Mulatto and Fleur-de-Lis were winners, and Jerry, Laurel, Humphrey Clinker, and Emma were not; and as a parting gift he beat Dr.

Faustus, Economist, and a good field for the Liverpool Trades Cup. Soon after that, he ran away with his lad, and broke down so badly after galloping several times round the field in front of Whitewall, that they had the greatest difficulty to support him back into his stable with sacks.

The Colonel. John Scott considered him in his prime, quite 21lbs. better than The Colonel, who was bred by Mr. Wyvill, of Burton Constable, and bought by Mr. Petre, as a yearling, in settlement of some confederate bets. The latter was short and pudgy, with fine speed, and high and fighting in his action, " ready to curl up into a mousehole, if he was reached, but very difficult to reach."

Charles Marson at Lord Exeter's. Charles Marson's ten years of service produced about £60,000 to the Exeter stable, as he won or received forfeit 207 times; and hence it is hardly to be wondered, that with such a sterling memento, his lordship stuck so long and so tenaciously by his Sultans. Previous to Marson's engagement, his lordship had seventeen horses at Prince's, but with no very great result; and Augusta, Holbein, and The Athenian, with Robinson up, were the first of the new era. When Sultan, of the lovely head, long back ribs, and muscular quarters, was purchased at seven, his legs had become quite fine, and he won one out of **The Sultan stock.** four races in the narrow blue stripes. The T.Y.C. was his *forte*, but he could get well over the Flat. He was a long horse, and many were wont to compare him to the prints of The Darley Arabian. In his last trial, a bad-tempered half-brother to Galata won, with Augusta second, and then his lordship put him out of training, and sent ten mares to him. His stock were fleshy and good doers; and for beauty, Vanish had no peer among them. Enamel by Phantom had been a successful horse for the stable before the Sultans were ready; and it was after the Two Thousand that the Burleigh agent and Mr. Tattersall raced off to Simon's Bath, on Exmoor, to look after his Rubens dam. Enamel got his name from the gold patches on one quarter. This colt's two remarkable white stockings were well known to all Newmarket; and his way of nodding his great, lop-eared, and flesh-nosed head, secured an uncommon affectionate look out for " Old Baldy" about the Bushes.

Beiram was nervous and irritable, and so wet through when he came to the July   Beiram. post, that Bill Arnull vowed he " would never want sweating again." Running, however, hardened his confidence, and he pulled up as dry as a bone. Being thrown up for two years effected nothing, and he came out in Rockingham's Goodwood Cup, only to break down. Even in his prime, a half-brother to Zinganee could give him any weight, and was considered by Marson the best he ever trained. This colt unfortunately slipped up on some wet bricks in his box, and was good for nothing afterwards. Green Mantle could get two   Green Mantle miles well; but she would jump all ways   and Varna. but the right one at the post. Nothing could be more deceptive in her trials, as she was beat to nothing by Bessie before the July; but her speed, when she meant it, was such, that a loss of forty yards in the Clearwell went for very little. Hers was a very glorious year with Lord Exeter, as Green Mantle and Varna were first and second in the Oaks, and Patron won the Two Thousand and four other races that spring before he went for the Derby. This colt had beaten her easily in an A. F. trial; and Lord Exeter, who would try three times over if it did not exactly suit him, and worked the weights by a clock, tried them in opposite directions on the same course, to be sure of the form.

Galata ripping them up.
Galata was, after all, the best of the Burleigh mares, and in the Ascot Cup of 1833, Will Arnull received the daring orders to " rip up Lucetta," and acted up to them most effectually. Her timidity was such, that Marson was obliged to train her alone, or else she would not have touched an oat. She was leggy, light-fleshed, and with large feet, and if she was held she would utterly beat herself, as she proved in a trial with Beiram. In the Port Stakes, Sam Darling had the cue to let her go, and finish them in the first mile. " *We'll catch the countryman,*" said Robinson to Will Wheatley, " *before he gets to the cords;*" but " *Well you may go and do it; I'll stop on this side of the Ditch,*" was Will's only reply. Lord Chesterfield, Mr. Payne, Col. Udny, and Marson were all at the Ditch gap, and Darling so literally obeyed his orders to "catch her by the head and come along," that there was soon a fearful spread-eagle of Emiliana, Archibald and Co. In fact, the Ditch gazers did not think it was a race at all, and declared that there was something running away; but Marson soon informed them, " *That's Galata; they'll never catch her,* " and he and Col. Udney each drew Will Chifney of a tenner upon it. It took a good deal to excite Lord Jersey; but on this occasion he was as pleased as when he jumped out of his phaeton after Cobweb won the One Thousand, and left the gout behind him. " *Hold her fast, Darling,*" he roared, as he galloped down the side of the course. " *All right, my lord,*" was the reply, " *If I was going to Bury I should win.*"

Darling's best race.
Darling was pitted successfully against Robinson in the dead heat for the Grand Duke Michael, between Muley Ishmael and Amurath. The first race was not so severe; but Darling had his orders to force the running as much as possible the second time. He did not like his job; but

Lord Exeter said, " *You've a great man against you, keep up your spirits,*" and "a pony" from his lordship, and a twenty-pound note from Lord George Bentinck, rewarded his steady riding. In the decider Robinson had a taste coming down the Bushes Hill, and Sam watched his shadow over the left, in the rays of the afternoon sun, and calling on his horse almost at the instant that he saw it glide slightly back, he got a clear length, and was never quite reached again.

The public had a notion that Cama- *Camarine and* rine was far beyond Lucetta in point *Taurus.* of speed, but had no chance with her over a Queen's Plate course; and that she required to run with her near leg first. If she started on the off one, said they, she swung it round so much, that, unless she had been steadied and made to change, she would soon have been in distress. Robinson, however, declares that the former was the very best mare he ever rode, and that Lucetta had no chance with her at any distance, and he knows nothing whatever of the leg peculiarity. Taurus stuck well up for two miles and a quarter, to her in the Jockey Club Plate, over the Beacon course. He had won an *A. F.* handicap so cleverly under 9st. 3lbs., that His Grace was determined to give him full Newmarket measure. Robinson made steady running on Camarine, to take the edge off his old friend's speed; but the victory was a costly one, and neither of them saw the post again. "Our Jim" felt so sure of the result in every way, that he went in vain to both owners to beg them not to run, but they would not heed him. Taurus was sixteen hands high, with enormous pace, for a mile and a quarter, and a very beautiful horse to look at. William Edwards bought him from Lord Warwick, at Tattersall's, and sold him to the Duke of Bedford. At three years old, he suddenly became a high-blower, but he was tried to have such speed for three-quarters-of-a-mile, that no other measure was ever taken of him. He was matched five times at half-a-mile, and, as he would be going best pace in forty yards, scarcely anything could get to his shoulder at that distance. His sons, Oakley, John o' Gaunt, King of the Peak, &c., were all in the Bedford stable when Admiral Rous became the Duke's "Master of the Horse."

The Duke of Bedford as a racing man. His Grace was very uncertain in his attendance at Newmarket. He seldom came in the spring, and looked upon the October meetings more as a tryst where he could meet his Whig friends, than his horses. He was very seldom through his stables, and cared for a race-horse about as much as he did for a unicorn. None of his winners were ever painted, as he considered it "quite an acquired taste." Admiral Rous persuaded him to have occasional trials, but the only one he ever attended in Edwards's day, was when John o' Gaunt was tried before the Newmarket Stakes. His heart was not in "The Bushes;" but roving back to the Cowper's Oak, of his earlier days, with Hercules and Marmion, waiting for the word to draw. Pearce's canvas has placed him once more among them, on his white Shamrock, with Colonel Higgins on his rat-tailed horse, Major Macginnes, Mr. Magniac on The Saddle (which Mr. Phillimore bequeathed to him when its Newmarket match days were over), old Sam Whitbread, on his odd-coloured chesnut, Captain Newland, and George Beers, on Cognac, looking as fierce as if he had just pulled down a fox, and was breaking him up in the spirit. At Tedworth, too, his Grace would be on the flags with Carter for hours to the last, tracing back lines of blood, and recalling the work of every hound in his own and the Grafton pack; but for racing he

The Oakley meet.

had no real heart, and merely wished his stable to pay.

John o' Gaunt was always tried to be better than Oakley; but he put out incipient ring- Envoy,&Magog bones, and no one ever knew how good the giant. he was. Edwards swore by Envoy, as the best, bar Ralph, that he ever trained, and the chesnut was an equal favourite with the Duke. He ran quite untried for the Drawing Room Stakes, and hence the House party had no reason to wonder that they had not heard of him. No horse required so much long walking exercise, in addition to his work, at least five days a-week; and the petting and lack of exercise at Woburn him made him so round and foul-blooded, that he could never be trained again. Oakley and Robinson " knew every post on the Flat," and over a T.Y.C. he was just about 5lbs. better than Celia. He might have run further, but his great muscular top hardly comported with his small knees and hocks; and as he showed a tendency to put out curbs, they dare not go on with him for a longer course. Magog was bought by the Duke for £300, from Mr. Ransome, and for three-quarters-of-a-mile he was immensely fast; but his leg gave way at three, and his temper soon after. He quite ate up to his weight, and when his rations were gone, he would have been ready to take his turn at a pig-trough.

The Earl of Albemarle was in the The late Earl of Palace stable at the same time as His Albemarle. Grace; but Barcarolle's Oaks chance was put out by illness, after she had won The Thousand, and Mr. Kirby's £400 cheque was ready. His lordship formed very little judgment about horses, and as Dr. Johnson said of his Derbyshire friend, " *His talk is of sheep and bullocks.*" He would, in fact, have never kept horses at all, but for the very laudable feeling that, as Master of the Horse, he had no right to see Ascot racing at other people's expence. Still, as is

M

often the case when owners take things easy, and do
not make their lives miserable by watching the market, his green-and-white cap had a good time of it
with Ralph and the Emperor; and he purchased
Royal George for £150 from Edwards, and sold him
to the foreigners for more than thrice that sum. The
ill luck of the stable seemed to concen-
trate itself on the Duke of Beaufort.

Bad Beaufort luck.

Whatever he bought, bred, or borrowed, turned out
badly, and when it really seemed on the cards, his
horse would tumble down, or run out of the course,
or go amiss.

Muley was a good runner, despite his
somewhat odd pins, and Muley Moloch

*Muley and Muley
Moloch.*

was rather high on the leg, and rather short-
quartered. His Champagne and York Derby wins
had made him a hot St. Leger favourite in Yorkshire,
but he never had a chance, and they hedged their
opinion after the race, by saying that his teeth had
been so bad that he lived on balls of meal for six
weeks before. Mr. Tattersall, who had the charge
of the Underley stud, was not a little fond of selling
them at Doncaster, and it was from Marpessa, one
of old Muley's daughters, and Alice Hawthorne,
his granddaughter, that Pocahontas and Thormanby
sprang.

Master Henry, the sire of Touchstone's
dam, is embalmed in Sam Day's memory,

*The grandsire of
Touchstone.*

as being one of his favourite platers; and especially
great in mud. John Scott had never seen Touchstone till the Liverpool St. Leger, when the brown
made his own running, and was beaten by General
Chassé. Godfrey Kirkley, who was with

*John Scott's first
sight of Touch-
stone.*

Mr. Riddell, trained him, and had him
as fat as a bull; but still Birdlime and
Inheritor, who had just beaten Physician at 32lbs.
for the two years, in the Cup, were behind him,
and Scott told Lords Derby and Wilton that he

felt sure he could win the St. Leger. The beginning was not favourable, as he was put in the charge of a drunken groom to walk to Yorkshire, and got loose on the Lancashire moors for hours, where a sailor caught him and brought him to Sheffield. After such neglect, he arrived at Malton in a *His mishaps and* painfully weak state, and a course of *medicine.* Peruvian bark had to be resorted to before they dared to work him. What with this and his jaundice, John Scott seldom had a horse which required so much doctoring. A record of the calomel and other drugs which he swallowed would form a portion of Whitewall history, as remarkable as the recovery of its Prince Lewellyn, who answered to the old ale and port, and won two races after he had been covered up in the stall as dead, and his grave had been dug in the paddock.

He had his final polish at Hambleton, and when Bill declared after the trial to ride Lady le Gros, Darling was applied to for Touchstone. However, Lord Sligo had been before-hand, and Sam weighed for Bran, and declares to this day that Touchstone stopped to him at the finish; while Bob Johnson "dodged backwards and forwards on Chassé before us and between us, all over the course."

Touchstone was only third up the *Mostyn-mile* Mostyn mile to Intriguer and Birdlime, *martys.* both of his year. Oddly enough, as soon as his flag was lowered, Blenkhorn led out his Leger successor Queen of Trumps for her maiden race, but although they were both at the same meeting the next autumn, and each walked over for two stakes, they never met at the post. In 1835, when he had just shown in good Cup form at Doncaster, he again failed up the Mostyn mile, but he was before Birdlime, who essayed that heart-breaking hill four times in vain. At five years old, he did a great thing with Hornsea and Scroggins at Epsom, the week before the Ascot

Cup, in which he beat Rockingham and Lucifer. His near fore-ankle was never very good, and even in his first Ascot Cup race, it had almost risen to the dignity of "a leg." Its chance of rising to it was furthered by the wild notions of the man in charge, who persisted in doctoring it during John Scott's absence at Manchester, with hot *Ascot Cup tremb-* oils instead of Gowland's lotion. Still, it *lings.* was 100 to 1 on him if the leg stood, though Connolly and Pavis had been clever enough to get on nearly £5,000 against him, and it was half-past twelve before Mr. Hill would release them. Joe Rogers was another of the sceptics at Death's, and expressed such a confident determination to eat him if he won, that John Scott could not refrain from subsequently sending his compliments, and a request to know how "he should like him cooked."

Touchstone's pe- Touchstone was a peculiar horse in *culiarities.* every way. He had very fleshy legs, and turned his hocks out so much, and went so wide behind, that a barrel could have been got between his legs when he was galloping. He went with a straight knee; and in short he was nearly the oddest goer that ever cleared its pipes in good air on Langton Wold, as he pitched and yet stayed as well. Ground made no appreciable difference to him, but he was desperately lazy at exercise, and could hardly be kicked along on most days. As a beginner he did not excel, and his fine speed was quite his greatest point. It was a very hard matter to catch him when he was once set a-going, and no horse pulled harder. If he was at all stale, it would never do to squeeze him too much, or he would swerve to the left like a shot. He just lived into his 31st year, and although that wondrous hind action in his walk rather failed him, and he was quite wasted over the back and loins, he could wave his flag and march very proudly round his court-yard at

Eaton. For two years he had been on the wane, but still he never had an hour's illness at the stud, and never had a dose of medicine in Cheshire till just before he died. He was quite a valetudinarian, and it was remarkable to see how on wet days he would retreat, quick march, to his shed, and stand earnestly watching the weather. There was apparently great pain in the head for three days before his death, and he took nothing but a little gruel, and scarcely any notice of Fisher, who had attended him for seven years. His feet were all taken off, and the greater part of his mane and tail, and sent to the Hall, and he was buried in the middle of the stable-yard.

Till within the last three years, he was a very sure stock-getter, but not His descendants. partial to young mares, nor to old ones till May or June. The latest Sire List contains 18 of his sons and 37 of his grandsons; and upwards of 100 of his mares are at the stud. He got his sires especially in every form, and we fancy that Surplice is the finest and biggest of them, Orlando the most beautiful and bloodlike, and Touchwood more like himself than any of them, but on a larger scale. His luck with distinguished mares was variable. There was Orlando from Vulture, Newminster and Nunnykirk from Beeswing, Cotherstone from Emma, Surplice from Crucifix, Assault from Ghuznee; but Alice Hawthorne and Lady Evelyn failed, Ellerdale, Inheritress, and Queen Mary missed; Refraction and Canezou were not very lucky; Miss Twickenham, Ellen Middleton Pocahontas, Barbelle, and Martha Lynn never honoured him with a visit; and Mr. Johnstone's Harriet was the last mare that went to him. He and Liverpool were selected by the late Duke of Orleans for four of his best mares, when with Edgar Pavis, and then with Charles Edwards, that true-hearted sportsman held his racing court at Chantilly. As a general thing, his stock were best at a mile, bad on their legs after three, and, like him, with no great action in their slow paces.

Jereed & Mundig. Jereed could live with him well at weights for age, and John Scott quite hoped to stand on him for the Derby instead of Mickle Fell, that anything but brilliant Brother to Mundig. It was not to be; he was all well at eight one night, but a secret foe got at him before five next morning, and a glance at his legs told the treacherous tale. Mundig was a very moderate horse, and Consol was his schoolmaster. Still he convinced the brothers so completely that he was worth backing for the Derby after his "Yorkshire gallop" in clothes with Marcian over the *D.I.*, that the double had to be promptly put on the touts. They had "got" one of the stable lads, and so the chesnut and Consol were started off, as if they had given up Epsom, and were going home, and then turned back after a six miles walk, when the lad had fully gazetted their departure for the North. Although the chesnut had never run in public, he came to 6 to 1 in a few hours, and those who had been most active in "drawing" the lad, immediately said that it "was a nice robbery, and the Scotts ought to be ashamed of themselves."

Mundig's Derby Day. When he ran for the Derby, Lord Chesterfield lent John a bad-mouthed pony, which took to rusting in the furzes. At last his rider got him straight and milled him well across the Downs, and at their next effort he cannoned a carriage near the winning-post. He was barely pulled off that, when Lord Jersey rode up: "*Well, John, I'm sorry for you—Ascot's won.*" "*Now't of the sort,*" said a cad with enough rags ready made on his back for a mop, "*the old beggar in black's won.*" "*Has he?*" said John; "*you're the man for my business;*" and flinging him half-a-crown, he rode off to meet his horse and congratulate the young heir of Streatlam on his eighteen thousand. Bill Scott never rode a severer race, and he had to shout as loud to Nat to keep his colt from hanging on to him, as he did in the Satirist Leger when he summarily ordered him to pull Van Amburgh to one side after coming round the bend, and "*let me have a shy at Old John Day.*"

Hornsea, Scroggins, Carew, and Gladiator were all contemporaries of Touchstone at Malton, and when the three first were tried with him, Scroggins was beat a distance. Hornsea and Touchstone were regularly laid alongside each other at 20lbs. in the Doncaster Cup, and the young one was the better favourite of the two at starting, and beaten a neck. The chesnut, the origin of whose wall-eyes once strangely puzzled a German, was a "good, steady horse;" but Carew, who separated Touchstone from Venison, Beeswing, and General Chassé in the Doncaster Cup of the next year, and beat a Goodwood Cup field as well, was really "very moderate." He cut himself down in the St. Leger, to serve the narrow thin-fleshed Scroggins, of whom John Scott speaks as "queer in the pipes, but smart." *Hornsea, Scroggins & Carew.*

Gladiator by Partisan was a very blood-like, dark chesnut, but rather delicate, and requiring remarkable nicety in his preparation. John and William Scott gave £100 for him, and sold him to Lord Wilton for £200, and a contingency of half the Derby and St. Leger. He lost the first, and never started again, but his price gradually rose to £800, and finally to £2,000. For Sweetmeat's sake alone he was worth every penny of it, but he also left Queen Mary the dam of Blink Bonny and the grandam of Caller Ou. His sire Partisan was a beautiful, short-legged horse with a lovely head, straight-hocks, and a clubby fore-foot. *Gladiator.*

Many of the elder trainers still recur to him fondly as "like a bit of machinery in his stride." His Patron, a half-brother to Augusta was very good; but Venison was the gamest and stoutest of his sons. Still that little fellow could never quite do himself justice, as his very long action hardly fitted him for forcing the running, as he was often obliged to do.

The mare Frailty was presented to John Scott by Mr. Petre, and was sent to Partisan, when she was rising five. There was nothing particular about her, but a very curby hock, which had sprung going round Ferguson's Corner at Catterick. Her Cyprian was

Early days of Cyprian.

sent for a few months before breaking to Mr. Hebden at Appleton, among the Helmsley Moors, near the haunts of the re-nowned Jemmy Golding, who when he was rising ninety-two, thus addressed John Scott, "*There are no hunters bred now a-days, Mr. Scott. I'll just away and buy some brood mares, and breed a few.*" She was made quite a pet of in that country, and knew the taste of cheese-cakes, and all that sort of thing; but Bill Scott did not think much of her Oaks chance when he "had a taste," and it hung upon her beating Aveline for a £40 stake at Malton, whether she went to Epsom at all. She had a hard time of it, as she walked into Surrey, and then back to Newcastle, and then home to Malton, and won both Oaks and Northumberland Plate, during the six weeks. Joe Wilkins the present Aintree trainer, conducted her on a pony, and they travelled on an average twenty miles per day. She was terribly high-mettled, and never trained after four, and Songstress, also a winner of the Oaks, and Meteora were her best foals. She never caused any death herself, and her ill-temper did not descend to her stock; but one of them, Artful Dodger, hit a lad who was washing his feet, with his hock on the jugular vein, and killed him outright on the spot.

Epirus, the Malton horse of '37, was Purchase of Epirus. purchased along with his brother Epidaurus from Mrs. Savile Lumley for £1,700, with a £500 contingency if he won the Leger, but it needed all John Scott's eloquence in a two-hours' confab to get them at the price. Epirus was untried, and "the young beauty," as his mistress termed him in her delivery order to Hornshaw, was disqualified, or else Elis's brilliant running, both as a two-year-old and with Bay Middleton a fortnight before, would have made the figure a much higher one. Langar filled a 25 sov. subscription at Tickhill Castle in the following year, and such was Lord George's admiration for Elis, that he took a fourth of the forty. subscriptions. The chesnut died there at last, and he is buried on one side of the hedge in the principal paddock, and Catton on the other.

Epirus could stay well enough, al- His training in the metropolis. though speed was his best point, and his trial, in which he gave Cardinal Puff 10lbs., seemed quite good enough for the St. Leger. He was the only horse that ever broke Bill Scott's collar-bone; and as John Scott adds, " the only one I ever trained in the streets of London." Owing to there being no North Western truck at liberty, he had to stay three days there in stables behind All Saints' Church, and he used to take long constitutionals from four a.m. up and down Regent-street. Sam Chifney had a heavy retainer, to go down and ride him at the Potteries, but he never looked near, and Nat got a winning mount on him.

Cardinal Puff bore a very distinguished The trial of Don John and Cardinal Puff. part in the great Don John trial, when the young one beat him at 12lbs. for the year. George Nelson's orders were simply to "*stand none of Bill's humbug, but come right through.*" Both Lord Chesterfield and Colonel Anson thought it madness to try at that weight; and at the far side of the hill, Bill thought the young horse had the worst of it. He accordingly shouted to George to ease a bit; but the more he shouted, the harder went "The Admiral." Bill suffered a little, and caught his leader on the hill, "fairly jumping over me, the moment he was touched with the spur." George, "who never made a mistake with the old 'un," gradually fancied himself in full The Colonel and command of The "Fleet," at Pigburn, "the Admiral." and at last demanded in his vinous valour from Colonel Anson, whether he called *himself* a Colonel. However, he rode over special to Doncaster in the morning, to apologize; and the Colonel, who had the keenest appreciation, for years after, of his antics and carols, on that memorable night, only replied, "*Never mind, George; I'm glad to be blown up on such an occasion; you only ride another Don John trial, and you may do it again.*"

Horse whims. Don John detested Bill Scott, owing, it was supposed, to his having hit him twice with a whip, in his box at York. All the carrots in the East Riding would not have reconciled them, and like Jack Spigot, it made him furious even to hear the sound of Bill's voice. The Princess took a dislike to every one at Whitewall, and after giving Jacob more trouble than half the stable to shoe, she ended by running John Scott and Markwell out of the paddock, when they went to see her at Bretby. It is a pretty general opinion among trainers, that horses cannot tell one person from another except by the voice, and that, in this re- A horses' know- spect, they are like the fairy "Fine ledge of sound. Ear." Ellerdale, for instance, took no notice of Tom Dawson, when he went to see her at

Admiral Harcourt's, some four or five years after she had left his stable; but the moment he said "*Coachman!*" she wheeled round, and struck at him quite viciously. Mentor was quite as odd this way, and he proved pretty well that the dislike arises from the association of the voice with the orders at exercise. Mat Dawson had him under his charge for a short time in Scotland, when his legs were wrong; and as he gave him no work, there was no raw established between them. Hence Mat quite laughed at the notion that the horse would not let him go up to him, if he heard his brother Tom's voice, and a bet of a new hat was made on it. They adjourned with some visitors to the box, and Mat got on most affectionately with his old charge, till there came Tom's whisper from behind—"*Poor old Mentor!*" and the whole party were dispersed in a second. Even General Chassé, as gluttonous a feeder as ever faced a manger, would pause in his swallow, and grunt if he heard Bob Johnson's voice; and Meretrix became so fidgetty from hearing Fobert's, at exercise, that he was obliged to employ a code of stick and hand signals to the boy.

Charles XII. was a very curious-coated horse, and very delicate at three. *Purchase of Charles XII.* Like Touchstone, he had rather a queer time of it on Blackstone Edge (over which Sydney Smith had years before proved himself such a Hannibal in the "Immortal,") as he stuck there for three hours, with every trace broken, on his return from the Liverpool Cup. In the same journey he had an equally narrow escape on the Liverpool platform, and hung on the ledge of it for minutes, without injuring a hair. He came into Mr. Johnstone's hands in rather a curious way. That gentleman had always nursed the wish, while in India, to own one of the finest horses that money could buy on his return. Accordingly, when he did reach

England, he commissioned Tom Dawson to buy him one for three thousand. "Better get two for that price" was Tom's counsel, and Hetman Platoff was priced to him at £1,200, and The Provost at £1,500. The latter was not up to Mr. Johnstone's mark, and accordingly a bid of £2,000 was made for Euclid. "*I'd sooner shoot him than take it*," was Mr. Thornhill's reply, and at length it was decided to give the £3,000 for Charles XII. Mr. Johnstone had a thousand offered for his bargain, but he refused it in real Thornhill style, and he was never prouder of his resolve, than when two years in succession he felt all the glory of winning the Goodwood Cup. At first Charles's stock sold pretty well at Doncaster, but at last he himself could only command a £20 bid. He was then sold privately for £50, but the vendee forfeited the £20 rather than take him. His tail was so short, and his back so down, that even Tom Dawson stood at the ring side and asked what he was.

Hetman Platoff had much finer speed,
Hetman Platoff.
although Charles stayed rather the best, but still John and Bill Scott always fancied, that if Hetman had not put out a curb, he would have been the A 1 on the St. Leger day. He was a wonderful weight-carrier, and of such boundless nerve, that he would have walked among a park of artillery and never moved a muscle. The Melton farmers first told John Scott of him when he was a yearling, and pathetically described him as half-starved in a field near Stillington, "with a half-bred colt, which had got master of him." Mr. Bowes and John made a rapid descent on that village, whose smoky alehouse and its indigestible Noah's Ark bacon dwell upon John's mind yet; but it ended in Colonel Croft selling the colt for 200 gs., and engaging to pay his St. Leger forfeit; and Mr. Bowes took half of him. The bad fare of the day was made up when Bill joined

them at The Black Swan, at night, and " Nancy"
Martinson waited on them.

Industry was pretty, but as nervous Industry and
as Hetman was bold; and the Brown Ghuznee.
Duchess she met in the Oaks was not of the Saxon
mint. Caroline Elvina, who went to help her, was
" without exception the finest-looking mare that
ever was at Whitewall;" and Ghuznee was " only
fourteen-three on the Oaks day; but a perfect rattler. The latter was also one of the many proofs
in John Scott's mind that " very superior-looking
legs go the quickest," as she had rest and green meat
for a fortnight after Ascot, and her sinews were quite
crooked when she was taken out of the box.

Launcelot had enormous speed, and
pulled even harder than his brother Launcelot.
Touchstone, with his head right into his chest. In
fact, hardly any one could hold him; and the hunting curb, which Bill selected for his St. Leger race,
was a most formidable affair. He had rather heavy
shoulder points, a short neck, and not very good
ankles, and John Scott considered him fully 21lbs.
better than Maroon. After the St. Leger he lay two
days in his box, and it is a miracle how he contrived
to reach The Salutation at all. Meteor, after the
Two Thousand, was in nearly the same plight, but he
was such a chronic cripple, that his lad had to chase
him about his box for an hour or two before a race,
to get him to " act" at all.

Satirist was soon forgotten at Malton, Satirist's St. Leger
but not the joke about his Doncaster trial.
trial. The Corporation Steward took up the chains
and held his peace, and the neat-herd, who was
charged not to tell any one, gave the office most
freely. In order to disappoint them, the Pigburn
party arrived at the Moor about half-past three, and
found only a few sweeps and Irishmen in attendance.
As it rained hard, they were most politely invited to

share the Rubbing-house, and then the Scott party slipped out and locked them up till it was over; and squared the "false imprisonment" with half-a-crown's worth of gin. It was rather a hard matter to bring off a trial at Doncaster, and on one occasion the blacking pot had to be freely used on their legs and faces, before the horses set out from Pigburn.

Atilla's trial. Attila's Newmarket trial at two-years-old was quite in the dark, and Colonel Peel's Hardinge and Sir Harry had just tried him half-a-mile on the limekiln-hill, when the renowned J. B. arrived with a lantern to reconnoitre. John Scott could not see the horses, but he knew from Attila's peculiarly quick and delicate step that he was coming away in front, two hundred yards before they finished.

Jacob's bet about Attila. He was a cheap £120 bargain at two years old, but not a lucky horse, as he was got at three times, and was coughing sadly before the Drawing Room Stakes. On the Derby day, after Jacob had discharged his plating functions, he stationed himself near the winning post with Charley Robinson, and waited there in the most boundless faith. A stranger presumed to doubt him, when he said, "*You'll precious soon see his white feace first*," and clenched his opinion by a sovereign bet. With a presence of mind, which Yorkshire can never cease to venerate, he added, "*I'll just tak hold of your horse's head, and I'll thank you, sir, not to stir fra the spot;*" and suiting the action to thé word, he secured his man and his money. It is on record that he and his companion gave away a barrel of beer to the multitude, and that in the hilarity of the moment he would have signed a week's truce with the touts.

Jacob on a tout hunt. That fraternity's experiences of the deceased are of a most doleful kind. He was long in partnership with an American dog, which

Mr. Harry Hill bought at a baker's in Knightsbridge, and sent for John Scott's acceptance as an Under-Leadbeater to Whitewall. The dog had been regularly educated to track slaves, and hence it took to touts with the highest imaginable zest. At times, the pair would come to a check at the foot of a tree, and when Jacob made his eye-cast among the branches, it became his turn to give tongue. "*Now I've got 'ther, thoo must, and thoo shalt come doon,*" and when his brown-and-white friend had enjoyed a good muzzled worry, the game would fly Malton-wards, bawling ten thousand murders. Well might one of them confide to his Malton allies, "*It's not that John Scott, but his old thief of a blacksmith and 'Captain' that I'm afeard on.*"

The old Pottery course is now so built upon, that the most imaginative mind cannot conjure up the idea that Attila ever won a Champagne Stakes over it, and that it ever witnessed a struggle between The Potentate and "The Alderman's" King Cole. King Cole. Marlow won no less than two dozen races on this son of Memnon, and the Buxton Cup three years in succession. He never had a horse so difficult to handle, as he always hung to the left, despite a Magogian pricker; and if the running was that way round, he could hardly be kept off the posts. Holmes, who got on him at exercise at Liverpool, voted it the worst mouth he had ever touched, but it was not inherited by his hunters and carriage horses, which were always at a premium in the district. At the first time of asking, he departed with Marlow down a lane at Bridge-north, but got such a refresher for it, that he wiped off his maidenhood very quickly at Ludlow. Marlow always considers that his Chester Cup was an enormous bit of luck. He lay in front with 7st. 8lbs., to the Castle Pole, and took the lead at the distance, and Lye, who watched nothing but Birdlime, could

never quite reach him, and was beaten a neck.
The Potentate always beat him afterwards, and was
a good 7lbs. better at least.

Marlow and old   Marlow, who began life as "a fea-
John Day.   ther" on the same day and in the same
race as Sam Rogers, got another good race for The
Alderman, still more out of the fire. It was a 100-
sovereign Stake, and all the money at Ascot; and
The Deputy went there on the chance of getting
his stake back, not to run. Accordingly Marlow,
who had sole charge of the colt, made this proposition to old John Day, when they met at scale;
but John could "settle nothing till I've seen my
Lord Lichfield;" and so saying, he seated himself on the weighing-chair, and called "eight seven."
Sam Darling sat there quietly tapping the toes of
his boots with his whip, and probably thought more
than he said, but Marlow did not fail to mark that
the generally accurate John, and Doe, the trainer,
had overlooked the 5lbs. extra on The Corsair, for
winning the Two Thousand. John then went to
seek out Lord Lichfield, and was not a little surprised when he returned with his lordship's consent
to give back the stake, that Marlow should meet him
with " *I've altered my mind; I'll have all or none;—
but we'd better make haste, its getting late.*"

It will do now, thought Marlow, when he had
John fairly in the saddle, and cantering and
whistling, and singing, as was his wont, down to
the post; but still he was not quite comfortable,
and he took care to get alongside of him, and
keep him in conversation upon things in general.
Mr. Davis started them, and they merely cantered to the distance; but when the black was
set going, he smashed up the chesnut in a trice,
and went nearly to the Swinley Course post before he could be stopped. The chesnut " wanted
no stopping;" but when John arrived back, Mar-

low placed eight twelve in the scale. "*I did'nt weigh that*," said John." "*I know you did'nt*," was the reply; "*but you ought. Where's the penalty?*" "*Fetch the bridle*," said John. "*Better bring the horse*," said Marlow; "*it will be a new kind of snaffle if it weighs 5lbs.*" John was fine weight as usual to begin with, and he could not stir the beam. "You did that very well, my boy; I give you great credit," he shouted to Marlow, as he rode past him off the course, and away he went whistling and singing once more. Job Marson and Taylor made the same mistake with Aphrodite, in the Doncaster Stakes, but one of the local reporters found it out, and gave Job the hint, to Nat's intense disgust.

Not to have a word on old Isaac and Sam Darling would be a strange omission indeed, and one that Warwick would not overlook in a hurry. Sam was ever true to his boyish impressions, and never thought either him or Hesperus quite so wonderful as Mantidamum, by Sir Solomon. On that horse, at Stafford, with 3½ st. of saddle-cloths, &c., he beat Dick Spencer and Jack Hayes, both great men on that circuit, but they had their revenge at Holywell, as they combined on Ambo and Stella, and fairly drove him into the Ditch. "*I'll have you some day*," he muttered, like another D'Israeli, when he met them in the weighing-house, and we should rather think he had. When Major Pigot gave up his horses, Sam, at his mother's particular request, did a little in the yard-wand way, at Oxford and Worcester; but he longed to wear the silk instead of selling it, and he went to Mr. West and old Sadler, at Bibury, to tuck up his cuffs in another cause, and carry out his great principle, that "any man may wait, but it requires a wise head to make running."

But we must put him on Isaac, who made his start on the Turf at the York

Sam Darling and Isaac.

History of Isaac.

August of '33, as the " gr. c. by Figaro, out of Jack Spigot's dam," and was beaten any distance in a two-year-old field, by Colonel Cradock's Emigrant. Like his half-brother, he had a pretty wayward temper, and paid the penalty of it. Sam first marked him in a Maiden Plate at Liverpool, two years afterwards, and took such a fancy to him, from the way he finished second to Luck's All, in the first heat, that he confided to Tom Speed, that he had got his eye on a treasure. He was sent by Mr. Ord Powlett, in the autumn to lead gallops for The Potentate, at Doncaster, and bolted near the Neat-herd's House, and took a little of " the bark off his leg." He was put up on the Thursday, and Mr. Sharpe began to bid for him; but stopped, under the idea that he had been fired; and when Mat Milton took a turn, Sam got close to him, and put it to him confidentially, whether " those great flat feet will ever suit the London stones." Hence " gr. g., by Figaro, 46 gs., Mr. S. Darling," was the sale entry; and Isaac Blades, who then trained him, was so angry that " such a rip should be named after me," that he cut Sam, and never spoke to him again.

The grey appeared in a Hack Stakes, winner to be sold for fifty, the next week at Liverpool; but Sam agreed with Mr. Sirdefield, who was second on Aratus, about the cross claim. The race was run off by moonlight; and near the Canal turn, the light-blue of Isaac was leading. " *Is it over yet?*" said Sam to Mr. Sirdefield. " *Oh! not yet, I think,*" was the reply, and Sam set the grey going again. He repeated the question over his shoulder at the distance, and then it was, "*Oh! yes. Yes! Sam! it is all up, now.*" When he next came to Liverpool, Harry his brother Sam Darling had taught him jumping with Lord Fitzhardinge's. He dwelt a little at his jumps, in consequence of being rather down in his eyes; but still he pulled off £176 over the hurdles. He got £30 more at a little Ellesmere meeting, on his road home, after Sam had run half over Liverpool in search of a Shropshire paper, which had the conditions. Isaac Day begged a mount at Bibury, and returned him with the assurance that his own back would never be itself again after the job; but he was ridden by Sam in almost all his flat races, of which he won forty-six. He went lobbing easily along, with his head out, and was great in dirt, as Caravan found to his cost, and went best when Sam kept shouting at him, "*Come along, old 'un.*" His victories at Warwick, when he belonged to its M.P., were looked at both from an electioneering and a racing point of view, and Isaac Day was sadly disappointed that he never could get Sam chaired. Amidst all his triumphs, he nearly died at Knutsford, and the guard of the coach went so far as to hail Sam, who was Newton-bound on his hack, and tell him that his horse was dead, and all Knutsford talking of it. Lear arrived at the races with the intelligence that he was better, and in a short time he succeeded in walking, by seven-mile stages, to Kynnersley, near Croome. Two miles was his favourite distance; but at half-a-mile less, Modesty could always do him. Still, if Isaac was beaten over a distance of ground, it was by a pace which left its mark upon the winner.

His Ditch-in race with the five-year-old I'm-not-aware, in which he had Weighting him for the Audley End. 22lbs. the worst of the weights, and made all the running, gave (Admiral) Rous such an opinion of him, that he put 10st. on him for the Audley End. "*I shan't want you to ride him, Captain Rous,*" said Sam, rather grimly, when they fell to chatting in front of the Rooms, next morning. "*What do you mean, now Sam?*" said the Admiral; "*Oh! I thought, Sir, you handicapped him to get a mount; according to your weights, there's not been such a horse in New-*

market since Sultan." However, taking the line through Roscius, there was not much fault to find with the weighting. A hurdle race in the November of '42, saw the last of him in public, and then Mr. Robins, of Stoneleigh Park, gave him a run out for four or five years, till he had to be shot for infirmity. Sam occasionally saw him in his retirement, but he "took no notice of me for good or evil." His skin now covers a favourite chair, and his portrait adorns the old inn sign at Bourton and many a bar-parlour down the Warwick and Worcester way.

The old Scottish cracks. Scotland's finest sportsmen seemed fated to die in their prime. "Willie Sharpe" still relishes his coursing at Knockhill and his training at Hambleton, with a zest which deserves better luck; and Lord Glasgow is as kind and dauntless as of yore, when he sent Actæon to the post against Memnon at York, and kept half Paisley in food during the whole of a hard winter. Mr. Merry has crept quietly on since he was content with the little Paisley bouts of poor Edgar on Beadershin, till he has made his yellow jacket a name of dread across the Border; but where are the other gallant chiels who were wont, year after year, to meet in the stand portals at the Caledonian Hunt? "The Inches of Perth, girdled as they are by the bright and brimming Tay; the short but trying bit of green carpet on the Frith of Clyde, where you are within hail of 'the auld clay biggin,' where the Ploughman Bard was born; the base of that grim grey keep, round which Forth winds its silver links; the fair regions of Tweed, or Musselburgh's dead flat margined by the snell and gurly sea," hold high festival for *them* no more. Sir David Baird, the hardest man, not barring Assheton Smith and Dick Christian, that ever fought his unswerving way through the bulfinches of Leicestershire, and Sir

Frederick Johnstone, live only by Mr. Gilmour's side in the Melton Hunt picture. Sir James Boswell can never again tell of the pluck and bottom of his Pugilist over Amesbury, or banter "The General" in return, when he reminds him of General Chassé and his Ayr dose of "Tincture of Myrrh." Lord Drumlanrig, "the doucest lad of them a'," no longer keeps the country side alive, and leads Joe Graham and his field across Dumfries-shire. William Hope Johnstone is no more among them, with an Era, a William le Gros, or The Returned, that winner of his two memorable four-mile steeple chases in succession at Eglinton Park; and Mr. Meiklam cannot whisper his last order to "Simmy Templeman," and then tell him how well the new blue-and-white stripes look, on which he has set a special loom to work, and bid them not mind the expense.

"The Turf, The Chase, and The Road," all drooped in Scotland when "Mr. Ramsay and the Hounds" ceased to be a toast in Mid Lothian, when his Lanercost or Inheritor were not under cup orders for Ayr, and when his mail-coach team, with himself or his good friend from Ury in command, no longer stepped gaily down Leith-street towards cannie Aberdeen. He had his summons when he had barely lived out half his time, and only last autumn the crape on the Caledonian Hunt scarlet, and the words of sorrow to his memory, told that one still more radiant element was wanting in the great gathering of Scottish sportsmen. "Eg- The late Lord linton" was one of them in every sense Eglinton of the word, and the thistle on his racing-jacket was no unmeaning emblem of his love for his "ain countree." No one enjoyed a game more heartily on the ice, the sward, or the racket-court; and there was scarcely a non-professional to beat him at billiards. "*Major quo non major*" was the neat tri-

bute on the monument of his favourite greyhound;
and old coursers will tell you exactly how his Waterloo took and worked his hare over the Flat; and
how that son of Dusty Miller beat Gracchus, the
Ashdown crack, on his own ground, and was looked
on, in Scotland, as the veritable champion of the
smooth interest against the rough. The history of
the " Eglinton Tartan" from the days when Queen
Bathsheba first bore it, till Corœbus and Fandango,
—that last great struggle between it and the Zetland spots, gave us one more glimpse of old times,
—needs no more recitals. Political duties claimed
him, as they had done Lord George; and he seemed
to have quite forgotten his way to Doncaster. "Nimrod" declared that the late Duke of Beaufort was the
most popular man in England; but the Earl of
Eglinton was the most so in the three countries
combined. The Irish loved him for his frankness,
his impartiality, his Vice-regal munificence and his
nice turns-out; the English reverenced him as the
soul of honour on their favourite Turf; and his
countrymen delighted in his hearty national feelings,
whether he was playing golf at St. Andrew's, or
laying his chaplet with manly eloquence in the
resting-place of Burns.

Sir James Boswell. Sir James Boswell had a strong dislike to dividing a race or a course, and
on one occasion he ran three No-goes rather than
give in. He also disliked exceedingly to see his
horses punished, and his last orders to his jockey
were invariably to that effect. In General Chassé's
case he was perforce obliged to be silent on that
head. The General's Ayr defeat by Myrrha never
seemed to be forgotten, and was married to immortal verse," in which the mare " only gave
her tail a wag," and of course won as she liked.
The " black and white stripes" men said with no
little truth that they did not meet the mare on equal

terms, as their champion was quite stale with a twelve days walk from Doncaster. Fobert has never yet been weaned from his first love by any of his "Spigot Lodge" flyers, and quite believes that in these times of comfortable railroad travelling, Chassé would have been a wonder. No one understood his peculiar temper better than poor Jack Holmes, or managed it so nicely in a race. He never would make his own running, and liked to come once for all a few strides from home. All distances and weights were much the same to him, but he wanted a severe hill to bring the leaders back to him at the finish, which was the reason that Liverpool suited him so well.

Myrrha was a low, cart-breasted mare, by Malek (own brother to Velocipede) out of Bessy, whom Mr. Sharpe rode as his Edinburgh hack, and, as in Enamel's and North Lincoln's case, there was quite a rush for her dam. She was traced, with some trouble, to a cabstand in York; but death had come to the rescue some months before. The people liked as much to see Sim (whom Mr. Sharpe first brought down to Scotland, when he was light weight, to Mr. Lambton) in the Elcho blue and black cap upon Philip, as Southrons did Nat on Lady Wildair. Philip was the death of Ballochmyle, and stuck to him so resolutely in some four-mile heats, at Gullane, on a very warm day, that the bay died in less than five minutes. The races had been removed that summer from Musselburgh to Gullane, on account of the cholera; and when that Caledonian Hunt was held at Cupar, in which Harry Edwards won his celebrated race on Terror, six or seven hearses went past during the afternoon entry; and the races almost seemed like a death-dance round the plague pit.

Myrrha and Philip.

Gullane was once the Malton of Scotland, and half-a-dozen horses busy at

Gullane.

their ∽ shaped work in the " myres " served last
summer to keep up a faint association with Lanercost,
Inheritor, and Despot, those knights of the straw
body and green sleeves, who were once the pre-
siding genii of the spot.   The house where all the
Dawsons were born and bred nestles at the foot
of the hill, on which stands the rude wooden light-
house, keeping watch and ward over the deep blue sea-
board of the German Ocean, and we could hardly wonder that I'Anson has always kept his" Caller Ou"
impressions, as the breezes " fresh fra the Forth "
swept over us that July. On one side the yellow harvest fields of East Lothian were waving; and Dirle-
ton's woods grow green and fair down to the very edge
of the beach.   Following the " gently curving lines of
creamy spray" to the right, the eye rests on the Bass
Rock,—ever clangorous with sea fowl, and standing
out blunt and bare from its wave-washed base—and
the cone-like eminence of Berwick Law ; while the
distant range of the Fife Hills takes us back to
Johnny Walker and his " dearies" before his View
Halloo was heard at Wynnstay.

Zohrab and Co.   Like Ambo, who revelled over the
Mostyn mile, and Charity, the third
Great Liverpool Steeple Chase winner, some of the
best Gullane geldings took to the road at last. Wee
Willie, Zoroaster, and Clym-o'-the-Clough, all came
trotting out at the sound of the horn, to take their
turn in the fourteen miles an hour Defiance; and
Pyramid, who led out of Edinburgh, when two bay
and two greys, cross-fashion, was Mr. Ramsay's
delight, worked himself stone-blind in the cause.
The old Ury lion was roused once more in his lair,
and horsing this crack coach from Lawrencekirk
to Aberdeen, and driving it many a stage, was as
great a boon to him as getting up his dog Billy's
muscle for another fight, or going through solemn
pedestrian exercises, for the same end, with " my

friend Tom Cribb." Even the gravest Scottish coaching days. Edinburgh professors liked to see the Ramsay coaches with their rich brass-mounted harness, and the scarlets and white hats, when the dashing young owner was on the box, and Alick Cooke, Jim Kitchen, George Murray, and Jamie Campbell were the reigning favourites.

Mr. Ramsay hunted the Carnwath Inheritor and the Ramsay lot. country as well as the three Lothians, and as he did not scruple to give 1,500 gs. for Lanercost, 1,000 for The Doctor, and 850 for Inheritor, " Nimrod" might well find in him almost the only breathing embodiment of his memorable *Quarterly Review* labours. His Inheritor was an old-fashioned weight-carrying hunter, with very long quarters, and big ribs and gaskins, but with rather a light ewe neck, and thinnish shoulders. Blinkhorn the trainer always compared him to old Walton, and said that his " action spoke vengeance ;" and Harry Edwards, after he had won two Liverpool Cups on him in '37, declared that he had not been on such a horse since Jerry. In The Trades' Cup (in which he carried 9 st. 4 lbs. the highest weight it has ever been won with), he fairly kicked Snyders out of the race at the post, or as Harry phrased it in the weighing-house, " *We* just gave Snyders one-two for himself, and settled him." Vestment was a more chubby, but an unlucky sort of horse. He split his pastern, running with Queen of Trumps, and " turned over here and there," and finally received such a severe cut to the bone, that he died of a lock-jaw. Despot was long, low, and dark brown; very honest, but with no great constitution ; and The Doctor, by Doctor Syntax, out of a sister to Zohrab, had especially fine quality, with nice symmetry, and ability to carry weight.

Tom Dawson considers Lanercost the Lanercost. finest-grown two-year-old he ever saw,

and when he came up at that age to Tupgill, he
could hardly believe he was the same yearling, " all
belly and no neck," which he had seen at The Bush,
at Carlisle, just after Mr. Ramsay had given £130
for him, because he was by his horse Liverpool. In
fact, his crest became so muscular, that " we might
have put a saddle on and fitted it." As a two-year-
old, he was tried to do a good thing with Aimwell,
on the High Moor; but forcing him on for the trial
spoilt him, and he went all to pieces during the winter, and had no business to come out at Catterick.
His defeat there by Jemmy Jumps was a sad disappointment to the Carlisle division ; but the spirits of
his nominator, " Jim Parkin," never failed.

Mr. James Parkin.   This Cumberland Squire was a singu-
larly handsome man, of a commanding
height which quite carried off his bulk, and with
a fund of mellow humour which never seemed to
fail, whether in the hunting-field, on the coach-box,
the yeomanry parade, or at his own table. When
the great North Road was in its glory, and the Glasgow, the Edinburgh, and Portpatrick mails used to
be changing horses almost together in Carlisle each
afternoon, and " the little Glasgow mail," with its
two horses, achieved its thirteen miles an hour, then
was Mr. Parkin in his glory too. It was strange,
indeed, if he wasn't seen waiting at The Bush door,
with his low-crowned hat, and his hands in his capacious pockets, and a droll good-humoured word for
everybody, from baronet to ostler, to work one of
them to Penrith ; or if the night was peculiarly inviting, as far as Lancaster. If there was a steeple-
chase or a horse show, he would be in the thick of
it, keeping every one on the grin with his quaint
comments and suggestions. If a Cumberland
Eleven had to be carried to Greystoke, or anywhere,
to play a match, he would invariably get up a team
of greys to take them ; and it was said that he was

so sincerely disgusted when the rail was first opened
between Newcastle and Carlisle, that, having business among the Black Diamonds, he went down by
the coach to Borough Bridge, and got on to the
Newcastle mail there, and home again the same way,
thus nearly doubling the distance. In fact, he was
so fond of driving, that there was a county joke
against him, that when in London he sent in the
driver and conductor one night to have a glass,
and then, utterly regardless of passengers and time-
keepers, drove the omnibus four miles to Hammer-
smith without a check.

His bachelor home at Greenaways was quite a
curiosity-shop in the way of driving-whips and fox-
brushes, and many was the quiet little party he used
to have there in the days of the Inglewood Hunt.
The hounds were then kept in kennels on the banks
of Tarn Wadlin, where the pike and the cranberries
flourished together, and on summer evenings we
used to have drags right round the edge of the lake.
The hunting field would have seemed as nothing
without him and his grey; and although his weight,
which at one time was fully twenty stone, precluded
his going across country, his knowledge of short
cuts, and his power of knocking a padlock to pieces
with the butt-end of his whip, or getting off and
fairly crushing his way at one shove through a fence,
with the grey waiting on him, combined to make
him a very rare absentee at the Whaw-hoop. For
racing he did not care much; but he nominated
Lancercost for all his three-year-old engagements,
and made one of the Cumberland quartet, which
used to book the inside of the coach or mail, and
go to Catterick, Newcastle, and Doncaster, to see
him run that year. They held the firmest belief that
he would prove to be one of the best horses the world
ever saw, and that Harry Edwards, who was then
living at Carlisle as a vet., and getting occasional

mounts from Alderman Copeland, or John Scott's stable, was the only man who could get him out.

Lanercostiana. And so he did at Newcastle, but The Hydra who was "not in the same day with him at home," got so near him that Tom Dawson was far from satisfied. He began to come very quick after that, and he was tried very high with St. Andrew before the St. Leger. Flat, thin-soled feet were always his bane. Walking up and down in front of Belle Isle he got a stone the size of a bean into one of them, which nearly lamed him, and stopped him in his work for the Liverpool Cup; and the next year at Chester (the scene of his daring attempt as an aged horse to give the fresh four-year-old Alice Hawthorne 51lbs.), his soles were quite festered, and he was nearly on his head at the Castle Pole. I'Anson used to say that his feet were as good as stable-barometers at last, and that he would fall lame as if he knew it was going to be hard." He was gross and sluggish to a degree, but became less so with age, and " passed his life in great eating and great work." The heavier the weight the better he liked it, as the three most celebrated Scottish geldings Zohrab, Potentate, and Olympic discovered at Eglinton Park. In fact, it seemed to make him much more lively, and Colonel Richardson always declared that "with thirteen stone he would pull walking."

Outwitting St. Martin. An incident at Dumfries proves how Lord Exeter's invariable plan of having a cut at the favourite for the off chance, is far too often neglected. Lancercost had beaten St. Martin twice at the Caledonian Hunt, and the pair came on to Dumfries and were both entered in the Fifty Pound Plate. In his gallop, Lancercost fell lame, and I'Anson had only time to get to the boy, and tell him to slip him into Mr. Wilkins's stable close by, before any one found it out. The leg was so big, that it was quite thought that the back tendon had gone, but fomentations through the night reduced it sufficiently to let him just walk on to the course. St. Martin's party had not got wind of it, and brought their horse to the post merely to try for a compromise. Cartwright's orders on Lanercost were to walk from the post, and pull up if St. Martin offered to make a pace. He was spared the precaution, as Lye turned his colt round, the moment the word was given, and left Lanercost alone in his glory.

The rivalry for the Ayr Cup was then so great among the Scottish dons, that Mr. Ramsay dare not trust to The Doctor (although at 2st. he had upset a great Liverpool pot on Deception that year) when St. Bennett was to do battle for Eglinton Castle and Lanercost was accordingly prepared for it.

His four-year-old labours that Sep- *Labours of Laner-* tember and October were equal to those *cost.* of a Hercules. On September 4th, he duly did the needful for St. Bennett at Ayr, tried Easingwold for the St. Leger at Catterick, the morning after he got back to Richmond, and then walked off to Borough Bridge on his way to Doncaster. At Doncaster he won a Four-Year-Old Stake, and divided Charles XII. and Beeswing in that splendid Cup finish of two. The next week he was at the Liverpool Autumn, trying to give Melbourne a year and 4lbs. in the Palatine, and Cruiskeen a year and 39lbs. in the Heaton Park; and running second both times. Thence he was sent back immediately to Glasgow by sea, and won twice against Bellona and Malvolio at the Caledonian Hunt. From Cupar, where he arrived the night before running, he was vanned to Kelso, where Zohrab and Bellona were no use to him for the Berwickshire Gold Cup; and then through Hawick to Dumfries, where

St. Bennett and Malvolio met him separately,
but to no purpose, in the latter part of that week.
Mr. Ramsay thought that he had gone to run for
the Cesarewitch, but I'Anson dare not risk it, and
with true Scottish caution preferred the certainties
near home. This brings him up to October 18th,
and as his five races had been mere exercise gallops,
and he seemed to get tone every day, I'Anson determined to put his head Heath-wards for The Cambridgeshire on the 28th.

Winning the Cam-   Between Dumfries and Annan his
bridgeshire.   troubles began, by the breaking down
one of the horses of his three-wheel van, which
was hardly big enough for him when he was
travelling night and day. For the last seventy
miles he grew so weary, that he stood on
his toes with his heels up against the door, and
propping his loin as he could. Hence when he
reached Newmarket he was so paralyzed, that he
"could hardly be abused into a trot," and to coax
him out of a trot into a canter was quite out of
Noble's power. There was nothing for it but to
cover him up from nose to tail in his box, till the sweat
fairly poured off him, and he was so fresh two or three
days afterwards that he positively "wanted to go
shopping on his road to the course, and not through
the shop door either." Still he settled down at the
post, and if Mickleton Maid had not mettled him up
so tremendously by the pace she made for Hetman
Platoff, to whom he gave 11 lbs., Noble could never
have driven him in a sharp finish with such a speedy
customer as "Bowes's Bay." This was the maiden
year of the two great stakes, and although some
high weights and those three-year-olds have run
close up for them since, neither of them has been
won by any horse at 8st. 9lbs. Lord George might
well say, "What a wonderful animal he is! he neither
sweats nor blows!" and it only proves that race-

horses will generally do their best thing, when they have been a little off.

His career after that was as variable as ever. There was that short-head New-castle Cup victory over Beeswing, with "The Young 'un" so handy at the finish, that it did not speak very highly for either the Cumberland or Northumber-land crack. Then he was snapped by Jem Robin-son on Beggarman at Goodwood ; and then Beeswing set him a task twice over at Kelso. With the high weight and The Doctor in attendance he gave her no chance in the Cup, although Bob Johnson offered £20 to £10 on his mare and lost it to I'Anson ; but she would have infallibly won after the dead heat, as the short preparation told in two miles, and there was nothing to help that time. Next year he was carried out twice in the Ascot Vase, first when Zeleta, and then when Miss Stilton bolted, and could never reach Satirist ; and then he won the Cup, making all his own running. After he was beaten "over the bricks" at Newcastle by Bees-wing, there was an order to sell for £2,500, which I'Anson did not think nearly enough. Even-tually Mr. Kirby gave £2,800, with some contingency (as Mr. Ramsay always maintained) about sending two mares gratis. No one expected to see him out again in '42, but John Scott wound him up only to experience the same see-saw luck, a brilliant per-formance at Chester, and a poisoning at Ascot. His stud career in England tapered away to nothing, but we are beginning to think of him again in the even-ing of his days at Chantilly, and reflect on the folly of overdoing a horse when he first goes to the stud, when we see Cosmopolite winning under any weight, and note that the dam of Nutbush is by him.

His after-career.

Between Lanercost and his dog (for which Goody Levy offered £50 and would have gone on), a most devoted friendship existed.

The love of Laner-cost for a dog.

Lanercost and Cabrera walked half-way to Doncaster
together from Swinton before the meeting of 1841,
and then the former was sent by the Malton Road
to Pigburn, to be delivered to John Scott. The dog
took no notice of the severance at the time, but
during the Doncaster week he was missing. It
seems that although he had never been there before,
he went straight to Pigburn, found out Lanercost's
box among all the others in the different yards, and
rushed in at stable time. It was a question whether
horse or dog seemed most pleased at the meeting, and
although the latter was treacherously coaxed out
with a cat, he would not quit the yard. During the
night, he climbed to a loft above the horse, and after
revenging himself for the cat cheat on all Jacob's fer-
rets, he departed for Doncaster, and met the bell-
man, who was calling him, in French-gate. The
fox, which a too confident hostler would pitch against
him, and the gentleman who would have another
peep at Lanercost in the van as the horse was crossing the Mersey to Chester, did not forget this sentinel very easily, and his dog opponents seldom survived their engagements.

Blue Bonnet.   It is a curious coincidence respecting
Our Nell and Blue Bonnet, which won
the Oaks and St. Leger in '42 out of Tom Dawson's
stable, that neither of them had ever run in public
before, and neither of them ever won again. Blue
Bonnet broke down twice as a two-year-old, and was
thrown up instead of going for The Ham. Dawson
got her quite sound by the following August,
and as with The Biddy turned loose to make
running, she beat the five-year-old Charles XII.
by a head at 2st., and scattered Galanthus, Moss
Trooper, and Aristotle pretty widely over the
High Moor, Tom Dawson had every right not
to be much frightened of Attila " with his Goodwood race on him," on the St. Leger day.

Whitewall never received a thinner- Cotherstone.
fleshed yearling than Cotherstone from
Isaac Walker's hands, and at two years old he was
always amiss. He was very fat before Doncaster,
and The Era beat him in his trial. Bill Scott said
he went fast and tired, and when he did not get well
off in The Criterion, which was alike fatal to
"Daniel" and "The West," and only ran a dead-
heat for the Nursery, Mr. Bowes said, "*I'll sell*,"
and John Scott said "*I'll buy*." No bargain was
made, and after Christmas he went into work again,
with All Fours, and as he was "always on the old
horse's back, and he never deceived us," Bill was sent
for, and so were Sim, and Nat, and Frank, and "all the
swells." Bill got on Cotherstone and Cotherstone's trial.
followed the old horse, but in the bot-
tom he felt so satisfied that he had never been on so
good a colt, and that it was a sin to show him up,
that he swung him a little out of the course, and
left the rest, Parthian, Armitage, Greatheart, Castor
and Co. to finish as they liked. Sim was the only
one who was up to it, but Colonel Anson was quite
sceptical, even under Bill's assurance that "*I
could have won to York*." However, Mr. Bowes got
on at good odds to win £20,000, but then came
the teething troubles. The horse was sent to Newmarket for the Riddlesworth, "quite beautiful from
fever," and in such pain that for a week he would
only lick cold mashes, but the teeth came through
just in time, and Lye lost £700 on his Pompey
mount.

The Two Thousand made him a hot Attempt to hocus
first favourite for the Derby, and the him.
effort to get at him at Leatherhead was worthy of
adaptation at the Adelphi. The man with the little
bottle of stuff in his pocket who pretended to be
drunk, the foray of Bill (who was quite a police-ser-
geant on the occasion), and Markwell into a cockloft

under the pretence of wanting a bed, the squaring of the carpenter, the finding of poisoned oats in an old stocking on the top of a clock, and a packet of brown powders in the church porch, are all clearly part and parcel of a tremendous "sensation drama." However, it all ended well, and Bill declared that he could have won if necessary by fifty yards.

A visit at Althorp Paddocks. We had not seen Cotherstone for seventeen years since the day he broke down so heavily at Goodwood. Hence we combined the coming-in of the new Spencer hound era and the going-out of the old blood stock one, into the same day; and when our Brixworth survey was ended, we drove off through Chapel Brampton, past Harleston Heath—so dear to Payne and his Pillagers—and very soon exchanged the flags for the foals. The paddocks are partly at Harleston and partly at Althorp, in the proportion of fifteen acres to eighty; and the former were planned by Squire Andrew, after whom the sire of Cadland was named.

They are delightfully roomy and comfortable, with a sort of grey antiquity about them which takes one back insensibly to the old Grafton and Bunbury days; and if these young occupants do not quickly learn to recognize and love Mr. Wilson, in his white hat, blue blouse, and extensive beard they must be most deeply ungrateful for his care. His aspect was a little startling and Republican at first; but we found his flow of animal spirits and quaint vocabulary perfectly unimpaired under the coming parting from his brood mares. He has done a little jockeyship in his day, and it was on Helena by Rainbow from Urganda that, twenty-nine years ago, he won the first race ever run over Chantilly. Isaac Walker and he were originally at Bloss's together, and it is somewhat remarkable that the one should have had the nursing of Cotherstone in his foal-hood, and the other in his old age.

A noble avenue of trees leads from "Cotherstone Hall" right down to Al- *Cotherstone in retirement.* thorp House, and the sweet white Wicket, which was grazing with her Storm foal in the centre of it, gave a charm to the scene, which made us doubly regret that even the inauguration of the Pytchley era should entail the dissolution of the Cotherstone cabinet. The door of another shed bore a plate of Wryneck, which recorded in almost illegible characters how she won 300 sovereigns for his late Lordship at the Newmarket Craven of '44. This mare was from Gitana by Tramp, and the first he ever bought. It is about nineteen years since Mr. Wilson took the head of affairs, and then Gladiator came for a season. The first Earl Spencer (the Shorthorn and Exchequer Earl) bought Cotherstone for 3,000 guineas in '44, before he broke down at Goodwood; and when he arrived in his van, his fetlocks almost touched the ground. He is "not much of a dandy now;" but on seeing the well-known bit of blue, he came whinnying up for a recognition. As it happened, he was quietly grazing; but he is for ever on the move for a regular set of constitutionals, which consist in walking round and round his paddocks, or on the sunny side. Well may his friend observe that "he looks as if he was matched against Mountjoy, and had nothing to do but to make haste." His jumping up is his oddest trait, and he sometimes greets Mr. Wilson by going off all fore-legs, just like a lamb.

His blood colts and fillies have been about equal in numbers, but the first *His stock.* fourteen out of sixteen foals after the horse was thrown open to *bonâ fide* tenant farmers, all fell colts. True to his sire's charter, he has very seldom got a chesnut. His blood has hit well with Slane's

and Priam's, and Mr. Payne had no reason to re-
pent his Althorp fancy in Glauca's and Farthingale's
year. The old horse does not now reside in "Cotherstone Hall," from which Stilton and nearly eighty
more winners may be said to date, and the lamb
must have claimed the major part of his nature, as
he has not left a tooth-mark on the ledge of the
wood. Stilton was quite his best, and if he could
always have been wound up as he was for the Metropolitan, he would have fought Stockwell and Kingston hard for the supremacy of '52. He gave
Evadne and Paddy-bird, both of his year, 20lbs.
easily, but he never got off at Chester, and was not
in the race till quite at the finish. The Chester Cup
has always been an unlucky matter for Tom Dawson,
as he has been second five times, and once second
and third.

Orlando's maiden   Orlando's first race at two years old
race.   was a Produce Stake at Ascot, in which
there was five to four on him, and great betting. All the seven had orders to wait, and John
Day Junior, who was on Wetnurse, considered that go
or wait he would be out of it. Walking down to the
post, he heard Nat, who was very cautious in money
matters, propose to Rogers to hedge rides, and he
accordingly chimed in with, "*Well, if it's a good
thing for Sam, it's a good thing for me; you'd better
let me do the same.*" "*A very likely thing,*" said
Nat; "*your little pony has no chance.*" "*Well!
well!*" rejoined John; "*never mind, I'll stay you
up, though you are on such a grand one.*" Mr. Davis
started them; three-quarters of a mile over the Old
Course, but the only response they gave to his "Go"
was to stop and look at each other. "*Mind I've
started you!*" he observed, and left them; and on
they walked for a hundred yards. "*This is a pretty
thing! none of you seem inclined to take the lead;
shall I take it for you?*" said Young John. Then

Robinson struck in, *" For goodness' sake, John, canter or do something, or my horse will bolt."*

Thus encouraged, John led the phalanx, which were pulling all over the course, at a slow canter; but when his mare got her feet on to the road for the Brick Kilns, he struck the spurs in and stole fifty yards in an instant. The others had to begin then, and Nat upset his horse with following her. John stopped his mare at the distance, and let Orlando reach his girths, and when he heard Nat's " CHICK ! CHICK !" he knew that the little man had begun to drive the crack. He could only sit quiet and hold his mare, and she just won a neck, tiring every stride. The Stand thought it was a false start, and when General Peel went to ask John about it, he thought it best to refer him to Jim, " the schoolmaster." And well might they call him that, and agree that for patience and fairness in a race he was unrivalled.

One of John's most tremendous races was on Wiseacre, who was a terrible *Young John Day's win on Wiseacre.* horse to ride, and finally fell lame in his joints, and went to nothing. The Ham Stakes at Goodwood was a very remarkable finish, and the handling on that occasion was equal to Sam Rogers's celebrated Findon win of last year on Caterer. John's orders were not to be second, and he went and tried to catch them at the distance. Then he suffered, and made another effort half-way up, and crept to the girths of the leaders, without asking his colt a question. Firebrand and Barrier were beat on his right, and he just thought he might land him, and getting up inch by inch, he hit him twice and just won a head. Nat trotted back on Chatham under the firm impression that he had won, and it was in vain for Sam to try and undeceive him. *" John Day won ?"* he said; *" he was beat off at the distance, and I've never seen him since ;"* John was so weary with the job, that he

could hardly sit on his saddle, and after he won the
Prendergast, the stirrup broke, and he made a second
finish by going to grass.

Death of Fran-   Franchise was the first great winner
chise.   for Alfred Day, and it was by the merest
chance that she was trained at all.   A purchaser had
his offer of three in a straw-yard.   He chose the
other two, and left her, although she might have
been his for £20, and hence her owner trained her
in despair.   At last, she broke her near hind-leg
short off in a gallop near Sadler's Plantation ;
the leg spun round in the air, nearly hitting her lad,
and she was left staggering on three, till William
Day galloped home for a pistol and shot her through
the head, as soon as there was a moment's cessation
in the plunging.

"Running Rein"   Of the fictitious hero of "The Run-
& St. Lawrence.   ning Rein year," a celebrated character
still observes most feelingly, " *What is the use of winning a Derby, if they don't let you have it ?*"   He was
own brother, it is supposed, to one of our most
celebrated runners ; and he got upset in his van
on boardship, and died soon after he was taken off.
Such at least is the legend of this dark offender.
St. Lawrence was one of the Irish division originally,
and began by running second for the Madrid Stakes.
No horse was nicer to wait with, and like Sweetmeat, a jockey could put him just where he liked.   He
never varied a pound from his form all the time that
he kept the clock at Danebury, and save and except
the yellow bay Spume, on whom he won fifteen
races, there was none that Young John loved better
to ride.   Speed was his point, and he never showed
it in a higher degree than when he beat Garry-Owen,
who gave him only 5lbs., over the T.Y.C.   He arrived at Danebury when he was four years old,
and became such "a calculating boy," that if he

found he couldn't reach home he would stop in the last hundred yards, and he did so in the Suffolk Stakes, and again across the Flat in the Craven.

The story of The Baron is somewhat on all fours with Touchstone's, but as the play-bills have it, "a period of eleven years elapses." John Scott was again on the Liverpool Stand with Earl Wilton and another nobleman, when he saw the chesnut beaten. He was as fat as a bull, and had bar-shoes and fearfully festered soles, and had been made twice the savage he was by muzzles. Still "The Wizard" thought he had a St. Leger in him. And so he went to Malton, and a very rough snappish customer they thought him at first. He was well physicked and then rammed along behind old All Fours, and as John Scott says, "took more work than I ever gave a horse in my life, and required more management." He was tried at Pigburn at the St. Leger distance to give As You Like It a stone, and did it with nearly a length to spare.

Iago, the Whitewall Leger horse of the next year, was quite as game, but he wanted speed. Still he would have outstridden the lazy Poynton at York, if Cartwright, who was riding Sheraton, had not got at the brown's girths for the honour of Mr. Meiklam and the stable, and given him three such stinging strokes on the quarters, that the horse, although one of his sinews had been cut by a hoof-hit in the race, dare not dwell any longer. Templeman was hard at him at the time, little looking for such a Blucher to aid him. Iago was rather short and high-legged, but for a horse of that make he stayed well. His head and back were beautiful, and his temper very good, but his stock were generally very short of temper and wind as well.

The B. Green two-year-olds. B. Green's and the Grafton scarlet were in every one's mouth in '47, and Hambleton began at last

> " To raise its head for endless spring,
>   And everlasting blossoming,"

till Voltigeur's Derby knocked it out of time. The party of which the ex-Manchester traveller was the ostensible chief had some thirty-five in training, and won thirty-two two-year-old races. In fact, every two-year-old they brought to the post that year contrived to rub off his maidenhood. At Chester in '49, they won ten races, the Cup among the number, with the eccentric Malton, who would not go into a stable, unless the door was a very wide one, and would then canter right in. Sometimes they could manage him blindfolded, but to make matters all right at Chester, they hired a coach-house. Teddy Edwards and Winteringham did the riding part for the stable, and Basham, who first rode as a feather at Stockton-on-Tees in '45, on sister to Andover's dam, had a few light-weight mounts.

Two-year-old trials. The confederacy gave £500 for Assault, the same for Chaff and Flatcatcher, £350 for Beverlac, and £150 for Swiss Boy; and acting on the approved fashion, bought their own brothers the next year. They tried them in November, but B. Green did not care to go and see it come off. " *It's no use my going to see it,*" he used to say; "*you can tell me what's first,*" and he comforted himself at home with his snuff and cigars. He also delighted in whist and billiards, and was very clever in watching the market, and managing his betting-lists. Before the trial, it was quite expected that Beverlac, who wanted no spurs, was the best of the three, but Assault won by two or three lengths, and Beverlac was beaten as far from Flatcatcher. The second trial ended the same way, and their forms never changed till Burlesque knocked up Assault, and he could never be got sound again. The trial was kept so quiet, that the public rather stood Beverlac, and 15 to 1 was taken about him at Chester for the Derby, a year before the race! Harry Stebbings had always an immense opinion of Flatcatcher, but he overdid it with him, especially in the St. Leger, by not giving Robinson waiting orders; and he refused, it was said, £3,000 from the French Government for him.

Danebury seemed sadly down on its luck in the early part of '46, as Old John was very ill at the Gloucester Coffee-House, and there were only twelve horses in training. Such a remarkable lot never followed each other at exercise before, as five of them won two Derbies, two Oaks, a One Thousand, two Newmarket Stakes, and four of the great cups; and Conyingham a future Two Thousand winner came later on in the year. Pyrrhus the First was bought as a foal with his dam Fortress for £300, after Old England was tried, and was half Mr. Gully's. Cymba and Mendicant were also there, but Cossack was the best of the bunch. John Day first heard of him from Dilly, when he was at Northampton races, and consented to accompany him to Mr. Elwes's of Billing, and look at two Hetman Platoffs for Mr. Payne.

The purchase of Cossack.

Dilly liked the brown, but thought the chesnut rather upright before, and too small as well. His companion was greatly taken with the latter, and after trying in vain to get him for £200 and a Derby contingency of £1,000, he sent a 200 guinea cheque, and sold the colt for the same sum to Mr. Pedley during the Gorhambury meeting. Mr. Elwes had asked Charles Marson to go and have a look at them, and Mr. Coape, who trained with him, would have bought them, but he did not just fancy the blood, and although he went past the very Park wall, he did not even care to look in. Had he got Cossack, the first and second for the '47 Derby would have been in his stable, and the heavy War Eagle hit would have been averted.

War Eagle.

Valentine threw all her stock leggy, and War Eagle was no exception, and fully sixteen-one. He pitched in his slow paces, but for a mile he was immensely fast, and if he was held, he would run on, but not go far when he was once in distress. His finest turn of speed was when he cut down Volley from the post at Doncaster. In the Cup he followed The Hero " just like clock-work," and came the moment Sam Mann touched him with the spur. Mr. Payne said of his Newmarket Stakes race with Cossack, that it was the fastest he ever saw. It was in fact like two races, as the pair came right away by themselves leaving a cloud of dust behind them. Mr. Bouverie would not hear of War Eagle waiting, but ordered him to " come away and beat them right out." War Eagle had a little the best of the start, on the whip hand, but they were soon at it, head and head, all the way up the cords. Sim never moved, but "felt for him," and when his horse answered his hand so truly, he felt sure that the Derby was over.

Cossack was a delightful horse to ride, never pulling, and always as ready as a shot, when he was wanted. A strong pace was his delight, and he could make it for himself, and except when War Eagle headed him coming down the hill, he led in the Derby from The Warren to the winning-post.

The Hero.

Hero was quiet when in front, and rather too free if he was behind, and liked to run big and above himself. He was rather shelly at three, but he thickened amazingly afterwards. In wet ground he could not move at all, and Footstool made a sad exhibition of him at

York in consequence. Young John Day was on him in his first race, the Woodcote Stakes, and his last the Goodwood Cup, and he has used one or two good hunters by him, Nelson to wit, with his harriers. Still as a sire he was not very valuable, as his stock from thorough-bred and half-bred mares ran rather small, and when fever in the feet set in, and he could hardly move in his box, he was vanned down to Hermit Lodge, where his Grace the Duke of Beaufort stays during the Stockbridge week, and shot and buried in the garden.

Chanticleer was a horse of great con-stitution, but always touched in the temper, and in fact "a perfect mad horse," when I'Anson first got him at Liverpool. Robertson stuck to his head in one of his frenzies, but he became so bad at last, that they were glad to get the lad out of the horse box by the window. He had thrown himself down in the box, and the stall had to be taken out before he would consent to go in it again. When he got to Hambleton, Harry Stebbings used to say, that he would just as soon be off the Moor when he was on; but I'Anson gradually got him quiet, and in the next year he did all his best things. Still he would not go up a passage, but roar his dissent like a bull, and kick by way of variation for a whole day. He was a free goer, and had fine pace, and if he was above himself he could stay with most of them, and go equally well on hard and soft ground.

Chanticleer.

Two miles over the flat suited Canezou best, but still she could stay much fur-ther if she had assistance. She always wanted much management in her training, and so did Springy Jack, a nice smart goer, but as heavy-fleshed as a bull, and quite competent and willing to eat up to his weight. There never was such a somnolent horse, as he would lie down and go to sleep for two or three

Canezou and Springy Jack.

hours, as soon as he had emptied his manger, and no training could keep his legs in order, with such an ever increasing top. Butler seldom rode a horse more desperately from the distance than he did him for the Great Yorkshire, and finished on him bareheaded; but Maid of Masham was not to be got rid of. If a jockey only sat as still as Sim did that day, she was one of the sweetest mares to ride, but a great martyr to windgalls in the knees, which were so bad that Tom Dawson did not wish her to run. And well he might not, as she took nearly an hour bringing on to the course from Middlethorpe, and they had to knock her about most unmercifully to get her warm.

Maid of Masham.

For Ellerdale, who won this stake for the same stable the year before the York course seemed to have a hidden charm, and she never seemed so unsettled, when she had to run there, as she generally did during her absence from Middleham. She was a delicate, second-class mare, and rather lacking in speed. Tom Dawson always says that her's is the only case he ever saw of a sinew slipping inside the hock. It occurred when she was at exercise, and she pulled up on three legs, and kicked so furiously from the pain, that he quite thought she had broken her leg. Full a fortnight elapsed before she could touch the ground, and she was trained no more. At the stud she threw winners to everything she was put to; and in the first five seasons, Ellermire, who beat the speediest field that has been seen in modern days at York, Ellington, Wardersmarke, Gildermire, and Summerside came in succession. Never did anything look more thoroughly the type of an English brood-mare as she walked into the Grimston ring, with the well-nurtured 1,500 guinea Nugget, looking as big as herself, at her side, and gazed round for the last time

Ellerdale.

at her Yorkshire admirers. It was 500 to 600 in no time, and so on to 1,120 guineas, but the untried Gildermire quite overlapped her, and got up to 1,260 guineas.

Such bidding quite petrified an old tyke, who was wandering round the outer circle. " *Oh, dear ! it beats me !"* he observed, resting on his staff; " *these gentlemen—they get fuller of money at the latter end of the day;"* and could only account for it by saying that she was such " *a well performed mare."*

The Yorkshire mind had been stirred to its utmost depth by attempts to solve the great problem, whether Stockwell would sell for more than " Westy." With true local pride they hoped he would not, but yet they felt sure he would, and the speculation in *crowns* and pots principally ran on the point whether or not the chesnut would touch five thousand, and the brown four.

Sale of Stockwell and West Australian.

St. Albans brought the former gallantly up, and the thousand soon became four thousand five hundred. We never heard such a price bid in a ring before, and yet there was no apparent enthusiasm. All of it was reserved for "The West." " *Here comes the pick of England,"* said they, as he emerged from a gate behind, and strode with his beautiful white reach head aloft into the ring. There was quite a thrill as the biddings slowly rose to three thousand, and a sort of burst of suppressed impatience and vexation when no one could beat Count de Morny. " *He can't be released,"* said a tyke close by us, in such a melancholy strain, and down went the hammer. There was quite a fond rush after him for a last view, but somehow or other he is only an ordinary horse to look at when his head is out of sight; and his stock, considering the chance he has had, justify the dubious verdict passed upon them when they first came out five summers since at

Tattersalls'. And so this grand sale passed into history; and when shall we see 20,689 guineas again made in one afternoon, twenty-three brood-mares averaging 409½ guineas, one brood-mare and her two brood-mare daughters making 2,990 guineas, and three St. Leger winners, chesnut, brown, and roan, standing up to the hammer in the self-same ring?

The late Lord Londesboro'. When all was over, we strolled quietly across the Park—so fresh and beautiful from the rain, that leaving such a spot made death seem doubly terrible—and lingered for a few minutes near the house, among its rich ribbon borders, its laurel banks, and its grotto.

The Armourer, with a skin as dark as Saladin himself, conducted us among his glorious collection of sword-breakers, thumb-screws, and coats of mail, and tried in vain to stir us up to enthusiasm upon horns of tenure and Damascus blades; and anon we took refuge from positively the last shower of the evening, under the gigantic tree which shades the remains of the retriever Sal, the faithful companion of the late Lord "in all his changes of residence and fortune."

The paddocks joined the Grimston plantation on our left, and just above the wall we could see the top of the gilt coronets surmounting the private gate which communicated between the two. His brood-mares were his Lordship's delight, and even his yacht Ursula, which won the Emperor of the French's cup, ranked second. In his days of comparative health he was always in his paddocks, on his bay pony, chatting to Jack Scott, and watching the yearlings as they ripened for Tattersall's; and when he could ride there no longer, he would be among them in his pony carriage. An accident in rook-shooting, which sprained or broke a small tendon in his foot, was the beginning of his last illness, and with the consequent loss of active exercise, his gradual break-up commenced, and no sea-breezes could fan him back to health. He left Grimston in September, and slept there but one night the following month, and then he bade good-bye for ever to the place which of all others he loved best. Grimston church is pulled down, and another has been erected on the site to his memory. The family vault is in an enclosure by itself, just to the right of the churchyard. Four small trees, cypress or arbor vitæ, mark the corners, and at the upper end a honeysuckle, which had half-fallen from its hold on the wall, leant over, and pointed almost to the exact spot in the vault, which contains that pale, fragile form we all remember so well.

Van Tromp was an exceedingly idle horse, and not at all deficient in speed. *Van Tromp.* The St. Leger day was his best, and he had won his race a mile from home. Marlow had backed him for the Derby for £200 after his race with Wanota in the Mersey Stakes, but he did not think him in his Liverpool form, when he saw him at the Derby post, and felt most keenly that any slur in the public mind should have ever been thrown on Marson. On the St. Leger day, he was quite a different horse, and we can only summon up three or four during the last twenty-five years that seemed to our mind just so ripe on the day. Marlow always considered that "The Dutchman" stayed better as he grew older, but that his staying arose rather from the fact that his speed was so tremendous that no horse could get him out, than from innate gameness, and hence for a really hard cup fight, when both were in their prime, he would have preferred being on Van Tromp. Never did horse win an Ascot Cup in such unflinching style as Van; but if Nat had persisted in waiting to the Stand, instead of trying to take up the running soon after the last turn, when he got nearly a length, Marlow would never have got a pull, and Van could never have answered to the whip as he did. Single-handed, Chanticleer ought always to have got the last run and beaten him, but still there was hardly 3lbs. between them either way.

Marlow and The
Dutchman.   Marlow's experience has been a pretty extensive one.   He looked after Waterwitch when Lye rode her for the Oaks, and spurred her almost in the hips.   His maiden victory was won when he was a lad at Lord Warwick's, on Gab at Cheltenham, beating his beloved Waterwitch, who, however, furnished him with win No. 2 before long. Still even his maiden win did not delight him so much as when he first got on The Dutchman (who was fully 21lbs. better than Elthiron), and followed Van Tromp up the gallop.   They only went half speed, but he returned him with "*Well! Mr. Fobert, I was never on such an one as this before.*"   Marlow never rode him in a trial, and always with a curb, as hard pulling was one of his specialties, and he once took the bit in his teeth, and gave Jack Sharpe a rough ride of it on Middleham Moor.   His stride was immense, and he always showed his fore shoes, but as a two-year-old, nothing could ever make him gallop except Escalade at Liverpool, and although he won by a length, Marlow smiled to himself when he read how "cleverly" or "easily" it was done, and noted how the seers dwelt all winter on "the fact, that this magnificent son of Bay Middleton has never been extended."

The Dutchman's
Derby race.   At the Derby, Marlow lay in the middle of his horses up to the mile-post, and found that he could beat all before him.   Round the turn, Hotspur came up so unexpectedly on the right, and so like a winner, that for the moment Marlow could not make out what it was.   Nothing was in the race after the turn, but the two and Tadmor; and as the Dutchman seemed all muddled and confused

in the deep ground, and perfectly inactive in comparison with his old self, there was but one thing, viz., "to sit and suffer." Hotspur went over the dirt like a swallow, and showed no signs of coming back till within three strides of home, when Marlow, who had a length to get, struck his horse twice (the only time in his life that he ever touched him), and the last stride gave him the short neck. He was quite sure he had won, as he said to the lad who was waiting for him, "*Old fellow! it's a tight fit, but I've just done it.*" Whitehouse is not certain upon the point to this day, but Marlow has no further remark to offer when he begins, than "*You won at the wrong place, George; you didn't win at Judge Clark.*" In the St. Leger, deep as the ground was, The Dutchman won all the way. The course exactly suited him, and he could have almost trotted in, if there had been a bet depending on it. He also won his match as he liked, and the Ascot Cup proved that Marlow had not overstated his hopes, when he said to Butler, who had a wonderful belief in Canezou that week, "*You'll see what a mess I'll make of you to-morrow.*" Arthur Briggs visited the great brown in France, and found him in what English trainers call "the condemned cells," near The Baron and Cossack, but he looked quite down, and very unlike his old Middleham or Rawcliffe self. With such views as our neighbours entertain on stallion exercise, it could hardly be otherwise. Still they contrive to breed many of their racers, with far better substance than we do.

His principal three-year-old rival, Vatican, was as full of quality as horse could be, but latterly quite the victim of temper. He nearly worried one lad walking from Ely, and savaged another in a corner. On a race-course he was very difficult to saddle, and once got loose at York, with his bridle off among the ditches. They

Vatican.

P

at last built a place at Hambleton, supported by pillars, where he could stand and hit nothing when he kicked. He was coy and very savage with his mares, and contrary to the usual rule, loved the satin-coated ones, and they had to use bluffs and all manner of double leading-rein expedients for service. As is often the case with very irritable horses, his stock were washy and small, and the fine cross of Slane and Venison was in his case quite thrown away.

Surplice.

Among the ten St. Leger winners, whose plates keep off the witches from the stable-doors of the Turf Tavern, the home-bred Surplice must not be forgotten, albeit we have got him a year out of his turn. He was a very early foal of January 24th, and Lord George took some Derby double event bets about him at Goodwood that July, and liked him still better when he got his measure at the end of the next year. He was then fifteen hands and rather leggy, and had arrived at

Accidents to Surplice.

that maturity in the face of two accidents, which made Cunningham tremble in his shoes. The first snow shower he was out in terrified him so much, that he dashed at a wall and performed a complete somersault into an adjoining garden. That did him no harm; but when he was being lunged he made a slip, and lay for a few seconds with his fore and hind feet right away from him, in such a perilous position, that it seemed all over with his back. Luck favoured him again, and he rolled on to one side and picked himself up unscathed.

The roaring humour.

No colt had a sweeter temper, and he was such a rare walker that he could almost get four times round the ring, when Loadstone and the other yearlings were doing it thrice. Nat and Butler paid him a visit when he was a yearling, and informed Colonel Anson and Lord George that, from the throppling noise he made in grazing, he must be a roarer. His Lordship stopped at the paddocks on his way from Welbeck to the races next morning, specially to listen; but as nearly all the other fourteen were similarly afflicted, he comforted himself with the thought that "*they can't all be roarers,*" and listened to these augurs of ill no more.

Siberia, the dam of Troica and Comfit, was Lord Zetland's first racer, and he gave only £35 for her, which was about the price paid for his Nickname by Ishmael, the dam of Augur and Castanette, and the grandam of Fandango. This old mare was eventually given to Bobby Hill, who sold her to Mr. John Bowe of Richmond, the breeder of El Hakim. Mr. Jacques had her next, and in his hands, she bred Massaniello, for which a thousand was refused as a yearling. Comfit's death was quite a tragical one. A gamekeeper had hung his white pony to the gate of the paddock in which she was grazing, and the mares became alarmed. Comfit arrived in a gallop at the gate, and tried to take it in her stride. She was within a month of foaling to Newminster at the time, and catching the top-bar with her fore-legs, she rolled over and broke her shoulder. Staggering on through the wood and holly bushes, she reached the door of her old stable and fell. She was carried to a short distance, and the foal, a fine colt, was taken from her immediately, but some little delay occurred in tying up the navel, and it lost a pint of blood and died.

Although the mares were pretty good and bred well, the Voltaire colts did not rank very high when Martha Lynn threw Barnton and Voltigeur to him. They were generally heavy-necked and heavy-fleshed, and it was these peculiarities which made Lord Zetland and one or two more of the Jockey Club men dislike Voltigeur, when

Beginning of the Aske Stud.

Death of Comfit.

Voltigeur.

Bobby Hill marked him as a yearling at Doncaster, and begged his Lordship to have a look at him. Their verdict was pretty well confirmed, when the colt came up before Mr. Tattersall's, and the " *Take him away!*" soon boomed forth, as not a soul there would give a hundred. And so he went back to Hart, to Mr. Stephenson's great disappointment, and he might have been cut for the hunting field, if Mr. John Brown (a nephew of " British Yeoman and Black Diamond Blakelock") had not once confided to Mr. Williamson, when they were out coursing near Sedgefield, that if he could only have it trained by Robert Hill, who had once looked after his uncle's horses, he would buy a racer forthwith, and that he had something in his eye.

Purchase and trial of Voltigeur.   Lord Zetland consented to allow the colt to come to Aske, on condition that he was lent to Mr. Williamson, and accordingly he arrived about the time of the next Catterick races. He was put along quietly till his Richmond engagement drew near, and then tried to give Castanette, who had just won at Doncaster, 12lbs. and a year over three-quarters of a-mile. His victory was so hollow, that they thought it could not be right, and tried them over again next morning with the same result. He had always thinnish soles, and ran these trials and his Richmond race in bar shoes, but Lord Zetland had him plated, and for the third time within the fortnight he was called upon to give the mare the same weight. His Lordship came to see the trial this time, and had Ellen Middleton put in to make a pace, and Cantab to scramble where he could with 16lbs. less than the crack, who had a white hood on and positively came in alone.

" *This is awful; we ought all to be downright 'shamed of ourselves,*" groaned poor Bobby when he saw his stable so completely cleaned out. It came off over Richmond about two o'clock in the afternoon, but

there was not a strange eye, save that of Mr. Rich,
M.P., to see it, and his sporting constituents were
not one whit wiser when the shades of evening descended. Their trial determined his Lordship to
give the £1,500, which was asked, with a £500 contingency, on each of the great events, and the luck
of "the spots" began.

Bobby Hill, who had a very intui- *Bobby Hill's train-*
tive perception of all stable matters, *ing notions.*
went at him forthwith, and never had a man a finer
bit of stuff to work upon, as he was never known to
have a cough or a swelled leg. To keep up a perpetual warfare against the latter was a great point
with Bob, and his favourite elixir was turpentine
and cream. He gum-bandaged nearly every horse
he had. If a privileged person asked him his rea-
sons on that head, he would reply: "*They're a
vast deal better for't.*" If a non-privileged individual
presumed to do so he would answer short: "*to keep
'em reet, to be sur.*" He was not the man to let
his horses be idle; but be his system what it
might, the three-year-old Voltigeur throve under
it. He could sweat week after week with twelve
stone, lad and all on his back, and quite deserved
his most glowing eulogy, "*his* legs and feet, my
Lord, is like *hiron.*"

When he had fairly broken down *Voltigeur at*
Castanette, he was carried on by St. *Epsom.*
Anne, but nothing came with him to Epsom. Job
had not a regular engagement from his Lordship in
'49, and did not ride in the trials, but he had been
sent for, early the next spring, and seen enough
to make him tell his Lordship and Mr. Williamson
at Catterick, that "*I think we'll be about winning
the Derby.*" "*He'll never gallop again till he gallops for t'money,*" said Bob, when he gave his colt
the wind up on the Friday before Epsom, and he
kept his word. The touts put out a very different

tale, and (although he had never been at more than half-speed) it was all over London on the Sunday, that he couldn't follow an Epirus gelding of Lumley's, which was lent to lead him up the gallop, and he went back to 30 to 1.

The Eglinton party, who were strong in their Mavors faith, declared that he had no muscle, but other eyes scanned him before the Wednesday, and he came back to sixteens. He was within an ace of being scratched on the Monday from sundry heavy forfeits attaching to his nominator, and there was a doubt as to whether Job could be released from another engagement to ride him, but the right resolve was taken, and the Aske housemaid who stood him, simply because he had "such a nice dark satin coat," won her money like a woman and a Britoness. Rhadulphus worked him between the two events, and as Doncaster drew nigh, those who consulted Bobby received these words for their comfort: "*He's fit for't job,*" or "*He's going tremendious slap.*"

Bobby's Lightfoot fancy.   The latter expression was most freely applied by Bobby to Lightfoot before Chester next year. He observed at exercise one day, "*Bedad, Mr. Williamson, that colt's a nailer; he stretched Voltigeur's neck as sure as I'm sitting on this galloway.*" John Gill thought he had got a Derby line for Neasham by trying him to give a Red Deer colt of the same year 19lbs. cleverly; and the latter was accordingly borrowed and tried at the same relative weight with Lightfoot. Voltigeur was put in to secure a pace, at weights for age with Bobby's delight (who received 9lbs. from Rhadulphus,) and pulled it off by a length, and it was all that Rhadulphus could do to beat the young'un, while the Red Deer colt cut up awfully. Job was on the young 'un, and rode him out severely to the finish. His trial seemed both to Gill and the Aske party to make him within 3 or 4lbs. of a Derby winner's form, but his Dee

Stakes exhibition was fearful, and he never could really gallop again. Hunting he managed fairly enough, and while Mr. Bell kept hounds, he performed very well with a whipper-in, and is still, we believe, at Thirsk.

Voltigeur's heart went next, and George Wallace and Hauxwell, who knew how *Voltigeur's decline.* gallantly he was wont to face that severe finish from the race-course, into the Aske grounds, found to their sorrow that he began to fail " from the Sweating Gates." It was all very well for poor Bobby to menace them with the pitchfork if they told any one ; the brown's match fate was sealed, and when they tried him after his defeat, Rhadulphus told them that he was fully a stone below his Doncaster Cup form. His stock, which are generally whole coloured, whatever the mare may be, inherit his tendency to be thick-necked (which he gets from Voltaire), with his very fine substance, moving, and temper. It is difficult to say, as it was with him, whether speed or staying is their especial forte ; but there is too often an unsound one among them ; and they take an immense deal of preparation.

His finest nick was with Mr. Chilton's *Vedette.* Birdcatcher mare, and from it came Vedette, with Blacklock blood on both sides. Seeing that luck had attended Mr. Bowes's nomenclature, he began the world as " West Hartlepool." Nothing could have been more unpromising than his yearling look, as his head was big, his middle like a brood mare's, and his hocks very far behind him, and hence much as his Lordship liked the blood, he wavered for some time, till Mr. Williamson used all his eloquence in favour of "the ugly one." At last the £250 went the right way, and unpromising as the beginning seemed, it is doubtful whether such a horse has ever been at Aske. He had quite as little notion as Fandango of leaving off, and for pace and staying as well, if the trainers and jockeys were polled, he would have as many votes as Voltigeur. When the chronic rheumatism was not troubling him, few had such action, and as he went with his head down, he seemed to " get all he stretched for."

He was the last horse that Job Marson ever rode in public, and Job told the stable that Voltigeur the second had been found at last. His first great trial was at Catterick before the Two Thousand at even weights, a mile and a-half, with Ignoramus and the four-year-old Gaudy, while Skirmisher received 7lbs. He just won it, but when he and Ignoramus were put together again over two miles of the same course, he gave Lord Fitzwilliam's horse 16lbs., and beat him half-a-length. This course proved fatal to both of them at last, as well as seven others from Aske, including Sabreur, Zeta, and Fandango, and in every instance it was the left leg which went.

Waking up Sabreur. Sabreur did not run at two years old; at three his action was odd; and the attempts to prepare him did not improve it. Bivouac gave him a stone, and did what he liked with him before Newcastle the next year. He was only prepared for a mile, and he showed no speed whatever in the Member's Plate; and as a forlorn hope, they decided to give him a gallop for " The Guineas."

There must have been an immense reserve of power about the horse, which he did not know how to use. As fate willed it, Ticket-of-Leave gave him a kick inside the thigh, just as they left the post. It might have broken his leg, but it did not, and mettled him up to such an extent, that he rushed through his horses, and the jockeys having no telescopes with them, saw him no more. In fact, he won by nearly half-a-distance, and although he was lame for a week after pulling up, he had his nerve fairly kicked into him. He never lost it, and his form and stride ever after were thoroughly altered.

Between him and Bivouac this happy kick made a difference of two stone, *His trial at Richmond.* and when he had a rough Cup course gallop on Richmond race-ground, ten days before York, he cantered away from Volatile with 2 st., Vanquisher with 18lbs., and Bivouac with 14lbs. less. The thing was done so openly, and so easily, that, although the public saw it, they had not the least idea what it meant. The Newcastle mode of cutting down the field did not answer at Doncaster, and the orders were given under the impression that it would be a false-run race, to suit The Wizard, who would be trying to stop the pace, if possible. It has, indeed, been singular ill-luck for " the spots," that after being disappointed of Rogers for Ivan, and just losing by a head—that neither Vedette nor Fandango should have been in the St. Leger, and that Sabreur should have cut himself down.

Nunnykirk was " a fair horse—nothing more," with slack loins, a sweet *Nunnykirk.* head, and still sweeter action. His brother Newminster was not so pretty, but better ribbed up. He was tried with the Exotic filly in the spring, and John Scott thought him a great horse, but he ran dead amiss for the Derby, and equally so at York, and even on the St. Leger day, he was not really himself. In fact, he was never exactly able to show what he could do. He went near the ground, with great leverage from behind, and his style of creeping along without any bustle was quite beautiful to see. We shall not easily forget watching him as he stole down from the distance in his canter, little as we expected that he could bring Aphroditè to grief. He was a bad walker, quite, in fact, one of the "kick up a sixpence school;" and Sir Tatton thought his slow paces so bad, that he declined the offer of him at twelve hundred. He

won no more after the St. Leger, and as a sire he
has knocked Teddington quite into the shade.   To
our minds, Oldminster, who spent his yearling life
in the Jervaux Abbey paddocks with Dictator
and Stanton, is the most perfect model that he ever
begot.

Teddington.

Sir Joseph saw Teddington at three
years old, and was wonderfully struck
with his action, and bought him with the mare from
a blacksmith, at Stamford, for £250, and a thousand
contingency.   He was a trifle clubby in one foot,
and had to wear a long shoe, but he very early
wound himself into the affections of Sir Joseph's
old groom, by the style in which he walked away
from all the others, when they were in the breaking
bridle, a test which is in nineteen cases out of twenty
almost the only sound one, by which a yearling's
horoscope can be cast.

His yearling form.

Sir Joseph made no bad bargain
when he took Fernhill, Sponge, and
everything else, at Fyfield, down to furniture and
stable-fittings, from Mr. Parr, for £3,000.   The
place, with its church tower and straw-thatched
buildings to the left, looks just like the snug home
of a well-to-do rector, with a strong tendency to
stock and white crops. There was only room for eight
horses there; but the bricklayers were soon set to
work, and now the accommodation is multiplied
eight-fold.   Fourteen yearlings came up from the
Leybourne Grange Paddocks in the autumn of the
next year, and of these a Venison colt, from Haitoe,
was the only one which did not win, or show some
running form. Teddington, The Ban, Aphroditè,
and Merry Peal were the most noticeable among
them, and The Confessor did not join company
for a month or two later. Teddingon's near
fore foot was still rather of the donkey order, and
although, by constant paring and attention, it was

got nearly right, there is a remarkable difference in the size of his plates, which remain as trophies on Alick Taylor's sideboard. As a yearling, he was always getting his head up, and running away with the boy, and hence his trainer was obliged to mount him for the first three weeks himself, at exercise, to get him a little into order. He had a rough gallop with the two-year-old Slang in November: but he did not seem up to his business, and was beaten a long way. In March they were tried again at 21lbs., and Teddington won so easily, that they were put together at evens, and with nearly the same result.

No jockeys rode trials at Fyfield in Sir Joseph's day, and five boys never His two-year-old trials with had a grander spin than when Tedding- Aphroditè, &c. ton, Aphroditè, Storyteller, Confessor, and The Ban finished in that order, with little more than a length between the lot. Teddington had half a length the best of it; but the very natural impression followed that all five were moderate. General Peel then lent his four-year-old Ione, which had cleaned out his two-year-olds at 10lbs.; but at 7lbs., Teddington finished a length in front of her; and when he tried her at evens, and three-quarters of a-mile, over again, he had just a head the best of it. He was short, and on high legs, the only form in which a short horse generally proves a clipper; but unlike most short horses, he never began well. On the whole, his two-year-old season, what with his tumble and his very close wins, was not a very prosperous one. After Goodwood he was thrown up in a box till October, and with Bacchanalian to lead him, went on till before his Newmarket race, when he was tried to be better than Vatican at 21lbs.

His Derby trial. Aphroditè, who was not remarkable as a stayer, was never measured with him after two years old, and in the great Derby trial on Middle Down, he gave 6 lbs. to Vatican, ran with Storyteller at evens, and gave Ban 21lbs., and Gladiole 2st. Gladiole forced the running at her best pace, but Vatican and Teddington (who was pulling over him) caught her half-a-mile from home, and the chesnut won so easily, that Taylor might well tell Fobert, when they met at Epsom, that now he knew through Vatican that he had a second Dutchman at last.

Derby anxieties. In fact, Sir Joseph thought the trial too good. A week before the Derby "the quicksilver fell," as the front of the shin of his off fore leg festered and filled all round. Stopping him, perhaps, did him good in every way, and the leg came all right; but he rather fretted with the change of stable at Epsom, and would do nothing more than pick the split peas out of a little corn, on the Derby morning. Still his heart was all right, and as Job said, "*I had only to spur him once to get him out near the turn.*" He came with such vengeance, that he almost ran over Ariosto. "*Where are you going to?*" said Nat. '*Beg your pardon, I can't hold my horse,*" replied Job; and he just heard Nat's ready rejoinder above the din of the thirty-two, "*I wish I couldn't hold mine.*" The chesnut was no great match horse; being in a cluster seemed to give him double confidence; and up a hill he was especially suited, as he was all hind action. Giving Little Harry 2st. 5lbs., and beating him for the Warwick Cup, was a very great thing, and even after his last Cup at Ascot, when he gave 9lbs. to a horse like Stockwell, who seemed fit to carry him, he was neither sick nor sorry. One of his back sinews began to give way that summer, and that he had not left his heart at Ascot was pretty well proved by the style in which he lived under 9st. 7lb. almost into the bottom in the Cesarewitch, for which he was only half-prepared. At the stud, the Vulture-part of his pedigree cut two ways, and although the action and speed have been good, the courage has been lacking as it was in his dam, and no cross, however stout, could correct this tendency.

Harry Stebbings never considered that Kingston was so fit as when he met Ted-dington for the Doncaster Cup. He had just been tried, to give Hungerford a year and 7lbs., and yet " the canoe" carried 12lbs. more in that race, and was only beaten a neck. The party were also deeply disappointed when he was beaten at Ascot by Grape-shot; but sadly as the hill told against his bad hind action, Basham felt sure that he was beaten on his merits, and revenged himself when he was taken off at Newcastle by backing Grapeshot to win him £800, and leading him back to scale. From $1\frac{1}{2}$ to $1\frac{3}{4}$ miles was about his mark, provided he had something to come away, and as he grew older he began worse in short races. Both Defiance and Lascelles were before him in a great finish for the Craven Stakes at Epsom, but he just defeated himself by trying to make a pace, and by an alteration of tactics with Rataplan in the Cup, he pulled off one of his best, if not his best victory.

Both fetlocks touched the ground after his Whip break down, and one of his legs filled as well. Sir Tatton liked the blood, and would have given 2,500 for him, but Mr. Blenkiron, who never will be denied, got him for 3,000. He died at Eltham, just as he was commencing his seventh season, within a fortnight of Omoo, whose *post mortem* showed that she was in foal with twins by him, one of which had begun to putrefy, and so caused her death. For his first two seasons, he got twice as many fillies as colts; but for the last three the numbers were balanced, and he seemed to get them with more length. An oak tree shades him, and a harvest has waved over the spot where that beautiful Knight of the Silver-hair lies buried.

The Cawston stud. The Cawston stud owes its celebrity to the advice which John Nutting the Eaton stud-groom gave Hemming, to buy Phryne at the sale in '45. He was sent to buy another, but she did'nt suit, and accordingly his lordship's 70 gs. was invested in the daughter of Touchstone and Decoy, which had just come out of training. Mr. Oldaker bid for her, and offered Hemming 10 gs. for his bargain, and " pay all your expenses as well ;" but her purchaser was inexorable. It seems that he had met Bill Scott in the interim, and been solemnly assured on that almost infallible authority, that he had got " a mare fit to breed you a winner of the three events if she's only used right." She broke to Pantaloon that spring ; but Elthiron was the result of second thoughts during the month that she was left. Pantaloon was also hired for the next season at Cawston ; and Lord John might well say to Hemming, as the white-reach tribe grew up round them, " That's the best day's work, Hemming, you ever did in your life, when you hired Pantaloon and bought Phryne."

Pantaloon and Phryne. Pantaloon was hired the next season for 150 gs., and then 200 gs. : and he never went back. The cross between this grand-looking chesnut and Phryne hit five years in succession. He had a curious hatred to a boy or a dog, and a peculiar partiality to a grey mare. Irish Birdcatcher had somewhat similar notions ; but he extended his antipathies to pigs and hens, and turned quite savage if they crossed his path. Phryne had spasms when she was in foal, and seemed to get no permanent relief from them except she had a goat to go with her, which had tired of his first love in the shape of his lordship's old charger Helen.

The Windhound rout. She was always the pet mare, and on that eventful afternoon when Cathe-

rine Hayes won the Oaks, and Windhound broke
loose among the fifteen mares, to "*get hold of
Phryne*" was Mrs. Hemming's first impulse. There
never was such a rout, and Cannobie, who was a foal
at the time, jumped a hedge and high rails on the
off side, and back through the gate to his little
dam, Lady Lurewell. To judge from A visit to Caw-
the hoof havoc in Dunkley's Meadow, ston.
there had been a second Windhound rout among
the mares on the afternoon of our visit, and it turned
out that the North Warwickshire had brought a fox
across it from Frankton Wood. The *troupe* were
quietly grazing in the next paddock, after the morning's alarm. Old Helen had long been laid with
Pantaloon and Rasselas under the holly; but the
flesh-coloured nose of the old Camel mare, the
crooked white reach of Miserrima, which knew no
crooked way up the Ascot hill, and Pearlin Jean,
with that white fore foot in rest, were all good to
descry. But, alas! the piebald pony, which roamed
amongst them, knew its good master's voice and step
no more; the new cricket ground on which he had
hoped that year to see Dunchurch beat Rugby,
was left half-sodded, and the roses and honey-
suckles, which were clinging to the clay-walls of
the "House that Jack built," told sadly that
another summer was fulfilling its course, but not for
him.

All knew and loved Lord John, and The late Lord
as a universal sportsman he was un- John Scott.
surpassed. Punt shooting, the leash, otter hunting,
with his red-and-white Gyp (which killed a thirteen-
pounder by herself, and then managed another,
which stuck to its tail), a bit of racing, or a little
patronage to "the lads of the Fancy"—whom he
brought up in great force under General "Dick Cain,"
to look after "The Brums" on a polling-day—were
quite in his line. His unfortunate lameness (which

arose from an injury to his ankle at a stone wall, out hunting) debarred him from joining, but he felt great interest in cricket; and one summer he took two Rugby men, at his own expense, right away to Scotland, to play in a match. In fact, he was always doing something, either out of doors or on paper, and he not only wrote an anonymous pamphlet on the currency, purely as he said " to bother my old friend Spooner," but he proved himself a hard hitter, when he had an occasional turn at polemics. There never was a more liberal landlord; but he quite enjoyed the joke when one of his tenants, who paid twenty-five shillings a-year for a cottage, and got two substantial dinners at the audit as well, told him that he really ought to have his rent lowered. His farms were remarkably low rented; and four or five years before his death, when he considered that the farmers were not employing enough labour, he spoke his mind in such a Downright Shippen way at a Benefit Society dinner at Dunchurch, that the poor fellows had to hang about the cottage doors no more with their hands in their pockets. At the time of the railway mania, he kept, like Mr. Assheton Smith, a regular look-out for the " theodolite scamps." They did The Squire of Tedworth, and managed matters comfortably enough, to his intense rage, on a very wet Sunday, when he was at church; but Lord John was too sharp for them, and when he and his watchers caught them at work for the Leamington line, they pitched into them, tore up their books, and sent them flying. He was, however, the last man to bear malice, and he got one of those he put to rout that day a most capital place.

Old Helen. His old charger Helen was by Octavian out of Lady of the Lake, and the first he ever had in his life. Once he rode her for a bet up the stone steps of the Bank of Dublin, when he was quartered there, to get a cheque cashed, and down again with value received. Her dislike to a jockey was extreme, and like Pickpocket, she insisted upon his getting up with a great coat on. Queen of the Gipsies, by Camel, was the best of her sixteen foals, and she went as a yearling for 90 gs., and turned out to be the speediest, bar Semiseria, of her year. Among his stud Lord John was very fond of Miserrima, "a good, fair mare," and the only one except Cannobie that was kept, when Mr. Merry purchased the lot, with Phryne, Catherine Hayes, Lady Lurewell, Blanche of Middlebie, Folkestone, Trovatore, &c. in it, for five thousand.

Independently of his blood, Lord John Hobbie Noble.
had always specially noticed Hobbie Noble from a yearling, in consequence of his hermit habits. No one ever caught him in company; but he would come to a whistle just like a dog, and his lordship would often take his friends out, after dinner, and call him up to the garden wicket to be looked at. The habit seemed to foreshadow "for the proud young porter" that a £6,500 cheque was in store for him, and that Her Majesty would send for him a second time to the front of her stand at Ascot. He was tried with Miserrima, who had just been second for the Oaks, at 16lbs. for the year, and John Day and John Scott both thought it must be too good to be correct. However, the former was pretty well convinced, the next year, after he had tried him with Little Harry before the Cambridgeshire, that he was a very great horse. Windhound was never much, although there is little doubt that he is Thormanby's sire; and The Reiver, who got very awkward in his temper, was a good stone below Catherine Hayes, when they were two-year-olds together.

The lengthy Cannobie, who was Cannobie.
left as a legacy to Hemming, was of a cleverer stamp than many of the Melbournes, and

could stay and race as well. He was coughing at the Derby when he ran third; but the public had not seen the best of him, and but for the severe strain which he gave his leg, by jumping the road at Newcastle, when he was following Heir of Lynne, two days before the Northumberland Plate, Mat Dawson quite believed that he would have ripened into a very superior Cup horse. Blanche of Middlebie seemed to be as lengthy for a foal as Cannobie was for a horse, and when we strolled to Cawston on our first visit with " Dick Over," and found her at Phryne's side, we thought that she and the firing of a chesnut yearling's hocks by the late Mr. Lucas's hand, were two of the finest pieces of workmanship we had ever seen in one day. She did not belie her promise in her two-year-old season, and swept £2,900 off the board. On the Friday before the St. Leger, she was tried on Weathercock Hill, at equal weights, with Sunbeam. Saunterer gave them each 26lbs., and came through from end to end, and Blanche, who was slightly carried out at the bend, was just half a length behind him, and rather more in front of poor Luke Snowdon and his first St. Leger winner. The black, whose performance under 8st. 12lbs. in the Cambridgeshire, and his reaching his horses like a flash at Chester, stamp him as one of the greatest wonders of the century, never lost his speed to the last; but his near fore leg gave way in the Doncaster Cup. He broke down hopelessly at Ascot the next year, and twenty-five hundred was his price to the Austrians.

Pocahontas.   Beyond being the sire of Miss Twickenham (the dam of Teddington) Rockingham did no good at the Stockwell paddocks; but The Baron, who came about the same time as Sorella, made a double hit in his second season, with Chief Baron Nicholson's dam, and Mr. Theobald's own mare Pocahontas. The latter had been to Muley

Moloch for the three preceding seasons, and was bought as a four-year-old for £500, after she was beaten for the Cup at Goodwood. She ran five times afterwards without success, and her last performance was for a Plate, at Chatham, where she finished second out of nine. She was then five months gone in foal with Cambaules, by Camel, but this grand cross was lost to the world, as he took the influenza, and became a roarer quite early.

Stockwell, her fifth, was a very fine colt; but every one assured Mr. Theobald that he was too big. John Lowry was a most consistent admirer of him, and as he was determined that he should have "an honest race," he begged his master, when he went to Brighton Races, to try and see Lord Exeter, and received as his answer, " Put it down in my book, my memory fails me." In due time his lordship arrived, and the white-faced chesnut was proudly displayed by John in the "burial paddock." His lordship thought him too big, but he went into committee with the old man, and after an hour of most anxious suspense, the latter strolled out to tell John, that he was to get his pet weaned as soon as he could, and that he was to go to Burleigh. The price was £180, and a £500 contingency if he won the Derby. This information was clenched with a present of a ten-pound note, and the promise of being put on at £50 to 0 at Epsom. The colt started in a month's time, by the earliest train in the morning, and by way of having something to " help him," through London, John hired a cab, and led him close behind it. Lord Exeter just made the purchase in time, as the old man died a month after the colt had left; and his stud, with the exception of Pocahontas and Sorella, was sold by Mr. Tattersall.

Pocahontas foaled Rataplan the morning that Mr. William Theobald

(marginal note: Early history of Stockwell.)

(marginal note: Birth of Rataplan.)

died, and Rataplan became the property of Mr. Thellusson, who gave him to his father. Lowry's earliest recollections of Rataplan were symptomatic of the after-vigour of the chesnut. *"He got up directly,"* says his historian, with admirable brevity, *" blew his nose, and sucked his mother."* Luck attended the mare, and when she and Sorella went to Willesden Paddocks, and the choice lay between Don John and Harkaway,* the trustees chose the latter for the future Prunella, and King Tom was the result. Thus from the nicks of three successive seasons, there came the respective sires of St. Alban's, Kettledrum, and Old Calabar. Stockwell made little out during his first season, as, with all his fine speed, he never could be made fit enough to get home. Still those who were near the judge's chair will have it that Mr. Clark over-looked him in the Prendergast Stakes, when he gave the race to Maidstone.

Rataplan's racing and training habits.   Rataplan always *" went proppy"* on his long pasterns, and at the best of times was only a middling beginner. *" Let him alone till he gets into his action,"* were the orders which his jockeys received, and his *"custom of an afternoon"* was to creep up to his horses at the half-distance, and make one effort. His shoulders, and not his heart, forbade a long struggle. When Sim rode him strictly to Mr. Parr's orders at Edinburgh, he thought at one time that he should never catch his horses; but, perhaps, his most wonderful race was when he won the Manchester Cup at 9st. 3lbs. Like Stockwell, his back power was almost miraculous, and if he threw up his heels no boy alive could sit him; but when he did get rid of them, he would walk straight off home to Ilsley. It was but seldom that he took these vivacious fits, and seeing that he generally

---

* We find that we were in error when we stated at page 83 that this horse was sold at Doncaster.

contrived to stumble about twelve times between his box and the Downs, it was never safe to take him without knee caps. There never was a lazier one foaled, bar Lanercost and Springy Jack, as he would lie full length while they plaited his mane, and go to sleep after feeding, with unerring regularity.

King Tom, or " Tom," as he was generally styled in the stable, was first
King Tom.
trained by Wyatt, at Myrtle Green, near Findon. During the Doncaster meeting of '53, when he had been beaten at Goodwood, and had won at Brighton, Baron Rothschild finally agreed, after some highly involved negotiations, to give Mr. Thellusson £2,000 for him. William King brought him up to London, and so on to Gorhambury, where he gave the two-year-old Twinkle a stone with all ease in his trial, and on the next Wednesday won the Triennial at Newmarket. He was a good-tempered, light-fleshed horse, and with fine speed, and ready for any distance that was set him. Before the Derby, he was tried at 8st. 9lbs. with Orestes 9st. 1lb., Hungerford 8st 2lbs., and Middlesex 7st. 2lbs. The last-named just beat him by half a neck, and the others were nowhere. On the Monday week before the Derby, he fell lame in the off hock, or at all events somewhere in the off-quarter, and as he did not do more than take a couple of canters between then and the race, it was no slight performance for him to separate Andover and Hermit.

To carry a high weight for three-
quarters-of-a-mile was Longbow's line,
Longbow.
as he showed so ably in the Goodwood Steward's Cup, but his long distance running, especially when he met Stockwell in the most muggy of days for the Great Yorkshire, was most wonderful. Foreigners are in the habit of giving wet hay as a roaring anti-

dote, and before **Larry McHale** ran his matches, John Scott gave him a ball of lard, with some shot in it, to try and keep down the lights; but with Longbow he used nothing but limed water.

Miss Bowe.

His dam, the sixteen-hand Catton-headed Miss Bowe, is still at the Knowsley Paddocks, in her thirtieth year, and as fresh and as shapely as many a mare of half her age. She has had no foal since Tom Bowline, and his lordship has ceased to send her to the horse since she missed to Paletot. Never did mare deserve better of an owner, or seem more likely to put in for forty.

Daniel O'Rourke.

Daniel O'Rourke, whose departure was thus solemnly heralded in a Turf paper, " *Daniel slept in London last night, previous to his departure for Austria,*" at 800 gs., was tried before the Derby, to give Champion 7lbs., and beat Backbiter at evens. Songstress gave him a stone, and a beating after the Oaks ; and he first had his temper spoilt when going in the van to Ascot.

" The West" finished him, as he was always on his heels up the gallop, and made him turn coward. At last he would kick and fly, and could hardly be got on to the wolds ; but Snarry's soothing manners put him all right, when the scene was changed to Sledmere. During his seven seasons there, Sir Tatton has bred upwards of 170 foals by him, and fully two-thirds of them chesnuts. He was not very lucky in getting colts from the Pyrrhus mares, and although he suited with the Hampton blood, his foals from the Sleight of Hand mares had more power.

Little Harry.

Little Harry was just the reverse of Mincepie, very good when the ground was not deep, and John Day liked him so much after the Bedford Stakes, that he got on at fifteens and twenties to one to win an independency. If

Danebury had a sad disappointment, Woodyeates had one of its grandest Chester triumphs that year, with little Joe Miller, who could get equally well through wet or dry. He Joe Miller. was never fifteen hands, very sweet-headed like his sire Venison, but shorter and most beautifully turned. Mr. Sadler bred him, and Mr. Farrance bought him for 200 gs. at Newmarket. In the Metropolitan Stakes he got knocked over by Miss Anne; but in the Chester Cup he got away in front from end to end; and Stilton, after his bad start, could never reach him. Grosvenor, in the same stable, was all the go for the Cup that year, and Davis thought so little of Joe in consequence, that Mr. Parker "got him" for £12,000, at 24 to 1 after the Metropolitan, and again for £6,000 over the Ascot Cup, at half those odds. Like most light-bodied and light-fleshed horses Joe stayed well, but he was cut for temper, and shot very early in the day, and honoured with burial in the centre of the Woodyeates yard.

The little wall-eyed Umbriel lured a few, including one of the cleverest Umbriel. men we have, into the belief that he was better than "The West." Sam Wheatley, who had West Australian. trained Haphazard and Agonistes for the then Earl of Darlington, and been stud-groom at Cheveley as well, gazed at the son of Melbourne and Mowerina with intense delight, and declared that he had never put his hand on a finer yearling. He, moreover, backed his opinion by getting on first of any one, and never hedging a penny.

Isaac Walker's annual jubilee comprises the ten days during which he takes Isaac Walker's annual appearance at Whitewall. the yearlings up to Whitewall, where he stays Saturday and Sunday, after placing them at school, and then proceeds to Doncaster as a finish. For five-and-twenty years it has been his habit to deposit his charges on the Friday before the St. Leger. In old days, Tom Carter would show up on that evening, and so would Ben Eddison, full of dry observations on society, and ready, when his county recollections of the Caunt and Bendigo tournament were evoked, to show with appropriate gesture, how " Bendy felled him like a *to-ad*." Bill Scott, who was never at the paddocks in his life, always addressed Isaac on these occasions, as " *Streatlam*," and John would only recognize him officially as " *Queen Mab*." Frank was always full of his husky chaff, confiding to Isaac what Mr Scott had said about him, and *vice versâ*; and so those merry days passed on.

Frank's first introduction to "The West." The splendid grunt of Frank when he first caught sight of The West, delighted John Scott and Isaac above all things. " *What's that?*" he said. " *That*," quoth John Scott, quite gravely, "*Oh! that's only a rough thing by Freedom; we'd better pass him;*" but " *what a pretty pair you are*," replied Frank, as he went up to introduce himself to his love at first sight. The trial with this colt and Longbow at 21lbs. for the year, was run three-quarters of a mile in a very deep ground, and the young'un won it, hands down. There were never any proved attempts to get at him, although the betting before Doncaster betokened that the " black cloud" was going to descend, and the great difficulties in the way of training him were his heavy flesh, and his tendency to a sort of off-and-on lameness, first in his feet and then in his ankle.

The West's Doncaster Jubilee. Frank and Isaac could never quite settle how far the Leger was to be won; and John Scott delicately said, that as Mr. Bowes would not be at Doncaster, of course Isaac must give the orders. Frank would have it, that it would do " *if I win by the length of my arm;*" but Isaac did'nt see it at all. " *None of your dodging*," said he; " *I don't like these heads and half necks; you make me shake in my shoes; let him out at the Red House, and see how far he can win.*" Nothing seemed so absurd to Frank as the popular idea of his horse not staying; " *Stay, indeed!*" he was wont to say in his fervour, " *he'll stay a thundering deal too long for any of them; the faster they'll go, the sooner it will be over; they'll wonder what's coming when I lay hold of them at ' White Willie.'* " It was of course gratifying to him to hear from Isaac that he had ridden the horse to his mind; but he rejoined, " *I was thinking of you all the way from the distance; the beggars stood stock still, or I'd have put you in a nice sweat.*" Isaac accompanied the horse home to the Salutation, and when John Scott and Hayhoe got there, they both saw that something was up. One might well say of the horse, that " he looks well;" and the other that he was " as bold as a hero;" for Isaac, in the exuberance of his enthusiasm, at having at last reared a winner of the double event, had poured a bottle of Champagne into the pail.

Catherine Hayes, who shares with Ellerdale the honour of being the best daughter of Lancercost, has always been a great favourite with Mat Dawson. She required drawing light, and is a particularly sweet-tempered, and wide-hipped mare, with her hocks close together. No action could be more easy and sweeping, and we have always maintained that to our eye nothing ever crept so beautifully up the Epsom hill. Her Nursery Stakes win at Goodwood, when looked at by the subsequent performances of the horses behind her, was a remarkable performance, as she won easily under the top weight, 8st. 7lbs., and gave Rataplan 14lbs., Ethelbert and Pantomime 13lbs., and Dagobert 2lbs. Mat Dawson never tried a two-year-old so highly, and as he knew her to be just as good at even weights as the four-year-old Kilmeny,

Catherine Hayes.

who had won The Steward's Cup that week at 6st. 13lbs., he had no Goodwood fears. After the Oaks, she caught cold across the loins, and had a heavy fringe of leeches applied on each side of her spine. Her action went sadly; but still she made a game wind-up of it, by giving Mayfair half-a-stone and "a long head" beating for the Coronation Stakes.

Goorkah's history. Goorkah claims a mention, but more for the peculiar manner of his dam's subsequent purchase. She belonged, with a mare called Fairy Queen by Brutandorf, to a farmer and bonesetter in Lanarkshire. Once on a time, he dreamt that he sold these two mares, and that Mr. Sharpe, of Hoddom Castle, purchased them, and he wrote off forthwith to apprise that gentleman of his dream, and beg him to hasten its fulfilment. Mr. Sharpe did not exactly see it in that enthusiastic light, and as Fairy Queen was blind, he declined her at once. With regard to Fair Jane, he said that he liked her blood; but that as she had been drawing coals from the station, and had been barren, he was only open to a swap for her with his filly Seclusion by St. Martin, a greyhound puppy (afterwards Cora Lynn), a couple of Dorkings, and a piece of plaid for trowsers. And so this novel bargain was arranged. She was in foal to Turnus, and as Goorkah showed some form, she was sent to Annandale again. At Kelso, Mr. Barber proposed to purchase her, and offered three hundred, but Mr. Sharpe would hear of nothing under five; and when another application came, he declared his ultimatum, by letter to each, and said that the first who gave that sum should have her. Both applications, as it turned out, were from the same quarter, and by the time the letter arrived, enclosing the five £100 notes, Hamlet was dropped.

Butterfly. Mr. Sharpe sold Butterfly and her dam for £70 to the Brothers Oates, and Mr. Eastwood took such a fancy to the former, when he first saw her as a yearling, that he purchased her at once, and sold half to Culshaw, who stipulated most rigidly that she should be called after his "herd matron"—that rare prize mould in which both Master and Royal Butterfly were cast and quickened. The luck he predicted from this process followed in due course. In her first trial with Buttercup, she was beaten, and although she won five times, she had some mischances as a two-year-old, getting knocked about at Beverley, and very badly off with Thormanby at York. Before she ran for her engagements at three years old, she had a rough gallop with Sparrow Hawk and Dilkoosh, and an Oaks win, and rare seconds both for the Ascot Cup and Northumberland Plate confirmed the promise which she then showed.

John Scott firmly believes that, according to his trial, Boiardo would have *Boiardo.* won the St. Leger in a canter. He was a rank roarer, and not a very taking horse in any way; but he now ranks high in Australia. Holmes, on Dervish, made all the running in the trial, and Sim lay last with Boiardo, who lost a shoe, and beat Acrobat very cleverly at the finish. Still Sim did not trust his leg, but chose Acrobat on the Leger day; and the severe pace which Dervish made from the start found out the crack's weak point.

Their victor Knight of St. George *Knight of St.* grew into more after, and left a most *George* beautiful, enlarged likeness of himself in Knight of St. Patrick; but when he won the St. Leger he was only just fifteen hands. There never was a more difficult horse to ride. He took a long time to make up his mind whether he would try or not, and then nothing but easing and coaxing, which Basham did to perfection, would make him put his good resolutions in force. Spurs and whip were quite out of the question. He always hung to the left, and nothing but a very severe pricker and long cheek to the left side of the bit, could keep him straight at all. As an Irish two-year-old he bolted once, lost twice, and won once, and his education was still in a sad state when he came to Hambleton with Game-keeper. He was ridden all the winter by Basham in a yearling's breaking tackle, and when he found that he could'nt bolt, going up the gallop, he went open-mouthed among the yearlings. His Derby trial was at 10lbs. with the five-year-old Kingston, and at evens with Eulogist, on the Saturday before Chester, and he won it cleverly. Kingston was, perhaps, not what he had been, although he fought out the Ascot Cup so well with "The West" that summer; but still the trial looked uncommonly hopeful. "The Knight," however, contracted a " gouty leg" before Epsom; his fore and hind feet caught, following Kingston up the gallop, and he cut his boot clean off, and into the flesh as well. Kingston was away on Her Majesty's service, the week of his Doncaster trial, and not liking to try "The Knight" farther, they made him give the speedy Corin an enormous amount of weight over a mile, and brought it off.

Virago.

There were more nuggets than Volti-geur at the Hart Diggings, as Virago was foaled there the year after his double event. She was advertised for sale as a yearling, at Doncaster, when old John Day slipped down, and tried to buy her privately, but Mr. Stephenson insisted on her going to the hammer along with Epinician. John Scott liked her, but left off at 340 and the next ten settled the job for Mr. Padwick. She was tried as a two-year-old in October, at 7lbs., with Little Harry, and William Day, who rode in the trial, was so pleased with her, that he increased the two thousand offer, which he made on the ground, to three when they got into the house; but Mr. Padwick was as firm as Gibraltar. After the Doncaster meeting of '54 she turned roarer; still old John could not bring himself to believe that she was so changed, and when the little, jumped-up St. Hubert beat her at something under weight for age, he thought him a wonder, and never blanched when " my boy William" assured him that at 18lbs. Lord of the Isles could quit Nabob when he liked in a mile.

This combination of Pantaloon and Touchstone, which had nicked so well reverse ways in the Phryne stock, was a thin, deep, flat-sided horse, who did not require very much work. His winding up for the Two Thousand, for which no horse ever came to the post more thoroughly fit, must have told on him, although he repeated his performance with Nabob on 4lbs. worse terms over the Derby distance afterwards. This was a great year for the threes, with Wild Dayrell, Rifleman, and Fandango also in it, and if the big and short De Clare's trial—to give Paletot 27lbs. over Leatherhead Downs, and manage old Bracken at evens—was correct, he would have been very busy at the finish. However, his ankle went in the effort, and he was seen in public no more till the Middlesboro' Show.

With the exception of Lady Flora, Mr. Popham had never had a thoroughbred mare, until he bought Ellen Middleton. Rickaby, his stud-groom, saw her advertised in *The Life*, and thought her Bay Middleton and Myrrha blood so good, that he was authorized to write to Bobby Hill for the price, and bought her unseen for fifty pounds, in the June of '51. As there was no very suitable horse near Littlecote, he was despatched the next spring on a little voyage of discovery among the stud farms. Harkaway, Ratcatcher, and The Libel were not to his fancy; Enfield could only offer Red Deer and the Earl of Richmond; and at last he came upon quite a seam of wealth at Barrow's of Newmarket, in Birdcatcher, **Don John**, John o'Gaunt, and Ion, and clenched matters with the latter, which was the last one brought out. Both the mares were sent to him, and after a month they were ordered home. Ellen Middleton had not been at Littlecote two hours before she turned to him, and was sent back that night.

The arrival of the first blood-colt produced the sensation which those little matters will produce in quiet country homes, and they sat up with Ellen for at least a fortnight before the event.

Birth of Wild Dayrell. When a colt appeared between 12 and 1 a.m., the butler was rung up and rushed on to the scene with his nightcap on his head, and a bottle of wine in his hand; and as it was necessary to remove the little stranger into a warmer box, he got a wheel-barrow, and insisted upon "*wheeling the winner of the Derby once in my life.*" There was nothing in that speech; but when Rickaby got home to his cottage about five on that April morning, he assured his wife there must be something remarkable for good or for evil about the colt, as he had just seen the strange sight of a wild duck and a wild drake actually sitting on a quickset hedge, close by the high road. That morning was indeed a remarkable one in Littlecote annals. It hailed the first blood colt Mr. Popham had ever possessed, and the first that Rickaby ever trained, and the latter never was at Epsom in his life till he fulfilled his threat of "bringing the money away."

His change of hands. At this time, Mr. Popham had no idea of training, and advertised both the colt and his half-sister for sale next year. Sam Reeves used never to tire of looking at him, as "the biggest and the best, &c." Jones, the Rockley trainer, bid money for him; and when Dagobert had put the Goodwood stable in love with the Ion blood, by winning the Chesterfield Stakes, Kent arrived and bid 500 gs. for the pair. As might have been expected with so big a yearling, the filly beat him in his trial, and Kent did not think that Lord Henry Lennox lost much when he was sent with the rest of his stud up to Tattersalls. Mr. Popham was in Scotland at the time; but forwarded Rickaby a commission to buy both back at 250 gs. and 50 gs., and he did so with, in both instances, very little to spare. And thus, as Lord George parted with a Surplice, General Peel with a Kingston, Admiral Harcourt with a Summerside, and Lord Exeter very nearly with a Stockwell, for lack of waiting a little longer, " Mr. Gordon" got rid of Wild Dayrell.

His early training was done in the most rural style. Two miles principally on the banks of *His training and trial.*

> " The Kennet swift for silver eels renowned,"

were marked out in Littlecote Park, as the winter ground, and at it they went, Rickaby leading the gallops on the five-year-old Zegra, an old gelding of Mr. Drinkald's, and his sons Tom and John on Wild Dayrell and the filly Creusa. The latter did not stand training long, and is now among Mr. Blenkiron's brood mares. In May the three adjourned to Lord Craven's, and had the use of his Lordship's Ashdown Park stabling; but still there was not time to bring out the colt against Bonnie Morn, at Stockbridge. They had no line except through Zegra, who had been tried and beaten two lengths by old Inder, and in the trial, an exceedingly rough one in clothes, the colt gave him about a couple of hundred yards over three-quarters of a mile, and never quite reached his head. The Newmarket victory was a very easy one, and the horse was fully sixteen one-and-a-half before they began with him for the Derby. Lord Albemarle was bought to do fast work for him; but he and Zegra were incompetent, as he used to run over them, kicking his heels, at intervals, into the air, so high that it was as much as Robert Sherwood or his lad could do to stick on. He soon stumped up Lord Albemarle, and then sixteen hundred was given at Lincoln for Jack Sheppard; and early in March they adjourned to Ashdown once more, with a whole regiment of touts in their train.

The stable of the two was like a fortress, and two dogs below, and Rickaby, who did the dragon, above, guarded the golden apple of Berkshire. It was thought advisable to keep Jack pretty fresh for the trial, and Gamelad was hired from John Osborne, and came with Robert Osborne in charge. Lord Craven and the house party used often to ride out at six o'clock, to see the gallops; but on the trial morning, ten days before the Derby, Mr. Etwall, Mr. F. Craven and Mr. Popham were also on the Weathercock Hill. Wild Dayrell was asked to carry 8st. 10lbs. and give Jack, whom they knew to be in form after beating Orinoco at Chester, 10lbs., and Gamelad, for whose sake Osborne had faithfully subsisted on salts and animalculæ for some twenty-four hours, about 2st. and a year. Zegra was nobody on that occasion, and like Gamelad was soon cut down; but Jack Sheppard and the crack went a splitting pace for a mile, where Jack fairly stood still. Mr. Etwall rode down to Charlton, to ask what had happened. Charlton, however, assured him that his colt was well enough, and added, "*I thought King Tom's trial a good one last year, but I never rode against such a horse as this before.*" And so every one there thought, when they saw him come in alone, with Gamelad toiling a full distance behind him.

The orders at the Derby were simply to " get quietly up the hill, and then stride along," and Sherwood did not make the pace so strong afterwards as they wished. Perhaps in the hard state of the ground it was as well, and either from that cause, or the horse hitting it when he ran into the quickset hedge in the paddock, before he could be pulled up, there was mischief in the near fore leg, half-way between the knee and the fetlock, by the end of that week, and for the first time in his life he was put into bandages. They went on with him for the Goodwood Cup, but the other leg began to fill, and it was all that Rickaby could do to prepare him for York. After his Doncaster break down, they tried to patch him up no more, and he began the Buccaneer, Horror, and Avalanche business. His mate, Jack Sheppard passed eventually into Mr. Saxon's hands, Mr. McGeorge got Lord Albemarle, and Zegra became Lord Craven's hack for a season or two. His foals have been principally mouse-browns; but unfortunately Alice Hawthorne's colt died quite early, and Rickaby has yet to prove if the same blood on both sides, but a degree farther off, will be as successful in his " Brown Dayrell" from a Cowl mare.

Ellington, his successor in the Derby honours, was ridden about at Admiral *Ellington.* Harcourt's after his two-year-old season, by the coachman, and made as handy at gate-opening as a hack,—the first time, perhaps, that a future " blue ribbon" has so passed the winter. One of those who won upon him got his hint in a curious way. His book was beating him, and in a half-desperate mood he sauntered down Piccadilly. Looking up at the clock above the Wellington Club, he saw that the hands stood at twenty-two minutes to eight, and just obscured the W.; and in an instant he had his cue, and felt so convinced he was right that he took the odds about the colt, to win £300.

Warlock was the most unlucky of horses the next year. He had sore shins *Warlock.* at Epsom, he fell twice at Newcastle, and he was

R

pulled up by mistake, after going once round, at
Carlisle, where Caller Ou also distinguished herself
subsequently by running against a post. The roan
was game and slow, and wanted a wonderful amount
of nice management, but still John Scott felt
assured that if anything happened to Ellington
at Doncaster he had everything else safe enough,
and so it proved. His finest race was when he
beat Fisherman by a neck for the Queen's Plate at
York.

Impérieuse was not regularly tried before the St.
Leger, but had merely a rough gallop with Warlock
and Forbidden Fruit, ridden by their boys, who were
not weighed beforehand. The stable saved stakes
with Blink Bonny; but though John Peart, who
was at Newmarket, had orders to lay the odds to
a hundred, he did not, and the telegram announc-
ing the One Thousand success, bore the welcome
postcript, " *None of the money hedged.*"

Horse eccentri-   The eccentricities of horses are end-
cities.   less. It was necessary to tie up Lucetta
by a piece of twine, or she would have turned nervous and broken everything. Pickpocket would
never let his jockey mount, except he had a coat
over his white satin jacket, simply because he had
once picked his owner's pocket of a white handkerchief, and turned so frightened at the flapping, that
he clenched his teeth and would not drop it. Bellona
blemished her hip in a horse-box, and would only
consent to stand loose in one after; and Lightning
would never go into a stable unless he was bluffed,
and then he would enter by himself. The love of
company is also a great trait in horses. It was said
of the Godolphin Arabian that when he had flat-
tened out his own cat by mistake, he missed it so
much that he pined from remorse, and savaged
every other cat that was put into him. If little One
Act had to make her own running, she would be

staring about on both sides for her companions; and
Gemma di Vergy was so exacting that no cat would
satisfy him for company, but Joe Dawson was absolutely obliged to have a lad there with a book or
newspaper all day, and another sleeping close by him
at night in a stall. The habit began when he was a
yearling. He climbed over a partition, no man can
tell how to this day, so as to get at the window, and
was espied with his feet on the window-sill, gravely
looking out into the yard.

St. Giles was the first colt that made
people remember that there was such a
horse as Womersley, and the ten of them which
started that season were all winners. He was skin
and bone when he came to Sledmere, and Sir Tatton
did not consider him ill sold at £300, when he and
Lanercost were exiled together. His stock were the
first that ever went up from Sledmere to meet Mr.
Tattersall at York August; and St. Giles, Greyling,
Companion, and another, all came back unsold.
For St. Giles, there was not a solitary bid, and William Day thought he was giving quite enough, when
he drew a 240-guinea cheque for the four. When
St. Giles had satisfied him, he came direct from
Chester to Sledmere, and not only bought his dam in-
foal with the 500 guinea St. James, and a filly foal at
her foot, but hired four Womersley fillies at 100 gs.
a-piece. The mare paid well, but the quartett were
duly returned as incapables in the Woodyeates sense
of the term. St. Giles was a big sixteen-hand
horse, who " did not come to hand easily," with
no great pace, but a glutton at a distance. Lord
Ribblesdale took him at the Sledmere price, and his
yearling trial was remarkably good. His race with
Skirmisher at Northampton was a very great one,
but the party were never more confident, and the
commissioner began his operations a fortnight before.

St. Giles.

Queen Mary's blood. Many of the modern cracks have been drawn out of the Doncaster lucky-bag, and Mr. Ramsay found himself wavering between Mendicant and Queen Mary on the morning of Foig-a-Ballagh's St. Leger. Something put him against the brown, for whom Mr. Gully gave 400 gs., and he got the bay for a hundred less. Strange, indeed, that one of the pair should be destined to win the Oaks and throw a Derby winner, and that the other should be the dam of Blink Bonny and grandam of Caller Ou as well. Mr. Ramsay died five years after, and there was so little promise about the puny Haricot, that I'Anson heard a remark in the crowd to the effect that "some madman has given twenty pound for her and the foal (Braxey)" (which is now in the Hampton Court Stud), and smiled to think that *he* had given the commission. Balrownie (a very good-looking horse), Blooming Heather, and Bonnie Scotland made about £6,000 gs., in stakes and sales, and then I'Anson was compensated for Queen Mary missing to Touchstone by the suspicions which ripened into certainty, when he had sent her Melbourne filly along for a few weeks.

Blink Bonny. She was the first of the family he ever trained as a two-year-old, and he never gave one more work, but a short T.Y.C. was not her line of business, and she was always a most moderate beginner. William Scott, Sir Lydston Newman's present stud-groom, took a great fancy to her, both for her own and his old Melbourne's sake, and advised Lord Londesboro' to give the three thousand which I'Anson offered to take for her after the Beverley meeting. This price was contingent on his being allowed to train her, and when he found that such was not his Lordship's intention, he raised it a thousand, and the bargain went off; and at the Northallerton meeting he refused £5,000 from Mr. Jackson. She throve pretty well till late in the autumn,

but then the dentition fever, which was always peculiarly severe with the Melbournes, came on, and she
sank, as Blooming Heather had done before her, to a
complete skeleton. She was always leaning to the off-
side as if flying from some unseen fury on the near,
and they only dare tie her up with a string to snap
if she ran back in one of the paroxysms. Newminster's teeth had punished him a good deal before
the Derby, but his state must have been bliss in
comparison. After the One Thousand, where her
looks fairly shocked the public, I'Anson told his
family that he wouldn't take £1,000 to 1d. about
her Epsom chance. Still on his return from Chester
she seemed to have got some relief, and although
she would seize her corn and then drop it as if it was
red-hot shot, she ate grass greedily, started her work
once more, and crept on very fast.

She seemed to improve on the journey *Her race for the*
up, and when she galloped with Strath- *Derby.*
naver at Epsom, she drew away from him with her
head down in her rare, old fashion. Charlton's orders
were never to try and win till close on the post, and he
did it without asking her a question. I'Anson
hardly knew what to think before they started, or
when the race was running. He twice thought she
looked like her old self at the whins, as she was
setting her ears back and flinging up her tail
as she always did when she meant vengeance.
Then although he swept the thirty backwards
and forwards with his glasses, he could never find
her yellow cap again, and when he did, he mistook
it for something else, till they were close at home.
On the Oaks day, her form was fully half-a-stone
better, but Charlton as nearly as possible broke his
stirrup iron, coming round Tattenham Corner.

Balrownie was troubled with sand- *Balrownie, Bloom-*
cracks, and was bad to train in conse- *ing Heather and*
quence. I'Anson thought he had tried *Bonnie Scot-*
land.

him high enough to win the St. Leger; but he injured his hock in his trial, and had to be stopped in
his work; and with a view to the Doncaster Stakes,
he was not ridden out when winning was hopeless.
Mr. Padwick gave £2,000 for him; and old John
Day was delighted with his trial, and so was Wells,
who rode him. He was a very unfortunate horse.
When he ran with Virago, at York, he was so severely kicked at the post, that the starter felt bound
to give him a little time to recover from it; and he
got pricked in his shoeing before he met Rataplan,
at Manchester. Blooming Heather shyed at a butcher's cart coming through London, and was still
quite stiff from slipping upon the stones, when she
went for the Oaks. Bonnie Scotland nearly broke
his leg at two years old, and never could be got
thoroughly fit. He had the greatest constitution of
the family, and was the most indolent at exercise
that I'Anson ever had to do with; and the last
heard of him was, that he had won the Great Prize
for sires at Cincinnatti, Ohio, against Lexington and
all comers.

Beadsman, the son of Mendicant,
Beadsman. had all the fine action of his dam, and
if people did pronounce him " a rum 'un to look at,"
they were more confirmed in their opinion when
his photograph appeared. There was not much
promise about him at two years' old, and if he had
not won a trial with a light weight on him at Danebury, he would have been probably put out of training. After the Two Thousand, he was tried to give
Fitzroland 6lbs., and won so far that Wells hallooed
to his lad to stop, as the touts were about.

Antonio, Anton, Of the three A's, Antonio, Anton, and
and Actæon. Actæon, which John Day had in hand
at one time, Anton was the smallest, and very neat,
but sadly touched in the temper; and if Vaultress
and Maid of Orleans still divide the honours of the

speediest Danebury mare, Actæon could probably
have beaten every thing of both sexes for half-a-
mile. Anton's luck was beyond the average in his
great three hundred-guinea match with Kent. His
near hind-leg had gone months before, and was kept
in perpetual cold bandages, but it just stood out with
the most careful nursing over the mile and a quarter,
and he won a neck. Antonio's A.F. match with Luff
was also a most brilliantly ridden finish. Wells on
Luff held the lead down the hill from the Bushes, and
Alfred Day, who could not take any liberties on his
roarer, got to him in the Bottom. Neither of them
dared to do more than touch his horse's mouth, and
when Wells stopped Luff half-way up, in order to
"reach home," Alfred drew up to his knee, and holding his bay there till the last few strides, just got up
and won by a short head. The old school, with all
their Robinsonian and Chifney memories, are bad to
beat, but the patience and tenderness of this finish
stamped it as a masterpiece on both sides, and none
spoke of it more highly than General Peel.

Marionette and Trumpeter were never
put together at two years old, but tried   Trumpeter.
collaterally with Pinsticker, who made out Trumpeter
to be 10lbs. the best of the two. On the Monday
before the Derby, they were measured, and John
Day again considered that Marionette had 10lbs.
the worst of it. The leg which had been hit at Bath
went very badly in the Derby, and the other followed
suit the moment they tried to put Trumpeter into
slow work again, and Harleston Paddocks has been
his destiny since. Mr. Harry Hill bought him for
220 guineas at the last "Corner" sale of the Royal
Yearlings, and it would be strange indeed if one of
the Hampton anniversaries comes off, without some
little jocular passage of arms between Mr. Hill and
Mr. Tattersall on the subject of that memorable
purchase.

Musjid was one of the Tickhill tick-

Musjid. lers, and Ariadne, The Moulvie, and
Cast-off were the other winners out of the lot which
went with him to Doncaster that autumn. Their sire
Newminster had two seasons there, and Langar,
Tramp, Catton, Barefoot, Interpreter, Juggler,
Cardinal Puff, Hetman Platoff, and Rataplan have
also flourished in turn under those ivied battlements,
girdled with a moat, and above whose tangled mass
of elm and sycamore, the gilt Tarrare stands out,
to tell of the "blue stripe" days when poor George
Nelson seldom missed a morning stroll to the
Castle.

Elis was foaled in the elder-tree box beneath it, and
"a great, strong foal he was," according to his accou-
cheur, John Hornshaw, and Slane saw the light in
these paddocks, when his Orville dam came to the
handsome Langar. The saddle-room box was Musjid's birthplace, and he only contrived to save his
rear by six days. He was the finest galloper
among them in the paddocks, but went so wide
and awkwardly behind, that the buyers at Doncaster all thought that he was lame. Mr. Gerard
Sturt first told Sir Joseph Hawley of him, and
advised him very strongly to go and have a
look.

No one would give the three hundred which Lord
Scarborough set upon him; and the colt went
home to Tickhill. Still Sir Joseph did not forget him, and on second thoughts about the middle of October the bargain was struck.

His Derby trial. In his Derby trial he was made to give
21 lbs. to Gallus, and Wells on Beacon, and something loose to make a pace, took what part they
could. For a mile it was a tremendous splitter be-
ween Musjid and Gallus, but the latter was told out
in the next quarter, and Sir Joseph felt sure that
he had the Derby again in his grasp. Wells

vowed forthwith that he had never ridden anything so good, and never expected to do again. The match with The Blacksmith the next year seemed a wonderfully good thing, but the Derby winner went dead amiss before the day.

Underhand's finest two-year-old performance was at Ripon, where he stumbled and ran Saunterer, who only gave him 2 lbs., to a head; while Skirmisher, who received 6 lbs., was just beaten as far. He was a very small colt, and was foaled at the Consett Iron Works, from one of whose functionaries he derived his name. Mr. Forster consigned him to Spigot Lodge, as a yearling; and one of his admirers from the works, who wanted a little outing, came shortly afterwards to see him. It was to him that Fobert and the world are indebted for a new wrinkle in the preparation of yearlings. " This and another colt," he said, "have run together from foals; but there never was such a promising galloper as this one, we know it, Mr. Fobert, for we've set the greyhounds on them regular." On cross-examination by Arthur Briggs, it was further elicited that Underhand had not altogether approved of being made a hare, and had once jumped a wall with the long-tails after him, and dropped without injury, on to the thatched roof of a pigsty.

His style of carrying his head very high impressed many with an idea that he was not a stayer. This was a mistake, but still about a mile and a-half was his best distance, and his great speed enabled him to get up through his horses from the half-distance, under very high weights. He always ran best in Aldcroft's hands, as his tender, patient way of nursing him pulled him through if it was at all on the cards. Dr. Syntax at Preston, and Beeswing at Newcastle, might be said to "farm the Cups," and Vampyre nearly had a monopoly of the Ascot Stakes for three successive years, yet no horse save Underhand ever ran in the same handicap for five out of his six seasons, and not only win it three times but finish by being second. Well might the "Black Diamonds" be found clustering round him like bees, year after year, waving their hats, and singing out excitedly from their platform stands, for minutes before the race began, " *Unney-hand wins; Unneyhand wins!*" We never saw his muscle so splendidly up, as when he won the Great Ebor Handicap at 9st. 1 lb. He never had a day's illness in his life, and his legs were as sound to the last as when he fled from the greyhounds.

St. Albans. St. Albans came to Fyfield about October, and pleased his Lordship and Taylor in a trial by giving Plumper 10 lbs. He was amiss all his two-year-old season, and so unwell after running third for The Ham, that Taylor assured his Lordship it would be death to him to start again that week. In fact, he put him into the van in Cantine's place at Salisbury, as he was far too weak to walk across the country. At Newmarket that autumn he made out very badly, but he began to come rather later on, and in a two-mile trial with Compromise, who gave him 25 lbs. for the two years, the six-year-old Clarissa gelding 6 st., and the two-year olds Conscript and Gwellyan, he won just as he liked. He was tried at Stevens' of Ilsley in the spring, and was in Godding's hands for the Metropolitan, and Chester Cup. This severe preparation knocked his legs about so much, that it was some weeks before Taylor could go on with him for the St. Leger; but he couldn't have made weather to suit the immense work his colt had to do, more exactly; and a rough gallop in clothes for the St. Leger distance with Plumper showed him to be more than 2st. the best of the pair. Luke Snowdon had never been on him till the day before the race, and his orders to come at the

distance resulted in the most decisive victory, since
The Dutchman's day. The outside of the fetlock-
joint of the off fore-foot had always been his weak
spot, and he was so lame on the Friday, that he had
to be blistered and thrown up as soon as he got
home. The Ascot Cup was fatal, and the weak
foot went hopelessly on that hard course as he came
round the bottom turn. Although he seemed more,
he was only fifteen-two when in training, of a remarkable rich dark chesnut, with a peculiarly proud
way of carrying his tail, and always ramping and
neighing about. His length and hind-quarters,
and great thighs and hocks were all fine points with
him, and his staying qualities most undeniable.

Ashdown is rich in something more
than mere historic fancies. It was Ashdown Park.
here that Miss Ann Richards, the strong-minded
virgin of Wiltshire, used to leave her coach and six
on the hills, and do beater's duty close by her dogs
all day, with her pole in her hand, and her kirtle up
to her knee, till :

> " Poor Ann, at last, was view'd by death,
> Who coursed and ran her out of breath."

Here, too, met the renowned club who made such
glorious matches, sang such merry songs, invented
such luscious puddings, and found such a worthy
chronicler in old Mr. Goodlake.

We first saw it on a peculiarly lovely morning, in
fact, the one which, after a dreary winter, seemed to
herald in earnest the welcome spring-tide of '60.
The South Berkshire hounds, passing under the
railway-bridge at Reading, on their way to a distant
meet, gave us a passing peep at country recreations
as we swept along to the Shrivenham station ; and
there, too, the very pointer, emblazoned as a trade-
mark on a whole heap of returned corn-sacks, bore

its silent witness to those sporting tastes which fairly permeate an Englishman's being.

Ride to the cours- · A friend's horse was duly in waiting
　ing ground.　for us, and we were soon cantering
along towards the hills, beyond which lay our coursing land of promise. An occupation road to the left led us past a farm, half hid in ivy, with rent-paying Herefords and juicy Devons lazily chewing the cud in its straw-yard, while the thrashing-machine kept relentlessly " crushing the air," not with its " sweetness," but its beetling hum, in the snug stack-garth behind. The farmer was as mellow and pleasant as his holding, and with a " Good morning!" and a few cheery words about Ashdown, we ride briskly on across the old pasture, and along the brook studded with willow-stumps, where the pike-fishers linger in the long summer days. A labourer with a waistcoat still deeper in its yellow than the straw-laden wain which rumbles along the ruts, re-calls us from the delights to the stern realities of Nature, as his wife addresses him behind the fence, in anything but the tones of the turtle; and anon we are climbing the hill to the downs in the wake of a little slipper, who is recounting his triumphs of " four years ago."

Once at the summit, and the downs seem to stretch away for miles in one vast, brown, rippling surface, with no sound to break their stillness, except the bleatings of the Hampshires, as they answer their newly born lambs; and the bullock language of the white-smocked ploughmen. The Vale of White Horse, so dear to Tom Brown's heart, furnishes a delightful sunny panorama, rich with trees, and water, behind us. In front is a strip of table land flanked on one side by a woodland dell, where the fox lies curled at the mouth of his earth, careless of V. W. H. horn and hound; while on the other is Compton Bottom, with its patches of stunted bushes

and undergrowth, and peopled with countless generations of "merry brown" and straight-backed hares.
The plough, that gentle innovator, has stolen a
march on those ancient solitudes at last. Teams of
oxen toil along the furrows and scare the partridges
in their track, while a group of farm-sheds and straw-
ricks remind us of a store-house in a desert, and
that civilization and rats will gain a settlement everywhere.

Now, a dark mass of carriages, carts, Notabilities of
and horsemen seems to be forming ahead, the field.
round the "Rubbing House," and we press on for a
true and correct card. The word of command is
given when the Earl and his party arrive, and the
tryer and slipper, both in scarlet, move down into the
Bottom to begin, while the foot people and the com-
missariat carts linger on the hill. The Ashdown
Cavalry are there, at least four hundred strong; and
when a hare does take the hill, and they all sit down
in their saddles and catch fast hold of their horses'
heads, the very ground seems to start and tremble
under them. Three or four daughters of a noble
house are in the throng, and one of them especially,
with a simple white feather in her hat, steers her
beautiful grey to the front, each time, with a grace
and dash that makes many a rugged courtier exclaim, that "it's worth coming to Ashdown to see
those ladies ride." A rigid costumier would have
been puzzled among that motley throng. Even the
two field stewards have no unity on the point. The
one is still faithful to the trim velveteen which was
in such vogue twenty years ago, while the other
communicates lustre to a spruce overcoat of faultless
whiteness, with cords and tops to match; and knicker-
bockers are all the fashion among the younger men,
with, as lawyers were wont to say in the good old
days of special demurrers, a little scarlet at the knee
and wrist, to "give colour."

Grave Scotchmen are there in plaid, from head to foot; while the rough shooting-coat and unshackled Doric of the East Riding mark the Yorkshiremen, who have come many a mile to back Glengarry in vain. Smart young jockeys leave Lambourne for the day, and are easy to pick out from their clever hand and seat; some of them on two-year-olds, to teach them to face a crowd and harden their confidence for future contests. There, too, conspicuous from his tall, active figure, is Grantley Berkeley, the mighty hunter and rifle-shot of *The Field*, fresh from the buffaloes and the other *spolia opima* of the Prairies. "Stonehenge," too, looks on, and gathers material for new chapters in his mind's eye on the sport, which he has made his own; while the editor of *The Life*, scorning to call horse or pony to his aid, be it hill or be it plough, is always in his place, near the judge, and scanning every turn with an ardour worthy of "The Sleepless Eye."

Coursers' talk.

Their talk is all of dogs, distemper, and fine young puppies coming forward or lost for ever to the slips; and a joke about a Macclesfield man, who advertised "a low-bred greyhound," seems to be keenly enjoyed. One takes up more general ground, and details plaintively that there were only three · waiters to forty-five diners at Lambourne over night, and that fears of coming frost had deterred the cautious landlord from speculating more extensively in his brother-man. Then there is a slight dispute between a little ancient courser on a pony and a young farmer, as to the whereabouts of the White Horse Hill. Neither of them will bate one jot of his opinion. One says that he has coursed up to it for 30 years, yea, even before the other was born; and the elderly infant doesn't at all see the overwhelming force of that argument, as he "came from the hill this morning."

And now the great match of sixteen dogs of "The World" against sixteen of Altcar Club, is renewed. Sixteen courses have been run off the day before, and the former has ten standing to the latter's six; but still Altcar does not despair, and the crowd predict that Rosy Morn, thanks to the Chadbury training, will come out as fresh as ever to-day. "There *she* goes" soon passes from lip to lip, as the first hare gets up in the Bottom, but it is not much of a course. The judge takes off his hunting cap and waves it to indicate that he will give no decision as to merits, and the flag steward waves both red and white flags accordingly. Somehow or other the white flag seems to win every course in the early part of the day, and people begin to follow luck instead of judgment, and, to try and back every dog on the "white" side of the card. Rosy Morn, however, does all that is expected of her; the brown and white crack from Yorkshire toils after her in vain, and there is no hat off that time.

But the course of courses is to come, "one of the old sort," as the white-haired Nestors affectionately say. In vain the hare makes for the hill, and the cover on the other side, which she has known of old. The two blacks won't be denied, but they have the problem of perpetual motion. to solve this time. "There's a picture of Ashdown!" says Mr. McGeorge as at last, after watching them work her for nearly three miles on the hill side, he sees them both lying down on the brow, near the Rubbing House, and the hare scampering away towards her old form in the Bottom. A painter might have followed the slips for inspiration all his life, and never lighted on such a beautiful "bit." Alas! poetry soon fades into a hard reality when the trainers "take up" their wearied charges; and then is heard the sad homily on the cunning Patience, that she'll "not get over such a towelling this season."

Beating the plan-   There is another pretty picture to
tations.   hand, as a small plantation is drawn.   A
few beaters go in, and the slipper crouches behind a
hedge with his dogs, while hare after hare scampers
towards him over the vacant space, with their heads
straight for the City of Refuge over the hill.   In
not one instance is it reached, though the hares are
nothing loth to charge the foot-people.   One is
picked up in such dashing style that the crowd in-
voluntarily raise a cheer, and a winner bears another
proudly back in his mouth, as if yearning for his
ovation as well.   From the style in which he grips
it, it looks at the distance like one of those troop of
white mountain hares, which a bewildered Southron,
(better read in the Pilgrims of the Rhine than British
Rural Sports), mistook for an elfin crew, as the High-
land gillies drove them up to him, and, throwing down
his Manton, fled on his lordly legs.   Another is so dis-
inclined to quit his hold, that it is only by the aid of
three men, one of whom pinches his ear, that his
fangs can be forced open at all.   But the day wears
on, and the hares begin to wax troublesome, and get
up by threes and fours, three hundred yards ahead
of the beaters.   Sometimes twenty or thirty are on
foot together, and they look nearly as big as foxes
against the horizon line, as they move restlessly about
in or stand derisively on their hind legs to listen.
But it is not for us to

> " Sing in venturous guise
> Of ricks and turns, and falls and byes,
> And all the courser's mysteries."

Suffice it to say, that when the ties of that day were
run off, the antagonists stood 4 to 4.   The next
day's post told of evens for the last time; and, before Saturday's sun had set, Rosy Morn, daughter of
Black Cloud and Riot, had vanquished the game
Sweetbriar ; and thus Altcar gloried in a double
victory.

But Effort, Riot, Sackcloth, Mocking Over the hill to Russley.
Bird, and even our old Cumberland
neighbour Truth are out of mind, as we skirt the
Bishopstown field, on another winter day, and think,
as we are obliged, from stress of ruts and mire, to
put into the fallows, that such a name as Trip the
Daisy is only a delusion and a snare.   Ashdown
Park and its ancestral avenue of limes lie away in
the homestead-dotted valley to the left, and just
above it is seen the quaint old Rubbing House upon
Weathercock Hill.   St. Lawrence, the two " Blacks"
—Tommy and Doctor—and Pretty Boy knew it well,
and it was there poor Luke Snowdon gave Brown
Duchess many a breather for the " Green and Gold,"
when Kettledrum cleared his pipes behind Dilkoosh
along the White Horse Ridge, and Dundee strode
his defiance on Bishopstown Hill.   Never before did
three such flyers hold three neighbouring heights.
Their grave and potent senior Thormanby is on the
Bishopstown side, and there too Leamington, Saunterer, Sunbeam, Hungerford, and King Tom were
sent along in their day, over the one and a-half miles
from the Craven Cricket Ground, to the Two o'Clock
Bush.

Once over that velvet turf, and Russ- A peep at Russ-ley Park.
ley Park is below us, with its mysterious
vista of beeches, which leads to nothing.   A St.
Leger and an Oaks winner are roaming under them,
and the neat stable-yard on the left holds not only
a Derby winner, and the mightiest second that ever
made the Scots "cock their bonnets" so boldly,
but the first favourite for the next year as well.   A
white reach and foot mark tell the tale of the massive sixteen-one Sunbeam, as she grazes quietly in the
distance with the weight-carrying Miss Anne, both
of them due to Lord of the Isles.   Little Lady
Lurewell carries her Wild Dayrell burden bravely,
and so does Russley's dam, and the whole-coloured

s

Catherine Hayes, as she loiters affectionately round
the house away from them all, and raises her sweet,
mild head for her wonted pat, as Mat Dawson comes
up. One of the very first Fisherman colts is in a
paddock beyond the yard, and, true to his Scottish
ownership, Newhaven is his name; and we find a
memento in-doors of his aunt Rambling Katie, in
the oxydized black duck inkstand, which tells its
own tale of York, and a kind-hearted owner dead
and gone.

Thormanby forms a pleasant link for
Mat Dawson between his old service and
his new. He thought "Old Alice," as we did when we
saw her at Cawston, a very hopeless subject, but the
spring brought strength, and she did not turn from
Windhound as she had done at the end of three
weeks from Melbourne, who got no foal that season.
It was in Sunbeam's year, that Mr. Plummer encountered Mat, and begged him to come and look at
"one of Alice's, which will suit Mr. Merry." Off
they went to the Turf Tavern, and Mr. Merry struck
a bargain at £350 for him on the Friday, thus carrying away as it were a Derby and St. Leger out of
the town at one stroke. Northern Light, Trovatore,
Lady Falconer, and Apollyon were in the yearling
lot that autumn, and he squandered them so decidedly when they did have a brush, that it was
thought advisable to hire the old mare. She foaled
a filly to Wild Dayrell, and it died, and then she was
barren to him again, and died herself, a mere steed of
Old Mortality, with an enormous gathering in her
udder, at Saunterer's paddocks.

Never did a two-year-old work much
harder than the chesnut, as he was out
no less than twelve times between Northampton
and The Criterion, in which his 3 lbs. to Thunder-
bolt stamped him. A severe course like Ascot and
the Newmarket finish always suited him best. When

Northern Light was beaten by Cape Flyaway (who was a first-rate tryer) at Bath, John Scott thought he had got the line, and sent Mat Dawson a friendly warning that he had a tremendous horse in The Wizard, and Mat sent back his compliments and his "Who's afraid?" The trial with Northern Light a week before had been high enough to allow of a margin, and as the chesnut had not a drawback, both trainer and owner considered that the Derby cheque only wanted Mr. Weatherby's signature. Twenty-four hours after the race their champion had a bad swollen gland, and as he required a great deal of preparation, it was not all plain sailing up to the Leger, where the infallible sign of turning a little awkward on going down to canter, was as fatal to the favourite as ever.

Mat Dawson had never heard of Dundee, till Thomas Winteringham *Dundee.* begged him at Doncaster to come to the ring side directly, as "They're just going to bring in Mr. Cookson's, and there's one by our horse." Strange as it may seem, Kettledrum was No. 1 on the list, and Dundee No. 2, and as Mat Dawson thought the latter a well-grown colt, and knew that Mr. Merry wanted a bit of Lord of the Isles, he put him in at 150.

Reeves of Epsom got one or two bids, and when the colt was knocked down at 170, he repented his lack of ardour too late, and begged Dawson to give up his bargain. Mr. Parr had one bid, but he did not go on, as his mind was rather set on taking home a Rataplan. He quavered between Kettledrum and Parasite, and got the one he wanted at 400 gs., but found that he could only act in dirt, and was infirm in his hocks, and a roarer as well.

Dundee bullied Russley, Folkestone, Starlight, and Sweet Hawthorn in his gallops in quite the Thor-

manby style, and although very backward, he was
tried very highly before Liverpool. A finish with
Lady Clifden, Big Ben, Dundee, and Little Lady
and not three-parts of a length between, is one
Liverpool may not see again, and Folkestone's defeat
of "The Lady" at Epsom Spring kept the stable
right. Once in form, and Dundee ruled for the season.
Brown Duchess certainly extended him at Liverpool,
in a splendid finish, for which the mare never got
sufficient credit that year, as he walked away from
her and Nemesis so completely in the Findon Stakes.
On paper, the Stockbridge race was a great one, but
the dead-heat with Maggiore at York weighed more
with the public than the stable. A young one
was not likely to improve with heats, but Mr.
Merry and Mat thought so little of Maggiore's
form, that they would have tried their colt higher
at home.

His break down. Dundee is rather a coltish, light-fleshed
horse, with a beautiful wind, a very
blood-like head, and fine thighs, but, like his sire, a
little upright on his fore joints. Custance always liked
to bring him eight or ten strides from home, and to
feel him "come like a steam-engine." Thormanby
left it to Sir William, Russley, and Folkestone to
try him among them, as he was almost too idle a
horse to do so satisfactorily. Dundee did all that was
desired, but there were indications two or three days
before Epsom, which made them watch the pointer
of the weather-glass very jealously, and wish themselves and the horse well out of it. Of his standing
another preparation, they had not a hope, and the
lower part of the suspensory ligament in the near
fore-leg went so badly, that after the Derby the fetlock touched the ground, and it was nearly forty
minutes' labour getting him back to Sherwood's.
Then it was another week before he could be got
into the van; three months of cold-water band-

ages hardly put him into a walking gear, and Habena was his first consort at Eltham.

A few miles over the downs, and we are among Tom Parr and his lot, which A peep at Benhams. do their long summer work on the Seven Barrow or Sparsholt Down, and in bad weather on the Charlton range. "*Puce and white wins,*" has now been heard from Weymouth to Kelso, for ten long years, and gradually the parchments of Letcombe Regis and Bowers, Benhams and the Manors of East and West Challow have given a solid significance to the cry. The Goodlake crest lingers in almost undecipherable characters above one of the gable ends in the most venerable of yards, where the green moss and the house-leek still cling to the thatch. The highly conservative corn chamber in the centre, whose stores have enabled so many thoroughbreds to face the hill, is still faithful to its wooden steps and rusty staddles, and gallantly defies all change. The ancient kennel of Glider and the other G.'s of the King of Wiltshire coursers is there, close by the box of Wyon and Tolurno, but nothing but a fir cone arch, round which the ivy is clinging, and an armless statue of Neptune among the wild flowers on the edge of the swan lake, tell of the old man's home. Kildonan was in Fisherman's barn, ripening (as it was then hoped) by a long winter's rest for Marlow's hand, but the Heron brown is not forgotten.

Mr. Parr still loves to tell how he humoured him with a long gallop or a Fisherman & Co. short one, but "never left him many days together," and points to the 65lbs. and the head-beating which he gave Misty Morn (the winner of thirteen races that season) at Derby, as the greatest triumph among his sixty-eight. The deceptive Lupellus has already died out of Benhams memory; but, wonder as he might seem in his day, he was never so fast as his little Punch of a brother Lupus; and it was the style in which Kildonan gave him 2 st., and Avalanche 9 lbs. over the *D.I.* which made Mr. Parr feel sure that Imaus would beat his half-brother no more.

Avalanche. Avalanche was one of the pots of treasure which Mr. Parr is ever turning up. Captain Oliver met him in the train, and begged him to take her for her forfeits, which he did, but she seemed so unpromising, that at first he only rode her as a hack. When the work on Sparsholt Down was over one morning, he rode her to Bowers Farm, where he intended to shoot, and her action in a brisk gallop across the plough at once decided him to train her. Her turn soon came, and she had to take Rattlebone's place in the Newmarket Biennial, when he fell amiss, and the trial at a stone with the four-year-old Indifference was so good, that her owner got on at 2,000 to 200 about her. And well he might, as whatever beat Indifference in a trial won its race. Still even Fordham, who can communicate his fine confidence to a nervous horse beyond almost any jockey of the day, could make but little of Indifference in public. In a trial at home, he gave Gaspard a stone, and a year cleverly, and yet at Stamford he was himself beaten by Wallace in a walk. According to this truest of tryers, Avalanche took the horrors after Ascot, but "The shooting pony" won between £4,000 and £5,000 in bets and stakes, and went to Belgium for 800 gs. more.

Caller Ou. I'Anson had almost made up his mind to send Queen Mary to West Australian in '57, but he changed his mind and chose Stockwell for her. He gave effect to his first fancy the next season, but she returned from Grimston with Caller Ou at her foot and barren. Scott told him by way of comfort that the little brown filly was a clipper, and that no foal in the paddock could come near her, when she galloped. She never lost a trial either at two or three years old ; and nothing in the stable could take more work, provided she was allowed to do it by herself.

In point of action it was Blink Bonny for choice, but their head notions were *Trials and peculiarities.* totally different. If Blink's jockey pulled hers up, she would have it down again, whereas if Caller Ou got excited and pulled about, up it went, and she would fight and wear herself out. Her first two-year-old trial was half-mile at even weights with the four-year-old Donati. Her victory was so hollow, that I'Anson tried them over again, and found it to be a true bill. Soon after that, a friend came through the stable, and casually remarked as they passed, " *If she could knock over Donati at evens, I'd give a thousand for her;*" but I'Anson never answered a word. After Beverley, he began to think that Donati was a deceiver, and the post-breaking feat at Carlisle did not improve matters.

On the Oaks day I'Anson had not discovered her mouth secret, and as Challoner did not ride her tenderly enough, she summarily shut up at the turn. Before York, she allowed Prologue to lead her in her fast work; but backward as she was, Starlight, whose heels were full of humour, never made her gallop there, and H. Grimshaw liked his mount so much, that he backed her to win him three hundred in the St. Leger. I'Anson's Doncaster hopes revived on Knavesmire, but still he offered her to Mr. Robinson of Australia for fifteen hundred. At Stockton she ran out two or three lengths, and the world did not know how good Oldminster was; and Derby did not at all convince her owner that there was going to be a Saucebox encore.

Her St. Leger race.   The arrangement that Grimshaw should come down for a week to Malton to ride in her gallops, was abandoned, and when she did come to Doncaster, he met I'Anson at the station and begged to give up his mount. In short, the night before the race, Lord Stamford had the refusal of her for £1,200, and if it had not been "all the money" she would most probably have never started. Challoner's orders to let her do what she liked with her head were carried out to the letter, and at the Red House she was going so well that he felt sure of a place. At the distance she was still going, and when Kettledrum came away, he felt that there was just one thing for it, and that was to tackle him and never let Luke have a pull. He found he had the best of the speed the moment he placed her alongside of the crack, who was running as game as a bull-dog in his difficulties, and there he sat, till the post was passed, not daring to move on her and touch her, and expecting every instant that she would cut it.

The youth of Kettledrum.   It seems but yesterday that we saw Kettledrum for the first time at Mr. Cookson's paddocks, in that unsatisfactory transition state of a yearling in January. He was short, and not the most elegant, but the strongest limbed one we ever met with at that age. Rataplan had been chosen for his dam Hybla, who was never broken, purely for the sake of the double cross of Whalebone, through The Saddler and The Baron. It has always been this celebrated breeder's theory, that whatever may be the best strain the mare has, a horse should be selected with the same. It was on this ground that Marmalade was sent to Lord of the Isles, that the double cross of Whalebone might unite through Waverley and Touchstone. The same end might have been effected by choosing Chanticleer, who also stood at Croft, but Dundee's sire got the preference on account of his Pantaloon strain, which always nicks well with Whalebone, either through Castrel, Selim, or Buzzard.

At Doncaster, many took against Kettledrum, as having far too heavy a top; but still he had a strong party, and it was then written of him, that " with that strong neck, and those wonderfully springy pasterns, it will be strange indeed if he does not race or stay, or both." Poor William Oates felt no peace of mind till Colonel Towneley consented to purchase; and if he had got his way, nothing would have stopped him for Dundee as well. The heavy top made the biddings languid. Messrs. Robinson and J. Dawson were " in" a few times; but Mr. Eastwood's nods came from the dangerous left with the regularity of a piston, and the crack fell beneath them for four hundred. Three times before had Col. Towneley nearly drawn a great winner in the yearling lottery. Oates had said a great deal about not going past Thormanby; and on the advice of Heseltine, who looked after his dam Peggy as a boy, money had been bid for Musjid; and Gladiolus was preferred; and but for Mrs. I'Anson and her daughters begging their father not to part with the blood, the joint offer of £500 for Haricot and the yearling Caller Ou would have been accepted. As it was, Mr. Eastwood bid 300 gs. for Caller Ou herself on the very Doncaster Thursday that he bought Haricot and Kettledrum for Colonel Towneley.

To get the young Kettledrum reduced *Training Kettle-* in bulk was rather a snail-like process, *drum.* and his first gallop was about December with Doefoot, who received 7lbs., and fairly danced away from him. At the next time of asking he was some lengths nearer; but he was a delicate feeder, and never took regular work till a month before the York August. His preparation had been so short, that although he got a bad start in the mud,

and regularly cut up the Lincolnshire regiment of Dictator Volunteers, who crossed the Humber next morning in the direst dismay, he did badly over the same course on the Friday, and ran some pounds below his form in The Champagne. His dentition was tedious, and hence the intention of coming through with him in the Two Thousand was abandoned. On a straight course he can make his own running, when he has had a little time to settle, but he gets his head up and crosses his legs immediately if he tries to do it on a round one. A tremendous pace is what he wants, and the style in which he stole along on the Derby day from Tattenham Corner,—ever handy with Dundee, when the bay came down the fatal hill into the straight like a flash; or flew up the Doncaster one as if he fairly revelled in the design of Rising Sun to break The Wizard's heart, and heeded nothing of 10lbs. to an Oaks winner,—was not a sight to be forgotten. The five-year-old Dilkoosh, who never told them wrong yet, was the stable barometer, and he was fully 5lbs. the worst of the two before the Derby. He was laid up with plaisters on his legs, long before the St. Leger; but from a collateral trial, they believed Kettledrum to be fully 7lbs. better than he was at Epsom. Perhaps, to our eye, he was not in such perfect bloom, but Yorkminster's flat refusal to help him up to the Red House was fatal, and instead of taking the fifth double first, he had to cast in his lot with Cotherstone, Coronation, Thormanby, and the baffled fifteen.

Col. Towneley's paddocks. His Doncaster and Epsom guardian had returned to his velveteen fellows, and their guns were echoing in chorus among the plantations on Beatrix and Middle Knowe, when with Wolfinden Crag as our beacon, we followed the windings of the trout-haunted Hodder. Above us were Staple Oak, Brennand, Whitendale, and Whitmore,

links in the chain of those everlasting hills, and
sponsors to Newminster and West Australian colts,
over which Heseltine, the Dr. Caius of the glen,
watches so tenderly. The "Black mutton," as the
Monks of Whaley and the Robin Hoods of the district delicately termed it in the days of the "Bold
Buccleuch," has departed for ever and aye since
the fiat of disparking went forth. Those who remember the killing of the last buck have long since
grown into greybeards, and when antlers were extinct, the curved horn of the Lonk King reigned pa-
ramount on the dark heather sides, and up the ash
and sycamore gullets of the Forest of Bowland, of
which Mr. Richard Eastwood is the Bow-bearer.
Two counties unite close by the Root Stud-farm,
and we might well ponder whether we should stop
in the West Riding to look at the Beeswing-like
style of the yearling Stella, as she stood ready to
greet us with the Voltigeur-necked Lamb Hill, and
the well-grown Nugget in their polished boxes of
home-forest oak,—or cross the elder-shaded stream,
to give her spotted namesake with Faith, Emma,
and Rosette, of Royal fame, a hearty Lancashire
greeting. It was well to be off with the old love
first, so we chose the Yorkshire side.

The old matrons Florence by Veloci- An hour with the
pede, and the hollow-backed Boarding brood mares.
School Miss still remember their Grimstone Paddock days, and enjoy an undying nine months'
friendship, when they meet again each spring.
Nelly Hill (on which Luke Snowdon won his
maiden race), Honeydew, by Touchstone, and the
white-faced Haricot, have nearly as great a bond
of union in Langdon Holme, and the little whitenose tip of Ellermire reminds us that the quickest
starter in England, a daughter of old Beeswing, the
dam of the St. Leger winner of the year, and the
mare who beat off the flying squadron of King of

Trumps, Hospodar, Kingston, and Ephesus, in a mile at York, are all confederates now. Rosaura, by Don John the germ of the stud, is there, with "fifteen or sixteen pure crosses, and yet one hair in her tail not right," as Heseltine observes in his fervour ; and so is her daughter Hesperithusa, the first foal and the first Cup winner that Col. Towneley ever owned. Her half-sister Passion Flower waits for an audience close by the edge of the pheasant brake, which fringes the holme, and Heseltine tells triumphantly how Doe-foot, their Liverpool Cup winner, went as a yearling to Doncaster with old Rosaura, and how they returned without a single bid. Two white hind legs marked a second slice of Touchstone in Amethyst, and the blood of Windhound and Melbourne, which lays rival claim to the honour of Thormanby's paternity, is united here in the whole brown Be Quick.

Patience, whom William Oates never failed to have a word with, and the old steeple-chasing Velocity, another of the h. b. brand, consort with the white-legged Evadne in the Smithy Paddocks, and Nightingale, who has nothing but "three event blood in her veins," gives back an answering note as the white Velocipede face of King of Trumps is seen approaching across the bridge from Holme Head to give us a meeting on the knoll. Pompadour, who could boast of nearly as proud a lineage as Repartee, had just joined the ranks from Middleham, and Castle Hill, Rappel, Deerfoot, and Ellerby fill up the boxes, which Stella, Lamb Hill, Goldfinch, and Campanile have left. And so year quietly succeeds to year, and yearling to yearling ; and perchance a third bonfire may announce the Epsom telegram from the summit of Staple Oak, and a cheer may be heard at last for a St. Leger winner, and "the white and black sleeves," in its own sweet valley of the Hodder.

CHAPTER IV.

STAG, DRAG, AND FLAG.

" I was lately in a company of very worthy people, where we had the Plea-
sure of a small Consort of Musick ; a good Hand on the Violin, and a Young
Lady (esteemed a top Mistress), sung and play'd on a very fine Harpsichord.
'Tis the Fashion (you know) for every one to commend ; and the most insensi-
ble Auditor, for fear of discovering his own Ignorance, must seem to be in
Raptures. The Lady performed to Admiration ; one stared, another talked
of Angels and the Spheres, a third wept, a fourth was ready to drop into a
Trance. At last a very honest Gentleman that sat by in a musing Posture,
having his Ears shaken with a longer and louder Quiver than ordinary, look'd
abroad, and gave me a Nod and Wink, with this ingenious remark : ' By Jingo,
I never heard anything better but a Cry of Dogs ; she draws out her Note like my
old Toler.' The Lady herself was not unacquainted with the Attractions of
Hunting, and (as she told me afterwards) she was more proud of this sincere
compliment from Toler's master than all the rest she received on the occasion."—
A COUNTRY SQUIRE'S ESSAY ON HUNTING.

So spake Old Toler's master, the sworn *Old hunting times.*
liegeman of the Prince of Orange,
with all the freshness of the time when it first became
the highest family ambition to have "a member for the
county, a lad for the living, and a fox from the family
gorse." An earlier generation had found pleasure in
chasing the yellow-breasted marten, and the bustard.
"Thick woods also extended from the village of St.
Giles westward towards Tybourne ; and Mary-le-
bonne was then also a great Black Forest, into which
the Queen used to send the Muscovite ambassador to
hunt the wild boar." How and where the last acorn-
eater was run into is involved in historical gloom ; but
no fox was found in Kensington Gardens after 1798,
when the gardeners combined against two litters in
the sewer "for carrying off water into the fosse
under the upper bastion," and shot one of their own
body in their undisciplined ardour.

The first Master of the Royal Hounds. Over fox-hunting, whether London or provincial, the old Master of Hounds to the King of Wales did not much care to preside. He busied himself more about beaver, marten, and float, and it was ordained by Forest law, that his hunting clothes should be bordered with their skins. His bugle was the horn of an ox valued at £1, and his protection extended as far as its note could be heard. He could only be cited to a court of justice early in the morning, before he had put on his boots, and whenever he had to be sworn, it was by his horn, his hound, and his leashes. Such was the Charles Davis of antiquity.

There are records of a tremendous run of seventy miles in the Merric King's reign, and the Duke of York with five others rode it from end to end. They took their stag near Lord Petre's in Essex, and lay there for the night, and on the earliest opportunity, the Duke repaired to Court, to give an accurate account of his saddle labours.

The Royal Staghounds. Towards the close of the eighteenth century His Majesty George III. was in the zenith of his stag-hunting. Earl Sandwich wore the golden dog couples; Johnson was the huntsman, and six yeomen prickers, with French horns, wound the *réveille* on Holyrood day. The fern-cutters never put in the sickle before that morning, and His Majesty seldom failed to give the field his greeting of the season, at Charity Farm, or Billing Bear. "Farmer George" met his hounds twice a week when he was at Windsor, clad in his light-blue coat, with black velvet cuffs and top-boots buckled up behind; but as he rode nearly nineteen stone, the hounds were very often stopped to bring him on to Reverence of the country people. terms. The country people loved dearly to see their King amongst them. We cannot cap the story which Bill Bean (who was hunting six years before the present century) once

begged permission to tell to the late Prince Consort,
when they were taking the deer in a cellar, that a
rustic of that Georgian era believed his sovereign
to have a lion for one arm, and a unicorn for the
other. Still we saw pleasant traces of the feeling
in an old workhouse dame, who told us how,
when quite a girl, she had seen the deer killed near
Leatherhead. Years had evidently created a little
confusion in her mind, between the gayer dress
of the huntsman, and the simple insignia of the
King, and so she spake on this wise. " His Majesty
had a scarlet coat and jockey cap, with gold all
about; he had a star on his heart, and we all fell on
our knees."

The runs were long, and the stags *The King out*
" Moonshine" and " Starlight" earned *hunting.*
their title from the time at which they were taken.
An own brother to " Sir Henry Gott" (a fine old
sportsman, whose hunting-groom always wore a
green plush coat down to his ankles), gave them the
severest day from Aldermaston to Reading, and as
His Majesty's horses were both knocked up, he was
seen returning to Windsor in a butcher's taxed cart,
and talking of crops and stock by the way. The
only emblem of royalty on these occasions was the
yeoman pricker riding on either side. At first, these
guardians of the night merely had their hunting-
whips; but when we were at war with all the world,
and a spy or highwayman had shot down Mr. Mellish, the Master of the Epping Forest lemon pyes,
on his return from hunting, two boys (of whom
Charles Davis was one), each with a brace of horse
pistols, were added to the hunting corps, and as soon as
the chace was over, they handed their pistols to two
yeomen prickers, in exchange for their horns. The
horse for His Majesty's statues was modelled from the
white Adonis, or the Hanover-bred Arrogant, which
were strictly kept as chargers. Perfection was a

favourite hunter, for many years, but the bay Hobby
was His Majesty's last, and best. By the royal
order, no hand but Mr. Davis's was permitted to
shoot him, and his ear is still kept among that great
huntsman's treasures, with the first hare (a white
one) that he ever saw killed.

The original pack. The original staghound pack, the
whole 40 couple of which were bought
by Colonel Thornton to go to France, were lemon
pyes, and black-and-whites, from 24 to 26 inches.
Their skins were rather thin, and their ears "as big
as cobblers' aprons," and in fact they seemed all head
and throat. For half-an-hour they were very fast,
and gave tongue like "Big Ben;" but after that
they sobered down, and never thought of racing like
the present foxhound pack for their deer, when it was
sinking. Kennel lameness was the Ascot scourge. In
vain did Sharpe adjourn to Brighton for a month in
the summer, and astonish "the languid bathers on
the Sussex coast," by taking a boat, morning and
afternoon, and making them swim after him till he
looked a sea-god among attendant Tritons, or rather
sea-dogs. They were as bad as ever before they had
been back at Ascot for a week, and until Mr. Davis
had a false flooring put, so as to admit a free current
of air, the effect of the sand upon the bog substra-
tum was never wholly neutralized. The Goodwood
pack were given to His Majesty in 1813, and sadly
the Sussex men grudged their departure. Their old
The Goodwood kennels were considered a model at that
kennels. time, and one *Sporting Magazine* poet
had been inflamed into writing a copy of verses in
the architect's praise. It is only the other day
that we turned aside for a minute under their ivied
archway, to have a look at such a memorable spot.
Two stone foxes guard it yet; but the South-
downs in the meadow beneath told how truly Goodwood had found a new love, before which, even the

horn and the " red cap with golden tassel" had to
bow ; and all those pleasant hazel copses, across
which old Tom Grant rattled the cubs so often
in the dew of the autumn morning, invite him and
his badger-pyes back in vain. With this pack a new
state of things began at the kennel. Mr. Davis,
whose father was " the hare-huntsman" to royalty,
left the harriers to become first whip, the Duke of
Richmond's men going on second and third, and
Sharpe blew his first blast on a Robin Hood, instead
of a French horn.

The Prince Regent, who used to draw George IV.'s hunting.
his deer supplies from the New Forest
each August, left stag for fox about '93, and with
Mr. Poyntz, their ex-master, as his manager, and
Sharpe as his huntsman, he took the H. H.
country and Albury Park, whose ale cellar alone
was valued at five hundred. His Royal Highness met the staghounds no more, either in his
royal father's reign or his own. Once he thought
of coming out again with the harriers, and had
his breeches and boots duly ordered, but he
never put them on. Mr. Davis's appointment
as huntsman in 1822 was quite after his heart.
" It delights me," he wrote, after it was gazetted
" to hear that you've got the hounds ; I hope you'll
get them so fast that they'll run away from everybody." Such was the handsel of that ever memorable career.

Mr. Davis was then thirty-four, and Mr. Davis's best runs.
had been exactly the term of a mi-
nority in the royal service, and spent a third of it
with the harriers. It needs a Bill Bean to truly
tell his triumphs ; of his stopping hounds when they
had a slow deer in front of them, and of the daring
talent of those casts, which none but the old stag-
hunters can fathom till they see the hounds again
striking the line. Mr. Davis's own ideas of his

fastest things centre upon two. The first was from Salt Hill to the "Oldaker kennels," fourteen miles within the hour, and he remembers it too well from the fact, that his rat-tailed Nimble broke down. Mr. Harvey Combe, who was then the master of the Old Berkeley, happened to be on the flags that day. They took out their watches to mark the time before any one came up. Lord Alvanley was placed second at the end of ten minutes, but he jocularly claimed to reverse the yachting rule, and claimed "some minutes to the good over Davis for my extra tonnage."

Fun in the Vale of Aylesbury. Richmond Trump gave them such a tremendous twenty miles from Aylesbury to Twyford Mill, that he was re-named "Twyford;" and he seemed so anxious to deserve the name, that he took them in his next run to Twyford in Oxfordshire. The first was a white stone day, in Lord Lichfield's first year of mastership; and Mr. Davis rode The Clipper, so called from being the first that was ever clipped for royal use. He had been originally in harness, and as he was up to sixteen stone, and his rider, even with a 7lb.-coat, did not ride above ten stone, he went through from end to end over grass in little more than an hour and a quarter. The hounds never checked for bullocks or anything else; and as Mr. Davis lay in the ditch with one arm round the deer's neck, he took out his watch with the other. For twenty minutes he had no companions, save the miller and his men, who were not a little astonished at the position of affairs; a gasping huntsman, "a hor-*ned* stag," and a pack baying like mad.

The Marquis at bay. Still Mr. Davis felt his position much more perilous when Earl Errol had established a club at Aylesbury, and went for a week into the country. The Marquis of Waterford came to see the fun, and a merry time there was of it at the White Hart. Mr. Davis slipped away early, and they determined to be revenged. When they had conducted one of Mr. Osman Ricardo's handiest horses into the big room, and made him jump over the chairs and tables, the next proposition was to " unearth the old badger." Recognizing whom they meant by the expression, Mr. Davis was out of bed in an instant, and almost before he could get his door locked, and a table and a chest of drawers thrust against it, he heard the horse coming up stairs, and the men of war with him. A fearful attack was made on the entrenchments, but they were not to be carried. Mr. Davis stood well to his guns within, and the landlord, whose patience had been exhausted by the horse's ascent, fought like a Trojan without, and "the old badger" lay curled in his earth till morning.

Ascot Heath seemed drear and strange, as we lately walked across it, to pay our annual May visit to Mr. Davis and the hounds. Two or three horses were slowly canter-ing round in their sheets, but even quite a summer sun overhead could not light up the scene; and it was one desolate expanse of brown ling and bracken, with here and there a solitary gorse flower. Time has dealt very gently with the veteran himself, as all the field allow that they never saw him go better or enjoy the sport more than during these two last sea-sons. His parlour is rich in picture history. Mr. Far-quharson and Jem Treadwell, by Mr. Davis's late brother, occupy the post of honour over the chim-ney-piece, and, in fact, the great majority of the engravings are from paintings by his well-known hand. Old Hermit, who loved nothing more dearly than the doubles in the Vale, is there in no less than seven positions, and Columbine, who finally went to the Duke of Beaufort's and bred some rare coach-horses, is not forgotten. The little chesnut Sepoy is

Visit to the Royal Kennels.

happily still ripe and ready for the Bucks side; but poor Pioneer's seven seasons among the stiffer fences of Berks are ended. The light-bodied and light-hearted Comus, who was ridden for a season by the Prince of Wales, after Mr. Davis had made him perfect, has been presented to the latter by his royal pupil, for a hack, and roarer as he is, the pair may do a great thing yet.

Pictures and testimonials. The earliest picture of Mr. Davis himself (who has ridden everything in a simple snaffle from that day to this) represents him as a lad of eighteen, whipping-in to his father with the Royal Harriers; and beneath it hang the series of English Hunt Pictures, which preserve so vividly the fine outline of the head of Tom Goosey, and the thunder and lightning features of the redoubtable Jack Shirley. The Silver Testimonial of '59 is in the dining-room, with Lord Maryborough's bust on guard. Lord Chesterfield's mastership is commemorated by a silver stag-group, and tributes of the same character are ranged daintily below it, and flanked by two horns, one of them the gift of the present Duke of Beaufort. Not the least among them is the hoof of a hunter The Miller, whose white fore hoof was selected in preference to his black, to show that popular prejudice as to soundness may err. Radiant, Byron, and Landscape of the beautiful skulls, are foremost among the hounds; and the Ripley Deer twice over claims his place, both in his paddock and going like great guns with his head quite low. The Miller ran for thirteen seasons; and went for eleven before he became cunning and useless. They seldom used to uncart him more than three times a season, and then Mr. Davis always put an extra guinea in his pocket, as he knew it would be a case of sleeping out for his men. This noted deer was a hero of Lord Maryborough's time, and looked such a rough unprepared thing, that Mr. Davis could hardly persuade his Lordship to hunt him. He knew his lines of country so well, that if he got a few hundred yards wide, he would invariably right himself; and at times he would swim a river, dodge down the opposite bank, and lie with his nose just out of the water.

In the kennel we begged to have Waterloo, of that rich-grey tan family *The Hound kennel.* by Woodman from Fife Wishful, and his sisters, Wanton, Waspish, and Widgeon (*my "Little Lady,"* as Mr. Davis terms her), drawn together. Then we had out the Rockwoods seven-couple strong— Relish, Rakish, and Rally on one side of the rails, and Ringwood, Rifler, Random, and Rasselas on the other. There they stood, almost a pack by themselves, and yet it was a mere oversight, which Mr. Davis sadly deplored at the time, which brought the first lot of them into being. The old dog was of course there, looking as meek but as yet sly as a Quaker, and runs well in his sixth season. He is from the old Goodwood sort, which Mr. Davis always finds to last the longest; but he is now the victim of kennel lameness, which has stopped him a good deal in his regular work. The lady pack go into Berks, and the dogs, which have more nerve for the crowd, take their turn across the Thames in Bucks.

A walk of two miles over the common, past the edge of the heath, and finally *Old Swinley revelries.* up a pleasant avenue found us at Swinley Paddocks. The house, where the Marquis of Cornwallis and divers ancient masters of buck-hounds kept such state, and where huntsmen and foresters drained horns quite as often as they blew them, has long since disappeared, and there is nothing save a large indentation in the ground, under the shade of some noble limes, to mark the tomb of all such revelry. High holiday was kept there when George III. was king, and each fourth of June came round. The

Master of the hounds gave a great dinner to all the
foresters, and farmers and twice or thrice the Royal
party drove over, and watched them while they
danced upon the green.

The Deer Pad-docks.   The Cotterill family live in a solitary
house close by, and the present man's
father and mother discharged the duties of deer-
keeper for 79 years. George Cotterill, the son, has
now held it for four, and passes quite a simple forest
life, without even a badge or livery for high days.
He knows no special festival of St. Hubert; but
sundry trophies of departed favourites hang round
his walls. Wild Boy's head is there, and judging
from it he may well speak of him as " the largest
deer I ever saw." There, too, in due array are the
four feet of Sepoy, of whom Cotterill has a vivid recollection as being not only a first-rate, but "'a most
amiable deer." His herd consists of about 21, and
stags were once all the rage; but the difficulty of getting them to run well between October and Christmas
has determined the question in favour of the haviers
and hinds. Many of the former are caught, and
cut as calves at ten days old, and then they never
have horns; while those which are selected later on
for their style of going, throw up one set of antlers
with soft tips after the operation. The Windsor
Little Park and Richmond Park stags have not done
well, and the best have come from the Great Park,
which may be owing to the breed having been more
crossed. The red deer from Woburn were the finest
strangers, as instead of the usual cat-hams, they had
quarters more like a horse, with rare backs
and gaskins to match. In Lord Errol's mastership, the hounds went each April to the
New Forest; Lord Palmerston used to meet
them there, and Mr. Assheton Smith and nineteen other masters of hounds were once in the
field together.

Nearly all the stags are born in Windsor Great Park, and the ill-luck which attended four that were bought for £80 from Chillingham in Lord Kinnaird's time, decided them to keep to the home-breds. *Deer diet.* Of this quartet Percy and Douglas did not run particularly well; and the other two, Robin Hood and Rob Roy, met with tragical deaths—one of them being spiked on some palings, and the other jumping over a railway bridge. Three runs in one season is a good allowance, and they have to be kept in tip-top condition to achieve that. Clover hay of the second crop, as the first is rather too coarse for their teeth, is given them at the rate of about 7 trusses per week for the 17, and to this are added 2 bushels of the smallest and heaviest old beans that can be got, with carrots, to vary matters in the winter. The deer-cart stood in a shed in the first paddock, on the door of which was nailed a foot, of apocryphal age; and the sick-house was in another corner, but with only Whimsy and her puppies in possession.

We were quite sorry to disturb a most harmonious and picturesque party of deer *Paddock exercise.* and cock pheasants in the next paddock. The former will come warmly enough round Cotterill at feeding time, but they would not fraternize with strangers at all, and we took care that they should show their action in three or four smart gallops. Richmond, with his fine antlers and great length, was far the most imposing among them, and he derives his name from having been dropped in the park of that ilk, to which he does the highest credit. He and The Doctor raced for the lead in the first heat, and in the second Sulky, who earned that unenviable name from his performance, or rather non performance, at Hawthorn Hill, took the lead and kept it throughout. As to the third, we have an indistinct idea of Lightning, a very small but nicely-made hind, cutting well in at the turns, and getting the lead from Jack Tar, the biggest there, but with not an inch of apology for horns, and of Red Rover finishing close up.

Carting the deer
On the day before hunting, a well-trained sheep-dog is called in to separate the chosen pair from the rest, and they are driven across paddock No. 3, to the enclosure in the corner, and so into a little house just big enough for a brace to fast in all night. It is very dangerous to go into them there, except with a large board for a shield ; and the pieces of hair strewn about prove how fierce some of the anti-Cotterill conflicts must be before he gets them righted. King Cole was quite a savage ; but as Cotterill used to say, " *I wouldn't care about his fighting the shield if he'd only fight the country.*" One side of this house has a moveable window, against which the door of the van is backed, and as the deer of the day has been adjusted, by dint of shield-fighting, into the half of the house nearest the window, he gets the first leap, and running up one side of the partition-board in the van and round the space at the end, naturally settles with his head ready for " putting himself on the country." The partition-board is then pushed up to the end, and the reserve deer has to jump in, and ride with his head to the horses.

Peculiarities of great stags.
A run from Farnham Common on March 1st, 1861, was the last great thing that the lamented Sepoy (who first showed his form on the morning that news of the fall of Delhi arrived) ever gave them. He was out once more on Easter Monday, and was taken, after a run from Maidenhead Thicket, six miles beyond High Wickham, among the junipers at Mapple Common, where very few were left to see him dodging like a beaten fox ; but he never lived to come back, and broke his leg that night, fretting over his captivity in a barn. They had hunted him four times a season since 1857,

and he is quite embalmed in Mr. Davis's memory, with Woodman, the Ripley, and the Hendon deer. He was not a very large deer, but good in any country; of "the straight bang-away sort," no sulkiness or subterfuge, never letting a hound see him till he was fairly tired, and invariably taking some distant hill for his point. He was originally bred in Windsor Park, and there was not a bite upon him after all his perils.

Red Hart was also a marvellous deer, of about the same size; but, unfortunately, when he got to a spot where he had been before, he never would leave it, even if he had another half hour in him. Occasionally he would make an honourable compromise, by running a short circuit and back again; but this was rather the exception than the rule. Cashiobury Park was a very favourite spot with him; and it was beautiful to see the hounds pick it out when he got among the fallow-deer there; and when Harry joined the red ranks once more in Windsor Great Park (where he is now enjoying himself for the summer) they actually stopped, and looked up to Mr. Davis for counsel, at the point where he entered the herd, after holding it for a few hundred yards over the foiled ground. The flints in the fair fields of Bucks play havoc with them; and Jack Tar, who has made the hounds sleep out two or three times, came to grief in consequence at last.

The specialty of the ten-year-old Harry of five season renown, is that he likes to *Harry.* finish in a house, and will never leave a wood if he is once there; and that he must have one particular run and that the Bracknell one. In fact, "*Harry and Brecknell*" acts quite like a charm upon the London men, and they would be loth indeed to miss it. They knew the length of his foot to a nicety that morning; and his temperament must be changed indeed, if he sends them back without seeing Bin-

field, Billing Bear, Haynes Hill, Ruscombe Lake,
Hare Hatch, Park Place, "then down the hill to
Medenham Abbey, and there we are" three times a
season.

Commodore is very great in deep ground, and
Cranbourne's forte is in a hill-and-wood country,
as he never dwells in it by any chance; and once
gave Mr. Davis nearly forty miles home of it, from
Garsington, near Oxford. Woodman, who was
then in his eighth season, would not be taken at
all, and went on jumping, at the end of a very long
run, among the fields near Highgate, till he broke a
blood-vessel and died. Two jumped over a railway
bridge, thirty feet into a cutting; and the renowned
Kit-Kat was hopelessly lost in his fourth season, and
no doubt became the prey of some venison-stealer,
He got into a large cover; and the heavy rain from
the boughs destroyed the scent so completely,
that they gave him up. Tom Wingfield sent
word, in a month's time, that he was in a cover near
Mr. Drake's; but he was no where to be found when
the hounds arrived.

The great Leices-
tershire staghunt. The late Marquis of Waterford im-
proved his Aylesbury recollections when
he was at Lowesby, and the "Great Leicestershire
Stag Hunt" was the earliest result. The preparations for the meet at Twyford were on a remarkable
scale. The stag was trained for days before in a
large walled kitchen-garden, and the Marquis with
a horn and a whip and a couple of little dogs kept him
in exercise for hours among the gooseberry bushes.
The hounds had one of their best pipe-openers by
running the drag of a clerical visitor, whose horse's
feet had been secretly aniseeded, and all seemed ripe
for action except the huntsman. He was a stranger,
and the grooms and second horsemen had got at him,
and made him so low-spirited by their geographical
sketches of the probable line of country, that his

pack was doubled in his eyes before he was told to lay them on. The stag made his point for the Queniborough-road, between Barsby and South Croxton, and then bent to the right, through Barsby village, leaving Gaddesby on the left. Up to this point the huntsman had gone well, and hallooing like a maniac; but his right foot was seen to fly up as high as his own head, crossing a ridge and furrow, and he was heard of no more. The Marquis on Saltfish was then left in command, and the hounds ran well for Brooksby, and down the turnpike road for Rearsby village. There the stag bolted into a farm-yard, and finally into a cellar, with his lordship and Tom Heycock after him, and kicked the spigot out of the ale barrel, and flooded the place before those eminent specials could secure him.

Riders were lucky who could find their way home, as the precaution had been "The Marquis's" freaks. duly taken of sawing the guide-posts in that part, and turning the arms the wrong way. Those between Lowesby and Leicester especially suffered, and are still braced with iron as a token. At all events it was a great day; and how the Marquis once rode to Melton and back, thirteen miles in the hour by moonlight, and jumped all the stiles between Twyford and Lowesby on his way back; how he fastened his horses into the fishing-boat from Lowesby Pond, and enjoyed the locomotion along the frosty road, till they took fright at Twyford Windmill, and leapt the hedge; how he and his friend Sir Frederick Johnson bought a gipsey baby for £5 (as a salve for having overset an encampment the night before, by means of a rope tied round each of their horses' necks), and in order to get rid of it, stuck it on to a hedge to shoot at, as they told the mother, till that nut-brown dame crept up behind, and nipped off with it; how he stopped a pulling horse, by riding him at a hedge, on the other side of which he had made a deep hole full of water, and exclaimed "There, old fellow, I have you now;" and how he missed buying Mr. Hodgson's lady pack, from looking too long at the dogs—will long be told at the midland fire-sides, along with the Great Leicestershire Stag Hunt.

Baron Rothschild's deer. Most of the principal herds in the kingdom have furnished deer for the Barons of "The Vale," but with very varied success. The five brace from Stowe failed, but two out of a trio from the Cheltenham Hunt went most famously. The Berkeley deer were middling, and the Knowseley ones were too tame, and lacked jumping qualities. One of the stags was, however, a brilliant exception, but after his first run from Pitchcote over The Vale to Tring Park, the hounds got him down in a muddy pool, near Lord Lonsdale's kennels, and Tom Ball on Billy the Beau could not get up in time to save him. Mr. Drax's were out of condition when they came, and were killed off very quickly before they were thoroughly fit. Those from Richmond Park went in pretty good form, but Sir Clifford Constable's,—which strained back to some of the originals, that did such service to the Hon. Grantley Berkeley when he kept staghounds at Cranfield Bridge,— showed, along with the too few which could be got from Woburn, the finest sport of all. Sir Clifford's were larger and lighter in their colour, but hardly so strong in their loins as the Woburn deer, and required very careful picking. Of the two breeds, they were the larger and the better scented, and were all sent as haviers with cropped ears.

Sir Clifford's deer. "Burton Constable" was the wildest and straightest going amongst them, and once when he was turned out at Wing, Lord William Beresford was almost the only man at the take near Oakley, in Mr. Drake's country, after eighteen miles by the Ordnance map. "Pipe-

maker," another of these Holderness flyers, was apt
to run a ring for the first mile, but when he did get
his head straight, ten to fifteen miles was his regu-
lation allowance, and if he had the chance he was
sure to point for the Claydon or Doddershall country.
From Perren's Farm over a very rough country on
to the hills near Checquers Court, was another of
his great things.

One of the hinds was, we believe, the heroine of the
run of nearly twenty-four miles over the Brill Hills, to
the turnpike on the Thame Road, close by Oxford, and
she never hung for a second, in the Wootton House
Woods. Roffey, the huntsman, killed his Little
Billy on this day, and Baron Nathaniel on Foscote,
and Mr. Crommelyn beat all the field out except
Tom Ball on Paddy, who had no second horse to
assist him. The shade of Little Billy was avenged
the next time she was uncarted, and great was
the lamentation over her. The Chesterton Hind
was also killed, but it was remembered in connection
with her death, how Tom Crommelyn went on Nonsense; and how the Hon. Robert Grimston and Bill
Golby jumped the Rousham Brook. Not content
with that, Mr. Grimston when only himself and two
others were left in the run, charged the Eythrop
river, brimming full, and swam out on a different
side to his mare

The best Woburn stag survived all his four season perils, and after giving them an infinity of good
runs, became so infirm in his joints, that he was
sold as a stock deer. His greatest effort was from
Golby's Farm to Dunstable, when only three rode at
the brook near Blackgrove Wood, and Mr. Oldaker
and another got in. One of the Woburn hinds was
drowned in the river below Thame in a run, which
told out all the gentlemen except Young Baron
Nathaniel on Peacock, and Baron Alphonze, and
they could not get nearer than Wootton; and Ribston

Pippin dropped dead under Tom Ball, a hundred
yards after he had laid the hounds on to another of
the hinds, which ran from Cublington to Hanslope.
The Duke could only spare a brace of these jewels
each season.   They inherited immense speed from
the large, wild park where they were dropped, and
their dark-red coats, smutty faces, and fineness in
the single, induced the belief that they had got some
high-bred foreign cross originally.

Harvey Combe the biggest havier

Harvey Combe. that Baron Rothschild ever had, earned
his name from having been taken in the old Berkeley
country.   He never waited or hung, and made up
for his lack of pace by his eternal bottom.   His
grandest run was from Aston Abbotts through Eythrop
to Thame.   He was brought out as second deer, and
by mere chance Baron Lionel, who was going home
with the hounds, met the deer-cart, which had missed its mark.   This havier was particularly adapted
for the Vale, as he did not care for being mobbed by
"the carrion," who pretend to hunt with the Baron,
and carry out their boast by starting off as their
only chance along the roads the moment the deer is
uncarted.   Still true to a favourite's fate, he died at
last in a cess-pool near Ledburn.   Another havier met
a rather more tragical death.   He was uncarted at
Wing, and went right over the Vale to Shardloes,
where everyone was beaten off except Tom Ball on
Economy, and Tom was obliged at last to leave his
mare on the road, and run over three fields to Mr.
Grove's Farm at Amersham, just in time to find him
impaled to his very back-bone on the iron palisades
near the house.   The white-faced havier must not
be forgotten.   He had strayed into the grounds of
Combe Abbey, and Roffey was sent down with ten
couple to catch him, and he proved himself worthy
of the toil in his first 1 hour 10 minutes without a
check.

The Barons Rothschild commenced their pack in the spring of '39, and The Baron's pack. Bill Roffey, who was great on the Carbonaro mare, hunted them till the gout gave him warning. Barwick, Tom Ball, and Fred. Cox have held the horn in turn. Fourteen or fifteen couple of Sir Charles Shakerley's staghounds, which were almost entirely of Cheshire blood began the pack, and they were strengthened with a draft from Mr. Harvey Combe, whose Osbaldeston's Tapster was used pretty freely. Gunnersbury by Osbaldeston's Falstaff from Cheshire Guilesome was one of the first and best that they ever bred, and was the sire of Dairymaid. Cheshire also sent a draft, and Berkeley Castle did the same for two seasons. Among the latter was old Paradox, who contributed Primrose and Princess, and some other beauties to the lady pack, but never bred a dog-hound straight enough for Baron Lionel's fancy. Fitzwilliam Marmion suited her best, but still it was the Feudal and Bluecap blood, the former especially, which made the Mentmore kennel so indebted to the Milton.

The smutty-faced Feudals were quite staghounds by nature. They broke themselves, and one word was sufficient to stop them. Sebright always declared that the old dog was one of the most sensible that he ever cheered. At one time there were five or six couple of the sort in work, and although his sons did not get their stock with quite the same substance, the taste for the slot did not dwindle. Fitzwilliam Bluecap was also represented by eight couple at one time, but their beautiful noses were rather counteracted by their head-long style. There were also a few in the kennel by Belvoir Rallywood (when he was at Brocklesby), and of Belvoir Kanter as well. With their introduction to "The Vale," they seemed to forget all about fox, and when one jumped out of a hedge-row and ran up a

furrow in view, close behind the deer, they let it
bend to the right without even noticing it, and went
straight over the fence.   There are now no hounds in
the kennel except what have been bred there, and, as
the Rothschild farms in Bucks have multiplied, about
30 couple of puppies are put out to walk.

Limits of The   During October, an old deer or two
    Vale.   are turned down on the Ivinghoe and
Chiltern Hills, on the Dunstable side, to give the
hounds a good half-hour or three-quarters with
blood at the end; and very early in November they
descend into The Vale, which is all doubles and
grass.   Winslow to Marsh Hill below Aylesbury,
and Mentmore to the Claydon Woods are the
limits of this splendid country.   Golby's Farm
is its Kirby Gate; but Aston Abbott's is its queen
of meets, as it generally secures them a run for
Hardwicke, or over the endless acres of Creslow Big
Ground.   The Rousham, the Hardwicke, the Creslow, the Winslow, and the Hulcoat Brooks have all
brought grief to heroes, and heroines as well, who
will try to be even with the huntsman, " even if he
goes through a canal."   Black Grove and Quainton
are the deepest countries, and there is scarcely a
hedge in them without a back brook to it.

The Rothschild   Baron Meyer hunts on both, but Mon-
    cracks.   day is Sir Antony's, and Thursday
Baron Lionel's day.   Baron Lionel has gone best
on Rachel the old bay steeple-chaser, who was wonderfully clever and steady among the doubles.   A
grey was another of his favourites; and he rode
Grouse latterly, till the black injured its coffin bone
on landing over a brook, and had to be shot that
day.   Sir Antony has been most at home on Peacock and Topthorn; and Sir Nathaniel's delights before he went to reside in Paris, were Foscote and
Scotsfoot.   As a proof of their good going, they
fetched a thousand guineas when they were sold

and the latter won the Cheltenham steeple-chase.
Baron Meyer's peculiars have been Hornsby, King
Charles, and Squib, and it was on King Charles before he received his knee accident, that he popped
over the very high post and rails by the side of a
gate, at which a whole crowd were waiting, and got
cheered for his style of solving " the real jam" difficulty.

Grouse, King Pippin, and Harkover Grouse, King Pip-
were the *élite* of Tom Ball's lot. He had pin, and Harkover.
won a steeple-chase on Grouse, a big
horse by Muley Moloch, at Aylesbury, and run
second to Dragsman at Chelmsford. *Waterloo* was
Grouse's original name, which was intended to point
attention to a wart that had been cut out of his ear,
and as he gave Roffey one or two falls, he thought
that he was rather blind. However he soon became
a top sawyer, and " galloped everything blind" on a
great day from Whaddesdon Windmill to Hudnall
Common; and Mr. Crommelin, who stayed the
longest, was glad to give in, four miles from the
finish, at the foot of Ivinghoe Hills. The chesnut
Harkover, who had won a steeple-chase near Oxford
with Bob Barker upon him, was a wonder through
dirt or at a brook. During their four seasons together, he never gave Tom a fall, and if there were not
too many casts, and he was not " rifled about" early
in the day, he was not to be beaten. He carried his
head up like a deer, and was ridden in a double-
reigned snaffle and a martingale, and although he
never seemed to see them, he " went at the doubles
forty miles an hour, as if he was going to eat them."

Still at this branch of science, he was not such an
artiste as the little King Pippin, whose praise was in
all The Vale, and who never required of Tom Ball
to open any gates. If there was no landing in a
double, he crashed through it, and out like a shot,
and once on a time, he jumped six or seven yards

U

over some trees and a saw-pit, which were ensconced on the other side of one of them. Such have been the trio of leaders in their day, and when Lord Petre was on his chesnut, the Hon. Robert Grimston on All Serene, Mr. Oldaker on Pilot, James Mason on Willesden, Cheslyn Hall on Brutandorf, Sam Baker on The Corporal, Mr. F. Knight on The Tory, Mr. Crommelin on Nonsense, Mr. Dawncey on a little chesnut mare as good in her way as his Alderneys, Mr. Lee on an old 'un of Charles Payne's, Mr. Learmouth on Jerry, and Will Golby, Will Eustace, and Morrice on their best, they have had to meet a field which it was a glory to cut down.

Bill Bean the arch-trespasser of England.

A word on Bill Bean and the drag-hunt. "What stable mind" in and round the metropolis is not cognizant of that arch-trespasser, once the very Apollyon of the farmers in the Harrow and Stanmore country—that ancient youth who was stag-hunting nearly ten years before the century began, and ready yet, in his disgust at the degeneracy of the steeple-chase age, to "jump my old pony Bean Stalk blindfold over a fence," which had been denounced at Hendon as presenting a premium on coroners' inquests. Still, a service of seventy years in the saddle has had its disadvantages. There are the books of doctors extant and deceased, whose testimony welded together would furnish some little account as follows:

"1792-1862.

"Mr. William Bean.

"To Messrs.————.

"Attending you when you broke both your thumbs, fractured the near leg (twice), broke the near ribs, injured the near knee, dislocated the near shoulder, ditto off shoulder, scalped your head, broke your nose, and other severe falls, £ , &c."

"*Actæon Nimrod, Esq., Tyho Paddocks, Huntingdonshire,*" was the name which his deer-cart bore. The yokels used to stare at it, and say, "*See, Tom !*

Bill Bean (the Arch Trespasser of England), p. 291.

what a long way they've comed." At one time he purposed inscribing on it, "*William Bean, Land Surveyor,*" but the conception was too grand and too dangerous. With the hounds he was more open, and duly branded them with a B. Hence another identity-puzzle arose among the rurals. Says Jack to Tom, "*What does that big B mean on the hounds?*" says Tom, in reply, "Why, Jack, you ain't half sharp this morning : it manes '*The Baron's,*' to be sure."

The deer-cart inscription was but a very faint index of the mission of that remarkable M. S. D. H., after whom so many tax-gatherers toiled in vain. When the Chancellor of the Exchequer's fangs were almost in him, he would "fold his tent like the Arab, and as silently steal away" into another district with *Splendour,* and the rest of the five couple, old Will White and the three brace of deer. Sometimes he would be at Willesden, then at Finchley, and anon at Golders Green. Be the kennel where it might, Captain Nesbitt and the guardsmen and a dozen or two more of "the upper ten thousand," &c., always had the office, but whether it was to be stag or drag, they never exactly knew. Five or six years ago the pack was given up, and Splendour, that meekest of hounds, who could carry half a belly-full of victuals, and three pounds of shot round his neck, and yet hold the lead, was given to Mr. Tom Mason, with whom he lately died. He had stood by his master in perilous times ; and when farmers would vindictively house the deer, and he " ran heel" to tell him they generally knew that their trespassing was over for that day. Bill was more fortunate when he merely drove his deer into a china closet, or when he coaxed a farmer, (who had been previously breathing out pitch-forks and slaughter against him) into a public-house, while his barn lock was being wrenched, and actually

The perils of the drag.

getting him to put on his coat and cap to see how he liked himself in the character of a British sportsman, left him at last to pay the score. But the drag was the thing after all, and in the trusty Will's hands, it became an engine of the deepest agricultural oppression.

Will White and his successor Kit. Will White had been originally an officer's servant in the Tenth, and when he was no longer in commission, his fine eye for country recommended him to Bill Bean. When he had duly fastened the aniseed cloth to his shoes, he would be told to come out at a certain milestone nine or ten miles away, and even if he had never been over the line before, he was certain to hit it to a half or a quarter of a mile. His finest performance was starting on Hampstead Heath, and going as straight as a pigeon to the ninth milestone on the Romford Road. *"There's London, Will, and there's Romford,"* said his master, pointing with his whip, and Will touched his cap, and waited to hear no more. He got over the widest brooks by making for a reclining pollard, and jumping with a sort of double-jointed spring from the top; and the hounds ran into him on the Bull's Eye night as he was snugly seated, after his toils, in a public-house at Hanwell. The customers were more tolerant of his aniseed flavour than the farmers. One of the latter went so far as to say that *"he's a regular nuisance; he injures our implements;"* and when he was asked to explain his dark speech, he replied, *" he goes and sits on them in the fields to rest himself, and leaves such a smell of aniseed that our men won't go near them."* On another occasion, he was taken up before a magistrate for trespassing. The complainant swore that he was only on the foot-path, but that he " knew he was trespassing by the smell," and was exceedingly surprised at the dismissal of the case. Dulwich Park was a great country for him, as it was in Chan-

cery at the time, and no one looked after trespassers.
The perpetual heats and colds killed the poor fellow
at last, and "Kit," his Irish successor, was generally
too drunk, either to run or drive. In his private
account of this malady, he threw the whole onus on
to the deer cart. *"Kit, my boy, one of them says
'It's a could morning for ye.' 'Faith and it is, says
I.' 'Kit, my boy, will you have a nip of anything?'
So I could'nt be off refusing. 'Kit, my boy, says
another, 'What deer have you got to-day?' 'Faith,
and it's not iligant in me to tell ye.' 'I'll stand ye
a little drop if you will.' So I had a little drop wid
him. Faith, and that deer-cart would make any boy
drunk"*

The two "Gunners" and Red Deer Bill Bean's
horses.
did well, but "Chunee" was one of Bill
Bean's best, although he did give him thirty-seven
falls in a very limited space of time. He was the
biggest and the stupidest of hunters, and received
his name from the elephant, which attracted so many
visitors to Exeter Change. A noble lord, who was
not averse to the drag, gave 200 guineas for him,
and declared that he would now "serve out all the
white gates in Yorkshire." In due time his lordship reported from his bed to Bill, that he had, in an
incredibly short time, run up his fall score to seventeen on him, and despairing of stopping him, when
he took the bit in his teeth, he had sent him at a hay-
stack, in which Chunee had buried his head eight feet,
and then tumbled backwards. Knowing his locomo-
tive antecedents, Bill replied that he could believe
all that and a great deal more of Chunee. His lordship also bought old Bag o'Nails, alias "Old Bag,"
who had lamed himself by jumping with Bill into a
gravel-pit. He could shuffle along very well in spite
of it, and it used to be said that "he was so lame that
he could'nt get up in time for the foxhounds; but he
was always ready for the drag at one o'clock."

Persecution of the farmers. The farmers said that they did not mind John Elmore as he was always so polite, and would stop when they told him; but " as for that Bill Bean, when we're ordering him not to go over one place, he only pops over another." In vain did they lock up their gates, pile hurdles on to them, and lie in ambush with pitchforks and other missiles, when they saw the *avant courier* of the Aniseed sweep by like the storm. One of them watched till nearly dusk, and then heard the hounds go past, as he sat triumphantly at his tea. He was in fact so astonished that he found himself reduced to asking Bill in confidence how he did manage in the dark, and was admitted to his confidence in return. "*Didn't you see us?*" said Bill; "*we ride with a bull's-eye on each stirrup, and a bull's-eye on our breast-plates, we can go just as well by night as by day.*" Well might the persecuted ones say ever after that when they heard the cry, "*There goes Bull's Eye Bill! it's no use trying to stop him.*" He was not always so good to know. The legs and the seat might seem like his, but as often as not there was an enormous false nose, a fiery red moustache of fearful size, and red wafers on the cheeks, which utterly destroyed his upper-part identity.

The great indignation meeting. Notices not to trespass arrived by every post, and the Uxbridge ordinary resolved itself almost weekly into an Indignation Meeting. "Bull's Eye Bill" must and shall be put down. The day for striking the blow arrived, and as the arch-trespasser sat under his own fig-tree at Willesden, a clatter of horses' hoofs down the road broke on his guilty ear. In a few minutes a phalanx of farmers presented themselves, and the very air seemed whitened with notices. Keeping his seat he received the "patent fulminators" from his foes with the most baffling courtesy. He marked and numbered each with a pencil as he received it. His countenance was unmoved, and wore the very slightest shade of contrition to be in keeping with the crisis. When the several notices were delivered a scroll containing their substance and all the names, was presented by a deputy on a sheet of foolscap. "*I can't read it in your presence, gentlemen!*" said Bill, "*it would not be respectful,*" and it was docketted with the rest of the papers. The situation seemed an alarming one, but ere another sun had set his line of action was taken.

Calling his first lieutenant to him, he made a masterly sketch of a drag-hunt for the morrow, which went through the very heart, or touched every farm in the round-robin. That afternoon he scorned all disguise. Once only he drew rein, and once more the oppressor bearded the oppressed. "*Why do I come here?*" he said; "*I come here, Sir, on purpose to be pulled up;*" and then he poured it out just like a leading article. "*The time had now arrived, when further concession became impossible, and forbearance a crime. If you begin, I'll begin. I've got all your signatures. You don't know what you've signed. I do. I've had counsel's opinion on it. That's why I was'nt here yesterday; I've been to my solicitors with that paper. I'll indict you all for conspiracy.*" And so saying he magnificently rode away, and he had rest from notices for nearly half a season.

How Bill attended to the notices.

Then the commissioners set at him, and he was charged for a whole pack. For once his spirits gave way, as he knew the chairman to be a man of wrath and endless notices, and that he and Splendour had not spared him. In fact Bill had never been off his place, and kept him, rushing wildly forth into his flower garden, in an attitude of protest, and once in his dressing-gown only and his slippers. It may be that those were nose or moustache days, but at all events

His graceful manners with the Tax Commissioners.

he did not recognize him till the case was called on. Then a flood of light gradually broke on him. *" William Bean,"* he said, as he put his nose down on the paper. *" What's your business? about dogs, I see ; Ah! hounds! Oh! stags.—Why! you're the man who'se always over my place. I've sent you several notices, I think."* One of the other commissioners, who wasn't altogether guiltless, and who keenly enjoyed the fun, winked at Bill, as much as to say, " Now Master William, he's regularly twigged you ;" and then folded his arms and placed his eyes on the ceiling to hear the end. *" I admit it, sir ; I admit it,"* said the crafty culprit, in his most unctuous tones, *" but really, Sir, your's is such a sweet, little, inviting spot, on the top of that hill, that I don't wonder at the deer always making for it."* Bill scored four by that slashing hit to leg. The prospect, as the chairman felt, was certainly very pretty, it was well that his brother commissioners and the public should hear that confirmed, and he was mollified as to the first point. Still justice must have its way. *" But* Mr. *Bean,"* he continued, *" you have a pack, I see, and you don't pay for them."* *" A pack, Sir,"* said Bill, more blandly than ever, *" I have only five couple. Mine is strictly a miniature establishment ; I have a miniature pack ; everything is in proportion. Would you favour me by coming to see it ? My benches are only made for five couple ; they could'nt hold five-and-a-half ; I am at your service any day, if you will favour me with an inspection."* And so point No. 2 was got rid of.

Oddly enough, the assessors had overlooked the *" Actæon Nimrod,"* &c., and only rested the third part of their case on the name not being behind as well as on the off-side of the deer-cart ; but Bill had quite got their range by this time. He accordingly went for the in-fighting, and involved them in such learned discussions upon stick-doors to admit air, a "thing absolutely necessary for air in the heated state of an animal's blood;" "might have difficulties with the Society for the Suppression of Cruelty to Animals;" "the impossibility of painting a letter on each stick;" that they gave him up as a bad job, and all the points as well. He returned gracefully to his friends and retainers, and he and Splendour trespassed worse than ever.

In 1833, Wiltshire had its first steeple- Jem Hills's steeple-chase. chase, and Jem Hills won it. It had its origin in a match which Mr. Horrocks made with Lord Ducie after dinner at Mr. Thomas Goodlake's, to match himself on one of his own horses against the whole of his Lordship's stud, one to the post, and Jem, who was then the Vale of White Horse huntsman, to ride. There was to be no mistake about it, and the conditions specified that it was to be "four miles straight a-head, neither to ride more than 100 yards along a road, every gate to be locked, and no fences cut." Mr. Robert Codrington, picked the ground from Tadpole Copse to Lyssal Hill, near Eyworth, all over the Water Eaton Vale, with bulfinches, gates, and two brooks to boot. The only guideposts were a flag in the Cold Harbour Road, and another on Lyssal Hill, and they were to get to them as they could. The adventurous pair met in scarlet coats and caps at Cold Harbour, Jem with five horses, and a goodly allowance of shot to make up the thirteen stone. As soon as they had been taken up to the top of the brow, and learnt the line, Jem knew that it was the "old chesnut mare's" day. The history of that steeple-chase is one of Jem's finest bits of recitative, and we heard it last November to peculiar advantage, when he was warmed to his work by the deep sympathy he had just received from the party on the grubbing up of Lyneham Gorse. Sometimes in his energy he fairly walked away from our pencil.

"The first fence," he always begins, The start. "was a double post and rails. We both

stood and looked at it. You see I wanted to find
out whether he'd take his own line or follow me. I
said, " *This won't do. Come, you have it first.*" He
said, "*No ! if you can't have it, I can't.*" We might
have been there all day, so I turned the old mare's
head and popped in and popped out. He followed,
and came over very prettily. The next was a great
bulfinch, with a ditch ; we got over that. I said,
" *Mind your next fence, we must both fall*" (we chat-
ted all the way.) It was a stiff fence—post and rail—
hedge and bank to clear. When we were coming to
it, he said, " *Don't let us kill one another, Jem ; I
won't ride on you if you won't ride on me.*" I said,
" *Give me plenty of room, and give him pepper.*" My
mare cleared twenty-nine feet, and his horse twenty-
nine-and-a-half. We sent them at it with such a
swing, I never saw a man so high in the air before.
I looked round and saw his horse's shoes glittering
the height of my shoulder. Then came the gate
into the Cold Harbour road. I said, " *Mr. Horrocks,
which of us shall have it first ?*" he said " *You do,*"
and we went over it side by side, our boots almost
touched. Same way through the bulfinch out of the
lane, like a bullet.

The plot thickens. Then we had some very small en-
closures with very big fences ; what I
call creepers ; my old mare, she could go the same
pace all the way; the country was tremendously
deep. When I found that he intended to wait on me,
I knew how to deal with him. Then we came into
a dirty lane, with a tremendous fence towards us.
I tried the old mare at it ; it knocked her backwards
into the ditch, but without getting a fall ; she recovered herself. I said, " *Now, Mr. Horrocks, you
have a try.*" We were very friendly all the way.
He said, " *No, Jem, if your old mare can't bore a
hole, my horse can't.*" So I put her at it ; I could'nt
help myself; and I got through. Well, he attempted,

and his horse floundered, and he nearly got off,
and there he hung. I looked back for my companion, when I'd got half-a-field a-head, and when I
saw him in his saddle, and coming full tilt, I eased
my mare. We had two miles to go then. It was
up rising ground, I kept pulling, and he kept pressing till he caught me, bulfinches all the way not so
big, we got very well over them, and came to a
barn.

Then there was a very large field down
to the last brook. Lord Ducie and all the   The last brook.
gentlemen were there. I was a hundred yards a-
head, when I passed the barn. I knew devilish well
that neither of our horses could jump the brook
(you know they always laugh at me about the
brooks.) The gentlemen kept hollering at him,
" *Now, Horrocks, come along, Jem's beat;*" and
he came down past me at the brook, as fast as his
horse could go. Believe me, the horse jumped right
into the brook, pitched upon his head, and turned
with his rump on to the other side, and there he lay.
I rode quietly down to the brook; Lord Ducie was
there on a fresh horse. He said, " *Jem, Jem! jump
it, the mare will bring you over, I'll give you a lead,*"
and over he went and jumped it beautifully. I pulled
up and sat looking at Mr. Horrocks in the brook. It
was quite a study. He was standing on the bank,
and the bridle came off; he fell backwards, bridle
and all, and the horse went sideways. Lord Ducie
was at me all the time, " *Come, come, Jem! he'll get
out.*" " I said, " *No, no, my lord! There's plenty of
time.*" Then I saw a ditch, which led from the
brook into the field at the opposite side. I stood as
long as I could to let the mare get her wind; the
pace had been strong all the way. When I thought
she'd had sufficient time, I let her down very quietly,
and waded her across the brook, to go up this ditch.
She made a plunge or two, and I went up it twenty

yards, and into the field. I had still three fences to
jump, and a gate at the finish. My mare was so
beat, I scrambled her on to them, and then we
scrambled out. The gate was locked, so I crammed
her round the gate-post between the gate and the
hedge. She was just like my old horse Bendigo,
jump anywhere, where he can get his head. So I
got to the winning-post, and into the farm-house,
and had a glass of brandy and water before he was
out of the brook. It was the only steeple-chase I ever
rode. I was to have ridden another the next week
at Cheltenham, only the horse broke down, and very
glad I was, I never care to ride another. Such is
the defendant's account of the great Wiltshire case
of *Horrocks v. Hills.*

First steeple-chase in Leicestershire.   It is now some seventy years since the
first steeple-chase was run off in Leicester-
shire. The distance was eight miles
from Barkby Holt to the Coplow and back, and Mr.
Charles Meynell, son of the great M. F. H., won it;
Lord Forester was second, and Sir Gilbert Heath-
cote last. There is very little oral tradition respecting it, except that Sir Gilbert's horse was rather fat,
that Lord Forester was the favourite, and that Mr.
Needham of Hungerton said to his lordship, " I'll
save you a hundred yards, if you'll come through
my garden, and jump the gate into the road."

Captain Becher.   From Noseley-Wood to the Coplow,
was the line of country on March 12th
1829, when Clinker's bridle came off, to Tom Heycock's great discomfiture, in a fall at the second fence
from home, and Field Nicholson won on Sir Harry
Goodricke's Magic. Capt. Becher (who made one of
the lot on Bantam) was entered to harriers in his native
Norfolk, as a copper-bottomed infant, on a pony which
no other boy could hold. A better berth than the saddle
was soon found for him in the Storekeeper's General
Department, and at sixteen, he was one of the staff

in charge of the field equipments to the Peninsula, and spent two or three years with the army of occupation. Ramsgate was his first scene of action after the peace, and his horse-flesh yearnings had the fullest scope in landing the troopers and mules, which "Champagne Tommy," of Pimlico, had furnished by contract, and making them swim a shore with the guy-ropes.

To use his own words, he "never had The palmy days of St. Albans. such a lark in my life," and when steeple-chases and hurdle-racing became all the fashion, under the auspices of Tommy Coleman, of St. Albans, he entered on such an amphibious existence for nine or ten seasons, that quiet householders who read of him almost weekly for six months of the year, began to have grave doubts whether he was an otter or a man. Tommy gave him a mount in the first hurdle race, which was got up specially to please the ladies, when races were established at No Man's Land. George IV., although within six weeks of his death, took such an interest in their success, that he requested Mr. Delmè Radcliffe to enter the Colonel and Hindostan, and beat Tommy's mare Bunter by a head, for the Gold Cup. Figurante was as simple as a young turkey, in hurdle matters, and Becher's orders were to get her between two others, so that she would find the hurdles (which had no stakes, and were separately fixed), "the easiest place to get away." Under this pilotage, she jumped in such style, that Lord Verulam told her owner "that's a deep fellow you've got on your mare; her feet were higher than our carriage when she went over." The first St. First St. Albans steeple-chase. Albans steeple-chase came off in that spring of '30. Sixteen started from Arlington church to the Obelisk in Wrest Park, near Silsoe; and Coleman so managed the line, that he could start them, and then by making a short cut, judge them as well. Lord

Ranelagh's grey horse Little Wonder, with Colonel Macdowell up, won the stake, which was worth about 300 sovereigns. The Colonel's orders were to watch nothing but Lord Clanricarde, who was on a little Irish chesnut; and one of the Berkeleys was third. The rest found their way into the Park from all quarters; with the exception of poor Mr. Stretfield on Teddy the Tiler, who had a fall in jumping a gate back on to a bridge after he had missed his line, and died in consequence. Coleman's general idea of a steeple-chase was two miles out and two miles in, and "keeping the line quite dark." Hence he concealed men in the ditches, with flags, which they raised on a given signal, as soon as the riders were ready. Other managers liked four miles straight, and after erecting scaffold poles, with a couple of sheets to finish between, they left the riders to hunt the country for their line, with no further directions than "leave that church on your right, and the clump on your left, and get to the hill beyond."

Tommy Coleman's volunteers. The March of '31 saw the St. Albans Steeple-chase in real form; and the carriages and horsemen poured in so resolutely for hours, that there was a regular block on the outskirts of the town, till Tommy gave the word. The horses came a week before, to train in Gorhambury Park, and other places about, and Moonraker created great excitement among the inhabitants, by jumping the Holloway lane in the course of an exercise canter.

Moonraker. Beardsworth, of Birmingham, had bought him out of a water-cart, and sold him, with his sinews quite callosed from work, for £18 to Sirdefield, who borrowed the crimson St. Leger jacket of the previous year for Mr. Parker to ride him in. The bay was fully seventeen at the time, not fifteen three, and with quarters as good as his head was ugly. Coleman in his blue coat and kersey breeches proclaimed mar-

tial law among the riders that day. They saddled
at his bugle-call in the paddock of his Turf Inn
(then called The Chequers), came out of the yard
three abreast, like cavalry, and marched up the town
behind. If their general caught any of them peep-
ing over the hedges, he was down on them at once,
and declared that for a repetition of the offence, he
would sentence the culprits to "run as a dead letter." Mr. Delmé Radcliffe was judge, and Bill Bean
on Chunee rode with them, as umpire, and had a fall
at a brook. The line began on the St. Alban's side of
Coombe Wood, leaving Haddons on the left, and
Colney on the right; but it was not nearly so formidable as the Aylesbury or Market Harboro' line,
and the finish was between two trees in Coleman's
Paddock. Moonraker beat eleven cleverly, and Wild
Boar, with Captain Becher on him, fell close at home,
and was bled so severely that he died next day.

The Captain had very nearly a share
in further bloodshed. A London law- A fierce lawyer.
yer claimed his bed after he had retired to rest, in a
double-bedded room with his father, and as he
stoutly refused to evacuate, the other thrust his card
under the door, and announced himself through the
keyhole as ripe and ready for the coffee and pistol
business next morning. However, Coleman reasoned
with him, and informed him in such strict confidence,
that the Captain had shot three men already, that
discretion and economy proved the best part of his
valour, and he disappeared so mysteriously from his
sofa, in the course of the night that Coleman " hunted
the country" in vain for his bill. Jack Elmore, who
made an admirable chairman, had, as Lord Palmerston observes, a similar " invitation." He settled
it very summarily, by saying that he knew nothing about cards and pistols, but he understood
punches on the head; so it too fell to the ground,
and as he had already put one man bodily out of a

window of that very inn, it was perhaps well for society that it did.

"The Squire" as steward.   Twenty came to the post the next year, and Moonraker, with Seffert on him, disposed of them once more. He and Corinthian Kate jumped the last fence together, and Grimaldi, who came in a different direction to avoid it, closed in with them at that point. Mr. Osbaldeston was umpire, and after lecturing them all in his raciest style, led the way on horseback to Ellenbrook Green. The troop would have been almost too much for Coleman that day, and, he might well say, " *Do face them for me, Squire, hold up your head like a Colonel, and be very decisive ;*" and indeed he was.

Grimaldi v. Moonraker.   " The Squire" was so dissatisfied with Grimaldi's defeat, that he offered Elmore £50 to make a five hundred match between the two, over his own farm, near Harrow. The referees, according to the custom in those days, carried the stakes in bank notes, sewn up in their pockets, and Elmore gave a capital spread to the Marquis of Abercorn, Colonel Anson, and several others at his farm. " The Squire" had a very slight opinion of Seffert as a rider, and requested to have " a bulfinch to begin with, that I may shake this fellow off ;" and when some friend told him that he himself was in a flurry, he poured out a glass brim full of sherry, and held it out as steady as a rock at arm's length, to reassure his backers. There was only one thing, he said, which he did fear, and that was being "ridden against by those London dealers." However, the only clashing was between him and Moonraker, but Colonel Anson ruled in his favour; and the course, which was a very light one, and without brooks, suited his fast grey exactly. Water was the grey's great bane, and in a race from Brixworth to Cottesbrook Cow Pastures, in 1833, the two brooks quite brought him to grief, and men had to get into one of them, and hold up his head.

Nothing daunted by this disaster, Grimaldi and Napoleon. "The Squire" determined to go on with his thousand-aside-match against Colonel Charritie's Napoleon, a slow half-bred horse, but a magnificent jumper. In the St. Albans Steeple-chase, Napoleon had been nowhere to him: but now there were two brooks and the Lem to be got over. The first two miles of the six was on a curve, and the last four straight; and the line was chosen from The Wharf to Gibraltar Farm, with the Windmill as the great land-mark . The Pytcheley, of which " The Squire" was then master, met at Dunchurch, and a perfect regiment of scarlets lined the Lem side, which was the thirty-eighth jump, and six from the finish. Said " The Squire" to the Captain before the race (for it was especially stipulated that they were not to address each other while running)—" *I don't like water, I can't swim like you*," and when they did charge it, they both went in headlong. It was thought that Napoleon would come up no more, but at last Becher's cap was seen, and then his horse's ears, and the pair floated a hundred yards down stream, the bay " fighting like a bad swimming dog." Napoleon got a hundred yards the best of it on landing; but he was fairly overhauled and beaten, and then a tremendous wrangle commenced. An envoy was sent back to see if The Squire had gone on the right side of a flag, before they would let them weigh in the granary, and Becher was so cold after his bath, that he told them they might send another man to look up the coroner. Eventually the stakes were withdrawn, and after being rubbed down and dressed, both of them went out hunting, and had the Lem again.

Bill Bean, who rode two dozen Viviana. steeple-chases, and won seventeen, was

x

on Grimaldi in the first Aylesbury race the next November year. The bold Field Nicholson was there,
but so was Becher, on Vivian, with both his wrists
bandaged. He fell over a gate, and got ducked in a
river; but got first past the winning flags notwith-
standing. This grandson of Swordsman was great in the
Vale, and as Becher said, he seemed to "gallop open-
mouthed over the doubles." Hence he was a most
dangerous horse if he made a mistake, but he very
seldom did. The present Lord Vivian bought him
for £30 from Dycer of Dublin, who had selected him
at one of his Repository sales for the Hon. Colonel
Westenra, M.F.H., by whom he was, we believe, returned, as unfit to carry his men with hounds. He
had been previously in harness, but he did'nt enjoy
leather, and had kicked a most respectable family
out of an Irish car. Lord Vivian rode him for one
season and part of another, and made him a perfect
fencer. He was so fond of his new business, that
after giving his Lordship a fall early in his first season, he got away, and went to the end of a brilliant
run by himself, and was one of the few, if not the
only horse, which reached Charlton Park with the
hounds.

In consequence of illness, his lordship gave
up hunting for a time, and sold Vivian to a
clerical friend, who resold him to Captain Lamb.
The Captain thought so lightly of his purchase,
that shortly afterwards when Lord Vivian had
gone to Leamington for his health, he pressed
the horse on him at £130, the same price that
his lordship had got for him; and the bargain only
went off, because the latter declined to consent
to his starting for the Debdale Stakes at Warwick.
Soon after that Captain Lamb discovered the full
truth of what Lord Vivian had told him, that the
bay was one of the best weight-carrying hunters ever
bred, and began to profit accordingly. His future

"orange cap, and purple" ally had never seen him before Mr. Osbaldeston challenged all the world with Cannon-ball; and he came in fact from Market Harbro' expressly to ride Vanguard. At the eleventh hour, the owner's own son decided to take the mount, and Becher was put on Vivian. The horse's coat was very long, and as Captain Lamb concluded that Becher had brought his own saddle with him, he was not provided with one, and there was a regular borrowing of a leather here, and a stirrup there, on the ground, to get one fitted up of the exact weight. The finish was up a tremendous hill, on which the gentlemen of three hunts assembled five hundred scarlets strong, and Becher by jumping a very great fence came up the ascent on the slant, and contrived to keep more in his horse to finish with.

A month after he had won at Ayles- Vivian v. Cock bury, Becher found himself once more Robin. putting his saddle on Vivian, to meet " *The* Marquis" and Cock Robin from Shankton Holt to the Rams Head cover. Cock Robin and Monarch were two of the best hunters that ever drew breath in Ireland ; and the defeated hero of this day, a smart brown, fenced so well and went so fast, that he got nearly three hundred yards in advance. For once in his life The Marquis, who was always in a hurry, was suddenly seized with a prudence fit, and in trying to avoid two tremendous jumps, which Becher was obliged to have, he got stuck in a dingle. The Captain saw his difficulty, and following some wheel ruts to the left, closed with him against the hill at the finish, which is quite as steep as " The Primrose." The Marquis always stood in fifty with The Captain, one to win, and was as good as a small annuity to him, as while the arrangement lasted, the former had only once the pull of him. On this occasion his lordship was rather wrath about his defeat, and said that he was " beat by the best

horse;" so Becher offered to run him back again
and change the horses, feeling sure that Vivian
would disagree with him before they had gone over
four fields.

Fun in The Vale. February found The Vale in its glory,
and there were two races, one for the
Light and one for the Heavies, the first of which
was set for half-past nine. Bill Bean was on Ro-
chelle, but he made too close a shave of it between
two trees, and was knocked out of his saddle, and
"left sitting." They were close at home at the time,
and Bill believes that, but for his accident, which
partially lamed one leg for life, he could not have
lost. He had not been over the ground like the other
riders, and not knowing the exact course of the river,
had to jump it, and a gate on a bridge as well.
Powell on Saladin got the better of Vivian this
time, and the Marquis on his Yellow Dwarf,
who looked exactly like a dun coach-horse, just
beat Mason and Grimaldi for the third place. Powell
did not win the light race on Lauristina, though
he distinguished himself quite as much by jumping over a treble, consisting of Grimaldi, Seffert,
and the fence; but the grey got up in time to be
second to Vivian. It was a great day, and Mr.
Davis who gave the starting signal, brought out the
staghounds as soon as the chases were over, and
uncarted one of his flying haviers.

Latter days and Early in the ensuing year, Becher was
death of Grim- again on the snaffle-mouthed Grimaldi,
aldi. among the brooks near Waltham Abbey.
This time he was more unfortunate than usual, as
he threw his rider on to some stubbs on his stomach,
and destroyed his powers of articulate speech for
hours, but still he contrived to steal to them and
catch them at the last fence.

The March of '36 witnessed the death of this memorable grey at St. Albans. He had hurt his back

and kidneys in a grip at Uxendon a few days before,
and Becher thought that he was dull, although he
jumped as steadily as ever. Three hundred yards of
deep meadow finished him, and he was scarcely past
the post before he reared and died. How he got
through his work was a marvel, as his kidneys were
proved on a *post mortem* to be one mass of congealed
blood. He was a perfect fencer, and if there was a
bit of sound ground he never missed it, but to the
last he would never do more or less than walk into
water, and all that the facetious Bill Bean could
suggest as a cure was to " water him well before he
started."

" The Marquis," Lord Clanricarde, Flacrow and the
Lord Macdonald, Sir David Baird, and Leamington.
the Hon. Mr. Villiers were all in " the Leamington"
of that year. Mr. Coke would not ride Flacrow, " because I should be beaten long before the horse," and
Tom Heycock, who was his deputy, was rewarded with
a golden shield for his side-board. Vivian with 7lbs.
extra " went as if his head was on fire," to the
lane before the last field, where he fell over a faggot,
which had been kicked out of the hedge, and could
scarcely rise at the last fence. Flacrow had gone like
a stumped-up horse, when he came out of the stable,
but he soon got his legs at liberty, and Tom was
cheered by the Marquis, when he caught him and
passed him in the lane. " *Who is Heycock?*" said
some Warwickshire men to Captain White. " *Who
is he?*" replied the Captain, " *Lord Heycock of
Owston, to be sure ; a very old title.*"

In the same spring, Vivian literally Lottery's begin-
walked over at Worcester, where every- nings.
thing else fell, and as the walk-over included a
flight of five feet rails done with hoop-iron, and a
ditch of four or five yards on the other side, it is a
mercy that he ever landed on to the Pitchcroft
meadows at all. His new rival, Lottery, appeared at

the end of this season at Barnet with young Henry
Elmore on him, and one of the strange, towering
jumps at a road in which he then indulged, brought
him over with a complete somersault.

St. Albans closed its career soon after
this, as the crowds were very unmanage-
able, and farmers began to be rusty about lending
their ground. To its last celebration but one, Prince
Paul Esterhazy gave a 100-guinea cup, in order that he
might see one more steeple-chase before he left
England. His highness and Coleman had it all over
again when they met at the Hampton Court Paddocks last year, and there was the Prince at 74 and
" as fond of riding and horses" as when he summoned
Mr. Anderson to present him with the cup, which
his Splendour had won. Although the tap-root was
dead at last, the sport blossomed every where in the
Midlands, and there was a match or two per week in
the Harrow country. Vivian carried a load of penalties,
and had Jerry and Cock Robin behind him at Dunchurch, but he could only contrive to repeat his
second at Leamington, where he divided Jerry and
Flacrow. Jerry was a tremendous horse for a
severe race, but with his 12lbs. penalty he was
only second to Conrad soon after at Northampton,
which furnished a line of the biggest fences and
brooks that living man had ever ridden over, in the
country about Wootton Hill. Milton Brook was
unusually swollen, and Mr. Payne lost a bet of £100
to half-a-sovereign, that all the horses did not get
over, and only one of them fell on landing. The
Marquis had got another of his tremendous leads
on Yellow Dwarf, but the shoemakers fairly blocked
him in at one of the brooks, and he had to pull his
horse into a trot. It was not done ill-temperedly on
this occasion, but it was a common trick of the mob
to dictate the line, by " the pressure from without,"
and they always set their faces most decidedly against

skirting, if there was a good stiff place which they wished to see negotiated.

Nothing more was heard of St. Albans after the December of this year, and Midnight appropriately closed the scene. Her prospects were, however, completely obscured, when her rider went to scale, as he could not draw his weight to half-a-pound. It was objected that the cart swayed about during the operation, but Bob Barker was not allowed to descend, and was solemnly carted in procession to Coleman's, only to try his weight once more with equal ill success. Mr. Anderson got the stakes, with Performer, and Lottery very much out of form, and ridden, for the first time by the renowned Jem Mason, was third. Six weeks after "Elmore's horse" beat a good field at Barnet, and then Mason jumped a flight of bullock rails extra with him on their route to the weighing place. The McDonoughs and Oliver came out about this time; Cannonball, Charity, and Railroad were heard of in the West, and the Nun began to be a familiar word in Warwickshire. Lottery had not quite come to his form, and Vivian was not quite done with, and for the last time the great rivals met in April 1838, from Drayton Grange to Flecknoe, and the one very big fence settled the question in favour of the junior.

Vivian v. Lottery.

Liverpool began its Great National in earnest the next year, and when True Blue and Bob Barker had done Charity over the hurdles, both of them with Lottery, Seventy-Four, three of "Harkaway Ferguson's," Railroad, Cannonball, and The Nun were among the seventeen which answered the saddling-bell. Becher was on Conrad, and went first to get him to settle down, up to what was then a fence with double rails, and a large ditch dammed up on the off-side. The horse made a mistake and hit the rails, and in a second, the gallant Captain had "formed to receive

Beginning of the Liverpool Grand National.

cavalry" by crouching under the bank. As for his
charger, he got back on the wrong side, and he lost
him, and the place, although sadly degenerated, is
called Becher's brook unto this day.

Leicestershire to wit.   The Whissendine was the last jump
that spring in the steeple-chase, which
marked Lord Suffield's mastership of the Quorn.
Mr. Villiers was first on Gipsy, and as the last horse
had to pay the second horse's stake, there was a fine
rear finish between Sir David Baird and Lord Cran-
stoun. Lord Desart was not satisfied at being behind
Lord Waterford and his 600-guinea Sea, and attributed it entirely to his fall; but a match of 100
sovereigns from Shankton Holt to Ram's Head, that
favourite old battle ground of Leicestershire, confirmed the first event.

Lottery's zenith and finish.   The Nun held her own pretty well in
the Midlands, Lottery bullied every-
thing when he had the chance; and when Gaylad
did the same, and no penalties seemed to stop them,
the handicap era gradually loomed. Lottery began
as Chance, and was licked into fits by Fop in a mile-
and-a-half trial; and then he was a performer at
Jackson's Grounds, where The Mite and Columbine
were heads and tails with him. He was a very
peculiarly-made horse, short in his quarters, deep in
his girth, but light in his middle and back ribs;
with a perfect snaffle-bridle mouth, fine speed, and a
very "trap to follow." When others could hardly
rise at their fences, he seemed to jump as if from a
spring-board. His jumping muscles were first brought
into such high play by putting him in a ring, with
flights of rails round it, and a man in the middle to
keep him moving, and he perfected his jumping education with Mr. Anderson's stag-hounds. After
his mistake at the Liverpool wall, he refused the
first fence, a post and rails five times at Faken-
ham; he showed his finest speed soon after that,

when he caught Seventy-Four on the post at Leamington; and he was scratched along with Jerry,
Seventy-Four and Peter Simple in the 100 sov. 25
forfeit steeple-chase, which was made up at Horncastle Fair, and which fell to Mr. Anderson's lot
with his blood-like Cigar. When Peter Simple and
Gaylad came out from Lincolnshire, his reverses began. He was third to Peter at Boston, and was
leading at Chelmsford when he came down in a
ploughed field, and left Gaylad who had 14lb. extra
like himself, to win it. Fit or not fit, Mr. Elmore
would have him out, despite all that George Docke-
ray could say, and it was owing to this determination,
that he was enabled to pay off Gaylad soon after at
Newport Pagnell. Later in the year he was beaten
a length in this country by Lucks All, who was ridden in most daring style by Tom Goddard. He was
giving away 29lbs., and the meadows were so flooded
that no one exactly knew where the brooks began
and ended, and five out of the twenty were all swimming together.

From '35 to '49, the Brocklesby men
did the legitimate thing, and never
"drooped and turned aside" either for
a fence or a handicap. Their annual steeple-chase
was for maiden horses, open to all England, and a
victory or a good performance added so much to the
value of their young horses, that they fetched very
high prices at Horncastle. The Brocklesby Hunt
Union Club was formed at Caistor in the November
of the first named year, and it got under way very
shortly at Rigby Slingsmere.

Tom Brooks of Croxby was its president, William
Richardson and William Torr its secretary and trea-
surer; and old Will Smith blew his horn, as the
starting signal. Lionel Holmes won the first race on
a mare of Mr. Hargreaves's, and was so determined
to lose no time after a fall, that he got on to her

Establishment of Brocklesby Hunt steeple-chases.

back when she was rising, and so to work once more. Flying Billy fell at the last fence but one, and lived to run for the Doncaster Cup against Touchstone, who beat him with nearly two distances in hand, to the infinite astonishment of "The Squire of Limber." In '36, the course was parallel to Barton Street, and Cannon-ball the winner jumped a sheep-fold in a corner as his last fence but one. A lot of men were sitting there to see the finish, and they "dropped like rooks off a rail," when they found him thundering among them. Captain Becher had a mount, and fell clean out of Laceby into Aylesby Lordship, but some one lent him a fresh horse, and he got close up with the leaders again, and sung a tremendous song about Grimaldi that night, and "the stile at the top of the hill." "I'd stay longer, gentlemen," he said in conclusion, "but a mount on Vivian is too good a thing to give away," and to Egham he departed forthwith. The Old Granby at Grimsby had a still more roystering party the next year, and George Skipworth was duly congratulated on coming all his length into the winning field, and being first after all.

Valentine an old grey, which had been lame and drawn a harvest waggon, had to thank Loft's steady riding for his win in '38, against a field of twenty-one; and Gaylad was nowhere to Ormsby the next year, and Peter Simple second. Better luck attended Gaylad the second time, but Peter Simple had a mischance some distance from home. As the maiden clause had been abolished ere this, Gaylad went in a third time, but he only won by the quickness of Captain Skipworth, who saw that the winning-wagon had been moved, and wheeled his horse round so as to go on the proper side of the flag. The owner of Croxby by Velocipede had to refund, and this little affair cost the fund £140. One county never sent out two finer steeple-chase champions than Gaylad and Peter Simple, but still neither of them could be said to be of the Lottery mint. Peter, for whom John Elmore offered seven hundred in vain, was a most beautiful horse to look at, and when he "paced he seemed fit to carry a king." He could go up to his knees in dirt; but his mouth was not first-rate, and he was far too impetuous at his fences. Gaylad, on the contrary, was not the horse to catch the eye, and had a forbidding head, and was rather light through his brisket. He went fast, and flew his brooks and fences magnificently, but he was not particularly clever at timber.

There is nothing connected with '42, except that Loft's Creeper won, and a cream-coloured colt called Paul Pry was Brocklesby steeple-chases 1842-49. the first entry in the mortuary tablets of the Club; and then for three years the fine, patient riding of Charles Nainby in the scarlet, had its reward on his own and his father's horses, the clever Crocus, and the two grey Tommies, Newcastle, and Northallerton. Crocus's was the last race which the second Earl of Yarboro' attended. His lordship delighted in seeing the thing done in good orthodox style, and hence the riders were all solemnly taken by way of prelude into a deep chalk-pit, to receive their instructions as to the line. Both the Tommies were sold for £200 a-piece, and but for a storm which prevented "Northallerton" from crossing the Humber to Beverley fair, he would have been sold for thirty some months before. In '46, Captain Skipworth did one of his best things on the hard-pulling Dubious; Lamplough crossed the Humber the next year with Salivation, and stole the race for the first time out of the district; and Mr. Oldaker wound matters up at twice, first by winning it with his Jenny Lind (when Pilot, whom Lord Gardner is riding yet, ran third), and lastly by a winning mount on Rachel. Twenty-two tried their hand

against the bay mare in vain, and then the silk
jackets were laid aside, and for thirteen seasons no
red flag has waved, to show the line to the lads of
the Brocklesby.

The horse world of London could boast during
this time of two men both equally great in their
line; to wit, "Old Tilbury" and Jack Elmore, the
hunter dealers. The former lived to nearly eighty,
and although he had signed no pledge, and received
no pewter medal as a signet of his allegiance, there
was not such a rigid tee-totaller, in the length and
breadth of Her Majesty's dominions. He never got
his full credit in this respect, seeing that the smell
of ale or spirits was quite as exhilarating in its effect
upon him, as if he had been in the Docks, and then
he could be handicapped to give weight to most men
in a story. In later life, he was generally black and
all black in his attire, save and except his white
neck-tie; and to the last his whole talk was of horses.

Mr. Tilbury the dealer. The conventional pun upon the first
syllable of the word had peculiar signi-
ficance in his case, as, barring a little water when he
could get nothing else, tea was the only fluid that
ever passed his lips. He was always very neat in
his dress, but short, and of the heavy-sternius build;
and it was this peculiarity which used to call forth
some funny remarks from "The Squire," when they
were going from covert to covert, in those merry
days when the two Georges, equally great in their
line, ruled at Windsor and Quorn.

His class of horses. He was never much of a rider across
country, and perhaps not a first-class
judge of a horse. As a general thing he seemed to
go for horses of a certain power and substance,
which would either frame into hunters or machiners,
or as he used to put it, "if there was not one there
was the other." When he first began, he had a little
wheel-wright's shop in Bryanston-street, Edgeware-

road, and let out buggy horses. From this humble spot, he went on to South-street, the scene of his fine tilbury trade, and rising at last into all his glory in Mount-street, began to let out hunters, and took a farm at Elstree, three miles beyond Edgeware. After that, he took 200 acres at the Dove House, Pinner, which afforded plenty of exercise and larking ground, of which his aid-de-camps, Newcome and Jim Mason (whom Bill Bean claims to have led over his first flight of park palings), and Jim Payne availed themselves to the full. Mat Milton, who was wont to say, that if he did lose his horse in the hunting-field, he could always *"pay five or six stout fellows and run him down,"* was then at the head of the crack hunter business in Piccadilly; but Tilbury's stud, many of which were purchased from the Elmores, was never under seventy. He would let them by the day or the season, and Count Matuschevitz and Mr. Harvey Combe opened very paying accounts with him. In fact, many of his sixty-pound horses would earn their fifty guineas per season, and if any accident happened, he had always another ready to send down. They were picketted out everywhere, all over the Midlands, but principally at Melton and Northampton; and he would ride enormous distances, week after week, looking them up and making arrangements about proxies.

He also did a little in the steeple-chase line, with his Culverthorpe, Prospero, and Tomboy, when Vivian, Cigar, and Lottery had brought up matters to a white heat; but he left off on the wrong side, both in this and his hunter dealing. The latter sadly dwindled a few years before his death in 1860. Mount-street, and a few common stamp horses still remained, with a small farm at Thatch End, adjoining the Pinner acres of his more glorious days, but the younger generation knew him not, and went elsewhere for their hunters.

On the box it might truly be said of him that

" Difficulties prove a soul legitimately great."

His coachmanship.   As a four-in-hand whip he had no
particular pretensions ; but his delight
was to have two raw young things in a break or a
curricle, and drive them in and out of places, and
along thoroughfares, which hardly any coachman
with the most metallic nerves would have dared to
essay. *" Such hands,"*—as a good whip once said to
us—*" never let them begin kicking ; knew just when
to stop them to a yard."* If a young horse would
not go on, he would sit as calm as a Mohawk Chief,
biding his time. To take his tilbury into a field,
and turn it neatly over, and step out of it, without the horse falling, was another sleight-of-
hand diversion with the ribbons, to which he was
peculiarly partial. He had all the quiet manner of the old school, and was very full of anecdotes, which of course grew on as his life-shadows
lengthened, till one or two of them became perfect sea-serpents. To the last he was faithful
The two French-   to the one about the two foreigners,
men and the   who hired horses from him to meet Her
Three Pigeons.   Majesty's at " The Three Magpies" on
Hounslow Heath. Their horses were so beaten when
they left off near Red Hill, that they were obliged
to leave them, and get a post-chaise. Then came
the difficulty, which Mr. Tilbury told with appropriate action and streaming eyes. They had forgotten the name of the inn where they had left their
hacks, and they only knew that it had to do with a
bird. *" Drive us to the Pigons,"* they said,
*" de birds of colour ; you do know—de black
and white Pigons,"* till they had utterly bewildered and exasperated their post-boy, and
were only helped out of the dilemma by a friendly
scarlet.

William Elmore, the father of the three brothers' George, John, and Adam, The Elmores. settled in Hampshire, and came up to town only once a week latterly. He was a very big man, so much so that he used to tell a story of a countryman, who could not be persuaded to tell him and his fat friend which way the hounds had gone. "*You don't want the hounds,*" he said, forking the dung into his cart all the time, with the most provoking coolness, "*you'd better both send your guts on by the waggon afore you go after them.*" Upon the subject of dressing, he was particular and sensitive, and equally so upon having a beef-steak pudding always ready for him on his return from hunting. Once when he did not appear till twelve o'clock, it had been disposed of in the household supper, but his peremptory orders from that day forth were, to this effect, "*If I'm away for a week, never take the pudding out of the pot!*"

The Elmores as hunter dealers. His son John was like him, rather a *bon vivant*, and inherited many more of his ways. George, the elder brother, and the master of the concern, was a quiet man, and hated steeple-chasing, but left his brothers to do pretty much as they liked. He simply said that the more they spent, the less there would be for them at his death. John was a better driver, but not such a good rider as Adam, who had wonderfully fine "show hands," and an imposing figure on a horse. Still he was not equal as a salesman to his brother, but quite the best buyer, so that their special talents blended exactly, and for many years they had quite a first-class business. Their head man, Old John Haynes, with his bent leg and top-boots, went hopping about to all the country fairs, and knew every likely farmer and breeder in the Midlands. He also took Worcestershire and Shropshire in his rounds, with all the sagacity of a truffle hunter; and never seemed to think that his masters could purchase enough. It was no argument in his eyes that the cheque-book could stand no more. In those days, before the rail, George Odell, Catlin, Sam Wilson, and the Drages used to buy up young horses in Yorkshire, and place them out with the Northamptonshire and Leicestershire farmers, for a year or two to be got handy, and it was on these fives and sixes, that the Elmores pounced at the Midland county fairs. Now, they are bought in Yorkshire as threes and fours, and railed up at once; and all the grand middle education is lost. The firm removed from Duke-street, Manchester-square, to John-street, Edge-ware-road, and after George's death in 1845, Adam stayed on there, and kept on the foreign trade, while John exchanged Neasdon for Uxendon, which he soon fitted up with a steeple-chase course, and cared very little more about business.

John Elmore at home. In his heyday, he was fully sixteen stone; but a slow consumption had gradually worn him down to about nine-stone-eight; and those friends who remembered so well his once florid and portly presence, hardly knew him again towards the close. He once farmed nearly a thousand acres, but latterly he held only one farm of about half that amount. As a judge of horses, and steeple-chasers in particular, he had no superior. A clever pony he dearly loved; and even the rough, hairy-heeled ones, which he did his farming on, had a character peculiarly their own. One of them would get over a fence, and regularly wait for him to follow and seize it by the tail, so as to be dragged up the bank on the "off-side." Like many of the old school, he was also right fond of a bit of cocking, and fought many a quiet "in-go" during the London season.

John Elmore's stories. He was the best of companions, and with some good story to tell of every

horse or sporting man that could be named. One
of Carlin the steeple-chase jockey especially delighted
him. " *Where have you been to?*" he said when·
that worthy did not arrive till some minutes after
the ruck. " *Been to, Mr. Elmore?*" was the reply ;
" *I had a fall, and a fellow called me an old brick-
maker, and asked me where I was taking all the clay
away to with me ; so I stopped and had a fight
with him, and so would you.*" Carlin was equally
ready to account for his absence on another occasion.
" *You told me,*" said he, " *to leave it all to the horse,
and I trusted to his honour, and he put me down—
that's a pretty thing.*" One about Bob * * * * * *
pleased him still more. Bob had sat up too late
with his friends, after ordering himself called early
next morning, and before putting him to bed
they had amused themselves with shaving his
head. Not being very particular in his toilet, he
never got a view of himself till he came to breakfast, opposite the pier-glass in the coffee-room.
He had the presence of mind to grasp the bell-
handle and summon the waiter. " *Waiter,*" he
said, "*where's that fool of a boots ? he's gone
and called the bald-headed old gentleman in the
next room ; and he's never called Bob* * * * * * at
all !" This story has been told in a variety of
ways, but Bob was, we believe, the great original
of it.

It was always " *my dear boy,*" when   Stag-hound
John Elmore wanted to impress an   diplomacy.
opinion on you; and to disbelieve him seemed
treason. It was said of an eminent manager, that
he had a voice which could lure a bird from a tree ;
and, as a friend of John Elmore's once said to us,
" *If John had done me out of ten thousand, I could'nt
have found it in my heart to blame him.*" The farmers, during the time he kept his stag-hounds, would
occasionally arrive at the farm, boiling over with a

sense of injury to their crops; but the interview generally ended in their stopping to make an evening of it; and then assuring him, at parting, that they would take it as a personal insult if he did not continue to pursue the very same line of conduct they had come to protest against. He was a great favourite with them, and was, in fact, almost free to hunt his stags for miles round Harrow without being harassed with trespass notices.

"The stag-hounds" were half-blood and half-fox-hound, and perfectly indifferent as to whether they had deer or hare in front of them; and he took to them the season after Mr. Anderson gave up his. He seldom kept more than half-a-dozen, and a brace and a-half of stags; but they went at it the moment the hay was off the ground, and would often be seen tolling along through crops of standing beans. He was a good horseman, but very excitable in a run; and the time to see him go best was when he turned out his second deer for a lark after luncheon. None went better with Mr. De Burgh's; and occasionally he would have a day with the Queen's, or change to fox with the Old Surrey and Lord Dacre's, and then spend a month at a time in Hampshire. His last hunter was Paddy, a very excellent horse under his weight, but a great savage in the stable.

Some years ago, when he had quite ceased to take a fence, he would go wonderfully on his fourteen-hand ponies, always the very best of their kind, whenever The Queen's came into the Harrow and Barnet country, and dash down lanes, however rough, with an energy which the most inveterate road-professors could only envy, and not dare to imitate in its integrity. If any of his horses had a thorn, he did'nt care how big the leg got; but he sent them hunting, to make it suppurate and come out.

Nothing pleased him better than to set five or six of his friends larking as they rode back from hunting by the side of the road, and to halloo at them all the way. Those were days, when he was in full health; but for the last few years one lung had entirely gone. When he wanted his horses trained, he would invariably put his stable lads on them in red spencers, and watch them while they jumped everything before them with hounds; and it was thus that The British Yeoman "got into a fine practice."

Grimaldi, Lottery, Jerry, Gaylad, The Weaver, Sam Weller, and British Yeoman bore the "blue and black cap," in turn; but Lottery was the only one he cared to talk much about. His friends used to laugh at this "Horncastle horse," who was lamed with larking the day he got him, but he always said, *"You may laugh—you'll see it come out;"* and well was his patience rewarded. When the horse had ceased to defy creation with Jem Mason under thirteen-stone-seven, if ever a friend went down for an afternoon, with "Jack" to Uxendon, he would order him to be saddled. *"Hang it!"* he would say, *"have you never been on the old horse?— get up!"* and be the ground ever so hard, or the fences ever so blind, he would insist on their backing him, one after the other, if there were half-a-dozen of them. He would turn him over anything; and occasionally it would be the iron hurdles between the garden and the paddock, or, for lack of a handier fence, he would put the rustic garden-chairs together.

He was in his sixty-sixth year when he died; and with him and "The Marquis"—the two original props—professional and amateur—of the steeple-chase have gone from amongst us. In these poor-spirited days, when too many owners think "the

grasshopper a burden" in the shape of 10st. 7lb.,
and rope away till they can blind the handicapper
into a stone less, we may well wish for a par-
ticle of the spirit which brought the Uxendon and
Curraghmore blues into "the tented field," and
made even St. Albans a place of real spirit and
renown.

A. I. 1861

Mr. Musters, p. 325.

CHAPTER V.

HORN AND HOUND.

" And Alvanley, too, shall Meltonia forget thee,
    Oh! never while wit and wine have a charm;
  Thou, too, wilt return, blithe as ever we met thee,
    And with joke, fun, and glee still old Sorrow disarm;
  And Chesterfield too, and our honoured De Wilton,
    With Plymouth and Stanley shall come in their train;
  And the Lord of the Chase and the Monarch of Melton
    Shall be Harry of Ribstone—Success to his reign!"

" You should go and see my old friend Joe Hewitt," said an *M. F. H.* to us, " I hear he's been giving them a capital lecture on foxhunting at Mexborough." The advice was too good to be lost, so away we strode from Doncaster on a January afternoon, down the short cut through that hazel cover, under the Conisboro' cliff, past the British School, whose rafters, on the testimony of the villagers, had rung again on that memorable night when Joe found his fox therein, and killed, after a brilliant burst of five-and-thirty minutes, from " The Platform Wood," and on to the lecturer's lair. He was full forty when he went to hunt Sir Jacob Astley's staghounds, in Norfolk, and that is more than forty seasons ago; but age has told but little on his tall, active frame. The walls of his snug little home reflect the triple phases of his hunting life. Two stags' heads hang in the ante-chamber; Joe himself is on Paddy, with the Badsworth Watchman, and Ranter, Cottager, and Glider from Lord Scarborough's at his side; and a stout man, in a buff waist-

Visit to Joe Hewitt.

coat, with gaiters, and a dog-whip, is neither more nor less than the Mr. Frank Fawkes, of his harrier days.

Service under Mr. Frank Fawkes. It was just 5 to 1 on Joe in his good master's mind, and he was butler, groom, gamekeeper, valet, and huntsman to him. They had not many horses between them; but still the stable cleared £500 in seven years. Scarlet was the livery of the hunt, and they used the privilege to the full, by never whipping off if they crossed the line of a fox. They gave one such a dusting from Hickleton Spinneys, that Lord Darlington expressed a lively belief to Joe, that "*you'll come into my dining-room, at Bilham, next.*" And Joe did arrive there shortly after. His lordship had run a fox to ground at Barnboro' Grange, and asked Joe to dig him out and bring him to Bilham. Late in the evening, Joe was duly announced, with "Charley" in a sack, and after showing his prisoner to the Duchess and the family, dismissed him from the front door to his old head of earths. Colonel Mellish cared quite as much, if not more, for the harriers than the Darlington and the Rufford; and mounted on the brown Lancaster, he kept the field alive. And so for seven seasons "Joe" used to make the hares tender on Mexboro' side, with old Master Franky's harriers, and "prepare them for the spit by the inflammatory process of an hour's run, with a ten minutes burst at the finish."

Joe stag-hunting in Norfolk. Two years after this merry little pack was given up (in consequence of Mr. Fawkes's death in '18), Joe departed to Sir Jacob Astley's staghounds, with Bill Turpin and Jim Shirley as his whips, and half the country came to see his first day. The stag took at once to a creek, and Joe's jump over it on Paddy, eight yards, and rotten banks on both sides, "put him right in Norfolk." Still they never expected to behold him again. He

wound his way over quicksands, where horse and
rider had never ventured before, on the beach between Morston and Wells, and only just got back
with his hounds when he had seen the deer picked
up by a boat, before the creek filled again. In
token of his jump, and his restoration to them, after
their terrible suspense, the field filled his pockets
with silver, till he could hardly button his coat.
Mr. Coke went specially to see the place, and introduced Joe to the Duke of Sussex and Sir Francis
Burdett at the next Holkham sheep-shearing, with
"*There's a fellow who's done such a thing as has
never been done in this county before.*"

After a couple of seasons Sir Jacob   Fox-hunting
turned to fox-hunting and did it well for   in Norfolk.
ten seasons, four days a week. The Burrow Kennels
soon had seventy couple in them, and a hundred and
fifty foxes were got together, in paddocks near Melton Constable, and kept there for four months.
Mr. Coke was very friendly, and told Sir Jacob to
quarter any quantity he liked on Holkham, so they
took him at his word, and turned down ten brace at
his front door. Still well disposed as the great landlord might be, they were " taken care of " by some
one, and scarcely two brace were ever hallooed away
again.

The steward at Gawdy Hall, which is   A new light on
just on the Suffolk border, was well dis-   fox-hunting.
posed; but had only been entered to pheasant and
rabbits. Trusting to his natural instincts, the first time
Sir Jacob met there, he rode furiously down the road
the moment he espied Joe and the hounds, and called
out, " *You're too late, huntsman, I've got all my men
together to beat the cover, and we've found such a
beautiful fox.*" He seemed to feel that he had acted
so prudently, and so strictly with a view to sport,
that as there was no help for it, Joe swallowed his
feelings, and did not care to undeceive him, but

simply inquired the line. It seemed a nice one over grass to a wood, and there was comfort in the hope that the fox might wait there. Sir Jacob and the officers from the Norwich barracks did not dwell much at breakfast after the startling news of that morning, and they were soon out of the Hall, and into the saddle. Luck was on their side ; one or two hounds feathered, and spoke to their fox when Joe held them on the line; they dressed him for five-and-twenty minutes in the wood, and ran into him over a fine open country almost without a check.

Fox-hunting lecture.   Still, even this anecdote of the dark ages of Norfolk did not satisfy us. We had come specially to hear the lecture, and as we had been duly told that he had "a most humoursome voice in drawing covers," we persevered till the horn came down. When the lecture did begin, and Joe was finding and then breaking up his fox, we sat aghast at the pent-up volume of sound, the perfect cave of Œolus, whose blasts we had let loose on that quiet street, and hardly dared to calculate the effect upon "rurals" and passers-by. Clogs seemed to come with measured steps as far as the garden-gate, and then become suddenly spell-bound. Joe's own head was his manuscript, and always has been, and a mere skeleton abstract was the only result of our pencil attempts to follow him.

"If I had a piano," he said, "I could make a devilish good run of it, and give plenty of music to it ; the piano should do the hounds. I begin with a single hound, then two, and so keep increasing. That's "*The try*" we don't find ; then we try another cover. *Yooi in, yoicks, yoicks! Push him up!* one hound speaks. In that case, I should give the piano a single tap. I should then call, if it was a hound we could depend upon, *Hark! hark!* to such an one ; if it still continues, and there's a fox on foot, *Hark! hark! to Watchman! Hark!* There I

want the piano for the body of the hounds. *Hark!
Get together! Push him up! Hooi!* that puts their
mettle up.

There's a *view halloo* [and indeed it was
one, more clogs seemed to be arrested in their
course, and we heard voices]—this is just the way,
only shorter, that I gave it them in the British
School; if there's a view halloo, then comes *Goneaway! Hark forard!* Now, you must begin with
the piano, it should make the hounds; now I carry
a great head. *Bless you,* gentlemen! Hold hard!
Yoi Gaurt! Come back!* You see the hard riders
have pressed the hounds too much, and they've over-
run the line; as soon as you see your dashing hounds
taking the lead, and your best hounds slackening you
may depend on it things are not all right. *El-loo
back!*

Now, gentlemen, do hold hard! You try back, and
generally make it out if well up; *Yokes!* there's a
chirrup; now I want the piano; there's another
chirrup; I want two strokes; the whole body are
sensible of it. *Have at 'em, my little fellows!* what's
leading? I say *Hark to Ranter,* or such an one;
then the whips and the piano go to work, and I carry
a great head till we kill. We're in a wheat field
now. *Bless you, gentlemen, do keep furrows!* Now
we view—*that's a Dead Halloo;* [and thankful indeed
we were that the whole village did not turn out at
the summons]. I get the fox, and keep him up,
hollering to get stragglers together. Then I told
them about Madcap; she was keen, she jumped up
and got hold of my ear; don't you see the mark?
you can feel a little knob there; I could have kissed
her to see her so anxious. That's the way the lecture goes on, I can draw it out any length that's
desirable. I gave them another lecture about my

---

* According to the accounts in the *Old Sporting Magazine,* a more
courteous huntsman never blew up a horn or a man.

visit to Raby Castle. I saw the Duke; his Grace remembered that fox and sack business at Bilham, though I had'nt seen him for fifty two years."

So much for Mexboro' and its cheery lecturer!

Fox-hunting 1790-1810. The closing and opening decades of the two centuries found hunting sound to the core. Meynell was "King of Quorn." Tom Oldaker, of "Huntsman's Hall," in his yellow plush coat almost to his ankles, woke up the beech woods of Chilton and the wild ridings of Easthamstead, with the three sharp bugle notes, which told that he had gone away, and the still more tuneful *La Mort.* The lady of Hatfield was first in the field, and last at the ball. Mr. Coke's hounds hovered between Castle Hedingham, Holkham, and Epping. The Duke of Grafton's dwarf pack were busy in Salcey Forest and the vast Whittlebury woodlands. Dick Knight's cheer was heard in Sywell Wood, and foxes were dying an honourable death of old age in Bedford Purlieus, despite all the talent of Will Dean. Petworth, Woburn, Brocklesby, and Belvoir, had each a family pack; and Cheshire mourned for its Bluecap, to ·which it subsequently erected an obelisk. Tom Grant was getting up and down the hills of Sussex like a flash on his chamois-footed steeds. Mr. Chute took everything that was too small for Tom, and kept up the glories of The Vine, which "The Iron Duke" nurtured so well in after years, and three times saved from grief. Lord Stawell was in the Holt Forest country, and Mr. St. John gradually changed back from hare to fox. Mr. Poyntz looked upon the killing of a May fox and a dance round the May-pole, when the Prince was at Albury Grange, as two vital points before he returned to Cowdray. The hounds and Tom Crane were always kept on the right of the line, whenever the army changed quarters in the Peninsula; and later still with Burdett, Whitbread,

Canning, and Romilly, as the line-hunters in St.
Stephens.

> " The sport of all sport was reserved for the day,
> When out of a bag they turned Lord Castlereagh."

The Earl of Darlington was long the *The late Earl of Darlington.*
Nimrod of the North, " with his chin
sticking out, and his cap on one ear. Many of
the old hands still speak of him as always having
his finger in his ear, or his cap in his hand, and
consider that his hunting was conducted on no
especial system. " He was all for riding, and
four couple of hounds in front, and the rest
coming as they could was the general order of
things." The stud, which was headed by the grey
Ralph, whose skin still covers an arm chair at Raby,
was first-rate, and worthy of their master. His Lordship came into the Badsworth country each spring
and autumn for six weeks at a time, and as he
had finished his own cub-hunting before the autumn
visit his hounds, which had been well blooded, pulled
down the foxes wholesale.

Squire Draper of Beswick and King's *Squire Draper.*
Huntsman for the East-Riding, has still
a strong traditional fame in Yorkshire. Foxes were
destroying the lambs to a great extent in 1726,
when he began his operations, and Sir Mark Constable was one of his chief supporters. He had
only £700 a year wherewith to keep up his old Hall,
and was blessed with three daughters and eleven
sons. Kickshaws he eschewed, and once a month
he killed an ox for roasting and salting. " All the
brushes in Christendom" was his chosen toast, after
he had drunk " King and Constitution," and a
leathern girdle round his drab coat and a rusty
velvet cap were his royal insignia of office. The
general effect could not have been impressive, as a
tailor who had come over from York to measure the

Miss Drapers for new hunting-habits, did not guess
him at his front-door, and he most rigidly exacted
two-pence for holding the horse.   On another occasion when one of the same order came over equipped
for riding, and said that he had left his horse elsewhere, he insisted on accompanying him to it, and
made him confess at the end of a two or three miles
walk, that his boots and whip were a pious fraud.
He was a little caustic in his humour, and considered
from what he had seen in his visit to the metropolis
that " a Yorkshire haft" could at least hold its own.
The drains of Holderness also suggest how he declined to assist a sufferer, on the short ground that
he was a " whipper-in, and not a whipper-out." His
daughter Diana, a regular " Di Vernon" in her way,
had a rare voice and eye to hounds, but died after
many perils in her virgin bed, at a good old age
at York, and she is buried with him at Market
Weighton.

The Yorkshire Ash, " the weed of the Wolds," had
Wolds. not begun to flourish in the old man's
time.   Beyond a few solitary elms and beeches, and
an occasional belt of firs, there was hardly a tree to
be seen on his vast hunting grounds of hill, valley,
and morass.   Except round the village garths, there
was not a gate between Market-Weighton and
Beverley.   The Wolds were covered with ling, to
which the bee-wives carried their swarms in order to
reflect its perfume and dark colour in the honey;
but there was not cover enough for ten miles round
Sledmere, to hide a goose, much less a travelling
fox.   The land was worth two-and-sixpence an
acre, and had hard work to pay that.   Barley
for future " Haver Cake Lads" was its only
white crop, and big-boned, and flat-sided black
and whites very faintly fore-shadowed the era of
" The Driffield Cow," which was almost as wonderful in its generation as the guinea-hen which

hunted running and flying with the Castle Howard
hounds.

The title deeds of the Middleton hunt The Wold hunts.
date back nearly 100 years, and seven
separate masters, and a triumvirate consisting of
Earl Carlisle, Lord Middleton, and Mr. Crompton
owned them till Sir Mark Sykes purchased them
from the first Lord Feversham in 1804, and hunted
them for two seasons at his own expense. The coats
of the club had light blue collars with a silver fox,
and " *Sykes, Goneaway !*" on the buttons ; and Sir
Mark mounted his men on Camilluses and Scri-
vington's, many of his own breeding. The hounds
were valued at 300 gs., when Mr. Watt and Mr.
Digby Legard formed a second triumvirate with Sir
Mark, and after a Middleton interregnum, Sir Tatton took them in 1811, and held them with only a
two-season break for two-and-forty years. Old Will
Carter and his son Tom Carter were huntsman and
first whip, and as Mr. Bethell and his successor had
given up Holderness, Sir Tatton's country extended
from Coxwold to Spurn Point. They always hunted on the Wednesday in the York country ; and
Sir Tatton (who was laying in a hunter stud from
four Camillus mares), used to leave Sledmere in the
dark, get on his hunter at Eddlethorpe, and often
ride forty miles home.

Every March and November Sir The Sykes hounds.
Tatton went to the Brandsburton
Kennels to work the Holderness side, which he
held for four seasons, till the present Holderness
Hunt was established, and Martin Hawke and
George Osbaldeston, who then lived at Hutton
Bushell, were the very life of the Hunt Club at
Beverley. The election spirit, which ran so high in
those days, did not penetrate within the walls of The
Tiger. It made no matter to the Club, that a hare
with a blue ribbon and " No Popery" round its neck

was sent to every one of the plumpers on one side; or that a fair electioneerer, who had expressed a wish to be a man for a moment, that she might pull a rubicund opponent's nose, received as her answer, "*You are welcome to do so, Mam, but it will burn your fingers!*" The young "Squire" was fresh from Brasenose, and if some clever cork-cutters had not lived near the bridge at York, and by their joint efforts promptly put in his neck after a tumble, that greatest and most versatile of all sporting careers would have been quenched very early.

The Badsworth. A season under Mr. Musters and two under Sir Bellingham Graham, brings the Badsworth up to the era of Mr. "Tom Hodgson," about 1817. Sir Bellingham left him twelve couple of hounds and three horses as a nest egg, and he purchased several couple of hounds from the Duke of Leeds, and kept the pack at Thorpe. Will

Engagement of Danby had been with the Badsworth dur-
Will Danby. ing part of Mr. Hodgson's mastership, and Jack Richards, Mr. Petre's huntsman, was so sure that he was just the man to work Holderness, that he wrote him to go over to Snydale, and apply for the place. Will was then with some harriers near Halifax, and on the first non-hunting day he set off at three a.m. in his top-boots, and at nine he stood before Mr. Hodgson. The energy of the man delighted him, and when he heard Will declare that "the distance mattered *nowt*, it was a bargain at a guinea a week," and Will walked back again the two-and-twenty miles, but "with a much lighter heart," to give his week's notice.

Waifs and strays To get the hounds together was the
for Holderness. next object. Before his draft was ready, Mr. Foljambe sent to say, "I know you'll take waifs and strays, so you're welcome to a young hound which has come to my kennel." It was duly sent in the boot of the coach and lost, and yet, utterly strange as it

Old Days in Holderness, p. 335.

was to the country, it came straight to Snydale, and was called Sensible in consequence. Young Will Carter happened to see it, and the moment his memory was confirmed by the earmark, he chal-lenged it as " Sister to our Driver." Still he begged Mr. Hodgson to tell his brother Tom nothing about it, as he has " far more than he can work." Ranter and Rosebud were all that Tom could spare in addition; but Sir William Gerard, Mr. Foljambe, and The Badsworth sent in some fourteen or fifteen couple. Ranter was rather undersized, but a rare hound; and although Badsworth Reginald could hardly crawl into Holderness, from kennel lameness, and was nearly hung on the road, he gradually worked himself sound.

In his time, Mr. Hodgson has built six kennels, and the lady pack of twenty *Kennel building.* couple which he sold to Lord Ducie for 1,000 gs. at his Quorn sale, were kennelled for a whole summer in a transmuted hovel at Snydale. It does not look worth as many pence, and has since then been the birth-place of Prologue and Virgilius, and the shel-ter of the old grey hunting mare Twilight. The last kennel he had a hand in was at Whiston, near Rotherham, in conjunction with Sir George Sitwell, who was " Master of the horse." Mr. Foljambe gave up part of his country to him; but Lord Scarbo-rough took the whole, and bought the pack from Mr. Hodgson when the veteran became the West Riding Registrar of Deeds at the end of his second season after leaving the Quorn country.

During Mr. Hodgson's sixteen sea- *Life in Holder-ness.* sons in Holderness, the hounds changed their kennels three times. Their first was at the Rose and Crown, Beverley, and then they were re-moved to other kennels in the town, and finally to Mr. Watt's, at Bishop Burton. The subscrip-tion never exceeded a thousand a year, and for

the first two seasons, it was barely £800 for four
days a week. At one time the work was so hard,
that Mr. Hodgson and Will between them had only
two horses that could get out of the stable at all.
As Will said, they were " *never bet yet;*" but when
a bye-day was asked for as well, Mr. Hodgson stood
firm on the ground, that it took " horses of cast-iron,
hounds of steel, and men of India-rubber" to
achieve what they were doing already. There were
never more than 36 couple of hounds in kennel; and
although the horses were only thirty-pounders to
begin with, two of them sold for £130 and £160 at
Quorn, after Mr. Hodgson had got five or six seasons out of them. Comical by Comus, and the gift
of Mr. William Maxwell (the present Lord Herries)
carried him for ten. Once he was scarcely off his
back for fifteen hours, and when his master's reign
in Holderness and Leicestershire was over, the old
black found honourable burial under an oak tree in
Everingham Park.

Will Danby's
sayings.
Will stipulated on going, as he did
when he joined the York and Ainsty as
huntsman, that he was not to wear gills; and the
sport did not suffer in either case by his resolve.
His speeches were not so caustic as that of a
celebrated brother-chip, who sat on his horse in the
middle of a heavily top-dressed field, and observed,
" *I've had fourteen boiling-house lectures, and I
shall now proceed to hunt my way out of this* 100-
acre field on purely scientific principles;" but they
were always straight to the point. On the legitimate duties and responsibility of the Legislature,
his views were not expansive. " *Mr.* —— *is to be
a Member of Parliament, Will!*" said one of the
hunt, as he was riding home with the hounds. " *Is
'er,*" replied Will. " *Well, he's good for nowt else.*"
Again, when a black coat, whose horse was rather
staring in his coat and hips sought counsel with him

upon the matter, he clenched it with, "*I think Mr.
—, you must keep your horse on chopped sarmons.*"
Nothing could induce him to have his portrait taken,
and when the ladies asked him to sit, he put the
question by, and said he was not handsome enough.
At last Mr. Hodgson conspired against him on this
point, and having decoyed him into treeing a fox,
he held him so long, and gripped him so fast as he
sat astride of his shoulders, that he got into a sketch-
book irrevocably in this highly-favoured position.

Master and man often rode five-and- *Dreams of the*
twenty miles to cover, and early in the *chase.*
spring, Will hallooed a fox away from Wassand
Wood, as the church clock was striking seven. Mr.
Hodgson called to give Mr. Constable notice, but
found the soup and fish on the table, and retired
without him to the enjoyment of a merry kill by
moonlight. This was nothing either to him or Will,
as they invariably "hunted in dreams," and Mr.
Hodgson had one of the most remarkable import at
Bishop Burton. Will had drawn sixteen couple of
the best dog hounds, to go into the Brandsburton
country as usual; when to his surprise, his master
appeared at day-break, and said, "*We must take
old Melody with us, Will. I've had a dream; she
must go, or we shan't get our fox.*" "*She'll disgrace
us, sir,*" replied Will, in the blankest astonishment,
as her toes were all down, and she was so nearly
worn out that she had not hunted five days that season; but Mr. Hodgson stood firm. A fox was
found in Dringhoe, and was lost beyond Wassand,
after running across the finest part of the country. Melody came on the line as she could, and
was of course missing when they checked. They
could make nothing out, and Will had held them
forward past a drain, where a fox had gone
to ground two seasons before, when Mr. Hodgson bethought himself to trot back. In a minute or two

he heard Melody's short yap in it, and digging up
to her, they found that she was baying their fox,
and almost touching him. Lavender was another
of Mr. Hodgson's handmaids, and so resolute, that
when her master saw his pack carry a tremendous
head to the top of Bempton Cliff, his heart quite
failed, and he knew that she must be over. His
prophetic mind was so convinced on the point, that
he pulled up, and went sadly home, dreading to
hear the end. Luckily only six went over, but she
was one. The late Ned Oxtoby, the first whip,
and a very valued servant of Mr. Hodgson's was
equal to the occasion. He peeped over the edge of
the cliff, and saw three hounds lying dead near the
fox, and the others bruised, and yelping on the
most remarkable crevices. By the aid of a rope, he
brought up Lavender and another, but a ledge prevented him from getting at Romulus, and he left
him with an aching heart, for the sea-gulls. When
he looked at the place afterwards in cool blood, he
declared that £100 a-year for life would'nt have
tempted him to go down. The reward was worth
the risk, as a couple of Lavender's eight puppies
lived and at the end of twenty miles, Will Webb,
who was then huntsman, saw the hounds swagger-
ing over a new arrival, and guessed that it was Romulus, who had backed himself up a cliff almost as
steep as a house side.

Holderness foxes.
The Holderness foxes of that period
were generally long, and dark-coloured
in the low country, while those on the wolds, which
Mr. Hodgson handled with his lady pack, were
rather bigger, and lighter in their coats. Five
were found in a rape-field, near Roos, which
they drew four times that day. One was chopped
to begin with, by being caught in a sheep-net,
and the four others furnished runs of different
duration from five-and-twenty to ten minutes.

As regards foxes' habits, Mr. Hodgson was a perfect Buffon. On one occasion he sent his horse to a farm house, and lay " stretched many a rood" in a dry ditch for hours, to see the vixen come and move nine cubs, which had been disturbed. When she did come, she proved to be the largest he had ever seen; but two magpies were chattering above her, and discomfited her so much, that she would not go up to them that night, and that long vigil was void. However, a sentinel was found, and his report was that she moved them to the opposite side of the field before daybreak, in lots of three at a time. Again he was summoned to a consultation by a farmer at Lowthorpe, to come over and see thirteen cubs. His man had disturbed them on ploughing a headland, and taken seven out of one angle of the earth, and six out of the other, both of which had only one common entrance. They were put in a stable with a half-door, and a lad sat up all night in the opposite granary, to pull the top part to, in case the dams came to them. Although the stable was half-a-mile from the earth, he had not to watch long; but the tarred string with which the door was tied, seemed to make them suspicious, and after scratching for nearly an hour at the bottom of the door they departed, and never came again.

Strychnined-rabbits and traps were then happily unknown in Holderness, and farming men, with "master's com-

Mr. Hodgson's Scurry Stakes at Beverley.

pliments," and consignments of stub-bred foxes and cubs were perpetually arriving at the kennels, to await further orders. On one occasion a litter was dug up at Sigglesthorne, and the farmer came with them himself. "1 will show you what I do with them," said Mr. Hodgson, and when Will had mealed them well, the trio adjourned from Bishop Burton to the bottom of the *T.Y.C.* at Beverley, with their burden in a couple of sacks. All four foxes ran together up the course, head and head, to the stand, as straight as if they were going down a furrow at Dringhoe, and then the old fox drew away from them, and straight to Bishop Burton Woods, while the others bent to the right.

Mr. Hodgson would never bolt a fox till he had been made safe, but on one occasion, he felt specially glad to let his fox have a second chance for its life. He had run one to ground in Sir Tatton's country, and was taking his hounds away, when the ladies and the gardeners arrived armed with pick-axe and spade, and full of complaints about peacock and guinea-hen slaughter. In vain did Mr. Hodgson propound to them, in his most chivalrous tones, the whole law of hunting on the point. His learning and sophistry availed him nothing. The fox was a regular ticket-of-leave offender, and they declared that if the digging occupied all night they would have him, and " the imminent deadly breach began." There was only one chance of foiling them politely, and Mr. Hodgson descending from his horse in his legal agony and leggings, commenced stamping wildly on the top of the earth, and succeeded in bolting him, and then bolted himself. However, he was enabled to send back the brush and mask to his fair persecutors, at the end of an hour; and his treachery was condoned. Still, as the ground had been opened he felt bound to lay their conduct before Sir Tatton. The baronet had deftly apologized for his hunter's rudeness in jumping away when the lady of Thorpe Hall came out to speak to him, by saying that " *it had never seen anything so handsome before;*" and his dictum in this equally difficult case was as follows:—" *Dear Hodgson,—Whenever the ladies tempt you to do anything wrong, get out of their way.*"

Practical jokes in Holderness. These were not Mr. Hodgson's only difficulties. An East Riding veteran

remembers why he did not care to sleep at The
Tiger again, when its merry club were having a
night of it in the next room, with Sir Bellingham
and Mr. Hodgson at their head, but the latter was
the victim of many plots in turn. They stuffed
his horn so full of egg and buttered toast, that he,
although he showed them a capital run from Kilnwick
Percy, he could not give them a note on finding.
Again, with Mr. Foljambe as the principal, they
disappointed him most grievously when he looked
for blood. A Bessingby fox had gone to ground in a
head of rabbit holes near Carnaby, and as it was
rather a dragging day, a few scarlets agreed to stop
and dig him out, when Mr. Hodgson went to draw
elsewhere. *"We've got him,"* shouted Mr. Foljambe, when he returned, *"in that sack; I know you
don't like much law, I'll take the sack myself, and go
into the middle of that grass field, and give you a
famous start."* The sack was accordingly held up,
shaken, and emptied. Alas! the hounds were still
more disgusted than Lord Middleton's, when they
were racing half a century ago for their fox from
Kexby Wood, and threw up at a stuffed one, which
was put to frighten carrion,—as they ran for nothing but an empty pie-dish, some plates, and a
mutton bone. The party had sent for a capital
lunch from Bessingby, and had never dug a yard.

On another occasion Mr. Hodgson
went to bed at eleven after a very hard   The biter bit.
day, and forgot to bolt the door. He was in his
first sleep, when he suddenly became conscious of
what seemed like a hairy pillow at the foot of the
bed, and waking out of a sweet dream of Dringhoe
and Blacksmith Gorse, viewed a party of his friends
dressed in hats and scarlets for the occasion, and
with spades and pickaxes in their hands, just putting
in a terrier at the foot of the bed, to draw a tame
fox. *"I know he's here, Will; I saw him go in,"*

said one in true Hodgsonian tones; but their victim
waited to hear no more, and in an instant the Gentleman in White dashed out into the passage, and
tried the first head of earths he could get to.   The
wife of one of the scarlet conspirators, who had been
listening for the *" Goneaway !"* just got her bed-
room door bolted in time, and he went to ground
in Lord Hawke's earth.   In vain did the unhappy
bachelor beg to be let in.   The key was turned
for the night, and *" No, no ! go on with the digging ;*
there's clean litter in the Badsworth Kennel, and
foul in the Holderness ; I'll stop where I am till
morning," was the only response.   And so he did,
and the pie-dish and the horn business were amply
avenged.

Captain Percy Williams.   Two troops of the Ninth Lancers
were at Beverley at that time, with
Captain Percy Williams among them.   It was under
Mr. Hodgson, to whom he often whipped in, that
the Captain first began his hunting career, and he
subsequently took charge of the hounds at the Oadby
Kennel during Mr. Hodgson's second season with
the Quorn.   The first time he ever handled them
was when they had a bye-day from the willow
garths, near Loughboro' and killed after an hour and
forty-five minutes in Stamford Park.   No one at

Mr. John Bower.   that time could beat Mr. John Bower
on his chesnut Marquis, or in fact upon
anything, made or unmade, even when at last he
could hardly hold the reins.   One of the finest
proofs of his horsemanship was in a very peculiar
run from Gransmoor, after a poacher with a lurcher.   His horse stuck fast in Barmpton drain,
and was utterly exhausted when he got him out. He
then hailed some ploughmen, and asked them if
they had seen a man, and learnt that one had just
fastened a dog to a gate, and run off.   *" Can any*
one of your horses get over a fence ?" said he, and

hardly waiting for a reply, and feeling sure of his friend Duggleby, the owner, he jumped on a raw young four-year-old, bare backed, with chains and collar, just as it was, and loosing the dog to run the scent, handed the filly over the fences, to the utter astonishment of herself and the ploughman, and ran into his game five or six fields beyond.

Mr. Ralph Lambton was one of the keenest disciples of Hugo Meynell. His brother, the father of the late Lord Durham, was one of the earliest of the sojourners at Melton, and kept a pack of harriers there as well. After leaving Cambridge without a shilling of debt (a rare feat which he loved to dwell upon), Ralph was a frequent visitor to Mr. Meynell at Quorn, and occasionally hunted with Sir Carnaby Haggerston, who was manager of the Belvoir during the late Duke's minority. His father General Lambton always said that he would leave his boy "enough to live upon, and keep a pack of fox-hounds with any squire in the county of Durham," and well he kept his word. For upwards of forty years did that son keep a pack nearly at his own expense, and infuse a Meynellian freshness into Northern hunting such as it had never known before. After the death of James Shelly, who came as huntsman to Lambton Park, with the Talbot pack (which were of Vernon, or rather Meynell blood), Mr. Lambton always hunted them himself, until he was in his seventieth year, when The Kitten fell with him in the middle of a grass field near Long Newton, and literally broke his back. He had injured the vertebræ in 1825, and made matters no better by a second fall, but there was no hope now, and for six years and four months, he faced without a murmur all the weariness of a sick room, with the calm heroism so peculiarly his own. A harder man or finer rider

has scarcely ever crossed a country. Once or twice
he was picked up for dead, when he had been
riding some raw four-year-old; and at last Mr.
George Baker of Elemore became so impressed
with the belief of his having an invulnerable body,
that he would not hear of his being called an iron
man, but carried the comparison a point further to
" those stub heads they make gun barrels of."

His habits of life.   He was a remarkably high-bred man,
in his look and address, and sat in Par-
liament several years for Durham. Boodle's was his
great resort when in town, but with the exception of
a few weeks in the season, he was rarely absent from
his hounds for a day. Few were more abstemious
and sparing in their diet, and he used to tell young
sportsmen, " You'll be lucky if you've no more din-
ner-bag at my age. He touched nothing from
breakfast till dinner, and rarely tasted any liquid
but wine. It was his boast that he was never
hungry or thirsty in his life. He always kept his
weight eleven-four to within a pound, and barring
his grey-head, he stripped quite young at sixty.
Such a Nestor in the field or in the coffee-room could
not fail to command respect, and the younger members of the Sedgefield Club always addressed him as
" *Sir.*" Scarlet with a silver button, and black with
a scarlet under-waistcoat, were the field and dress
livery, when the club was in its bloom; and Lords
Durham, and Kintore, Sir Hedworth Williamson,
and his son, Sir M. White Ridley, Sir David Baird,
the Messrs. Lambton (his nephews), Admiral Dundas, Mr. Spiers, Messrs. Shaftoe, Mr. Harland of
Sutton, &c., &c., are names well remembered at
Sedgefield, where it was duly held in November
and February. Of horses he was no very great
judge, but liked to buy thorough-bred young ones;
and Volunteer, Firebrand, Undertaker, Doctor,
Zephyr, Hermit, and Hannibal were among his

best. No one was a more regular hunter of a country; no matter how rough it might be, every cover
heard his boxwood horn in its due proportion, and
that cheery "*Yi, Haro! Forrard. Yi, Haro!*"
which came booming out in all its melody when his
hounds had settled to their scent and seemed inclined to run hard.

Mr. Lambton went to very few ken- Mr. Lambton on
the flags.
nels; but when he did go to Belvoir, he
told Goosey that he had quite spoilt him for home,
and that he should return perfectly downhearted.
He hated a short-necked hound, and made an immense point of good shoulders, as the best preventive
of lameness, but for legs and feet he cared less than
hound breeders generally do. They seemed to lose
their nerve entirely during their Quorn season. Old
Talisman, Whipster, and Forester would look round,
and when they saw the Melton Cavalry coming,
they never stopped for a scent, and in one instance
went nearly three miles across country without one,
at tip-top pace, and no Treadwell or Tom Ball could
stop them. Sometimes they did not taste blood for
three weeks together; but when they and Treadwell
fell on quieter times in the Berwickshire country,
and they could run away over the bogs from the
horses till they seemed like little terriers on the cliffs,
they soon got back their old form, and rendered a
capital account of the Cheviot Hill foxes.

Of a stale hound, Mr. Lambton had His hound feeding.
an immense horror. He kept a large
pack, and gave those that were not hunting long,
steady exercise, and brought them out as fit as
fighting-cocks. It was a saying of his, that if he
saw a hound tire, he felt as if he could hang himself.
Fresh pudding and flesh, and none of the latter on
the day before hunting, were the great points of his
feeding system, which he nearly always superin-
tended in person; and Fenwick Hunnam his feeder,

who had scarcely ever seen a hunt in his life,
quite coincided with his master, and was most
oracular on the subject of condition. " When
hounds ar'nt done to," he used to say, " as hounds
should be done to, they neither do credit to themselves nor them that's consarned with them. They
may kill a fox in a shabby short of a way, but when
they have to work for a second fox, and he's a strong
'un, they disgrace themselves, and them that's consarned with them ; I'll not have my hounds treated
in no syke way." Fenwick was a most faithful fix-
ture, and so were all Mr. Lambton's servants. He
did not give very high wages, but he knew how to
inspire their loyalty, and his butler, and housekeeper, his second groom, and several others lived
with him from fifteen to fifty years. His head
man, John Winter, was with him at Cambridge, and
never left him till his death.

Mr. Williamson's When he was at last laid to rest, Dur-
mastership. ham was aghast at the blank, but the
Marquis of Londonderry headed the subscription,
and came out in scarlet again, and charged the
fences, as he had done the Cuirassiers at Waterloo,
and Mr. Williamson became master for two seasons of the " Wynyard and Durham Foxhounds."
The Lambton hounds had been sold to Lord
Suffield, and Mr. Williamson had to put together
such odds and ends as he could get, late in the summer of '38. Mr. Foljambe, who has so often been a
friend in need on such occasions, sent a draft, and so
did Sir Tatton Sykes, and Sir Matthew White
Ridley, and others, Mr. Williamson was his own
huntsman, and steadied his wild, young pupils most
wonderfully before the season was out. His woodland labours were well repaid, and in his second
season, although he had to bring an unusual number
of young hounds into the field, they carried a head
and went the pace. Those who had played with the

drafts of the previous season, began to be reminded of " the flying ladies" of old Ralph Lambton's heart.

Once again the old Sedgefield country was in peril, but as the renowned yeoman-farmer, Dickey Wood of Close—who was always in front on Buckram or Bagsman, or a raw four-year-old, or an " auld gunner" out of the plough—expressed himself, my Lord Londonderry came forward once more and " kept the tambourine a rowling" without any subscription. His Lordship bought the hounds, with a rare stock of old meal, and brought them to Wynyard, and with John Glover, a pupil of Walker's from The Fife, as huntsman, and a friend of Mr. Williamson's as field-master, soothed the shade of Ralph Lambton once more, with the most remarkable run that the country has known.

"The morning" (Feb. 16th, 1841), says its chronicler, " was calm and dull, and the little wind that was blowing was from the South-West. The field was not numerous, as the Wynyard family were abroad for the season. Our meet was at Newbiggin, and before the hounds had been in the old cover at Foxy Hill (our first draw) three minutes, and almost before they had time to find him, Tommy Arrowsmith the whipper-in hallooed him away at the south-west corner of the Ten Acre Gorse. The field were stationed at the other end, and the hounds were away and half over the first field with a blazing scent, before the leading men could get to the Halloo. Facing as fine a piece of country as hounds ever ran over, we were evidently (barring accidents) in for a run of the old sort from Foxy Hill, and so it proved. After pointing for Newton Grange and Sadburge, he turned north-wards over Newbiggin Bottom, which was very deep, and the ' stell' brim-full of water, crossed the water by Dales House, leaving Barmpton a little to the left, and then straight for Byers Gill, to the south-west of Great Stanton, crossed the Sedgefield road, sank the hill to Little Stainton, and had another turn at the ' stell,' rather broader, and quite as full of water as we had found it above, and so straight to Bryan Harrison earths.

" Up to this point the time was 45 minutes. The hounds were on the earths for two or three minutes, but the body of them (18 couple as it afterwards proved) came out of the small plantation round the south side of the earths, and settled to a fair holding scent, and away across the Darlington turnpike road near Newton Grange, and the Yarm Road near Oak Tree, where they had their only check of importance, and had slow hunting down by Traffick Hill to the river

Tees. We had then run 1 hour 25 minutes in Durham, the first 45 minutes as hard as we could split over about 17 miles of country. Then the river Tees, swollen nearly up to the top of the embankment, and sweeping down with a volume and rapidity which might have deterred any fox, brought us all to a stand. Such as were left of the field and the celebrated 'black coat' of the country concluded that the day was over, when up came John Glover, who naturally, after such a run, was anxious to account for his fox, and cast them along the embankment, not thinking that the fox had crossed. After holding them along it for a few yards, every hound dashed in, having winded their fox from the opposite side, and in an instant the torrent was carrying them down at twenty miles an hour. After being carried down about 300 yards every hound landed, and they quietly cast themselves back exactly opposite to the spot where they had taken the water, struck the scent into Worsell Gill, and away up it, with as fine a cry as if they had just found. Now! Mr. Glover, a pretty business you've made of it! It's a 100 to 1 against their being got home to-night. Worsell Gill is full of wild Cleveland hill foxes, and the chances are the hounds will go straight to the Hills. 'Where is the nearest bridge?' says poor John. 'Yarm or Dinsdale,' is the reply, 'and neither of them nearer than three miles,' chimes in our friend of the black coat, and with a countenance as black with despair at the thoughts of the hounds out all night. John Glover is an entire stranger to the Yorkshire side of the Tees, and Arrowsmith almost as much, and the notes of hounds going direct south from the Gill, is dying away from the ear in the distance! Horses are nearly cooked, as well they might be.

"Fortunately the manager was able to get a fresh horse at the Dinsdale Hotel, and with John and the whip crossed at Dinsdale Bridge, and held on towards Pickton, in the direction of which the hounds seemed to be bending from Worsell Gill. Between Pickton and Appleton, the cry was heard again, and at Appleton we found them still ahead, and at Enter-Common they had crossed the Great North Road about ten minutes before us, going straight down for Lord Alvanley's Plantation in the Bedale country. At Cooper House, near Cowton, and at least twelve miles from Worsell Gill (where the hounds entered Yorkshire), we heard a halloo, and found a countryman with the fox and eighteen couple of hounds baying round him. Every hound took the river at Traffick Hill, and they were all up at Cooper House, and had killed their fox according to the countryman's account in about 1 hour 20 minutes from crossing the river. The reis no doubt that they had changed foxes at Bryan Harrison carths, the only hounds wanting at the end of this extraordinary run being those which were recovered at Foxy Hill, where they had run their first fox back to cover, and some still think it was a fresh fox from Worsell Gill. And so ended this wonderful day."

Sir Harry Main-
waring. Cheshire is truly faithful to the memory of the venerable father of its hunting field, Sir Harry Mainwaring. He was hale and vigorous to the very day of his death; and, although the glories and hospitalities of Peover had ended, he was as cheerful as ever at seventy-six, and fond of a little quiet cub-hunting when Sir Watkin's or the Cheshire came within reach of his quiet village home at Marbury. He assisted the late Mr. Heron for many years before he was Master himself; and his dynasty, which lasted for nineteen seasons, came to a close in '37. Will Head was his huntsman for several of them, and then came his favourite Joe Maiden, who bore such a distinguished part in those memorable days whose memory is embalmed in the Warburton songs. Sir Harry was a capital judge of a hound in kennel, or in his work, and made a tour of the best kennels every year. However promising might be the stories he heard of a hound's work, he never would breed from him, unless the kennel used him themselves; and the excuse " we have a good deal of the sort" was wholly lost upon him. He liked a large hound, and was most particular about legs and feet. Bedford, Gloucester, Gulliver, Bangor, Whynot, and Marquis, of the direct blood from the first introduction of hounds into Cheshire, were his favourites; and when he gave up the pack, it would have been difficult to find many superior to them in England; while the hunt had three or four men among its first-flight dozen who would bow to none. The day was never too long for Sir Harry in hunting, and no man ever kept a country better together, or hunted it more fairly. It was his boast that during the whole of his mastership he was never five minutes late at the cover side, and yet he had sometimes immense distances to reach from Peover. When there, he would never allow more than five minutes' law. He always wore flannel, never drank spirits, never had a rheumatic pain or headache in his life, and was always an early riser.

His best hunters were Brown Bess, an eighty-pound one-eyed mare called Alice Grey, Virgo, Delamere Lass, and a little chesnut from Shropshire, which he bought for £50, and sold to the Rothschilds. He had also a wonderful long-tailed brown hack, called Sweetbread, from the fact that she was purchased from a Knutsford butcher for £18, which always kept up a perpetual-motion canter to covert, whatever the distance might be. Across country he was a good performer, when the day was not too misty; but being very short-sighted, he carried his eye-glass in the handle of his whip, and required a horse to pull at him a little, so as to keep him straight. The Vale of Chester and the Nantwich country he liked best; and Seighton Gorse in the former, and Ravensmoor Windmill, Warmingham Wood, and Bradfield Green in the other parts were the principal places and meets in his day.

Tom Rance's history. Tom Rance was born with the century, and lived full a third of it with the Cheshire, as first or second whip, under seven masters and six huntsmen. His ambition was never stirred to be more than the successor of Zach Goddard, the "Father of English Whips," and he uniformly declared that he would as soon break stones as hunt a pack of hounds. The family seems to be subject to coincidences. His father and grandfather both died at sixty, but he has safely passed that age, and goes out with his spade on long-earth stopping excursions, with all the zest of youth. Again he is one of ten, and he has begotten ten in turn. He began by whipping in to harriers, near Yarmouth, and came on from there to Mr. "Dick Gurney," of Thickthorn, near Norwich.

Dick Gurney. This stout gentleman first "broke out" with ten or eleven brace of gery-hounds, and Tom had to lead them gallops, and act as slipper on field-days. He then kept six or seven

Dick Gurney, p. 351.

hunters for The Puckeridge and the Pytcheley, and
said that he only weighed sixteen stone.   Tom rode
second horse for him, and he led home the great slap-
ping Sober Robin, when his near fore-leg gave way in
the Ware country. Robin was fully sixteen-and-a-half
hands, with remarkable couplings, and rather a hot
temper of his own; and in his hey-day, Mr. Gurney
refused a thousand guineas for him over the dinner-
table.   Clinker was another of his best, and so was a
thickset chesnut mare. Tom always gave his master
five-and-twenty minutes before he brought up the
second horse, and delighted to watch him crashing
away with no spurs, and nothing but a dog-whip.
If a horse did refuse, he would " cut a life-time out
of him ;" and he would discharge the best groom he
had if he found him putting his horse over a leaping-
bar. Six of them fetched upwards of 1,800 gs. when
they were sold off at Tattersall's, and Master Fray was
bought in.   When " Dick" was not hunting, he had
plenty of time on his hands, and had abundant consolation in his snuff-box, the contents of which he
used to fling about so profusely in church that he
would set the pews behind him off sneezing.
   It has been well said that—

> " The Ethiop Gods have Ethop lips,
> Bronze eyes, and woolly hair,
> The Grecian Gods are like the Greeks,
> As keen-eyed, cold, and fair ;"

and perhaps it was on this principle, that the great
Pytcheley welter-weight set up as his idols, an
enormous pair of twin Scotch bullocks. Once, if
not twice a day, he pondered fondly over them, and
when they had been feeding for three years he had a
van made to take them to Smithfield. The best
died before the day of departure, and the other
never went after all.   Southdown rams, one of which,
Thickthorn, he hired from Mr. Webb, for 200 gs. a

season, were another of his fancies, and, taking him all in all, Tom considers "*he was a right 'un.*"

Tom in Cheshire. From his service, Tom departed to Baron Rothschild, as pad-groom "for two months, as near as a toucher," but the Baron released him at Lord Delamere's request, and in 1830 he met Sir Harry at Vale Royal, and accepted the seals of office, which he held to the end of the '61 season, till his eyesight became too dim. There was no finer characteristic of the man, than his genial tone and polite manner of steering his hounds at the end of his drooping whip lash, through a crowd of horsemen in a narrow lane. "*Jest stand a one side, gemmen, if you please; beg yer pardon; a little mossel, to let the 'ounds paass: thank ye, Sir; now gemmen, be so good; thank ye, Sir;*" and the feat was accomplished. Stimulated by these gentle blandishments, every one felt proud of the room he made, and quite a party to the safe conduct desired. Conciliation was the key-note of all his addresses, except to a transgressing hound, and there Tom was not forgiving, and rigidly included any previous conviction for riot in his sentence.

Tom's table-talk. Of course we wandered off to have a word with Tom on the Forest, and found him most communicative, on the few little points we had to ask. "We had four horses a-piece," he said, "when I came; we had no second horse that time of day. We lost the Wrenbury and Wickstead country; that's all done away with; we used to go to Wrenbury, and stop the week.

Head, Maiden, & Markwell. "Will Head was here when I came; he was a good little huntsman, a determined little fellow, but not so much so latterly. Joe Maiden came from the North Warwickshire; they were great times, few could go with him; resolute, determined chap was Maiden across country; so

persevering; never liked to lose a fox. No one
knew better how to handle a pack of hounds than
poor Markwell.

"'The foxes are sadly changed; so many Foxes and their troubles.
of 'em turned down; very few straight
forward foxes at all now; keepers level the old 'uns
off, and the young 'uns, a hignorant lot of little
devils, they know no country; they've no parents
to show them, or yet larn them the country, and it
ai'nt likely they can find it for themselves. We had
very straight-forward foxes in the Wrenbury country; the Chester country was never the same
as the Wrenbury country for good foxes; they
might chance about Saighton and Waverton to pick
up a good one, and take it to the hills. We had
two devilish good runs from Wharton Gorse to The
Willingtons; time Maiden was here; one fox from
Beech House cover, Hurlestone Gorse they call it,
used to go away regularly, at the lower end for Rad-
nor, and on for Peckforton Wood, up by Ridley. We
ran him three seasons, and killed him at last. He
was a greyhound fox; regular leggy one. They
used to send me to the old corner at the lower end of
the gorse. He knew us—before the hounds got there,
you'd see Charley walking off quickish. These
foxes on the hills, bless my heart and body, they
don't half rouse them. We want two or three days
amongst them, then we'd get some better foxes in
the country; they want well rousing; that was a
great point with Captain White; he made us stick
to the hills and drive them down.

"I have had a good many accidents; I Tom's disasters.
beg your pardon, gemmen; I lost my
eye, when I was twelve,—with a gun; it's given me a
deal of trouble; the first time I felt the other so bad,
was at feeding time, the hounds and everything
looked like a cloud of sulphur. The Manchester
doctors have been trying their hands on it; I think

they've cleared it a little; fire seemed to come out of it; and then something like a bottle screw, a black wavy thing from the eye to the ground. I could hardly see a fox at last; I dare say I missed some of them my last season. My horse once ran away with me, and broke the bridge of my nose against a bough; I couldn't blow it again for weeks; then a stub got into the blind eye, and I pulled it out; but when I broke the corner of my rib, I was in furious pain all the day. I still never gave in.

Sir Harry Main- "Sir Harry, he was a good 'un, coming
waring. up with his glass in his whip-handle; never a rattling rider; his two greys and a bay horse Briton I liked best to see him on; he would come on his hack be it where it would, and his hunters met him from the kennels. He liked General of the old Galloper sort, and Hannibal and Hotspur; the best we had we lost in the madness; we put eighteen-and-a-half couple forward after it; we had the *sweetest* pack before the malady.

The Cheshire "I beg your pardon, gemmen; talk
green collars. about riding, I saw Mr. Wilbraham Tollemache take the river Weaver brimming full close by Nantwich: he had a black, snaffle-bridle mare; she slipped back again, and he jerked himself clean over her head on to the bank, and pulled her out. "*That's well done, Tollemache!*" said Lord Delamere, and in the next field but one they ran to ground. Mr. Tollemache stripped, and met us going on for Aston Gorse, in an old farmer's clothes, and rode the run; he rode little thorough-bred things; he was a neat horseman, and had a deal of nerve. Sir Richard Brooke was a very good one, as long as he could last; he'd go as long as he could go; never nursed his horses. Mr. Glegg would take a line to himself, wide, always with the hounds, not as some of these young'uns do; if they see the hounds a little at fault, they go by them and make

the fences crash again. Mr. Smith Barry was a
fancy rider, he rode to his horse; he was rather on
the larking system, jump off and make horses come
over gates and stiles after him. I've seen Mr.
Warburton go along pretty well; he has his glasses
on; he's obliged to take them off and polish them
a bit, when we get to slow hunting. Colonel Cholmondley bruises along, I've heard him make these
wire fences rattle a bit; Captain White he was a
clipper; he could ride and keep them in first-rate
order too.

I beg your pardon, gemmen; there are great
changes; men and country; they were all small
fields, ditches never cleaned out in that Saighton
country; now it's like a garden; for two miles round
these cops are kept high and narrow, cut sharp as
the ridge of your hand to keep the harriers off;
they're getting a little flatter, horses get their hind-
feet on them; there's a deal of bone-dust about this
country now; it alters scent; the hounds stop and
peck at it, it's a bad fault these bone-dust fields;
and there's so much of this goano used. I beg your
pardon, gemmen, but I must go, I've some earth-
stopping." And so all the richer not only by these
notes, but by a fox's head, and some teeth which
Tom considers a worthy breast-pin for the highest
earthly potentate, we parted from the worthy old
fellow, and watched his thin, upright form disap-
pearing through the mist on his midnight errand.

One word for varmint "Old Zach," Old Zach Goddard.
the great link, in whipper-in succession,
between Tom Moody and Tom Rance—who died
some six or seven years since, in his seventy-second
year. Like Jem Morgan, he had four sons who all
followed his profession. Besides Jack, the inventor
of "Tailby Thursdays," and Ben late of the Bicester, there was Jem, a very determined fellow
who died when first whip to Ben Foote with Mr.

Villebois; and Tom, who was very distinguished
as a steeple-chaser and first whip with the Pytcheley, but he too died young, and is buried near Jack
Stevens and Jack Woodcock at Brixworth. Zach
was only five foot six, and never much above nine
stone; and it was when some one said to Mr.
John Warde, "If I had hounds I should so like
to get all men like Zach," that he made his much
quoted answer: " *Oh! you should, Eh! fond of light
weights; I don't know much difference between heavy
and light weights, except that the one breaks horses'
backs, and the other breaks their hearts.*" Zach
had a large fund of natural humour, and many
a tale to tell of the days when he was second
whip under Nevett to " Glorious John," who made
their place no sinecure during cub-hunting. The
men slept over the stables, and he would often wake
them with the thunders of his stick at three in
the morning, to " come and give those foxes a second
touch." However, they were of Billy Lackaday's
opinion on bell-ringing, and never got up, unless he
" persevered," and came at the door pannels a second
time.

The snooze in the Park. One sleep he never forgot to remind
them of. It was a hot summer's day,
and the three agreed to take a copper of ale, and sit
out with the hounds in Westron Park. Zach vowed
that he could keep awake, if no one else did, but
they slept well on into the evening, and when they
awoke, there were only two hounds left. One by
one they had slipped off home, and the old gentleman had let them in. It was quite a matter of discussion who " dare and go face him first," when they
saw him hovering in the distance, about the kennel,
but he put them out of difficulty by meeting them
and ironically asking after his hounds. Another
day he dropped on to Zach on the hat question.
Once a year he allowed each of his men a dog-skin

hat, and Zach's had been ordered a month. Not
seeing him at church, he asked Zach the reason, and
he at once laid it on to his shabby hat. "*Oh ! that's
your excuse, Zach?*" he said: "*a very poor one, Zach ;
if you had the best hat in England the parson would
not let you wear it ; you'd have to pull it off.*" Zach
didn't quite see his way out of this argument, so he
simply told his friends, "Squire had me there; old
man done me again." It was on a hat too that Mr.
Warde's great New Forest story turned. " I never
knew the nature of a bog," he used to say, "till I
went to Hampshire. I saw a good hat on the top of
one, and there was a head in it, and the head said, I
don't care for myself, but do help to get my horse
up, he's in a bog below."

Zach was with "Gentleman Smith"
for a time, but he was best known dur- Old Zach's career.
ing his seventeen seasons with Lord Middleton
in Warwickshire. His scream was almost un-
earthly in its shrillness, and he trusted to the
natural organ under all circumstances. Once,
when Harry Jackson had broken his thigh he was
in command, and Lord Middleton told him to blow
his hounds away from Woolford Wood. He put
the horn to his lips, and then he said, almost in a
passion, "*Hang it, my Lord; you know I never could
blow a horn,*" and he flung it away in the mud.
In his latter days he became kennel huntsman to
Mr. Bradley, in whose service he remained, much
respected, during the time that gentleman kept staghounds, and he turned out the pack in excellent
condition for their celebrated runs with " The Nob,"
and " Water Witch," &c., over the pastures of Warwickshire and Northamptonshire. When his days of
service were over, he would come to Heythrop, when
Jack was there. His ankles were weak from rheumatism and a number of severe falls, but he
would often come out on a mule and see Jim and

Jack rattle the cubs about. In the evenings he would take his pipe out of his mouth to give them a "Southerly Wind" or "Tom Moody," and a series of those view halloos which the Woolford and Farnboro' sides of Warwickshire knew so well. Itchington was a horse he liked to talk of, and the mention of his Grassini, which died when his Lordship lost so many, was enough almost at that lapse of time to bring out a second flood of tears. He swore by "Mr. Shawe" as the best huntsman, and Woodman the best hound he had ever seen, and the picture of the last, and Grassini's foot were the only memorials of his wood-craft, which he cared to keep.

Celebrities at Bicester. The Bicester country had the good fortune to be held, with the exception of Lord Sefton's one season, by only three masters for nearly seventy years. Early in the century there was not a chimney corner to be let in its little capital, and upwards of a hundred hunters were stabled there. It kept its prestige amidst no small attractions elsewhere. The Billesdon Coplow day, than which the late Lord Jersey used to vow that he had never known a colder, had sealed the fame of The Quorn country years before; and it was not suffering in Mr. Assheton Smith's hands. John Warde was with the Pytcheley, and "Mr. Shawe" with the Belvoir. Still the Bicester men were quite content with Stephen Goodall and Sir Thomas Mostyn's four days a week, and the choice of Tom Rose and the Grafton, or Philip Payne and the Badminton on the other two. Sir Thomas, with Mr. Griff Lloyd, as his factotum, lived at Bainton, close by the first set of kennels. Lord Jersey hunted with them when he was not at Melton; and when he was not on Gipsey, he generally rode the Hon. Mr. Vanneck's second best horse, and as generally beat him. Mr. Vanneck (who gave 700 gs. for two to Mr. Lloyd, of Aston) was far below him as a horseman, and John Warde used to say of him that he had seen him ride all round a field, and come out at the same place. This statement was rather qualified by its invariable conclusion. "*If he had not been a Melton man I'd not have shown him up.*"

Sir Harry Peyton went straight on Spartacus, and Mr. Harrison of Shelswell would give any money so that the twins Lindow and Rawlinson (who was great on Spread Eagle), might not have a pound the best of him in a fast thing. Sir John Cope and Mr. John Moore both joined the throng. Lord Stamford's nephew, Mr. Booth Grey, lived with Mr. Drake, who was very regular at the cover side, but he never rode hard; and the walls of "Hetters" or "The Cocked Hat," as it was termed, witnessed the good fellowship of Sir Charles Knightley, John Tremayne, twenty years member for Cornwall, and "Mr. Tom Pennant," from Wales. The latter was a very fair horseman, but Mr. Tremayne was more for hunting than riding. Sir Charles united the two, in an eminent degree, and although Guidepost had a high character, and was named to correspond, his Consol and Tilton (which he purchased for 250 gs. from Mr. Harrison) were far better. Baron Robeck, the Swede, backed himself for 20 gs. when the Pytcheley found at Holderby, to follow Sir Charles on the latter over the three first fences, and came to grief at a bridle gate. Tilton surprised Mr. Assheton Smith when he came over occasionally to reconnoitre, and he said of him that "he pulled for two hours after he seemed beat." It was remembered as characteristic of the man during one of these visits, that on a Claydon Woods Day, when he could not get his horse to face his fences, he got off him at last, and flogged him away in his fury up a lane. Lord Anglesey's "winter officers," as the hard riders of the Seventh were called, were often at the cover side, and

so was Jacob Wardell, one of the Billesdon Coplow
men. As his friends dropped off, Jacob gradually
gave up fox-hunting for wife-hunting, and set up a
regular agency-office for the purpose. His latest
report of himself upon the subject was, that he "had
married no end of people."

Sir Thomas was nearly as fond of his
four-in-hand as his hounds, and nothing
pleased him so much as to get behind
a team of old hunters, which had only been in harness
for a day or two; wait till they had done their
shindy, and drive them for their first lesson 150
miles to his house in Wales. He was one of the
B. D. C. Club, which preceded both "The Whip"
and "The Four-in-Hand" Clubs; and Squire Annesley, with his strawberry roans; Mr. Harrison,
with his bays; and Sir Henry Peyton with his greys
used to delight in doing their twelve miles from
Oxford to Benson, down the Henley Road. Sir
Thomas was not a keen fox-hunter, and if he felt
any great enthusiasm he never showed it. Stephen
Goodall used to say that he was a good but a most
provoking man, as "you never could judge from
his face, whether he was pleased or angry with
the day's sport." He was, in fact, rather idle, and
a sufferer from gout, which kept him out of the
saddle for the last five years of his life. All his
horses had short tails; and if he was regularly put
up, he would go very straight on the chesnut Mar-
cus, or Park Keeper, which had graduated in Leicestershire. He drove down punctually from London
every April to make the draft, and generally looked
over them in the dining-room. A few were put
back the first day, the final pick was made on the
second, and the naming came off on the third. As
he then said, he had them thoroughly in his eye,
and he could have drawn them without a mistake,
when he saw them again in the autumn.

Sir Thomas
Mostyn and
the B. D. C.

Stephen Goodall, p. 361.

Stephen Goodall came from Quorn,
and Harry King, who was whip, with
Will Lepper, and afterwards head-groom, rode many
hundred miles in search of suitable horseflesh for
him. Cyclops formed part and parcel of his
Leicestershire baggage, and Prince, Trinket, Con-
vention, King Charles, and Chawbacon, were picked
up in Harry's rounds. Ragman latterly became
Stephen's cover hack, but he never had more than
four hunters at the beginning of the season. Although they lived in a perpetual state of sore back,
he never lamed them, and really tired them less than
men of half his weight. When a horse suited him,
it generally lasted him till it was worn out.

Ragman was too often disposed to put him
down, and wallow whenever they went through a
stream. " *Coom up! coom up!*" was his constant
adjuration, " *I don't want a toast in the water
to-day.*" Trinket would also watch for an opportunity of favouring himself, and he would sometimes
lie down when they were breaking up their fox.
Stephen made it a point never to get on King
Charles till they had found, and then there was a
pass word in the hunt, " *Are you all ready? Yes,
my lord;*" in allusion to what Buckle had said (touching his cap) to Lord Jersey, when his lordship once
acted as starter at Newmarket. There were very few
rides in Stephen's day, and the paths in Claydon
Woods were such an utter bog from end to end, that
if they kept changing foxes his horse soon got beat.
If any one asked him his weight, he generally replied
rather angrily " *About a quarter of a ton;* but the
best gauge of him and his five-foot-five, is his scarlet
hunting-coat. Poor Will Goodall, who was always
a great pet with him, and just eight years old
when he died, used to produce it solemnly from a
cupboard, on state occasions, for his friends to try
on, both for warning and encouragement, and

accompany the ceremony with a tune on the veteran's horn.

Stephen in Kennel.   From old association, Stephen used the Quorn sires in his kennel, and liked a large hound. Seventy couple came in from quarters in Wales his first season, and the first draft of fifteen couple was sold to the Duke of Beaufort for 150 guineas. Lady was sent to the Quorn, Sultan soon after Stephen came, and then to Quorn Ranter, and five-and-a-half couple, Lucifer, Libertine, Lexicon, Loyal, Lydia, Lovely, Lazarus, Lictor, Lashwood, Lightning, and Lawless formed the two litters. All of them were entered; and some of the best hounds in England sprang from them. Lady generally ran hare till the fox was found; but she was beauty itself, and her head among foxhounds was much what Rosy Morn's is among greyhounds. Madness came into the kennel through a bite from a strange dog, as they were trotting along the road from one cover to another, and nearly 12 couple had to be put away. The rest were chained up in a large barn, and after watching them carefully for three months, Stephen signed a clean bill of health. His whips were always at the kennels at six in the summer, to feed and clean out the puppies; and if they were not there at the moment, they would hear the well-known clearing grunt, which preceded: "*Young man, you must have had fish for breakfast, and you've stopped to pick the bones.*" For the whipcord he was a most vigorous advocate, and used to take the pack once a week to Stowe Park, to show them the deer and hares. His great talk was of Quorn, and his proudest remembrance was pulling down a hedgerow fox in the Loughboro' country, after three hours, with a few couple of old hounds, and a most ticklish scent. He was wont to represent himself on that occasion as a perfect deliverer of shepherds and hen-wives.

Of his old Shropshire lieutenant, Tom Moody, he seldom spoke, except to say, that he thought him fonder of fishing in the Severn than hunting, and fonder of ale than either. One of his stories about him was that they went into the servants' hall for an hour or two at the meet, to wait till the frost had got a little out of the ground. *" Now, Tom, there's something to do to-day,"* said Stephen ; *" don't be too free with the ale."* *" Right, I won't, master,"* replied Tom. *" I'll sit opposite you and you tread on my foot if you see me getting on too fast."* So far so good; but a Newfoundland dog, which had crept in unobserved, pressed Tom's foot when it shifted its position, and Tom mistaking the signal, called out in the most injured tone, *" Oh ! hang it, master ! I've only had one horn yet !"* Tom Sebright's father made one of this memorable group of huntsmen and whips.

Stephen lived two or three years after leaving Sir Thomas Mostyn, and had the use of old Ragman till his death, and a man, from Mr. Villebois', for one season, and then Tom Wingfield the elder reigned in his stead. Ben Foote helped to carry him to his grave in Hethe church-yard ; and Griff Lloyd was rather disappointed at not being asked to read the funeral service.

This curious character and fellow of All Souls was the rector of Christleton, near Chester, and curate of Newton Purcell, in Oxfordshire. He made no sermons, but said that he was a better man who knew how to make a good selection, and, like old John Day, he generally fell back upon Blair. He read them in a low impressive tone, and never pitched his voice. They did say that he would put off marriages and burials to suit the hounds; but only once was he caught napping, and then he preached a Christmas-day sermon in February, and never found it out till he got to the words " The anniversary of this day." He lived with his cousin at Chesterton, bought the hay and corn, and well earned his title to be called the " Black Whipper-in," when he went to work on his rat-tailed Ascham (which delighted him by throwing up its heels whenever he mounted) in the woodlands. He was very faithful to the family jacket, and whenever it won at Holywell he would wave his stick, and hit his hack and shout right lustily " *Yellow one first.*" Liverpool races he seldom missed, and made one at the annual race banquet of the " Double Dandy," who was several stone heavier, and in fact so big that he had to wait a day when his servant mistook the tenor of his order to take two seats in the mail, and returned after securing one in and one out.

Griff Lloyd's power of bearing fatigue. No one could go through such an amount of fatigue as " Griff." He would come by coach and chaise from Christleton to Swift's House during the cub-hunting season, get there about twelve o'clock at night, and be up and off at four, ten miles to cover; and he has been known to go back to Cheshire, always on the outside, the same night. If he was at Bainton or Swift's House he thought nothing of riding thirty miles to Shuckborough Hill, home again, and then out to dinner on a pony. Chaises on such occasions he regarded as the merest delusions. With hounds he was very persevering, and always fond of getting a nick in a run. If they were in a narrow dirty lane, he would call to the man before him in the blandest spirit of inquiry, " *Where did you buy that horse of yours, sir?*" and before he had time to answer, Griff would go to the front of his victim, and give him the dirty reversion of his heels. His voice in covert was magnificent, and when the hounds were slack in drawing Stratton Audley Gorse, which was unusually thick, the field would look round for Griff

Jem Hills, p. 365.

to aid them, and after a few of his stentorian cheers they would make it shake again, and the fox was hallooed away in no time. The joke he liked worst to hear of, was that of the young polecats, which Stephen Goodall did not fail to treasure up against him, and produce at all seasons. His terrier worried a nest of four, as he thought, near the Bainton Kennels, and he was so proud of Vixen's exploit, that he nailed them up, and called Stephen to look and commend. Alas! the clearing grunt that time again heralded the words of doom, " *Well! Mr. Lloyd, you have done a pretty morning's work, you've killed four cubs for us!*" It was rather a bad job, as that same season a farmer's dog scratched eleven out of a bank, and killed them, and the farmer's tribulation was such, that he kicked the lad who was with the dog clean out of his yard, and declared that he " would sooner have lost a flock of sheep." When Sir Thomas Mostyn died, Griff took a house at Chesterton, and lived there in the hunting season, till his health began to go. At last a groom rode hunting with him, or he might hardly have known his way back. Hunting was still the theme of his discourse to the last, and he only survived his absence from the field for two seasons; and there never will be his " marrow" again.

Jem Hills was born with the century, which thus did a good thing early on; *Jem Hills.* and he whipped-in when he was ten, and marked his pig-skin jubilee in 1860, by not having a single fall that season. The fine weather, and the pleasure of slipping down the fifty-three miles to Didcot in some two minutes under the hour, determined us lately to go and have a quiet afternoon with him, at the kennels. On a July day, when the sun lights up the market-hall, and those nice old-fashioned houses, there is no pleasanter little town than Chipping Norton; but from its high position, no winter

residence could be desired more exactly in keeping
with "the man who could'nt get warm." Failing to
find Jem at the old spot, we turned to the left
through the church-yard, where old Zach lies; and
skirting the station, we found ourselves, after a walk
of a mile, at the new kennels. They are more in the
centre of the country than Heythrop, whose ruins,
after so many decades of ducal revelry and hound
entries, are handed over bodily at last to the rats and
to the owls. Tar Wood is sixteen miles distant, and
Jem and his men only sleep out for New Barns.

View from the kennel. Although there is a pretty steep road
to mount from the station, still when
you are fairly at the kennels, you seem to be in a
sort of bason among the hills. Jem, looking remarkably well, but with his right hand tied up in
consequence of an attack of the old chalk-stone
enemy, swept the horizon for us, with the eye of a
general, as we stood by his garden wicket. "Boulter's
Barn," of happy memory, was in front of us, in the
shape of a clump of trees, clinging unobtrusively to
the side of a hill; and beyond it we were requested
to believe in the existence of Churchill Heath, on
the principle of the groom who accepted the artist's
explanation, that although he might be invisible in
the picture, he was coming up the other side of the
hill.

The Heythrop covers. For the gazer on Churchill Mount
the chain of covers which have long since
prompted the saying, "Better by half shoot a child
than kill a Heythrop fox," take up the tale, as the
eye sweeps into the opposite valley, and rests on
the three hundred acres of the Brewin, where the
long and white-legged foresters have their earths;
on Churchill Heath, which is too damp for lying;
the oaks and the ashes of the Norrells; but, alas!
on no Lyneham Heath. Well may Jem bewail that
extinct gorse in the "Give me back my Legions"

vein. "*None of your grubbing,*" as he invariably
says to Mr. Langston's agent, when that gentleman
tries gently to lead his mind to the great subject of
agricultural improvement, with axe, steam-plough,
and tile: "*You've grubbed enough: I'm afraid of
you.*" Then he will propose his annual compromise,
which was repeated again that day: "*You may grub
up Churchill Heath and The Norrells, and Sand Pits,
if you'll give us back only twelve acres of Lyneham
Gorse.*" Over these past and present battle-grounds
the eye roams off once more to Merry Mouth, and
up a fine hunting vale to Gawcombe Wood, looking
like two globe-shaped hollows, then leaving Odding-
ton Ashes (the noted hermitage of wild outlying
foxes) to the left, and so on to the spire of Stow-on-
the-Wold, the village of the noted May and October
horse fairs. There, too, is Seisingcote Wood, creeping up the valley towards Evesham, and there too,
almost in front of us, are the quiet groves of
Daylesford, to which, "when under a tropical sun
he ruled fifty millions of Asiatics, the hopes of
Warren Hastings, amidst all the cares of war, finance,
and legislation, still pointed," and to which he at
length retired to die. Warwickshire, Oxfordshire,
Gloucestershire, and Worcestershire all meet hard
by the Four Share Stone to the right of the Park;
and between us and it, as we wrap up that stirring
Mount panorama, is the expanse of Kingham Field
still bearing all the signs of recent enclosure, and
alive with double fertilizers and ploughs, in which
the Herefords and a few "doubtful" Shorthorn heifers
are contentedly toiling together.

The stables, like the kennels, are
built of Chipping Norton sand-stone, The kennels near Chipping Norton.
with rooms above for the grooms and
the whips. The geological formation of the ground
changes at this point, and the stables are on
clay, and the kennels within twenty yards of them,

on sand. Save and except four clever-looking
hacks, one of which Jem considers to be the best
£25 bargain he ever made, there were no horses to
be seen, as the whole eighteen were at Little Compton, in yards and other loose places. Mr. Charles
Simmond's contract with the hunt ceased some four
or five years ago, and ever since then it has horsed
itself. Pamela and her litter of Hector puppies
were the sole tenants of the loose-box of Bendigo,
a great horse, but not more loved than Sailor, Betsy
Baker, and the yellow bay. The field is on a slope,
and a very beautiful one for hounds to spread themselves over. At the bottom is a small orchard, where
they lie under the apple-trees with Jem in the summer, and dream of rich red foresters past and to come.
In the snow, such is the confiding or rather chaff-
ing nature of those foxes, although Jem has brought
about a thousand brace to book in a quarter of a
century, that they sometimes come to meet *him*, and
a brace played such antics close up to the kennels a
few winters ago, that the whole pack was in an
uproar till Sam got up and view-hallooed the in-
truders away.

There was no maiden nurse about, and we merely
heard the story of Dairy Maid, who brought up five
cubs and a puppy in days when Goosey and Shirley
both adopted the system. We thought that there
would be some music in the Nathan key, after the
clouds of chaff which have descended upon Jem's
devoted head by reason of him ; and accordingly it
soon burst forth, " *Talk about horses ! that's a
daughter of ' the clothes horse ;' I was never to get
Nathans with short legs.* " Welcome, her sister,
was not of her stamp behind the shoulders,
but it is an unspeakable comfort to Jem that she
wanted no entering. She always joined the pack,
when they came to Tackley Heath, and made
a hit down a field of swedes, which will be men-

tioned in connection with her to the end of her days.

Jem had then hardly set his house in order, but there in full array was the fox which got drowned in the trap. "Two dog foxes like wolves," preserve his race, as far as size goes, in the Forest. One of them had already licked Jem two or three times, so that he breathed vows of vengeance on the smallest allusion to the case. Still, amid this warfare, he is not neglecting more peaceful pursuits; and although he has no Young Chipping Norton eleven in training to take the shine once more out of the crack Forest Club, the cricket spirit which he acquired in Broadbridge's and Wenman's day has not died out, and he has recently been umpire in a match at Deddington.

He claimed to have four hundred foxes at that moment within his pro-

Heythrop foxes.

tectorate, and barring one with white toes, which he killed at Worton Heath, he has seen no approach to hereditary white pads lately. He rather thought of getting some Scotch grey-hound foxes for a cross, but did not succeed. This failure does not seem to weigh upon him, as, contrary to the generally received horse and hound notions, he attributes the stoutness of his foxes to the fact, that the blood has been kept intact for generations. One of the patriarchs which had baffled him most rancorously for two or three seasons came to hand at last, after 1 hour 45 minutes from Langley to Wroughton. The crafty old foresters of Will Long's day would hardly recognize Wychwood now, as, with the exception of four hundred acres at each end, the whole of the forest has been stubbed up, and the consequence is, that the cub-hunting, which once began on the 1st of August, is now delayed till the middle of September. Some of Jem's best runs have been after a frosty morning; and when other people did'nt

hunt, the Heythrop would have their fun if they
threw off at two o'clock, and, to use his
energetic expression, "*fairly fetched it out of the
fire.*"

Making-up forty   The last great Tackley Heath day of
brace.   1859-60 began at half-past one. Hunting had seemed an impossibility, and, in fact, they dare
not draw the Great Tew country, but a clipping one
hour and thirty-five minutes rewarded them for their
pluck. Up to February 20th it was a capital season, and they killed 39½ brace, and then for their
last six weeks, do what they might, they had not
scent enough to complete their 40 brace. However,
their last day produced an old dog fox, who broke
twelve times from the top of the forest, and at last
went a four mile gallop straight along the turnpike-
road, and brought Jem to a complete stand-still at
the cross roads. Things looked so critical that Jem,
as a last hope, proposed to Mr. Hall to go and chop
a lame fox which had been hanging for some days
about a little spinney. Still he felt sure that his
hunted fox had gone round towards Chorlbury, and
that, if he came back, he should hit him over the
wall; and so it turned out. Keeping along the wall
en route to the lame-'un, he heard a view halloo at
last, and ascertained that his fox had just gone into
Boinall, so beaten that he had to jump three times
at the wall before he could get over. The hounds
could just hit it on the grass, but could hardly speak
to it in cover, where a vixen did all the work for
half-an-hour, till at last Helena dropped across the
beaten fox, and pulled him down.

Of course, we had a cup of tea and a little conversation; and of course, we found Jem in a most
"affable" mood, in every sense of the word. We
discoursed of the forest and its changes, which seems
a very delicate subject. "Its nearly all grubbed
up," he said, "and the deer killed, red and fallow;

we used to go through hundreds of them on the drives. Lords Churchill and Redesdale have left only a bit of it at the top and bottom, where the foxes must fly. The old foresters get puzzled, and they can't dwell; they get lost, and dare not touch certain covers and go down wind. It's a black thorn and hazel cover, with grass. They used to put a six-foot hedge, with thorns outside, to keep the deer out. The foxes smeused, and the hounds would jump at the fences, and lose their eyes or get staked and drop into the ditch; that's done away with now, that's one little comfort, but there's no badger hunting."

Debarred as we were from seeing Jem at this game, we pressed him to set it before us, which he did as follows : "Twenty couple are useless, if you want to kill without the brisket dodges, they can't smother or bite him to death. Five couple which really like it," he went on to say, "will stick to it and catch a badger, where there are lots of cubs about. Lord Dillon and Mr. Webb didn't believe me, so Lord Vaux came and had a night of it with them; hot supper at Ditchley. We sent a man at twelve to sack the hole. The run of a badger is very odd ⅃⅂⅃⅂⅂⅃, and so on. We got on to it at the bottom of the Park, and picked it out into the Oak riding. The cubs were up, and the vixen came squalling across the rides, after the badger and the hounds, a hundred yards behind. We gave him an hour-and-a-half in the Park, and then to ground, and brought him home at three. I used to be with the hounds under a tree, and put a man to sack the hole, and watch. They'd be out eating beans like a pig. Three and four season hunters did it best. The Rocket sort were good at that game, and Platoff was very great. If another hound spoke to a fox, he'd come back to me. His note for a badger was short and deep, and for a fox

Jem and the badgers.

light and clear. He'd bay them, but he'd not turn them up. Harlequin knew the brisket dodge, and we dare not take him out. Badgers and foxes go very well together. They tell me that they killed nearly all the badgers in one of the woods in Sir Tatton's old country, and that there was one found next day, and it was lying curled up in the earth with a fox. They're friendly enough, but the foxes are the lazy ones, and the badgers do the digging, and right they should. I killed nine badgers the first season I came here, and some of them with terriers. Once I turned one out in the frost with a couple of my terriers, Cribb and Fan, and they shuffled along well. They held him till I walked a couple of miles and got a sack."

Glories of Cribb the terrier. "Cribb would fight a red-hot poker till it became cold; his jaw-bone was quite bare; there was not a bit of under-lip, and he'd put out a fire with his feet. That's why they called him 'The Fire Eater.' You had only to say '*Kill that cat*,' and it was done. Still he would bear any amount of teazing, and never fought till I told him. I kept him two years after he was blind; he would make his bed at the badger's door, and get in next morning, and go creeping along by the wall to find his head. He was a biggish eighteen pound dog, and he'd draw a cover beautifully. They would go to his cry. I have got Jack, a great grandson of his now, and he'll draw and find foxes with any hound. Never speaks to riot. Jack threw his tongue last season, and out came a hare. Mr. Hall was there. '*Oh! Jack, Jack!*' he said, '*You've made a mis-take.*" Then out came a fox close under the hedge.'"

Jem's early days. We then tried back a little for Jem's earlier days, when "grubbing" troubles were unknown. It seems that he whipped in to Bob Bartlett and the Duke of Dorset's harriers at

Noel House, near Seven-oaks in Kent, while Tom
whipped in to the Surrey. The Duke was a fine,
tall, young fellow, of nearly six feet; and he was
killed larking a horse over a wall near Dublin.
"I did a little whipping-in when I was ten," said
Jem, "but his Grace would have it; — he was
all wrong—that I was too little to be trusted for
fear of accidents, so I was left at home with the little
grey hack, and precious savage I was about it. I
had four brothers with hounds, we were by an
earthstopper from a huntsman's daughter, so we
couldn't be better bred. My father was a quarry-
man and stopped earths as well. My word, what a
hand he was, stopping all the old quarries about
Godstone! I was with the Duke three seasons, and
wore a green coat. After that I was pad-groom,
and whipped-in to Tom with the Surrey for seven
seasons, then to Colonel Wyndham, then to the
Badminton and Lord Ducie, and so on here. I
knew this country well when I was with his Grace
and Will Long, and the hounds used to come to
Heythrop on September 16th, and the Duke on the
first of November, and we carried on the game till
Christmas. Then we had six weeks in the Badminton country, till February 16th, and then back
again here till April.

"I had the present Duke here in '57.
I had told him how fast Harlequin was,
and his Grace said he should like to see
me prove my words. Mr. Hall had a special meet
for his Grace at Bradwell Grove, and we had the
largest field I ever saw out, foot and horse. I like
to see foot people, they enjoy it so, and they never
interfere with me. I've got them in pretty good
training. We killed a brace in Bradwell Grove,
then we found in Winrush Poor Lot, and ran to
Aldsworth Village into a coal-hole. His Grace said,
'I should like to see this Harlequin of yours catch

Special day for the Duke of Beaufort.

a fox in six **fields.'**　We turned him up, and the fox
came back to the top of the wall, and all the hounds
viewed him.　Then he ran a mile along a green
lane near Aldsworth, and we had a regular lay on.
Harlequin led a hundred yards out of the pack, the
fox went under a wall **and** Harlequin over, up a
bank to a plantation, he wrenched and turned twice
all by himself, through the **fence into** the next field,
and pulled him **down.'　His Grace said,** that he
'never saw such pace **in a hound before.'** It was
a rare day's welcome to the **present** Duke, and the
hounds were as steady as beagles.　**Fast hounds are**
the thing, **give him** what **old** Philip Payne called
'palpitation **of the heart' in the first ten** minutes
and you'll do.　**Lord** Valentia says **I've** 'no business
with more **than two** couple;' and Captain Anstey's
only for allowing me one hound.　He says, '*Jem
knows exactly where the fox is going with all this lifting
and telegraphing.'*　Captain Anstey **was the** only
one who followed the Duke of Beaufort into his two
countries, and he's going yet.

Blooding future masters of hounds.
"I blooded the present Duke at Heythrop in the deer park, **close beside an**
elder tree, and I did a **good** day's work.
The Duke **was only** speaking of it the other day;
he remembered all about it; he said, '*I got a good
scolding for giving you a slap on the face, but you did
put it on so very thick.'*　I blooded Lord Granville,
he was master of the buck hounds then—he'll be
leader of the Lords now; he was a **good** deal older,
so I got **no slap** that time.　**He quite** enjoyed it.
When the meets were at Heythrop, the two Mr.
Baileys, **from** Bath, the two **Mr.** Worralls, Mr.
Rawlinson and Lindow, **Mr.** Webb of Kiddington,
Mr. Evans of Dean, and Mr. Holloway of Chorlbury, were the cracks.　The Sixth Duke was among
us then on his horse **St.** George.　Will Long had
Bertha, Gimcrack, and Milkman then.　I rode the

first a little when she was five years old. I liked a grey
mare Tilberena best. His Grace bred her, but she
was a wicked one—the grooms could'nt ride her, so I
begged to have a try. I made conditions, mind you,
that if I killed her I was not to be blamed; and the
Duke told me I might kill her if I liked. She was
a devil certainly at first, but I got her to carry me
as quiet as a dog horse. She was one of the best
looking ones I ever saw, and a rare galloper and
jumper, I never rode anything like her. She
knocked them about right and left when I had gone,
so they sent her to the stud. In '26 we hunted the
Forest only spring and autumn. There were 8,000
acres of it then; if they cut a place, they put a
large fence to keep the deer out; it was well rided,
and the hounds pressed the deer hard if they got a
scent. Ditchley Wood's only half what it was, I'll
tell you what, there's only one-third of the cover left
in the country to what there was then. We used to
pay £160 a-year for gorses, which are gone Cooper's
Gorse, Hilbury Gorse, and Dunster Gorse, all stubbed up.

"The scent is twice as good from
Brewin to Northleach as from Brewin   Scent symptoms.
to Aston, and the fleeces of the Cotswolds are better. You know pretty well how the scent is by the
hounds. If there is a nasty blue mist, there is no
scent. Even in Gloucestershire where the scent is
far better, they'll not go into cover, make any excuse.
A little black cloud will stop them in the middle of
a field; when you can hear well, there's a scent; if
it's bad hearing, it's a bad scenting day."

Then we had the great story of the   The South War-
Warwickshire killing their fox at last,   wickshire's
which despite any delicacy towards Jem   triumph.
must be given in all its details. "Well, you will
have it," said Jem, "so you must. I had always
been teazing them about never getting across the

turnpike-road, which divides our countries, and they
sometimes got quite riled, when I offered to have it
sodded. Well, Mr. Henley Greaves was master
then, and poor George Wells—a sterling good fellow
and huntsman, was George—lived with him. They
found at Woolford Wood, and carried a good head over
Larches-on-the-Hill, down by Cornwell, over the
hill by Boulters Barn, Sarsgrove to left, Sarsden
Village; they *were* astonished to see a pack of
hounds there, and Jem not at the head of them.
Then on to The Norrells, through it, and killed him at
Puddlicote Quarries. That was enough. Mr. Greaves
and George Wells, and all of them,—it was our Hunt
Meeting that day,—they came to the White Hart
and regularly had me up before all the gentlemen, and
Mr. Greaves presented me with the brush. '*Jem
wouldn't sod that lane as he promised, from Stow to
Bloxam, and so he's quite entitled to this brush.*'
George Wells stood there grinning, poor fellow.
Then the gentleman said, I must of course not re-
ceive it without a speech, and they said I ought to
have a white sheet on. So I took it, and I said,
I'll have it mounted in silver, with an inscription,
'*This is the brush of the fox which took the South
Warwickshire five-and-twenty years to kill.*' So I
gave them it back pretty well. Mr. Greaves said,
'*Well, George! I think we'd better not have brought
it,—Jem's down on us harder than ever.*' I tell the
South Warwickshire men now, that I know it was
only a three-legged one out of The Norrells, and that
I've missed one since. The real truth is, if I can
find a fox on these hills and get him over that road,
and sink that fine scenting vale of theirs, when he's
half beat, I can hook him, but if they find a fox in
that Vale and bring him on to our cold hills, its
a good reason why they lose him.

"They say I don't like water, and
they've got a picture of me stepping

Dislike to water.

into it. There was a huntsman's dinner at
Banbury to Wingfield, Stevens, and myself, the
farmers gave it, first-rate fellows; and they were all
on me about it. I said very well, when we're at
North Aston, and the fox goes over the brook,
I'll pound you all. Going down from Doddington
next time, I called up my second horseman; he was
on the grey mare Julia. I said, go and stand under
the thick hedge on the opposite side of the bank from
where we draw. We drew first on Dean Hill.
Cooper and Selsby were great at water, and they
said, '*Come along down this field.*' There was a
tree across, I turned my black horse loose and ran
across it, and got on the grey, and George went
back for the black. I said I should go across the
brook at a place where not a man in England dare
jump it, and I was right. I always go in and out.
Another time when I got to a brook I kept hallooing
them on, forty or fifty of those Oxford boys, and I
popped down to a ford, 100 yards below, and crept
up the other side of the hedge; the hounds checked
on a fallow, and I heard them say, '*We've done
him,—we've left the old 'un behind.*' '*Have you?*' I
said, and I peeped through the hedge, '*The huntsman's here, and he don't want you to hunt them.*'
So I did them again."

"Poor Will Goodall was so fond of the   Cricket remini-
brook business. Such a carpentering   scences.
he used to have the day after they had been at
Melton Spinney with those rails at the fords, 'to keep
the tinkers out,' as he called them. He was very
fond of cricket: he went and fielded for a friend,
when The United came to Grantham. He jumped
about so in his white cord breeches; I had great fun
watching him. I used to play a great deal; when
the game went against me the better I liked it. Old
Jem Broadbridge used to make me go in first, when
things looked odd. When Brown came to play with

the Brighton Club, we practised a fortnight throwing balls at each other's wickets, to be ready for him. I was one of the Petworth Club, and we went to Brighton to play them.

Broadbridge said, '*Do go in first, Jem, they're all afraid of these shooters.*' I got three runs off Brown, and twelve runs in all; Lillywhite bowled me. Brown was a great fellow, six feet high, his balls came like bullets; they were all over the place, three long-stops could'nt handle them. I never lost my wicket with a catapulta, I knew how to watch the machine; I was in with a catapulta up at the Forest, and I went and fetched seven off it. I watched where he set it for leg-stump, middle or near stump. Once I took a young Eleven to play this grand Forest Club, and dressed them. I lasted them out each time, and made 130 runs. We wanted five to win. '*Don't you move your bat,*' I said to the last man; they shouted, '*That's not fair, Jem.*' I got the next over, and I got seven, and we regularly chaffed the Club. I've not played them since. I always leave off a winner. Once I shot a pigeon match for £10 a-side; I won that, and I'll shoot no more. I've played one single-wicket match, and beat my man, and they'll not catch me at that again. I've ridden this steeple-chase and I won, so I may say that I've never been licked."

Clarke's sanctum. With an idle afternoon on our hands, and a clear sky overhead, we left the train at Chippenham, and faced the 10½ miles, heel and toe, to Badminton, to see that first Wonder and Spangle entry, which united the scarlet and black collar of Tubney, with the green plush of the Duke. The road is nice, but too flat to be interesting; and we were right glad to find ourselves in Acton Turvile, and then among the pretty cottages of Badminton, one or two of which seem perfectly clustered over with vine and ivy leaves. We found Clark almost roofless, as his

house was being enlarged, and he was living in the
village *pro tem.* ; but still he stuck to his snuggery,
which seemed like a sort of oasis in a brick-and-
mortar wilderness. Mr. Morrell's well-known print
occupied the place of honour above the fire-place, on
each side of which hung the heads of Vigil and Ade-
line. Old Trumpeter, who was put away soon after
he came, looks out of canvas, in company with the
young Harlequin; and beneath them was Trouncer, a
relic of Clarke's service with Sir John Gerard. Shamrock and Grimaldi, two Old Berkshire friends, Hor-
lock's Statesman (sire of Friendly and Filagree),
poor Will Goodall, Hercules, and Philip Payne, found
their place as well; and there, too, was Clarke himself on Topthorn, cheering Forester and Bobadil of
Tubney renown ; while Farmer, who died under
his first whip after a great Craven run, at Lambourne, has left him his foot as a forget-me-not,
for the side-board.

The "blue and white" scalp-board with The kennel beau-
its fringe of pads, pleasantly keeps up ties of Badmin-
the connection with Kingstown, who ton.
stands near the kennels, and the yearlings which
were coming forward for John Day. During the
last four seasons, the average of noses has been 73
brace, and in the last they reached 91, the largest
number, we believe, on record. His Grace can
generally count on five hundred head of foxes in a
country, which is about forty square miles in extent,
and from 14 to 15 brace are killed each season off
Mr. Holford's property, which abounds with game.
So much for true-hearted and industrious keepers,
and an owner who has not one face for the master of
the hounds, and another for his own men ! This year
(1860) was the first of the Tubney cross, and the
result was to be found in twelve out of the twenty-
one litters, from which the entry had been selected.
Nearly 38 couple of dog hounds were on the flags,

ranging from 23¼ to 24 inches, with Hengist even
slightly over that standard.   The half-faced Fleecer,
Clarke's friend of seven seasons, was there, by Fitzhardinge Furrier from Heroine, and so back through
Fitzhardinge Flourisher, and Beaufort Fairplay to
the Furrier fountain head of honour.   There, too,
was the gay-coloured Forester, Wonder worthy in
looks of his mate, and Wrangler, Sailor, and Sportsman of Warwickshire Saffron descent.   Termagant
and Tenderness had spoken up elsewhere for Harlequin, who was with his sister Honesty, the prize
Tubney Cup holders in "the Hercules year," and blest
with a remarkable head, which marks him among
ten thousand.

Limner had been put away, but his Legacy and
Loyalty were left, and so was his Paragon, strain-
ing back to Beaufort Warlock on one side, and from
a dam the very last of the Beaufort Potentates.   Sportsman, Prodigal, Sparkler, and Whynot were among the particulars, and Trimbush, who
had been in training for the hound match.   Spangle
the fifty-guinea matron of the Tubney sale prospered
in her generation after she came to Badminton, and
did her work well as an eight-season hunter.   Her
rare Wonders inherit her somewhat smutty face, and
Woldsman in his work exactly resembles her.   Jack
Jones bred her, and Clarke entered her, and looked
forward to raising a pack from her when she died.
She leaves eight couple of them in work, and a
couple of handsome ones coming forward.

Among the matrons were Vistula and Vestal,
Sanguine, and Vigil of the Warwickshire Saffron
sort, in which Clarke delights, as "there is no end
of them;" Wisdom, too, of the old badger-pie sort,
Harriet, Hasty, Pleasant, and Pastime, and Coun-
tess, with Skilful, who has a deal of the old Sunderland head and crown.   It would never do to forget
Friendly, the yellow-pied Handmaid, or Caroline.

There, too, was the grey face of old Spangle, and the very handsome Fallacy. Honesty and Toilet, both Tubney Cup winners, were in the throng, but as yet they had bred from neither of them; and so were Rarity and Playful, to tell of old Remus, who had been recently put away in his tenth season. Faithless by Flagrant, and Woful by Belvoir Comus, were there with Baroness; Seamstress was the least among that fair and good-tempered array, and never did two sisters show better than Waspish and Woodbine, as they passed side by side through the wicket.

If you ask Will Long about his old Badminton pack, he will generally reply *Recollections of Will Long.* that he would lay his life down for Prophetess by Plunder, and Tuneful by Warwickshire Tarquin. Still Dorimont is the burden of his discourse. The day when the sixth Duke ordered him to draw Stowe-on-the-Wold, fifteen miles away from Badminton, only twenty minutes before dark, or when the seventh requested him to bring out Milkman in a frost, and lark him over some flights of hurdles in the straw-ride, are still specially marked in his memory, but not more than the work of the old dog in Ditchley Woods, when he had been for months on the retired list. His blood comes up in all the best strains in the kennel. Rufus and Remus have it through their dam Rarity by Rutland, a capital son of his, and it can be traced in Wonder through Fearnought to Gaiety. Remus was the cleanest in his fore-hand, but Rufus had most power, and was nearest the ground, and decidedly the best of the two, and the Duke of Rutland and Sir Richard Sutton used him freely.

Mr. Childe of Kinlet first began hard- *The dawn of Leicestershire.* riding in Leicestershire, to Mr. Meynell's great disgust; and after Lords Forester and Jersey came with "the splittercockation pace," he declared that he "had not had a day's happiness." He and

Tom Tit knew no troubles till then, and his
horses used to rear on their hind legs, and jump
gates and stiles standing, in the most sober and
comfortable way. In fact, it was the regular Muster's régime; getting through a country, and not
over it. The Bull's Head and the George at Loughboro' were the head-quarters, and a hundred horses
would go past the window in the morning to cover.
Mr. Meynell hunted the whole of the original Quorn
country, from Clifton Gardens near Nottingham
to Market Harborough, thirty miles away and the
Leicester harriers, whose patrons met once a week
at The Bell, enjoyed themselves under his wing and
got his small draft. Mr. Cholmondley, Sir Stephen
Glynne, Sir Harry Featherstone, and Prince Boothby
were great at Loughboro', and Brooksby Gate was
the first meet of the season in November. Gradually Melton was discovered to be more central, and
the attractions of the Belvoir and "Lord Lonsdale's
Tuesdays" brought Loughboro' to grief, and the
opening day to Kirby Gate, which for sixty years
never lacked Mr. Sheldon Cradock's presence on
horse-back, and at last in a chaise.

The Quorn country.   Fourteen masters — Sefton, Foley,
Smith, Osbaldeston, Bellingham Gra-
ham, Osbaldeston, Southampton, Goodricke, Holyoake, Errington, Suffield, Hodgson, Greene, Sutton,
and Stamford—have reigned since. Still through
all the changes of tillage and draining, Sixhills,
Shoby, Widmerpool, and Willoughby held the
best scent then, and hold it still. The Forest
still continues to be what Mr. Meynell said of
it, "the finest scenting country in the world;"
and the best for breaking young hounds. The only
part of the old enclosure is Charley, which remains
the same as it did sixty years ago. All was then an
open sheep-walk of heath and stone, and without
any fence or even a tree, save a few hazels and

oaks, for miles. The foxes were as wild as hawks, and were generally found among the Whitwick rocks near the present Monastery, where Mr. Meynell and his men would dig for hours. The four M's of the Old Club and Mr. Cradock of Loughboro' gradually took the management of the covers, and the subscriptions when Mr. Assheton Smith had the hounds and about £3,500 a-year, were paid as punctually as a bank dividend. "The Blue Coats" were in their glory, and among them "Gamboy Henton" who spoke to his own nose down a drain, when Meynell's Gamboy could not. These flyers would "hardly open their mouths under two hundred;" and Jonathan King of Beeby would take a horse out of his stable for no one. "Come and ride him," he used to say, "and if you like him, three hundred's my price."

For his tackle, Mr. Smith still stands confessedly the first man across Leicestershire, and except Sir David Baird, very few attempted to go so straight. The fences were higher then, and no caps were worn, and both of them would have their clothes torn off their backs, and their flesh from their faces, rather than not go every inch of the way with hounds. As Tom Heycock used to observe of Sir David, "If he did get a fall, and you thought he was out of the run, he would always pop up by your side." Mr. Smith brought his little horse Benjie into the country, and as he said then, so he said to the last, that his present horse was his best.

It was another of his axioms, that the great secret was "learning how to gallop," and he had to put out his highest proficiency on the Mondays; when Messrs. Rawlinson and Lindow would invariably come to ride against him. "He would often ride for a certain fall, when he wanted to make a cast," and no one knew how to

fall off better. He studied it as a science, and when
his horse was at all blown, he always sent him at
timber a little aslant, so as to get free of him
easier if he made a mistake. People knew what
unmade, uncertain-tempered brutes he rode, and
when he did something quite out of the common,
they cheered him. This made him very tenacious,
and if any one followed him over any of those " sensation jumps," he was quite crabbed and seldom forgot
it. One man he was never jealous of under any
circumstances. Speaking of the finish of a run he
said, " No one was there but myself;" and when
some one suggested Tom Gamble, he replied, " *Oh,
he's nobody ; he's always there!*"

He once rode against Sir James Musgrave, near
Clawson, in the days when hunter pairs were all the
fashion at Melton Thorns, but Sir James changed
his black without his observing it, and jumping the
locked gate at the bottom, left him pounded and in a
fearful passion. From Broderip Oak over the Vale to
Lydiard Wood, was another of his great rides, when
Lord Kintore had the V. W. H., and he was gracious
enough to say to his Lordship, " *Well! old friend,
you had just the best of it!*" Be the country what
it might, he never gave it a thought, and Mr. Davis
always says that he was " the best stag hunter of us
all," when we went into the New Forest.

The Billesdon   One of his greatest Leicestershire
Brook leap.   leaps was the Billesdon Brook, which he
leapt in a place where it was a regular ravine. The
bank had rather curved in, and it required at last
thirty-four feet to cover it, and a plashed hedge on
the opposite side. The field saw him coming up the
turnpike from the Coplow to Billesdon ; and for the
first time in his life nursing his horse. He knew
what was before him, and then rushing through the
crowd like a bullet, he went at it determined to do
something tremendous ; but Lord Aylesford followed

him, and got over with a slight scramble on the other side. Dick Christian jumped the same brook, on Mr. Maxse's grey King of the Valley in his steeple-chase, and the measurement from hind foot to hind-foot, was thirty-six feet. All Mr. Smith's escapes were as nothing compared to one of his friend Mr. Coke's when he went to stay with him in Hampshire. Seeing a nice practicable fence, he charged it, but not only found himself dropping all in a heap into a deep lane, but right in front of a horse and cart. This vision so startled the horse, that it dashed forward, and drew the cart right over the legs of Mr. Coke's hunter, as it lay on the ground, and lamed it for many a week after.

Mr. Smith seemed to relax towards no one so much as Mr. Greene, whom he *Training little Will Burton.* considered his best pupil, and there was also an exception in favour of little Will Burton. He determined to give Will his first lesson, when he was little more than four stone. Putting him on one of his steadiest hunters, he observed by way of prelude, "*Boy! if you don't stick close to me, you'll never see your mother again!*" Having made this first and last appeal, he proceeded to give him a lead over some hog-backed stiles, and chose one so close under a tree, that the little fellow's hat was knocked off. In a minute his master was down picking it up. "*Rare fun this, boy, isn't it?*" "*Yes, master,*" said Young Hopeful, "*but if we don't look sharp, we won't see the hounds again.*" The retort suited his grim humour to a nicety, and he chuckled at the thoughts of it long after poor little Will was in his grave.

At that time, the hounds spent alter- *Will's hound education.* nate three weeks between Quorn and Bowden Inn, where Lord Plymouth, Mr. Maxse, and Mr. Maher also sent their horses, and Mr. Smith told the story of the hat so well at Serlby, that the hero of it was summoned to be looked over and tell his weight.

This occurred so often afterwards that Will began to think that "master will never have done showing me to the ladies." In other respects he was a precocious pupil, and in his leisure hours he clipped his master's cat. It came up as usual to be stroked by Mr. Smith at stable hour, and an enquiry soon fixed suspicion on the culprit, who said he " thought it would make her handsome." We do not know whether the punishment, blended as it was with the deepest instruction, would suit the authors of the Revised Code, but it simply consisted in writing out and then spelling over to his master, twenty of the hardest hound names in the pack.

Old Tom Wingfield, who had a peculiar habit of always catching his horse up, before he took a fence, never got on with Mr. Smith in kennel. Tom smoked morning, noon, and night, and we have no doubt does so still at eighty-seven. Hence " *Send that fellow to me, when he's sure he's done his pipe,*" was the general form of cabinet council summons. There is a good deal of truth in what Dick Burton always says to George Carter, " I had the lion, you had the lamb," as Mr. Smith grew much milder latterly, and he took the dog-hounds into the open, and George the lady pack and the puppies into the woods, without at all interfering with each other. There never was a better man to get away from a big wood. He would not speak a word after they found. There was no " *Whey ! confound the horse,*" as with Mr. Codrington (when it wasn't stirring an ear), but he kept quietly moving in the ridings; and when they broke he was at them like a shot.

Mr. Hames of Glenn. In Leicestershire, Mr. Hames of Glenn was his great hound secretary. He would put out twenty couple of puppies for him, and go round twice a-week to shepherd them. "If you don't keep the one well," he used to say, " I'll send you two; and if you don't keep the two well I'll

Dick Burton, p. 387.

send you the dam and the whole litter." His good humour had its effect, and they came in from quarters like bacon pigs. Mr. Hames's enthusiasm did not die out, and they used to say in Mr. Osbaldeston's day, that if he heard Dick Burton crack his whip as a signal on passing through the village, he would have run out of church from a wedding or a funeral. A fox with a mangy brush and loins in Shankton Holt was a great card with him, and he named him "Jack." "I'll back old Jack to-day" was his offer, directly they found; and they never could succeed in killing him.

It was in Lincolnshire that "The Squire," after a capital season up to Christmas Eve, underwent all the agonies of "the great frost," which never broke up again till past the middle of February; when hunting men felt like the exiles of Siberia. After that, he had three things good enough to make the fortune of a season, one of them with scarcely a check seventeen miles from point to point, with Jim Wilson and Tom Sebright checking him all the way over Tower Moor, to keep him out of the Heath. It was all grass and no plough in Lincolnshire then; drains have now made the top of the soil light; and sheep no longer rot almost up to their hocks in water, so that the labours and difficulties of those days must not be judged of by the standard of the present, when there is a stable of 70 or 80 hunters to pick from, and sometimes 120 couple of hounds out at quarters. *"The Squire" in Lincolnshire.*

The picture of Dick Burton and the hounds is the key, as far as sires go, to the finest Osbaldeston blood. Dick is not on the Big Grey, which "had always one spur in him, and the other never out of him," but Cervantes, one of his own making. Walton Thorns has just been drawn blank, and Vanquisher by Musters's Proctor, always one of the last out, comes up flying a stile. He *The Osbaldeston hound blood.*

cc 2

was one of the most beautiful dog-hounds at Quorn,
not so fast as Furrier, and, like him, he never,
smeused. The farmer who walked him at Hutton
Bushel, sent him in with the comment, that he ought
to be a very good hound, as "he had eaten the mistress' prayer-book one day." The old black and
white Vaulter lies down near the yellow-pied Pilgrim, "such a dog for ribs and thighs, and eight
inches round the arm," who looks wistfully up in
Dick's face, waiting for the word to move on to
Mundy's Gorse. His sire Rocket by Vernon's
Rallywood also shows those grave, long features,
which were such a type of his road wisdom, and
Furrier comes cantering up to the group, in which
Mindful, his companion in the Belvoir draft,
bears part with Nabob "an owdacious stinger,
with a true Brocklesby head." The yellow-pied
Hermit bears testimony to a Beaufort draft, and
there, too, are Primrose, and Rosebud the faithful
consort of Furrier and one with Rocket in the Vernon pack purchase. The little terrier Nettle is
almost the "dearest of them 'a'" to Dick. Her dam
used to ride to cover in Lord Middleton's carriage,
but Nettle despised all such help. Dick often tells
how she was somehow or other always first, second, or
third over the rides for an hour and twenty minutes
in Martinshawe Wood, and then pitched in to her
well earned fox for the first time; how she went in at
a badger with her legs under her, when she had
hardly a cheek-tooth left, and how she honourably
retired when "The Squire" had jumped upon her
at the last fence but one before the fox went to
ground after a very fast thing.

The Squire's
hound tastes.
Blood rather than size was "The
Squire's" aim in kennel. Four couple
and a half of Rockets, none of them less than four
season hunters, three couple of Vanquishers, and
26½ couple of Furriers were the cream of the pack,

when he went to the Pytcheley. Over the great
grass-fields of Kelmarsh and Oxendon, the "Furrier ladies" for two seasons especially, were in
their greatest glory. He had made them so handy,
that at a signal they would divide in their cast, but
latterly they were always flashing over the scent,
when their fox doubled back, or dodged; and four
or five scurries with different foxes, too often made
up the journal entry at night. When they did settle
to one, and blew him up in the open, "The Squire"
might well say "they don't fly like pigeons, they fly
like angels."

Never was he known to go in a car- *The Squire's scorn of fatigue.*
riage to cover; and he never seemed to
know what fatigue was. "If you will have two
horses, you shall have two packs a-day," he said to
the Quornites, and as he never went to sleep after
dinner, he wouldn't have objected to a turn with a
third by moonlight. Tommy Coleman, who often
cut in for a half-mile gallop at his side during the 8
hours and 40 minutes of his great Newmarket match,
declared that he could see no difference in him at the
20th and 200th mile; and yet some of his horses,
old Guildford especially, pulled hard. He rode it a
race all the way, standing up in his stirrups. There
was always quite a set-to at the end of each four
miles; and he would blow any one up if they attempted to help him on to his fresh horse. When
all was over, he insisted on riding into the town,
and Mr. Gully was so grieved at seeing fine training
and stamina so fearfully taxed, that he said "Really,
Squire, you ought to have a whip over your shoulders
for taking such liberties with yourself!"

An acre of manuscript might be filled *Meltoniana.*
with the sayings and doings of the hard-
riding men of Melton, back to the days when Ralph
Lambton was treasuring up for Durham County use
every waif and stray that fell from the lips of his

St. Hugo; or when Lord Sefton set the whole
country talking, by jumping the Decoy Brook near
Bunny on his grey. He carried top weight about 20st.,
and won in a tremendous fast thing of 20 minutes,
" a stone a minute," as he afterwards said.

General Gros-   Then there was General Grosvenor
venor.   equally quaint in his way at Newmarket
or at the meet, where he would sometimes arrive
from Brooksby, with a perfect cloud of grooms after
him, by way of giving his hunters exercise. " You
ride no more for me," he said to " The Vicar" after
he had ridden Dœdalus, " you lay so far out of
your ground, you nearly frightened Mrs. Grosvenor
to death." A dislike to sleeping out was another
of his leading features. A bed was at his service
after he had dined out in the Cottesmore country,
but he could not make up his mind. At last he
sent for the housemaid, who was a woman of short
stature, and asked when it had been slept in? " I
slept in it, General, only last night," said she.
" *You slept in it*," he replied, looking her well over,
You're not big enough to air a bed: order my car-
riage."

Mr. John Moore.   Mr. Moore wielded well the power of
the Old Club, and did " the coffee-house
part of the business" by keeping men together, and
gathering in the subscriptions quite early in the season. He was a thin man with long legs, and " daylight knees" in his saddle, and always a quiet rider.
Like most of the men of that period, he never liked
to be asked too little for a horse. Wright of Syssonby offered him one in the spring at rather a low
figure, but he returned him after a trial, and a dealer
bought him. The next season Wright espied his
old friend at Thorpe Trussells; and it was a perfect
bit of news for Mr. Moore, when he was told
" You're sitting, Sir, on the same horse you
were on at the end of last season; I suppose I

asked you a hundred too little." He was also
a little of an epicure, and his friends used to
tell him that they had heard his Shorthorn solilo-
quies at cattle shows: "I should like to have a
rump-steak out of you." Once he was regularly
taken in when he was yachting abroad. He
found, as he thought, a young lamb tethered to a
stake, and gave five shillings for it. He had, as it
seems forgotten the size of the sheep of that country,
and only thought of the Bakewells, and it turned
out, as he said, with disgust, to be "an old tup, and
as strong as a Billy Goat."

" Harden your hearts and tighten your
girths," was Lord Alvanley's great watch- Lord Alvanley.
word at the " View Halloo," and it was magnificent to
see him go over the first half-dozen fences. Twenty
minutes was his allowance, or about five more on an
average than Lord Sefton. He butchered his horses
along when they would go, spurs well home and reins
slack; and Prick Ears understood him best. Once
when he was on his white horse, they found at Whissendine Pastures, and as all the steam was in him, he
came right out of the crowd, and had the brook first.
The horse got in, and plunged his Lordship's hat to
the bottom, and to the end of the day he persevered
on bare-headed, and with his horse perfectly black,
or rather pyebald from the slush. He had a skew-
ball, but the weight did not suit him, and his Lordship
announced after one ride, that he was sure that
" the horse would commit suicide rather than carry
him again."

A woodland day he abhorred. " What sport have
you had to-day, Alvanley?" said one of his friends
when he met him coming home rather glum. " Oh !
beautiful, we've been up Tilton Wood, and down
Tilton Wood, and through Tilton Wood, then we
went away from Tilton Wood, and back again to
Tilton Wood, and they'll very likely finish at Tilton

Wood." On another day, he declared that he had been quite beaten in the "Whole Art of Riding made Easy," by a Circus man from Leicester, who came out to see the fun in a property scarlet, and on an old grey trick-horse. Near Quenby Hall, the man pretended to ride at a gate, and when the horse stopped short, he threw himself over his head, and made such a series of somersaults that the field thought that he and his top-boots would never come to earth again. Spending, his Lordship termed "realizing," and defied any one to give a more philosophical definition of it; and when his servant told him that he was sorry to say that the corn-factor had turned awkward at last, he asked what was the state of his confectioner's mind, and on learning that it was favourable, he said, " *Oh ! that will do : give 'em biscuits !*" His finest stroke of policy was when he gave away a whole boat-load of coals to the poor of Melton, and the inference from this liberality was so favourable, that he had a roaring credit for months, at the expense of the Navigation Company.

Mr. Maher's "Old Tommy." Be it Erin-go-Bragh or Shugaraoo, or anything else, Mr. "Paddy" Maher never used anything but a snaffle. Mr. Frank Forester introduced a great change into the cover horse system, as he generally rode his own there, and this prevented the grooms from running riot as of yore. In Old Tommy, Mr. Maher had a veritable treasure, as he seemed to have a private key to the run of every fox. He was such a wizard that Mr. Burton ordered his lad never to keep his eye off him, and go exactly where he did. Old Tommy was indignant at this, and when he could not shake him off, he pulled up, and sitting down on a gate began to read the newspaper. The lad thought that Tommy would be lost that day, and rode on; but when he was wanted, the veteran was there to a minute, and Mr. Burton had to look into space for his second horse. The lad explained matters, and acted so rigidly in future up to his directions, "If Tommy gets on to a gate to read the paper, get up beside him, and ask him to edify you as well as himself," that Tommy and he became fast friends.

There was a story against Mr. Maher of the way in which he tried to trick Old Tommy, who was on a horse with about the same walking pace as his own. He held that going on one side of a wood was much shorter than the other, and sent Tommy to come along it with the strictest injunction not to break from a walk; but (seeing from an opening in the wood that he was making as good time as himself), stealthily started to canter. Tommy saw it and did the same, and got to the meeting place first. Mr. Maher was exceedingly angry, and was not at all satisfied with the explanation, that Tommy had seen him canter just after he came to the wood corner, and saw no possible harm in doing the same.

Mr. Maher outwitted.

Many compared Sir Francis Burdett's seat on Sampson to a pair of compasses across a telescope. He cared little for personal comforts, and his Westminster and provincial supporters who believed (after they had seen him seated at a window teaching it to his boy), that he did nothing but study Magna Charta all day, would have hardly known "Old Glory" as the fox-hunting devotee in those two little rooms which had once been part of the stables, at Kirby Hall, or dining out after hunting, and stopping all night in his dirty but historical top-boots. He had a soul for subscribing as well as hunting; and he and Lord Plymouth each gave £400 to the Quorn. In fact, if he only hunted once in a season, he gave £200, and Mr. Sheldon Cradock tells no story with more zest than how on hearing of cover wants, he asked for his

Sir Francis Burdett.

if anything came upon him suddenly, he as often as not put his foot in it, and his rider down.

Captain White. Captain White graduated with " The Squire" in Lincolnshire, and was the friendly go-between, who arranged that he should purchase Quorn from Mr. Assheton Smith His first day in Leicestershire was on "The Widow," at Scraptoft, and they had eight minutes from The Laurels, very sharp, to ground. They went back and found again, and had eleven miles. Mr. Smith saw the mare, and her young rider so forward, that although his temper went from being bogged almost immediately after, he did not forget it. The next time they appeared was in a very fast thing from Billesdon Coplow to Slawston Windmill. Only five were left in at last, and when Mr. Smith saw his brook acquaintance down, he caught his mare for him, and only gave him a warmish exhortation to be quick, as with scarcely a breath left in him, he staggered over a fallow.

Putting up hunters at the Old Club. Putting up horses for auction at the Old Club was quite a business each night. Parties were often made on purpose, and after a couple of bottles of claret, business became quite brisk. Each owner had one reserve bid, and it was quite a sight the next morning to watch the different horses change stables, to the great bewilderment of the grooms. Several were very sweet on The Widow the first day she came out, and "*four hundred*" was put under the candlestick. The Captain's reserve bid was a hundred above that sum, and after the Billesdon Coplow day, Lord Middleton did not scruple to close for her. Mistakes frequently arose from the habit of having hunters of the same colour and style. Sir James Musgrave, who would give good prices at the end of the season for horses he had seen go well, had three greys, by Fitzjames, (for which he paid a thousand guineas to a Shropshire man), so alike that the grooms and their owner only knew them; and Captain White had two equally "winsome marrows," in his dark chesnuts. The Quorn had had a very fast forty minutes, and The Captain had been in the front rank as usual with one of them, and come a tremendous cropper into a green lane. Luckily his groom was close at hand with the other, and as not a soul knew of the change, it was sold for four hundred at night.

Harlequin, by Sir Oliver, was the best horse venture The Captain ever made, and was bought out of a Derbyshire team, for £100, when he was four years old. He had two splints his first season, but the bone grew up to them, and his action and blood made him quite equal to fourteen stone. He made his debút at Easton Wood, and a few of them had two miles over the plough and back before the field knew what was going on; and they then changed foxes, and ran to Woodwell Head. The style in which the horse had jumped on and off a little bulrush island, during the run, got so bruited about, that when Lord Plymouth heard of it, coupled with Mr. Standish's report of his action across ridge and furrow, he determined to have him at any price. It was eventually agreed that he should give Pedlar and a £900 cheque for him; and as The Captain sold the latter for £250, he made a clear thousand guineas of his horse. His lordship had got four falls off his 400-guinea Assheton, the first time he rode him, and was glad to sell him to Mr. Holyoake; but he never repented buying Harlequin, and vowed after riding him for seven seasons, that he was the only one he ever liked. He was a perfect snaffle-bridle horse, and the only instructions The Captain gave with him were, " Don't bully him, my lord; hold him nicely for three fences, and then sit down on him, and send him along." From hip

to tail he was all muscle, and Mr. Gilmour said of
him, that he "only seemed to gallop over an ox-
fence." There is, however, always a set-off to luck,
and his brother Jupiter met his death, by a stake
running into his chest, just as the hounds were
killing; and General Grosvenor insisted on giving
him honourable burial in the centre of the middle
riding in Stockersten Wood.

Mr. Maxse pound-
ing a couple. What Harlequin or Merry Lad might
have said to it is a different thing, but
even The Captain and Admiral Berkeley* confess
that Mr. Maxse with all the weight fairly set them
over four oak rails, at the corner of Harlesdon Wood.
Cognac, who took them with his chest, and drew
the stumps right out of the ground, and his rider
looked back when the crash was over, and said,
"*Ah! I always thought you were a pair of soft ones!*"
This was the third or fourth flight of rails which
Cognac, who was very fresh after a frost, and in one
of his rushing humours, had served out that day.
Mr. Campbell, of Saddell, had introduced him into
his Melton song, and therefore he was more
talked of; but Mr. Maxse was quite as fond of
Treacle and the Baron, both of which he purchased
from Sir Bellingham Graham; and it was for the
latter that Captain Ross, who yearned to be the
steeple-chase champion, offered him a thousand
guineas in vain.

Merry Lad. Captain White bought Merry Lad from
Mr. Tilbury, for £200; but although he
did not go the length of Lord Cardigan's Dandy,
who danced about on his hind legs, and flew at everything at the cover side, till they were obliged to
bring him in blinkers; he was very restive at first, and
required to be flogged out of the yard. His great
day was one from Thorpe Trussells, by Great Dalby
to Rolleston, where they killed in a ditch. He

* Now Lord Fitzhardinge.

played first fiddle with the Captain for some twelve seasons, when Alice Grey took his place, and he was used in harness at last.

To see The Captain starting for the Scurry at Croxton or Heaton Park, and calling the young ones to order at the post was a very grand sight, and often in the middle of the race, a series of most sonorous Tally-hoes were heard from the same quarter, to make the impetuous ones go a little faster. Dick Christian has already told of the Waste Walk on the Kettleby Road; but the Captain had harder work than that when he had to get off 10lbs. in two days for Theodore, when he was staying at Heaton Park. During the last two miles of one walk, he was so beat, that in order to have something to force the running, he picked up a bag-piper, and was marching in state behind him up the flower-garden, on his return, with a face like a furnace, when the house party encountered him. *The Captain at Croxton and Heaton Park.*

Besides profiting by the countless riding hints, which he received from Mr. Assheton Smith, when he first came out, Mr. Greene went into strong practice on off days, over his own Rolleston estate. He would invite parties to course there, and mounting one of his best hunters, ride so close up to the dogs, that at times their owners would be a little nervous lest he should jump on to them. He negotiated the ox-fences and wide ditches with which the estate abounds so brilliantly, that dog owners often said, that to see him at work was worth all the sport among the hares. *Mr. Greene of Rolleston.*

His hand and seat were so light, that he went by the name of "The Fly," and he seemed to tell his horse more by knee-pressure than anything, exactly what he expected of him. When he came out cub-hunting within the last two or three seasons, on a little chesnut " Nat " (which *Style of riding.*

Mr. Richard Sutton had bought from its name-sake at Newmarket), the finest horsemen thought it quite a head-and-hand lesson to watch him gradually soothe the little gentleman, which would fly and kick about in every direction, into a quiet canter. Horse handling was a science he had quite thought out, and we remember well his delight when we sat with him, the last time we ever met, at the Alhambra, and saw Mr. Rarey have his first interview with King of Oude. He always said that he endeavoured to make his horses take their fences a trifle aslant, and he "came up to them," as a first flight friend writes us, "with bounding strokes to the last, when he slackened his rein, and allowed them to exert their full power, the fling almost invariably bringing him safely into the next field."

The riding of his later years. Latterly he hunted about two or three days a-week, in a quiet sort of way, but enjoyed it as much as ever. In fact, he said that in one or two runs he had "never ridden more up to the mark when he was one-and-twenty," and nothing gave him greater pleasure than a remark of Lord Gardner's : "*I say, Greene, you're cutting the young 'uns down.*" He had a great "eye forward" for hounds, and stoutly carried out the maxim, never to take timber if you can avoid it. He repeated this to Goddard (who was riding side by side with him in a fast thing by Holt two seasons ago), and Jack often tells how beautifully he suited the action to the word, and popped his horse through the hedge close by the gate-post and into the front rank in an instant.

His horses. The white Glanagyle, which was given to him by Mr. Otway Cave, was his cover hack for nearly fifteen seasons. He always rode it in the Park when he came to town, and it is now finishing out its days with Sir Frederick Fowke.

He seldom kept more than six hunters, and was not given to change. "The bay mare" never had a name; and after her, Muley of whom he records in 1835, " I was never carried better in my life," and Don John "very clever," were in force some five-and-twenty years ago. Fanny, Asparagus, and Symmetry were in his stables together ; Syssonby stood very high with him ; Phantom, who was out of one of his own mares, won a Hunters Stake at Northampton ; and Alice Grey, little Piccolo, and the water-loving Mrs. Caudle carried him to the front, during his memorable mastership. The first was given away to a tenant, and Mrs. Caudle was bought in for 230 gs., when half worn out, and carried him for some seasons after that.

He kept a rough journal of every day he was out; a little limp-backed red book, tied with a red ribbon. The entries till he became master seem very slight, and those who expect to glean much of what took place in 1835-39 would search in vain. With Mr. Hodgson's two seasons, his writing ardour seems to have been quickened, although once or twice we detect a mere pencil entry, the gist of one of which is, "*rode Norton, a fall.*" "*Rolleston, lots of foxes,*" occurs several times, but the great Assheton Smith day of 1840 has merely these three lines : " *Assheton Smith, met at Rolleston, we had about two thousand horses and thirty carriages, Prince Ernest present, rode Don John.*" However, a Leicester newspaper extract, pasted into each end of the book, puts the flesh on to this skeleton entry. Among the more varied entries are " stopped the hounds in consequence of a mad dog;" " Laughton Hills, excellent day, was on my horse twelve hours ;" " Coplow, only our old fox, plenty at Barkby Holt ;" and then comes " Kilby Wharf, found one of the best foxes I ever saw." " Waterford's hounds at Somerby, turned out a stag,

His hunting journal

rode Norton," shows that steady and orthodox
as he was, he could not resist a peep at "The
Wild Huntsman," and "1 hour 45 minutes"
was his reward. Two runs with Mr. Hodgson's
seem to have delighted him most in the whole of the
seven years' chronicle, which we have glanced at.
One of them, January 20, 1840, is described as "a
great run, two hours from the Coplow, killed, one of
the finest runs I ever saw, carried brilliantly by
Harlequin." To the other, of December 9, 1840, he
applies the terms, "best run I ever saw; ran from
Thorpe Trussells to Spinney at Rolleston Brook, 52
minutes. From Halstead to Rolleston not a horse
within half-a-mile of them, 22 couple, and all up;
rode my grey mare, and she had decidedly the best
of it, and not beat."

His great Thorpe   Latterly he rather leant to the belief,
   Trussells run. that a run in his own mastership from
Thorpe Trussells to Rolleston Gorse, was perhaps the
best of the two, and Tom Heycock is with him on
the point. There were twelve horses in Twyford
Brook, and full fifty per cent. of the remainder were
beaten off in Tilton Bottom, Mr. Greene on Retriever,
Tom Day on Cossington, and only five or six others
being able to get up the Skeffington Vale. How he
and Tom Day ever got such a pack put together,
astonished all Leicestershire; and not one blank
day went into the diary during his six seasons.
He took great pains with his foxes: one of the broad-
backed, short black foxes which Captain White sent
him from Derbyshire went, like the celebrated Manton Gorse ones of two seasons since, and gave him
three runs from John Ball, before Tom could bring
him to book. As an M.F.H., none were more
energetic or popular both with the gentlemen and the
farmers. If the meet was thirty miles off, he would
never miss it, and he would saunter down to the
kennels at Billesdon on every non-hunting day. It

was at that village that Mr. Grant had his studio while he was engaged on the Melton Hunt picture, and spent some weeks at Rolleston while it was in progress.

It was beautiful to hear Mr. Greene Mr. Greene at home. talk of hunting, especially at the head of his own table. He was all animation, and you hardly knew whether most to admire the conciseness and spirit of his descriptions, or the delicate grace with which he kept self so completely in the back-ground,—giving every first-flight man his due, and hitting off his peculiar style. He was tenacious of his old friendships and early predilections. "Holyoake," for whom he acted during his mastership, Goodricke and Bellingham Graham were ever on his lips; and the riding of Lords Wilton and Gardner, and Mr. Gilmour, a theme which never grew old; but still he did not grudge the younger men their laurels. Fairness and kindness were great features in him, and no one had finer tact in settling a vexed question, or putting two men together, when they had begun to fight a little shy. To give another chance was the great rule of his magisterial life, and young offenders might well say appealingly, "*Take me to 'The Squire!'*" He delighted in a little farming. and never seemed happier than when he had his tenants round him at the rent dinners, and invited Sir Frederick Fowke and Mr. John Marriot, and perhaps one or two of the neighbouring clergy to dine with them. Latterly he was a good deal in London, and loved dearly to meet his friends Sir Bellingham and Mr. Maxse (who had been at University College, Oxford, with him) in his daily visits to Boodle's, or to have a chat with Mr. Payne and "The Squire," at the Arlington. He often dropped in at Tattersall's on a Monday, and if he did not care to accompany Lord Berners, who always came to dine with him in Upper Baker-street

on the evening of the Private View, each Christmas,
he amazingly enjoyed judging the hunters at the
Leicester Agricultural Show.   Up to the last winter
before Mr. Smith died he was a regular visitor at
Tedworth, and it was there that he renewed his
acquaintance with Mr. Coke.

His latter days.   An affection of the heart had given
its infallible warning some ten years previously, and he should then have given up hunting. He
would stop for breath at the bottom of Bushy Close
Hill between Billesdon and Rolleston; but it was
not till his grey Topthorn gave him a fall at a hedge
and back-dyke between Norton Gorse and Barkby
Holt, about twelve months before his death, that he
really began to fail.   He had never recovered the
loss of his nephew, who was to have inherited
Rolleston ; but when the shadows began to thicken
round him at last, he was enabled to look more
steadily into the future.   Last October he took
a friend into his stables to show him Topthorn and
Crinoline, and his eyes filled with tears, when he
said *" There they are, I shall never want them again."*
To many he seemed wasted, and he thought so himself ; but when his groom Shield weighed him just a
fortnight before his death, after a lapse of two years,
he was within a pound of what he had been in
1855.   *" Eight stone one, Shield "* he said, *" Is
that all you can make it ? that was exactly my
weight when I was at college."*   He seemed to take
heart from this, and not only ordered a new whip
and scarlet, but rode over to Leicester the day before his death to try a horse at Hames's.

The meet at   The next morning was the first monthly
Rolleston.   meet of the hounds at Rolleston.   He
was in more than his wonted spirits at seeing so large
a field, and Sir Frederick Fowke, Captain Baily,
Mr. Tailby, and so many of his friends round him.
It was quite a summer day, and the servants said

they "had never seen the sun shine so brightly on
master before," and thought sadly afterwards of the
old country omen, when they knew the end. While
the second breakfast was going on, he sauntered
down to the sunk fence, to have a word with the
master and Jack Goddard. "I never saw a nicer
lot," he said, when Wildboy and Welfare, the cup
winners, and two couple more from Sutton's Lively,
had been pointed out to him;" you're just getting
them the size I like so much."

Shield had taken the fine edge off
Crinoline when they had looked them His last hunt.
through, and there was soon a view halloo on the
Tugby side of the gorse. The fox bore away by the
keeper's house, leaving Loddington Village on the
right, and so on to Launde Park Wood. Jack Goddard's horse hit him a sharp blow on the muscles of
the back in a somersault over some rails near the
Uppingham Road, but he picked himself up in
fearful pain, and on his Poet once more; and Mr.
Greene caught his last glimpse of the chase as Mr.
Tailby led the field up Skeffington Vale. He had
got a good start, but he jumped no fences, and between Rolleston and Skeffington Wood, he suddenly
turned quite pale, and said pressing his side, "*I feel
very ill, Shield; I can't ride to-day.*" A little
brandy rather restored him, and he cantered and
trotted along homewards. "*Shield, I've done with
them,*" were his last words to his faithful groom as
he gave him his mare, and he never crossed that
threshold again.

He sat down in his arm-chair in the
dining-room, and had scarcely asked for and his death.
a little brandy, and said that he thought he had
ridden too hard, and felt "that odd sensation again,"
when he bowed his head and died. The thoughts of
a lingering death had always possessed a peculiar terror for him, so much so, that he often declared that

he would rather be shot down in a battle or a battue. His wish was fulfilled, and a mere lad took him up in his arms, and laid him just as he was, in his scarlet coat and boots, on his bed in the east room, which he had specially chosen as his bed-room, so as to see his hunters go out for exercise each morning.

The sale day. The coat of arms keeping their grim dog and boar guard in the entrance-hall with " Love and Loyalty" to the last, stood out sad and unchanged amid the dreary havoc of the sale day. The billiard-table was blocked up with the claret-warmer, the china, and the books. The chair in which he died was on the terrace, waiting to be car-ried away by its new owner. The Billesdon Coplow, "The Whissendine appears in view," "The Melton Hunt," and the pictures of the hunters were ticketed on the floor, and turned with their faces to the wall; while a crowd were pressing round the gay, sweet-topped Topthorn, and the slashing,* hard-pulling Crinoline in the meadow, or following the auctioneer, all eager for a relic if it were only a spud, into every nook and cranny of the yard.

It was indeed, "after me the Deluge." Rolles-ton was there still; the silver firs with their quaint rectangular branches near the knoll once so dear to the Quorn; the deep claret shade on the fish pond in front of the house, from which genera-tions of foxes had filched the ducks and swans and received a free pardon; the cross by the old grey church worn on the south side with pil-grim's knees; and the dark boat-shaped arbour at the top of the dark yew walk, where Mr. Assheton Smith and his pupil so often sat and gathered inspira-tion from the view of the top end of Rolleston Wood and Goadby with its "tremendous" vale,—they knew no change, but there was now another lord of the soil, and the heart of the place was gone.

Sir Richard Sutton's style of going Sir Richard Sutton.
was rather slow, but straight. He was
never anxious to be first and did not seem to ride for a
place, but took the fences just as they came. Even
when quite a young man, he never cared to go beyond
a certain pace. Hedge and ditch he liked, but to
timber and water, the latter especially, he was not
very partial. He liked Emperor quite as well as
Whitenose, who gave him six or seven falls in one
day, and he went well on Snowdrift, which he purchased for 250 guineas from Sir Tatton, and named
from the circumstance of his being obliged to return
to Sledmere that day, to borrow a snow-plough so
as to enable him to get on to Mr. Osbaldeston's
at Ebberston.

Thrussington Gorse, Barkby, and Scraptoft were his
most favourite Quorn meets, and he always said that
he was not sure that he had done a wise thing in
gravelling the Burton country wood rides, during
his long mastership, as instead of the field being
left fetlock-deep in them, they could get away and
interfere with his hounds. If he was pleased after
a run, he had a peculiar way of putting his whip-
hand on his hip, and holding his horn against the
pit of his stomach, and snapping his little dark
eyes.

Nothing perhaps delighted him so Hunting incidents.
much as Daphne the grandam of Dry-
den, of whom Will Goodall said that no hound
"brought so much intellect into our kennel." On
this occasion, Sir Richard ran his fox from Shoby
Scholes to Lord Aylesford's covert, and Grimston
Gorse, and right up to Belvoir, and to ground again
in the middle of a field near Shoby Scholes. Daphne
rushed right into the drain in her stride, and was working there up to her shoulders when Ben Morgan came
up, and on hearing of it from Ben, Sir Richard got
off in his delight to clap her. He enjoyed no

hunting-field joke more afterwards, than that of a labourer waving to him at a check. When he got to him, and asked how long the fox had been gone, the man scratched his head, and replied, seemingly in all sincerity, "*I seed him at five o'clock, when I wur a foddering the beasts.*" Well might he say to Lord Wilton, "that man must have a great opinion of my hounds." He did not care for hounds being very level if they worked well; but he never forgot it, if any of them were too free of tongue. Giving away the old and young draft, generally about five-and-twenty couple, was a great fancy of his, and the huntsman was allowed £70 in lieu. He was going very deep latterly into the Belvoir Guider blood, when he had done as much as he cared to do with Trueman, whose dam Pastime came, like Wildair, in a Brocklesby draft. No one exactly knew why he took such a fancy to Trueman, but he and old Bluecap were the only ones which shared his carriage to cover, and stood in with him for the lunch of cold chicken or pie, with which it was always stored. Trueman was a fair dog, but never ran to head, and crossed well with the Brocklesby blood, and Affable by Vine Grampian.

Early days of Will Goodall. Will Goodall was placed in Mr. Drake's stables under his father, when he was eleven, and after three seasons as cover boy for Mr. Tom Drake, he was put on as second whip under Wingfield. Dick Simpson was first whip, and judging from the style in which he had seen Will from a boy "jumping the church walls like a hare," he knew that he should have a lively colleague. Will had had his early perils, as Flounce dragged him fully twenty yards across the stable-yard at Shardloes before his father's eyes. As he grew older, he "had an aching tooth to be with Jem Hills," who had just then come to the Heythrop. His father, who had been a hunting-groom for eight seasons in the Belvoir country, wrote to Tom Goosey, but there was no answer, and the lad still pined for change. Nothing might have come of it, but Mr. Cox once said to him before Lord Forester's brother in the hunting-field, " I am told you want to leave, Bill ; they tell me the Duke of Rutland wants a whip." Mr. Forester hearing this, struck in and said he was not aware of the fact, but promised to write, and in ten days, which Bill described as a life-time, his Lordship sent for his weight, and ten stone was the reply. Another letter arrived from Belvoir to say that he was to go down directly, and he saw the '37 season out, beginning on his first morning at Woolsthorpe Cliff Wood. Goosey received him in a very candid way. "You must not mind," he said, " if I give you a good blowing up in the field ; I'm as likely to do so if you're right as wrong." This great huntsman told his mind to his whips without circumlocution, but to the field it was generally prefaced with " I beg leave to say." " *You jumped on that hound, Sir, at the fence, and I beg leave to say, Sir, you buried him as well,* " was his ironical remark to one of them.

Will's was latterly a very forced voice, and summer and winter he generally said he had a cold. He was broad across his shoulders, Will Goodall at The Belvoir. and big in the legs, and seemed at least two stone above The Emperor's mark ; but he always nursed his horse, and this added to his immense quickness of eye, brought him where he was He also rode Light-heart, Knipton, Swing, Multum in Parvo, Nimrod, and Melton during his last season. The two first were his best, and it was Lightheart by Greatheart from a mare of Mr. Frank Grant's, and bred by Lord Forester at Willey, which carried his successor Jem Cooper so well on the Hose Gorse day, which first marked his maiden year. The end of Will's ambition was to get his foxes over the Nottingham turnpike by Lord Plymouth's Lodge, from Melton

Spinney, and so by Goodricke's Gorse into the grass, but it was scarcely once in a season that he had this felicity.

Two runs on February 15th and 21st of his last season pleased him, so he wrote us, more than any he had ever known. In the first they were hallooed forward to a fresh fox, when their old one had crept in somewhere near Culverthorpe, after "1 hour 50 mins. of regular blazing." "From Dembleby Thorns," he adds, "they went away like pigeons in flight, the horses, and even many of our good men melting away like snow in summer; they ran from scent to view; and killed him by themselves (with the exception of 15 minutes from Culverthorpe), as hard as ever they could split, for 3 hours 22 minutes. I was first into the last field, and the only person who saw them course him, and his Grace was in the field when they caught him. We were the only two, but Mr. Frank Gordon, Mr. Hardy of Grantham, and Mr. Housen, Mr. Brooksner, and Jem came up to see them eat him. Sir Thomas Whichcote's horse stood stock-still one field away." We had no further particulars of the run of the 21st, than " We had a regular trimmer ! Oh ! such a trimmer, which few men live to see. The hounds did not get home till one o'clock the next morning. With their first fox they had 2 hours and 10 minutes to ground nearly in view, and with their second 1 hour 50 minutes. They tired every one out and ran into him by themselves charmingly; it was all over our best country with both foxes."

Goosey had a story that he was never driven but once from cover by a foggy day; and "then I beg leave to say I had done my best, for I drew a turn-pike-road, and thought that the trees on the other side were the cover." How, Will's genius would have dealt with this emergency, it is difficult to divine, but he used to declare that when a Humby Wood

fox beat him in the morning, he went back again in
the evening, and had a lot of old men and women with
lanterns in the rides, and so worked on till he had
just time to get home, and save Sunday. He considered that he had kept all Goosey's quality in the
kennel and that he had got length with Rallywood;
and he swore by Trusty by Foljambe's Forester, and
in fact all the sort, as such close workers and steady
hounds for an afternoon. Almost his last piece of
advice to Ben Morgan, when he told him, "I've
had many rough falls, but none like this," was, to
use one of the sort, Alfred from the celebrated
Nightshade, and he had one more word ere they
parted for the glories of Comus and Guider.

Tom Sebright was wont to say, that
he first learnt to be so fond of hounds, Tom Sebright.
by running after the late Mr. Villebois' pack, when
he hunted the Romsey side of the Old Hampshire
country. Time scored him on its page at Stowe-on-
the Wold in 1789, and it dealt very tenderly with him
to the close. His father, Tom Sebright, who died
there in his eighty-sixth year, was quite a huntsman
worthy in his day. He showed all the science of a
" master forester," when he hunted the New Forest;
and nearly to the last, he would trot out on his pony,
to meet Jem Hills, when he came to Heyford Village.
No wonder that such a keen hand wished his lad to begin early; and at fifteen Tom was duly entered with
Mr. Musters, who soon observed his fine hand and
quick eye to hounds. He went from the Annesley
kennels, to Sir Mark Sykes, who was then master
of the North Riding Hounds, in conjunction with
Mr. Digby Legard, but his style of riding was too
tremendous. Hence when " The Squire" came after the drafts which he wished to add to his new
purchase of the Monson pack, Mr. Legard said to
him, " *You may take the whip as well: we've tried
him three seasons, and he kills all our horses.*" And

so this brilliant pair crossed the Humber, and hunted the Burton country, and the Southwold woodlands, and worked their way round through Nottinghamshire to the Quorn.

Tom in Leicestershire. We have dwelt so often before on Tom's Leicestershire career, that we are not going to " run heel" now. He never hunted the hounds except when " The Squire" was away, and that only happened twice, to speak of—when his mother died, and when he broke his leg. Tom's day had very nearly ended in the canal near Stragglethorpe. They had found at Ella's Gorse, and away by Widmerpool, into the Vale; and the fox, after running the towing path a short distance, took the water. He was viewed over, and as some one must go, Captain White swam it on Pilot; and Tom tried to follow. Half way across the horse sank like a stone, and was drowned, and Captain White had no little difficulty in rescuing Tom, by fishing for him with the lash of his hunting-whip.

First day in the Milton country. Mr. John Moore recommended him to Earl Fitzwilliam as successor to John Clark, and he headed this celebrated pack for exactly forty seasons. He came in March, and the first meet was at Bedford Purlieus; but the hounds kept changing their foxes, and his lordship decided to have a turn at Sutton Wood. Tom rode Thorney that day, and the decision with which he lifted his hounds for five hundred yards over the plough, and did not allow his fox to dwell for an instant in Abbot's Wood, made the old hands say, that " there's no mistake about our new man." Monk's Wood and Bedford Purlieus were latterly very different to what they had been in the dykeless days of Will Dean, when horses had fairly to skip from one sound bit of ground to another in the ridings, and Tom found no better places for making

hounds steady. Aversley Wood foxes had always
an honourable mention, and he looked upon them as
quite the wildest and the best. The Soke of Peter-
boro' with its Castor Hanglands and Upton Wood,
was a very favourite place for his infant school in
the autumn. " When there was a scent," he used
to say, " hounds run as well there as anywhere;" but
taking the season through, he leant to Barnwell
Wold. Of Morchay Lawn he was also very fond,
and it was there that he entered George Carter to
the country, three weeks before the season closed,
in the April of '45.

We loved to stroll out with the old Scenery about
man and the hounds into Milton Park, Milton.
and by judiciously leading up to her, induce him to
talk of " Relish," a name which he used to pronounce with as much unction, as Robert Hall was
wont to throw into " Mesopotamia;" and we mis-
chievously got him to say it for the last time, just
before we bade him good-bye on the show ground
at Yarm. He was one of those fine, sterling characters which well repaid the study; and the whole
place and its accessories seemed so exactly in keeping with him. The rick-backed church, with its
crooked wooden belfry, the Fox Hounds sign nailed
to the elm, the straggling thorn clumps at the edge
of the park, over which, under a cold December sky,
the withered clematis was hanging in rich tracery,
like the veil of a bride, the Nen creeping on its
" lazy Scheldt"-like course along the broad meadows of Overton, the white sun-dial on the wall
of the steward's house, and the quaint intermixture
of the martello tower, with the thatch and the ivy
at the kennels all blended so thoroughly with him,
and his honest pride of being part and parcel of an
old English home.

During the summer he spent nearly Tom on the flags.
all his time among " my lambs," and

cared very little to wander afield. The Yarborough, Beaufort, and Belvoir kennels were what he principally used; but during his last two seasons he dipped deeply into Mr. Selby Lowndes's Royal, an old-fashioned-looking dog, and rather wild in his work. "*Ah! my lad, the dam is the secret,*" was his constant remark to young huntsmen. Like most reserved men, he was tough in his opinion, both in the field and the kennel, and no one but the boiler knew what the puppies were by, till they were ready to go out to quarters. He hung very much to the notion that in breeding two negatives would make a positive, both in style of work and make, and enforced it pretty generally in all his correspondence. It was delightful to hear him tell, almost under his breath, when you asked after the cream of entry, that they were "perhaps *just* the most beautiful I ever had," and believing himself most implicitly, summer after summer. "A thing of beauty" was most truly his "joy for ever." If he was showing one of his hounds, which he thought a a little out of the common way, he would indicate his delight by thrusting his hands deep into his breeches pocket, and kicking out his little right leg. He would then draw his hand over the hound from the head to the stern, and remark, in his gentle tone that "it could'nt be more beautiful if it had been spoke-shaved."

The kennel after his death. To stroll among the hounds, as they lay cub-dreaming on their benches was quite like entering a congress of woodland senators. Old Hardwicke, the winner at Yarm, had ended his line hunting, after his sixth season, and was there no longer to tell of the Harper sort though eleven couple of his puppies may. One of them was the last that Tom gave any directions about, and he requested George to call him "Hardwicke," and send him to Mr. Strixon's. Foreman sat up, showing in his wise countenance all the intelligence of the Feudals, which enabled him to be pilot so often; and near the one-eyed Fugleman, was Bachelor, who "kept Greenwich time" for Tom, and Rasselas, with that ancient grey-dished face, which always made him remark, without any disrespect to dignitaries, that he "had a head like an archbishop." Friendly of the Feudal sort, for which Milton has to thank Badminton, and repaid its debt with Hermit, had also devoted her best years to the pack; and with his paw on her, and his brother the line-hunting Bachelor's white-face on his own quarters, old Bluecap takes his snooze. Susan, and Shiner with his long tan features, speak up well for the Shiner sort; and the Feudals are here again, with Finisher, who lies with his smart head over the ledge. The badger-pied Ferryman, from Hardwicke's sister, which Tom was always quoting as "the neck and shoulders to keep in your eye," is also in the group, full of honourable scars, and with a split-up ear, which show that he will have his cub dividends in full.

Tom's manner was rather phlegmatic; and he never wearied of enforcing *Tom in the field.* the trite maxim, "that so much mischief is done by being in a hurry." When a fox was found, his scream "made you shake in your saddle;" but still his View Halloo was hardly so musical as his predecessor's, John Clark. In hound language and horn blowing, none could excel him, even when he was long past the thirty to sixty era, which he spoke of as "the prime of a huntsman's life." His language to the field, was remarkably courteous and guarded, even under deep provocation. If a fox was headed right into his face, he seldom got beyond "*Odd Rabbit it altogether!*" and if a whip did not put hounds to him immediately, or mistook orders, he appealed most forciby to "*Rays and Garters!*"

to aid him. Perhaps he tried too high for the majority of whips, and not only expected great excellence too early, but was a little impatient if he did not find it. Although very kind in his nature, he was decidedly chary of his professional praise. He would listen to some eulogy on a whip or huntsman whom he knew to be far below proof, and observe as a closer, with his little, short laugh, that he " might have made a good boiler if he had been properly brought up to it ;" or else " he can halloo and blow the horn." Then, perhaps, he would put down his lip, and sum up a horse with, " when the wind was in him he was good enough." The fast talkers he always dismissed with the comment, that they were " not always so fast over the country, when it came to the contest."

Style of hunting. In the great woodlands, where he was so quiet, and always there, it was beautiful to see the hounds fly to his horn; and nothing pleased him so much as " to give him a rattling good turn round, and get them close at him before he goes away." His broad bald forehead, of the Old Noll mould, was a treat to look at, when he lifted them to their fox, which he never did till they had made their own cast first. He was not fond latterly of long casts forward. " *Odd Rabbit it ! let them hunt, gentle-men,*" was all his desire ; and then came his cheery " *Catch them if you can now.*" At the death he was almost nervously anxious lest the horse-men should tread upon his darlings ; and then, if the master was out, there came the fine retainer- like courtesy and touch of the cap: "*A dog fox, my Lord!*" Never but once did any one of his three Milton masters speak a word of reproof to him. " *Tom ! Tom!*" said his late lordship, in his quiet way, when he had been left behind at Washingley Wood, " *you rode away from the master of the hounds.*" " *I blew my horn three times, I assure you,*

my lord, before I left the cover," was the answer.
Nothing more was said, till his lordship broke the
silence, as they rode back to Milton, with *" Tom!
don't let the sun go down upon my wrath ;"* and Tom
often said afterwards " This was the first and last
scolding I ever got at Milton."

Along with this story and the deeds
of Thorney, Patriot, and "The Squire,"
he generally got in a word for Mr. Hopkinson,
his hero of that great day from Barnewell Wold,
when they killed in the ploughed field, near Pap-
ley Gorse. Hounds and hunting were his unvaried
theme, and latterly he had rather a curious habit of
exaggerating the distance of a burst when he was
giving the points of a run. *" Then right away"* was
his mode of delineating it, with a triumphant wave
of his right hand into space. His friend John
Payne used often to quiz him about it, when he went
to smoke his pipe with him in the evening, and tell
that octogenarian sportsman what they had been
doing. *" Right long way that was, Tom; rare long
round I should think ; about two or three miles, Eh ?"*
and then, if Tom added that they " went as straight
as a pigeon," he would good-humouredly drop on him
again, with *" a pretty pigeon that would be !"* and
being thus duly cautioned, Tom had to begin
again.

He considered the season of 1847-48 as his best.
For the first ten seasons at Milton he kept a diary
of the sport, and then he tired of it. His hound-
book, on the contrary, was a perfect Talmud in his
eyes, but it was not till within the last three seasons
that he began to entrust its treasures to print. He
stuck to his few old cronies whom he
had known when he first came into
the country, and as he saw them dropping off
one by one, he could cheerfully say that he " had
had a very good innings," and tell George Carter

Describing a run.

Tom at home.

E E

that they would " soon be changing houses." Frank
Buckle used to hunt with him, and they were, of
course, acquainted; but Frank was " on the other
side of the question," and came very little to Milton;
and Tom felt sure that " he cared a good deal more
for bull-dogs than hounds." Shirley and Goosey
were his earliest friends among the huntsmen,
and when they or any of their juniors came over, he
would solemnly take his pipe out of his mouth, to
announce that he was " bomb-proof," and then
"puzzle out the sort" with them into the short hours.
One or another of his neighbours ploughed up his
close for him, and helped him in his few farming operations; but his heart was in the gorse and
not in the granary. He hardly ever went near a
race-course, till Ignoramus became too much for his
philosophy, and then he not only timed a visit to Old
George Carter, in order to see the colt run at Stockbridge, but duly appeared at the Grove Kennels on
the eve of the St. Leger.

He once only had an impulse to shoot at a private
pigeon-match, and scored with the best of them.
The joke of his beating Lord Fitzwilliam's
game-keeper was much too good to be lost, and
he found himself promptly figuring in a true and
correct list of the crack shots on that occasion. His
mingled dismay and disgust when he got hold of
the paper, and found himself and his deeds gazetted
in full, as if he had been some Professor of the
trigger, is remembered by his family yet. Except
for a little fun with his grand-children, he never
took a bat in hand, although as a young man he was
a very fair player. His early veneration for " The
Squire" was not unconnected with his powers in
that line, as when Lord Frederick Beauclerk broke
his finger at Nottingham, there were few all round
players who could cope with " the little wonder."
" The Squire's" bowling was as rapid as his riding,

and when he played two of the best of the Notts Club
for fifty guineas aside, he made eighty-four, and
howled them both for seventeen.

A likeness of him, in cricket cos- Tom's snuggery.
tume, with his bat under his arm, used
to hang above Tom's fire-place; and his driving-
match was equally honoured. The walls of that little chamber presented a curious, unpretending med-
ley. A *Sporting Magazine* print of his father,
holding sweet converse over a half-door with New
Forest Jasper, was kept in countenance by the blue
and white prize tickets from the Yarm Show. An
old mare's hoof was grouped with the late Lord Milton's spurs ; and The Billesdon Coplow, " Reynard's
last shift," and " An Earth-stopper" comported well
with the rusty high-crowned hunting cap, which had
its peg on one side of the writing cabinet. Patriot,
with the hounds Hardwicke, Marplot, and Rasselas,
from his son George's hand, some portraits of the
Fitzwilliam family, and his two horns (about the
disposition of which he left special directions in his
will), adorned his drawing room; and he never
wearied of telling of the old black, which carried
him so well over Kimbolton Park palings from
Leighton Gorse. In his prime no man was more
determined, and be it timber or water, he was in his
place as quick as lightning, whether he was on Re-
former, Blucher, Clipper, Zara, or the fidgetty Martingale. He liked also to tell of Mr. Osbaldeston's
Orange, which won the Cup at Lincoln, and carried
him over six gates in succession on one day ; and
his best water jump in Lincolnshire, was on a Scriv-
ington horse, with a middle like a cow, and carrying
the saddle on his shoulders. He liked big well-bred
horses ; and Hellaby exactly suited him during his
last season, as he could sit down on him, and let him
go along at a nice lobbing pace when the hounds began to run.

Sport of his last season. The cub-hunting in his last season (1860-61) did not begin until the middle of September, which was later than he had ever known it; and before the woodlands were " regularly stripped for business," he attended the pleasantest meet of his life at the Huntingdon Town Hall. His Grace the Duke of Manchester was in the chair, and handed him, with many kind words, the 800 guineas in a silver cup, to which 293 of his friends had subscribed. The old man could hardly speak his thanks when he received " the treasured heir-loom," and sketched the past very briefly, but he " came again" later in the evening, and told them how, when he could cheer hounds no longer, he trusted to fill the Cup, and bring it to his cottage door, when the hunt went past, and drink " Success to Foxhunting," with them once more.

The next season began nicely, and he soon wrote to tell us of a day from Farcet Fen, which had greatly delighted him. They found in some coleseed, and the fox took a ring in the fen, &c., " then right away to Washingley Woods," and was eventually killed near Buckworth Great Wood. He added, " It was about eighteen miles straight; time a little more than two hours. This was one of the old-fashioned runs I have seen in this country some years ago. I do expect this season to be one of sport, the country is in such good condition for hounds; and the greatest advantage will accrue from the hard riders not being able to ride over them, which is a great pleasure for me to see." One of the principal events of his last March was the clashing with the Pytcheley in Oakley Purlieus, and packing with them up to Boughton Wood, where the forty couple divided, Tom and Charles Payne going away with one lot (which was, oddly enough, made up nearly half-and-half from each kennel) and running their fox to ground; and the four whips with the other, which lost their fox near

Brigstock. Thirty-five brace was the return of the season, which " was altogether a satisfactory one," and his last day was at Laxton Hall, on April 24th, when he unfortunately killed a brace of cubs.

A fall from his grey mare near Win- First symptoms
wick, in March, was the first cause of of illness.
the mischief which gradually brought him to his end ; and it was strongly suspected that he had broken a rib. For a man of his age and weight the fall on the side of a bank was a severe one. He hunted the hounds again, but his cough never left him, and it became so troublesome to himself and the congregation, that for the first time for many a-year, his wonted seat at church was vacant for Sundays together. The summer brought no apparent change in these symptoms, and going to the Hound Show at Yarm increased them. These shows were latterly quite a bright spot in his life. He looked upon them as a little private bout between himself and Ben Morgan, and after he had beaten him with Hardwicke and Friendly, he never failed to tell that "they were rattling good fellows at Redcar." Ben had beaten him in his turn with Warrener and Languish at Middlesboro', but Tom was most philosophic under such reverses, and instead of railing at the judges, he forgot all his rivalry in "the social cloud," and hoped on for another year. The next August he was ready for another trip North, with three-and-a-half couple and a terrier, to Yarm, and he said for weeks before, "I'll drink their good healths that can lick me with my Bachelor and Hercules."

To get up Old Tom after dinner, and Tom at Middles-
cheer him till they got a short burst out boro' and Yarm.
of him, was quite a tent feature of these meetings ; and the respect which was shown to him both by masters and huntsmen gratified him not a little. Others might go in mufti, or unorthodox hats, but he

always attended in full costume as the professional
Premier of the Noble Science, and those hound shows
would have seemed to lack *solidarité* if he had not
been there.   He looked quite a link between the wood
and the woodlands, as we met him in his scarlet
with the green plush collar and his dark corduroys,
strolling along the dock side at Middlesboro', and
a forest of masts bristling in the back-ground;
and there was a still more remarkable link between Yarm and Leicestershire, as the Quorn
huntsmen of '19, '39, and '59, himself and the two
Treadwells, stood side by side.   His son Harry
was whipping in to him that day, when he
brought up his Friendly and Bachelor before the
bench for the Champion Cup, and from the whispers
which went on, and the notes which were made by
the Bench, it seemed morally certain that Tom would
be there or thereabouts again.   Then came the
pause, and Mr. Tom Parrington as clerk of the
council stepped up for instructions.   Poor Will
Boulton was beckoned to, and once more he and
Bonny Face were on the boards.   Then "Ben" got
the office, and Captain Williams taped Middleton
Languish, and cast a very longing eye on her as she
retreated.   Tom seemed to have gone to ground for a
space, but he did not peep out in vain from behind
the half door.   For him too came the welcome signal, and he darted forth leading Bachelor, and then
handing him over to Harry, positively made a run of
it back for Friendly.   "*That's all you want*," said
Sir John Trolloppe, the last entries were made in the
books, and Tom stood second.   However, there was
balm for him in the other classes, and when the
cards of victory, red, white, and blue, were placed
in front of the compartments, Mr. Hill's, Lord Middleton's, the Bramham Moor, and the Milton all
bloomed like a bouquet, and nearly twenty pounds
was Tom's value received, when he marched amid a

perfect chorus of view halloos up to the chairman.

He might well tell his doctor that he The last party.
had been at rather a gay party at Yarm.
His cough grew worse after the journey, but he thought that "one of my old doses would set me up again," and he was anxious to invite a few of his friends, who were not able to come to the testimonial dinner, and get that off his mind before the cub-hunting began. That wish was fulfilled, and Mr. Percival of Wansford, the Goodliffes, John Core, and two or three others sat round his board once again, and noted how cheerfully he spoke of what he hoped to do for them the next season on the Thrapston side, and how he dwelt on the kindness of Mr. Fitzwilliam, when he gave his health.

He generally required a little pressing, but he was no laggard that evening, when "*A Southerly wind and a cloudy sky,*" was called for according to custom. Although his cough fairly broke him down when he had got through two stanzas, and he was excused the rest, there was all the wonted animation in his "*Have at him my boys,*" "*Hi wind 'em !*" and his face shone again as he spoke to his hounds in that chorus, and found them doing everything he told them. There was such character about him and the song, that when you had a chance, you didn't like to lose it. Then George Carter and his father dropped in unexpectedly at night, and the horns were got down, and Tom talked like a composer upon Chase music in general, and fairly beat old George out of the field, when he challenged him to a tune. A stroll down to the kennels before tea, and a little more chat about the cubs and Yarm closed the evening, and only one or two of those old friends ever saw him again. It was a meeting he had long set his heart on, and it proved his farewell.

His last illness. A few days after, he took the hounds out for their Tuesday's exercise as usual, intending to give them a long trot round by Upton. He had scarcely gone three miles, when he pulled up, and told George Carter that he felt very sick, and ill with a pain in his side, and that they must cut it short. "If I had had any further to go, I should have dropped," were his words when he got off at the kennel door, and gave Carter the list of the hounds to draw for hunting next day. He was in such pain and profuse perspiration, that his daughter, who met him near the wicket, fancied that he must have had another fall, and he required no pressing to go to bed. For the first part of his time he dozed a great deal; his efforts for breath could be heard all over the house; and he was so restless that he hardly knew night from day. On the Friday he was better, but the pain returned next morning, and the action of his heart was so feeble, that the doctors dare not grant his request for leeches. He thought but little of kennel matters, but merely sent for George Carter to tell him about Mr. Strixon's puppy, and asked him on leaving after his "little Georgy, poor little boy," whom he had always liked to see among the hounds. George told him that he had taken out six-and-forty couple into Thistle Moor and killed a cub, but he made no comment.

His death. His son Harry and his son-in-law helped to nurse him by turns, and sat up with him the night before he died; and fresh water from the pump was all he longed for. They saw that there was no hope, but still his appetite seemed suddenly to return, and when his dinner was brought him next day he did think it "looked like business." Once more he hoped for life: "See what a dinner I've eaten, I shall be up in three weeks; I don't want to leave you yet." He then insisted, as it was Sunday, on having two glasses of wine as usual, to drink his

time-honoured toasts, "A good health to you all,"
and "The master of the hounds." "*That's not
enough,*" he said, "*to drink Mr. Fitzwilliam's health in,
Winifred,*" when she only poured out half a glass,
but he could do little more than taste it when it
was given to him. The toast he had drunk Sunday
after Sunday, for those forty seasons, made him
wander back to the hounds; "*Don't you see them?*"
he said to his daughter, "*they're all round my bed;
there's old Bluecap, and Shiner, and Bonny Lass
wagging her stern.*" "No, no, father," she replied,
"you're mistaken." "*Ah! they're gone now;
strange, isn't it, I should see them so plain? Oh, dear!
my eyes deceive me; they're only flies.*"

The window was open, and the sound of the church
bell floated into the room. In his days of health it
had never struck on his ear in vain, and he spoke to his
little grandchild and told her not to be late. "*Are
you dressed for church, Harry?*" he said to his son,
who sat and watched him at the bed-side, but he
was hardly conscious of the answer, and almost before the bell was down, his own last summons had
been given and obeyed.

and burial. They laid him at Thorpe, by the side
of his Dorothy and his son. Her loss
two years before, had almost bowed him down.
"She helped me through many a hard trouble;
nothing but her tender care made me the man I
have been, but God's will be done." It was thus he
told the grief, which in his quiet nature sank so
deep; and those who knew him best, knew too how
truly he had spoken through the lines, which he
selected for her head-stone:

> "Restrained from passionate excess,
>   Thou bidst me mourn in calm distress,
>   For those who rest in Thee."

And there the old man sleeps; and as we passed
away from the spot, and lingered for a mo-

ment by the grave of Will Dean "aged 79," and read how "all fall alike, the fearfull and the brave," we might well think how long and brilliant had been their career, and what pages might have been added to the annals of the Chase, if "The Master of the Donnington," Will Goodall, and Sir Harry had not died in their prime.

FINIS.

Printed by Rogerson and Tuxford, 246, Strand London.